PRAISE FOR LAURIE R. KING AND

O Jerusalem

'Mary Russell is never less than fascinating company'
Los Angeles Times

'Fabulous reading, breathless excitement, and the myriad
pleasures of watching great minds at work'
Booklist

'Excellent . . . King never forgets the true spirit of Conan Doyle'
Chicago Tribune

'Outstanding examples of the Sherlock Holmes pastiche . . . the
depiction of Holmes and the addition of his partner, Mary, is
superbly done.'
Mystery Women

'The great marvel of King's series is that she's managed to preserve
the integrity of Holmes' character and yet somehow conjure up a
woman astute, edgy and compelling enough to be the partner of his
mind as well as his heart'
Washington Post Book World

LAURIE R. KING lives in northern California. Her background includes such diverse interests as Old Testament theology and construction work, and she has been writing crime fiction since 1987. The winner of the Edgar, the Nero, the Macavity and the John Creasey awards, she is the author of highly praised stand-alone suspense novels and a contemporary mystery series, as well as the Mary Russell/Sherlock Holmes series.

By Laurie R. King

O JERUSALEM

LAURIE R. KING

Allison & Busby Limited
13 Charlotte Mews
London W1T 4EJ
www.allisonandbusby.com

First published in Great Britain in 2002.
This paperback edition published by Allison & Busby in 2012.

Published by arrangement with Bantam Books,
an imprint of The Random House Publishing Group,
a division of Random House, Inc., New York., NY, USA.
All rights reserved.

A CIP catalogue record for this book is available from
the British Library.

10 9 8 7 6 5 4 3 2 1

ISBN 978-0-7490-1162-8

Typeset in 11/16 pt Adobe Garamond Pro by
Allison & Busby Ltd.

The paper used for this Allison & Busby publication
has been produced from trees that have been legally sourced
from well-managed and credibly certified forests.

Printed and bound by
CPI Group (UK) Ltd, Croydon, CR0 4YY

For Dorothy Nicholl,
and in memory of Donald,
with love and with gratitude

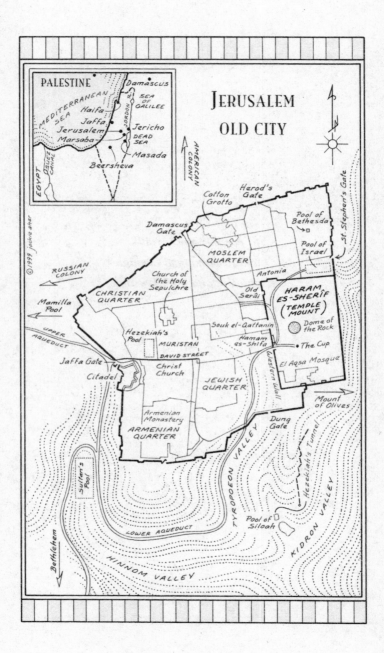

If I forget thee, O Jerusalem,
let my right hand forget its cunning.

— PSALM 137:5

EDITOR'S REMARKS

THE STORY THAT FOLLOWS IS a chapter in the life of Mary Russell, whose handwritten manuscripts I was sent some years ago (along with a puzzling collection of other objects, most of which have their explanations within the manuscripts themselves). The present volume, however, is published out of sequence, as it describes events that took place in 1919, during the period of the story I transcribed and published as *The Beekeeper's Apprentice*. The Russell/Holmes saga has now reached 1923 with *The Moor;* yet in the current work, *O Jerusalem,* Russell is still little more than the great detective's apprentice.

There are two reasons for this break in the proper order. One is simply that when I first read the manuscript, an entire section seemed to be missing, creating a gap I was not able to bridge until twenty-three neatly typed pages arrived in my mailbox, with a Slovenian stamp cancelled in the city of Ljubljana. (Yet another oddity in the already mystifying provenance of these manuscripts.) Secondly, even without the since-closed gap, the current story links up closely with another manuscript dating to the winter of 1923–1924, to be published in the near future. Thematically, the pair forms a neater sequence than if *O Jerusalem* had been inserted second into the series.

A word about this story's setting may be in order. In January of 1919, the Palestine that Ms Russell entered was freshly under British authority. The previous October, British forces had broken the back of German/Turkish control over the area. The year before that, in late 1917, the holy city of Jerusalem had been freed from four centuries of Turkish control. The Paris peace talks opened on 1st January 1919, bringing together Emir Feisal, T.E. Lawrence, Chaim Weizmann, and the other authorities charged with hammering out policy and boundaries, while in the Middle East itself, unrest continued to seethe in a climate of tragic misunderstanding coupled with basic disagreement. In March, rebellion broke out in Egypt; in April, five Jews and four Arabs were killed in a series of outbursts; in September, a riot took place in Jerusalem.

The twentieth century is only the latest chapter of bloodshed in the story of the Middle East, for the history of Palestine is a litany of warfare. The Hyksos and the Egyptians, the Philistines and the Assyrians, Egypt again and Babylon were followed by Alexander, the Seleucids, and the Romans. Persian gave way to Moslem Arab, Crusader failed to hold it against Saladin; even Napoleon tried to take Palestine, losing a war to fly-borne eye disease.

In the midst of all this fighting, in the early centuries of the struggle for control over this precious land bridge connecting three continents, the small walled town of Jerusalem came into being. Built around a spring in the desert hills, on a patch of rocky ground amid three valleys, there the people lived, and there they built their holy place. Weapons evolved from bronze to iron, the city wall grew thicker and higher, and eventually, with tremendous feats of engineering that ensured the supply of water during a siege, the town shifted uphill from the life-giving spring. The holy place at its centre remained.

The Temple that defined early Judaism, the centre of cultic worship, was laid atop a hill. Over the centuries the Temple was damaged and repaired, devastated and rebuilt anew. In the first century of the Common Era, a troublesome rabbi and carpenter from Nazareth was paraded alongside the walls of the holy enclosure, to be executed on a hill across one of the valleys. Forty years later, the Temple was finally razed, its stones overturned, the city laid waste, its surviving population dispersed. Two and a half centuries later, the Roman Empire converted, to follow the rabbi it had executed, and under the resulting Byzantines, Jerusalem became a Christian city in a Christian country.

Then Islam rose up out of the south and covered the land, and the followers of the Prophet Muhammad claimed the Temple Mount as their own holy ground, and built on it their houses of worship, ornate and intricate, passionate expressions of geometry and colour. Crusaders arrived and were thrown out; the Mamelukes ruled; and the Ottoman Empire reached out from the north to occupy the land as far as the Red Sea, until that empire too became corrupt and weak. In the second decade of the twentieth century, General Edmund Allenby pitted his clever mind against the dying empire and in September 1918 achieved his victory in the fields of Armageddon. The British declared a protectorate over Palestine, and began the process of impossible decision-making – decisions whose effects and implications have shuddered through the years to the present day.

There is, I am obliged to say, no clear evidence that the following tale is true. Granted, many of the people mentioned in it did exist, and most of the physical landmarks described by Ms Russell – the Cotton Grotto and the Haram es-Sherif, the cisterns, streets and public baths, the monasteries in the desert – are there to this day. Even the Western Wall was then as she describes it, a dank stone courtyard measuring some fifty yards long and ten deep, crowded round by the high dwellings of impoverished North African Muslims. Still, there is no proof that this heretofore unknown chapter of Israel's history actually took place. Then again, there is no proof it did not.

– LAURIE R. KING

AUTHOR'S PROLOGUE

The education of a scholar is greatly benefited by travelling in the
pursuit of knowledge and to meet the authorities of his age.
— THE *Muqaddimah* OF IBN KHALDÛN

DURING THE FINAL WEEK OF December 1918, shortly before
my nineteenth birthday, I vanished into British-occupied
Palestine in the company of my friend and mentor Sherlock
Holmes. The reasons for our temporary exile I have given
elsewhere,[1] but as that adventure had almost no bearing on what
we did while we were in the Middle East, I need not go into it
in any detail here. Suffice it to say that our Holy Land sojourn
was by way of being a retreat, distressingly near ignominious, a
means of distancing ourselves from a disastrous field of battle
— England — while we patched the wounds that our bodies and

[1] See *The Beekeeper's Apprentice*

our self-respect had sustained and assembled plans for the next stages of that campaign.

We entered the country, a British protectorate since the autumn's triumphs over the Turks, under the auspices of Sherlock Holmes' brother, Mycroft, an enigmatic and occasionally alarming figure whose authority within His Majesty's government was as immense as it was undefined. Given the necessity of our temporary absence from the United Kingdom, Mycroft had presented us with a choice of five venues, in each of which he (and hence His Majesty) had tasks with which he needed help. Holmes, in a spontaneous and utterly unexpected recognition of my increasingly adult status in our partnership, had ceded the choice to me. I chose Palestine.

A note about Arabic:

Arabic has more grammatical forms than English. For example, 'he' and 'she' take separate verb endings, and 'you' can be masculine, feminine, or plural. English translators often resort to 'thou' and 'thy' under the mistaken impression that the pronouns impart an Arabic flavour to the translation. To my mind, the only impression given is a stilted and thus inaccurate one, but then a literal translation is quite often not the best. I have therefore rendered Arab and Hebrew speech into their most natural English equivalent, and if the reader is disappointed not to find a story peppered with 'Thou son of a dog!' and 'By the beard of the Prophet!' so be it. Personally, I have always thought pepper an overused spice.

Similarly I have rendered the names of people and towns in the orthography of English usage: Jerusalem rather than the more exact Yerushalayim, Jericho instead of Yeriho, etc.

— M. R. H.

Chapter One

I

I began to learn another alphabet, and meditate on words that hissed and words that gasped.
— JEROME, *Vita S. Paulii*, TRANS. HELEN WADDELL
(*The Desert Fathers*)

THE SKIFF WAS BLACK, ITS gunwales scant inches above the waves. Like my two companions, I was dressed in dark clothing, my face smeared with lamp-black. The rowlocks were wrapped and muffled; the loudest sounds in all the night were the light slap of water on wood and the rhythmic rustle of Steven's clothing as he pulled at the oars.

Holmes stiffened first, then Steven's oars went still, and finally I too heard it: a distant deep thrum of engines off the starboard side. It was not the boat we had come on, but it was approaching fast, much too fast to outrun. Steven shipped the oars without a sound, and the three of us folded up into the bottom of the skiff.

The engines grew, and grew, until they filled the night and seemed to be right upon us, and still they grew, until I began to doubt the wisdom of this enterprise before it had even begun. Holmes and I kept our faces pressed against the boards and stared up at the outline that was Steven, his head raised slightly above the boat. He turned to us, and I could see the faint gleam of his teeth as he spoke.

'They're coming this way, might not see us if they don't put their searchlights on. If they're going to hit us I'll give you ten seconds' warning. Fill your lungs, dive off to the stern as far as you can, and swim like the living hell. Best take your shoes off now.'

Holmes and I wrestled with each other's laces and tugged, then lay again waiting. The heavy churn seemed just feet away, but Steven said nothing. We remained frozen. My teeth ached with the noise, and the thud of the ship's engines became my heartbeat, and then terrifyingly a huge wall loomed above us and dim lights flew past over our heads. Without warning the skiff dropped and then leapt into the air, spinning about in time to hit the next wave broadside, drenching us and coming within a hair's-breadth of overturning before we were slapped back into place by the following one, sliding down into the trough and mounting the next. Down and up and down and around we were tossed until eventually, wet through and dizzy as a child's top, we bobbled on the sea like the piece of flotsam we were and listened to the engines fade.

Steven sat up. 'Anyone overboard?' he asked softly.

'We're both here,' Holmes assured him. His voice was not completely level, and from the bow came the brief flash of Steven's teeth.

'Welcome to Palestine,' he whispered, grinning ferociously.

I groaned as I eased myself upright. 'My shoulder feels broken and – oh, damn, I've lost a boot. How are you, Holmes?' It was barely two weeks since a bomb had blown up just behind him as he stood tending a beehive, and although his abrasions were healing, his skin was far from whole.

'My back survives, Russell, and your footwear is here.' Holmes thrust the boot at me and I fumbled to take it, then bent and pulled it and the one I had managed to hold on to back over my sodden woollen stockings.

'Why don't they put more running lights on?' I complained.

'Troop ship,' explained Steven. 'Still a bit nervous about submarines. There're rumours about that some of the German captains haven't heard the war's over yet. Or don't want to hear. Quiet with the bailing now,' he ordered. Taking the oars back in his hands, he turned us about and continued the steady pull to shore.

The remaining mile passed without incident. Even with the added water on board, Steven worked the oars with a strong, smooth ease that would have put him on an eights team in Oxford. He glanced over his shoulder occasionally at the approaching shore, where we were to meet two gentlemen in the employ of His Majesty's government, Ali and Mahmoud Hazr. Other than their names, I hadn't a clue what awaited us here.

Looking up from the bailing, I eventually decided that he was making for a spot midway between a double light north of us and a slightly amber single light to the south. Swells began to rise beneath the bow and the sound of breaking waves drew closer, until suddenly we were skimming through the white foam of mild surf, and with a jar we crunched onto the beach.

Steven immediately shipped his oars, stood, and stepped over the prow of the little boat into the shallow water. Holmes grabbed his haversack and went next, jumping lightly onto the coarse shingle. I followed, pausing for a moment on the bow to squint through my salt-smeared spectacles at the dark shore. Steven put his hand up to help me, and as I shifted my eyes downward they registered with a shock two figures standing perfectly still, thirty feet or so behind Holmes.

'Holmes,' I hissed, 'there are two women behind you!'

Steven's hand on mine hesitated briefly, then tugged again. 'Miss Russell, there'll be a patrol any minute. It's all right.'

I stepped cautiously into the water beside him and moved up to where Holmes stood.

'*Salaam aleikum,* Steven,' came a voice from the night: accented, low, and by no means that of a woman.

'*Aleikum es-salaam,* Ali. I hope you are well.'

'Praise be to God,' was the reply.

'I have a pair of pigeons for you.'

'They could have landed at a more convenient time, Steven.'

'Shall I take them away again?'

'No, Steven. We accept delivery. Mahmoud regrets we cannot ask you to come and drink coffee, but at the moment, it would not be wise. *Maalesh,*' he added, using the all-purpose Arabic expression that was a verbal shrug of the shoulders at life's inequities and accidents.

'I thank Mahmoud, and will accept another time. Go with God, Ali.'

'Allah watch your back, Steven.'

Steven put his hip to the boat and shoved it out, then scrambled on board; his oars flashed briefly. Before he had cleared the breakwater, Holmes was hurrying me up the beach in the wake of the two flowing black shapes. I stumbled when my boots left the shingle and hit a patch of paving stones, and then we were on a street, in what seemed to be a village or the outskirts of a town.

For twenty breathless minutes our path was hindered by nothing more than uneven ground and the occasional barking mongrel, but abruptly the two figures in front of us whirled around, swept us into a filthy corner, and there we cowered, shivering in our damp clothing, while two pairs of military boots trod slowly past and two torches illuminated various nooks and crannies, including ours. I froze when the light shone bright around the edges of the cloaks that covered us, but the patrol must have seen only a pile of rubbish and rags, because the light played down our alley for only a brief instant, and went away, leaving us a pile of softly breathing bodies. Some of us stank of garlic and goats.

The footsteps faded around a corner, and we were caught up by our guides as rapidly as we had been pushed down in the first place, and swept off again down the road.

This was the land my people had clung to for more than three thousand years, I thought with irony: a squalid, stinking village whose inhabitants were kept inside their crumbling walls by the occupying British Expeditionary Forces. The streets of the Promised Land flowed not with milk and honey but with ordure, and the glories of Askalon and Asdod were faded indeed.

The third time we were pushed bodily into a corner and covered with the garlic- and sweat-impregnated robes of our companions (neither of them women, as close proximity had quickly made apparent, despite the cheap scent one of them wore). I thought I should suffocate with the combined stench of perfume and the nauseous weeks-old fish entrails and sweetly acrid decaying oranges that we knelt in. We were there a long, long time before the two men removed their hands from our shoulders and let us up. I staggered a few steps away and gagged, gulping huge cleansing lungfuls of sea air and scrubbing at my nose in a vain attempt to remove the lingering smell. Holmes laid a hand on my back, and I pulled myself together and followed the men.

We covered perhaps six miles that night, though barely three if measured in a direct line. We froze, we doubled back, we went in circles. Once we lost one of the dark robed figures, only to have him rejoin us, equally silently, some twenty minutes and one large circuit later. With his reappearance we changed direction and started a straight run, inland and slightly north, which ended when I came up short against the back of one of them and he, or his companion, seized my shoulders, spun me around, tipped my head down with a hand like a paw, and shoved me through a short, narrow doorway into what felt like a small cave, clammy with cold and holding a variety of odd (though for a change not unpleasant) smells.

I was completely blind, and stood still while at least two people moved around me, closing doors and what sounded like window shutters, rustling gently (their feet, I suddenly realised, had always been nearly noiseless) until the man behind me spoke a brief guttural phrase in a language I did not know, and in front of me a match scraped and flared, outlining a shape as broad as a monolith. The bright match dimmed, and when he stood upright to shake it out the light that remained was gentle and warm, like a candle – or, I saw as he turned towards us, a small oil-fed wick burning from a pinched clay bowl.

I spared no attention for the light source, however; my eyes were on the two men as they moved across to a corner of the room, shrugged their outer garments on a rough table, and turned to face us.

I was prepared, of course, for the two men to be Arabs, given their names, clothing, and the Moslem greeting back on the beach, but when I saw the reality of my companions in this tiny space it was a good thing I had Holmes with me, because I might otherwise have bolted for freedom: We had been dropped into the hands of a pair of Arab cut-throats. Their dark eyes and swarthy faces were nearly hidden between their beards and the loose headcloths they wore. The younger man was dressed as a dandy, if one can picture an Oriental dandy with curling moustaches, long bead-tipped plaits around his face, kohl encircling his eyes, and smelling of flowery scent, with an ornate curved scabbard stuck through the left side of his belt and a pearl-handled revolver on the right. A heavy gold watch on his wrist showed the wrong time but echoed the gold thread of the thick cords that held his headcloth in place, and the crimson colour of his boots matched the red in the flamboyant embroidery that ran up the front of his long waistcoat. The other man was older and more conservatively dressed – or rather, the colours of his garments were quieter, the embroidery more subtle. He wore the usual long-skirted Arab robe, although he too had both knife and gun (a long-barrelled Colt revolver). His face was bisected by a scar that tugged at his left eye and continued down into his beard; the younger man was missing two of his front teeth, which when he spoke revealed a slight and oddly sinister lisp.

I had lost a cousin two years before in the town north of here, cut down along with one of his children when the Arab inhabitants had risen against their Jewish neighbours, massacred a number of them, and driven the remainder from their homes. I did not want to be in the same room with these menacing individuals, much less dependent on them for food, drink, and instruction for the next six weeks.

Holmes seemed quite oblivious. He studied his surroundings as he unbuttoned his damp woollen jacket, peeling it off stiffly along with his haversack and dropping them both onto the rough bench that slumped against one wall. He turned to the men. 'I do hope you are satisfied,' he said in a low drawl. 'I imagine we shall have sufficient demands on our energies in the next few days without your continuing with these little games.' The two Arabs did not react, although their gazes seemed to sharpen somewhat. 'Which of you is Ali Hazr?'

The younger, more colourful man tipped his head briefly to one side. 'And you are Mahmoud Hazr?' Holmes asked the other. The stocky older man with the scar lowered his eyelids briefly in confirmation. 'I am Sherlock Holmes, this is Mary Russell. Gentlemen, we are at your service.'

His generous offer did not seem overly to impress the two

Arabs. The brothers looked at each other for a moment of wordless communication, then Ali turned his back on us and went to the back corner of the tiny room, where he dropped to his heels and began to assemble a handful of twigs and sticks into a small fire. Holmes opened his mouth, and then I could see him make the decision to shut it: Mycroft had chosen these men, and we had to trust that they knew what they were about. They had worked hard enough to get us here undetected; they would not light a fire if it was not safe.

I glanced over at Mahmoud, and found his black eyes studying Holmes with a mingled look of amusement, approval, and speculation. When he felt my gaze, his face closed and his eyebrows went down, but as he turned away I decided that, Arab cut-throat or no, the man was not unaware of subtle undercurrents.

'What is wrong with you?' he asked Holmes. His English was clear, though heavily accented.

It was Holmes' turn to assume a stony expression. 'There is nothing the matter with me.'

Ali gave a brief bark of what must have been laughter. 'Some movements pain you,' he said, 'and you flinched when I pushed on your shoulder. Are you injured or just old?'

It was, I had to admit, a valid question under the circumstances. Evidently Holmes too decided that the men had a right to know with what they were being saddled.

'I was injured, two weeks ago. It is merely the remnants of sensitivity.'

Ali sighed deeply and returned to his fire, but the answer seemed to satisfy Mahmoud. He walked over to the makeshift table leaning against the wall and bent to a heap of bundles that lay beneath it, coming up with a fringed leather pouch about the size of two fists. This he shook once, to attract Ali's attention. The younger man looked up, and the two shared another brief, wordless conversation before Ali shrugged and reached around the fire for an object like a giant's spoon, a shallow pan with a long handle, which he placed on top of the burning sticks before standing and moving away from the fire corner. Mahmoud took his brother's place at the fire, dropping to his heels and pulling open the drawstring of the leather pouch. He plunged his hand in, came up with a handful of pale, grey-green beans, thumbed a few of them back into the bag, and then poured the rest into the skillet. It appeared that we had earned the right to a cup of coffee.

Holmes had already warned me that in Arab countries, coffee-making was a long, drawn-out affair. We sat in silence watching Mahmoud's utterly unhurried motions, swirling the beans across the pan. The small green dots changed colour, grew dark, and finally began to sweat their fragrant oil. When they were shiny and slick and nearly burnt, Mahmoud picked up a large wooden mortar and with a flick of the wrist tipped the contents of the coffee skillet into it, spilling not a single bean. He set aside the skillet and took up a pestle, and began to pound the beans. At first the coffee crackled crisply under the pestle and tumbled back into the bottom of the mortar, but gradually the sound grew soft, and a rhythm grew up, the pounding alternating every few strokes with a swipe at the sides, where the coffee clung. The resulting sound was like a cross between a drum and a bell, quite musical and curiously soothing.

Eventually the coffee was reduced to a powder, and Mahmoud set the mortar and pestle to one side and reached for the incongruously homely English saucepan of steaming water that Ali had set to boil, filled from a skin hanging off the rafters. Picking up the tallest of three long, thin brass coffee-pots, he poured the ground coffee into it, followed by the steaming water. After a minute he skimmed off the foam and allowed the coffee to subside, then poured the mixture into a smaller pot with the same shape. He added a pinch of spice, stirred and skimmed it again, and finally poured the tar-like coffee into four tiny porcelain cups without handles that nested in the palm of his hand. It was unlike any Turkish coffee I had ever tasted, fragrant with cardamom and thick enough to spoon from the cup.

After the ceremonial three cups, we ate, tearing pieces of a flat bread, cold and tasting of raw flour despite being flecked with burnt bits, using the pieces to scoop, spoon-like, into a communal pot of some sort of spiced and mashed pulse or bean, also cold. It was a makeshift meal, but it served to fill our stomachs, and its completion seemed to mark a degree of acceptance on the part of our hosts. They wiped their fingers on their robes, cleared the cups and empty bowl to one side, and proceeded to pull out a couple of beautifully embroidered tobacco pouches and roll themselves cigarettes. Holmes accepted Mahmoud's offer of the pouch, papers, and a glass of cold water; they were not offered to me, but I declined as if they had been, and waited impatiently for the male tobacco ritual to reach a point where speech was acceptable. Eventually, the silent Mahmoud looked at Ali, who seemed to feel the glance and take it as a signal because he immediately reached into the front of his robe with his left hand and took out a thumb-sized knob of soft wood. His right hand went to his chest and drew the heavy, razor-honed knife from its decorated scabbard, and to my surprise he proceeded to use the unlikely blade to whittle delicately at the bit of wood. After a few moments, his cigarette bobbing dangerously close to his black beard, he paused in his carving and raised his eyes to Holmes.

'So,' he said. 'Do you mind telling us what you are doing here?'

CHAPTER TWO

ب

Geometry enlightens the mind and sets one's mind straight . . . The mind that turns regularly to geometry is unlikely to fall into error.
– THE *Muqaddimah* OF IBN KHALDÛN

I WAS BEGINNING TO WONDER the same thing myself, and in fact, the question was to run like a refrain through all the activities of the next few days. What was I doing here?

'My brother, Mycroft, suggested that you had a problem we might help you with,' Holmes replied. 'That is all I know.'

'A "problem",' Ali repeated.

'His word.'

'So you come all the way from England to help us with a problem you know nothing about.'

'I am regarded as something by way of an expert on problems,' Holmes said modestly.

'Or is it that your brother, Mycroft, wants you to check up on us?'

'I should think if that's what he wanted, he would have indicated we might not trust you, but it's difficult to say. Mycroft is something by way of an expert on keeping things to himself.'

Ali made a growling noise in the back of his throat and fingered his knife impatiently. 'Why did you come? What brings you here?'

Holmes made no further effort to dodge the question, although the answer was a thing of unvarnished humiliation. 'We were in danger of losing our lives in London, and needed to get away for some weeks in order to gain the upper hand on our return. Mycroft thought we could as well make ourselves useful as hide in a cave somewhere.'

'So we are to be your nursemaids?' Ali said with incredulity.

'Absolutely not,' Holmes snapped, his voice suddenly cold.

'You are an old man and she is a girl,' Ali retorted. 'You may have dyed your faces, but you can't even speak Arabic.'

'I speak the tongue as one who was born to the black tents of the Howeitat Bedu,' said Holmes in an Arabic that was apparently as flawless as he imagined it, for Ali looked at him in surprise and even Mahmoud cocked an eyebrow. 'Russell speaks Hebrew, as well as French, German, and a number of fairly useless dead languages; her Arabic is progressing rapidly.'

It was an exaggeration, but I promptly dragged up a sentence I had laboriously constructed during our boat trip here (ten days spent primarily on intensive lessons in Arabic and intense games of chess) and I parroted it to the room. 'My Arabic lacks beauty, but the bones are strong and it grows in the manner of a young horse.'

I was afraid they would ask me a question, at which my ignorance would be laid bare, but Ali picked up where he had left off.

'Very well,' he said, still in English. 'You speak with a beautiful accent, but there is more to life here than language. We do not have time to set our steps by yours.'

'If we lag behind, leave us. An hour in the bazaar to supply the portions of our costume the boat could not provide, and we are ready.'

'Dressed as you are, everyone in the market would know your business.'

'Then you will have to spend the hour for us,' Holmes said, as if in agreement to a proposal. Mahmoud made some slight noise, but when I glanced at him, his face was without expression.

'But you look wrong,' Ali objected. 'You have strange eyes. The girl even wears spectacles.'

'The spectacles are an oddity, but not an insurmountable one. As for the eyes, Circassians often have blue eyes. So do Berbers, who often have yellow hair as well. Berbers are also known for being strong-headed, which is even more appropriate.'

'We have no beds,' Ali cried in desperation.

'*Maalesh,*' Holmes said. 'But as an "old man" I suppose I am meant to need my sleep, so I will wish you a good night.' And so saying, he kicked off his boots, wrapped himself up in his greatcoat, and turned his face to the wall. I followed his example; eventually the others did as well. They could, after all, scarcely lie in comfort on the carpets and bedclothes they no doubt had in their possession when their two soft Western guests slept on the packed-earth floor.

Between the discomfort, the nocturnal activities of a variety of four-, six-, and eight-legged residents, and the gradual mid-night suspicion that our hosts were more than unusually troubled by our visit ('They could have landed at a more convenient time,' Ali had said to Steven), I did not actually fall asleep until I had heard the pre-dawn wail of a distant *muezzin* calling the faithful to prayer. I woke when the door opened and shut at first light, but by then I was numb enough to call it comfortable, and dropped back to sleep until Ali and Mahmoud swept back in, their arms filled with bundles.

Their shopping expedition had not changed their temper. Mahmoud went silently to the corner to build a fire for coffee while Ali came perilously close to throwing his purchases at us and kicking us awake. (In truth, the room was so small that dropping the things and pacing up and down amounted to the same thing.) I blearily pushed my stiff bones upright, put on my spectacles, shifted back out of his way, and reached for the nearest twine-bound parcel.

My heart sank when I saw what it contained, and I sat rubbing my face and wondering where to begin. Ali's idea of a suitable garment amounted to a rough, black, head-to-toe sack with a hole for my eyes combined with too-small, thin-soled, decorative sandals with narrow straps that hurt just to look at them.

'Holmes,' I said. He looked up from his gear, which was similar to Mahmoud's, only plainer. His mouth twitched and he looked down at the wide belt in his hand, and then he relented.

'This will be fine,' he said, and stood up to begin the change of identity. 'Russell's, however, will not do. She will need the clothing of a young man.'

'That is not possible,' Ali said flatly. 'It is *haram*.' Forbidden.

'It is necessary, and no one will know.'

'She could be stoned for dressing as a man.'

'It is highly unlikely any judge would approve the punishment, although a mob might use it as an excuse to throw some rocks. If you are afraid of being placed in danger, then we shall leave you.'

Ali's hand gripped the shaft of his knife so hard I thought the ivory would bulge out between his fingers, but the blade remained in the sheath.

'You will not accuse me of cowardice, and she will wear those clothes.'

'Actually, no,' Holmes said, completely ignoring the man's fury and sounding merely bored – an old and effective technique of his. 'She will not wear those clothes, or anything like them. No *burkah,* no bangles, no veil. She will not walk behind us, she will not cook our food, she will not carry water on her head. This is not, you understand, my choice; I should be perfectly happy to have her clothed head to foot and in a subservient position – the novelty would be most entertaining. However, she will simply not do that, so we must either live with it or separate. The choice, gentlemen, is yours.'

His state of undress had reached the point at which I had to turn my back, so I missed the non-verbal portions of the discussion that followed, and many of the words they used passed me by. Still, I did not need a translation for their emotional content, nor did I need to have Holmes tell me why Ali had left so precipitately, since all the women's garments left with him. I turned back to find Holmes transformed into a Palestinian Arab.

Mahmoud, through all this, had placidly gone about the business of making coffee, and had now reached the stage of shaking the pan of near-black beans. He glanced up and caught my eye, then lifted his chin at the table leaning against the wall. I went over curiously and picked up the small, worn, leather-bound book that lay on the rough surface. On what would be the back cover in an English book but was the front in Hebrew or Arabic, there was a short phrase in faded gold Arabic script.

'A Koran?' I asked him. He continued shaking the beans. 'Yours?'

'Yours,' he said briefly, and followed it with a flow of Arabic that Holmes translated. '"Start with the knowledge of God's Book and the duties of your religion, then study the Arabic language, to give you purity of speech."'

'Is that from the Koran?'

'Ibn Khaldun,' Mahmoud said. The name was familiar, that of an early Arabic historian whose work I had not read.

'Well, thank you. I will read this with care.'

Mahmoud reached for the coffee mortar and poured the beans into it, and that was that.

Once his mind had been turned to the problem, Ali did an adequate job in producing the long-skirted lower garment and the loose woollen *abayya* that went over it, and the heavy sheepskin-lined coat I would need on cold nights. The sandals he gave me were still thin-soled, but they fit, and the cloth he brought for my headgear was better in hiding long hair than the loose *kuffiyah* my three companions wore. He even demonstrated how to wrap a turban that looked sloppy but stayed firmly fixed.

I smoothed the skirts of my *abayya,* wishing I had a mirror, and allowed the men back inside. Mahmoud nodded, Ali scowled, and Holmes checked to see that all the ties and belts were done correctly.

Physically, I would pass as an Arab youth. There was one more difficulty, however.

'Do we still call "him" Mariam?' Ali asked sarcastically. '"Miri" would be more useful.'

Mahmoud thought about it for a moment, then cast a sly glance at his partner. 'Amir.'

Ali burst into laughter, and I had grudgingly to admit that the name was amusing. *Mir* indicated a relationship with a prince. Ali's suggested *Miri* would indicate that I was owned by the state, the property of a prince or commander; in other words, a slave – which, although it might prove accurate, depending on how much drudge labour the men got out of me, was nothing to be proud of. *Amir,* on the other hand, was far too grand for an itinerant boy, and I could hear already that it would be a source of amusement every time it was pronounced. Still, it seemed that I had little choice in the matter: 'Amir' I was, ridiculous or not. *Maalesh.*

Ali and Mahmoud were anxious to be away – or, Ali was anxious, while Mahmoud firmly dedicated himself to closing up and moving on. We packed away our clothing and the kitchen (the coffee-pots and mortar, one saucepan, the goatskin for water, and a large convex iron pan called a *saj* for making the flat bread we seemed condemned to live on) and made ready to slip away.

My first sight of Palestine by light of day was of a rain-darkened expanse of rock. The hut was set into a crumbling hillside, its bricks the same dun colour as the surrounding stones; when I glanced back fifty feet away, the structure was all but invisible. I turned my back on our shelter, and set off into the country.

After a mile or two, I asked Holmes if he knew where we were going. I thought perhaps the two Hazrs had a house in Jerusalem or in the foothills, but it seemed that the bulk of their possessions – tents, stores, cooking pots, and mules – had been left with friends some ten miles outside of town. I gaped at Holmes, then at Ali.

'You mean, you don't have a house?'

'A hair house,' he said, the Arabic name for a tent. 'Two, now. And a third mule.'

'We're to be gipsies? In these shoes?'

'Not gipsies,' Ali corrected me scornfully. 'Bedu.'

'For heaven's sake,' I muttered. 'Couldn't Mycroft afford to get his people a house?'

Mahmoud the silent spoke up, contributing a string of Arabic that could have been a deadly insult or a recipe for scones. I looked to Holmes; he translated.

'He said, "Better a wandering dog than a tethered lion."'

'Oh,' I said doubtfully. 'Right.'

It looked, then, as if we were to be Bedouin Arabs rather than members of a more settled community. Not, however, the romantic, deep-desert, camel-riding Bedu brought to fame by the exploits of then Major, now Colonel Lawrence and his Arab revolt. These two travelled a cramped little hill country on mules – God's most intractable quadruped – T.E. Lawrence was at the Paris peace talks, and romance was fled from the land.

I stifled a sigh. Even General Edmund Allenby, my own personal hero of the Middle East – soldier and scholar, terrible and beloved commander, brutal and subtle builder of campaigns – would be far beyond my reach in this guise. If I so much as caught a glimpse of him, it would be from a rock at the side of the road while the general flew past in his famous armoured Rolls-Royce, splashing me with mud.

Instead of a sojourn in a marble-floored villa filled with carpets and cushions, I would be on foot, in crude sandals, sharing a tent with Holmes, and with no private toilet facilities for miles. I thought about lodging a protest at least about not being given my own tent, but decided to let it be for the present. We had slept in close proximity before, when need be, and until I could arrange something else, sharing a tent with him would be better than sharing a tent with all three males.

The afternoon wore on, the rain lessened, and I succumbed to enchantment. The thrill of being in Eretz Yisrael, the exotic sensation of the clothes I wore, the glory of watching the sun move across the sky and smelling the brilliant air and the cook fires and the sheer intoxication of Adventure made me want to dance down the stony road, twirling my rough garments about me. I did not even mind too much that we were heading away from my own goal of Jerusalem, nor that we had still been told nothing whatsoever about our mission by the two close-mouthed Arabs. I was in the Holy Land; much as I craved to set eyes upon the city itself, holy ground to three faiths, the countryside would have to suffice for now.

After an hour, we were forced to stop and pack gauze around the painful chafe of my sandals' toe-straps. The discomfort did not put a halt to my pleasure, though, and the cup after cup of cool water we dipped out of an ancient stone trough fed by a roadside spring filled me with the sensation of communion. I did not complain, at the footwear or at the heavy burden I carried, and I kept up with the pace our guides set.

The sun was low at our backs as we walked along a dusty road with groves of young orange trees on either side, when abruptly first Mahmoud and a split second later Ali stopped dead, their heads raised, their postures radiating alarm. I could hear nothing but the insistent lowing of a cow, smell nothing other than the sweet evening air of the orange grove. I glanced at Holmes in a question, but he shook his head to show his own incomprehension.

Ali wheeled about and bundled us off into the trees, where we threw off our packs while Mahmoud retrieved a well-cared-for Lee Enfield rifle from one of the larger bundles. Ali slipped away into the dusk, pearl-handled revolver in hand, while Mahmoud gestured for us to follow him.

Holmes spoke in a low voice remarkably free of impatience. 'May I ask—'

'No smoke,' Mahmoud answered curtly. 'And the cow has not been milked. Be silent.'

We approached the farm buildings with caution and indeed, aside from the loud complaints of the cow, an unnatural silence lay heavy around us. We took up positions behind a shed from the deserted-looking house and barn, and waited.

A quarter of an hour after he had left us, Ali stepped into the open farmyard and trotted across to us. He spoke to Mahmoud; Holmes translated for me.

'Whoever did this is gone. The two hired men are in the trees, shot in the back. I saw no-one else.'

Our companions exchanged a look, and separated again, Ali towards the barn, Mahmoud into the shed. It proved to hold only an assortment of farm equipment, but we heard a shout from the barn, and when we got there, Ali had lit a paraffin lamp and was kneeling next to a man who had spilt more blood across the earthen floor than I would have imagined possible. A dagger very like that in Ali's belt jutted from the man's chest. The theatrical sight of the curved hilt and the copious blood nearly shocked a gust of laughter out of me, so closely did it resemble the corpse in some stage melodrama, but the urge to giggle passed in an instant and another reaction took over.

A bare two weeks earlier, Holmes and I had been bombed, hunted down, chased through London, and finally shot at while standing in an office of New Scotland Yard; a sniper's bullet had exploded the window beside me, missing me by inches. I thought I had left behind the blinding terror of the exploding window and the hard slap of lead on brick, but I had not; now I plunged straight back into the dry-mouthed, heart-pounding state as if no time at all had intervened between that attack and this one.

'Oh, God, Holmes, she's here,' I found myself saying with a whimper. 'She's here waiting for us, she must have known where we were going. Someone in Mycroft's group has been bought. We have to get out of here, Holmes, we can't trust these men, we can't trust anyone, we—'

He caught me and shook me, hard. 'Russell! Use your brain. It is not us. She could have had us any time in the last day. This is not about us, Russell. Think.'

I stared at him, and the panic retreated, my vision slowly cleared. I swallowed, nodded, and Holmes released me.

Still, two men were dead, and this one would be soon. If it wasn't to do with us, what was it?

Mahmoud had bent over the dying man, so close his beard brushed the man's shoulder, and was speaking forcibly into his ear. 'Yitzak,' he said, over and over again until the still figure stirred slightly and the blue eyelids flickered.

'Yitzak, who did this?' It took me a moment to register that he was speaking in Hebrew.

'Mahmoud?' the flaccid lips breathed. The embroidered skullcap the man wore was dislodged by his faint movement. It tipped and dropped away to the earthen floor, revealing thinning hair, a circle of pale scalp, and a clotted head wound.

'We are here, Yitzak. Who did this?'

'Ruth?'

'Ruth and the children are not back yet. The carriage is not in the barn. Your family is safe. Who was it, Yitzak?'

'Man. Saw him. With. The *mullah*. Last week.'

'The *mullah* who preached in Jaffa?' Yitzak blinked his affirmation. 'It was one of his men?'

'Two. Not his. I—' Yitzak coughed wetly and groaned, and that was all he told us. Ten minutes later his breathing ceased. Mahmoud stood up, looked at the drying blood on his hands, and went outside. While Holmes moved in a circle around the body, examining the scuffed ground, I stood and listened to the sound of a hand pump and the splash of water. When Mahmoud came back into the barn, the entire front of his dark garment was wet. He picked up the lantern from the floor, and inclined his head towards the door, a clear gesture that we should leave. Ali protested in Arabic, something about Ruth and the children seeing this.

'We must not bury him,' Mahmoud told his brother.

'We must go.'

'We cannot—' Ali began.

Mahmoud moved slightly, a matter of drawing himself up, and Ali stopped immediately. Mahmoud's face was dark with rage, not at Ali but at what Ali was forcing upon him. I took an involuntary step back, and hoped fervently that I would never have that look directed against me. 'You will go and tell the neighbours,' Mahmoud said forcibly. 'We will meet you on the road. *Insh'allah,*' he added: If God wills it.

Ali glanced at us and nodded, but before he could turn away, Holmes spoke for the first time.

'Why did the killer leave his knife?'

Mahmoud stood with the lantern in his hand and looked at Holmes; neither he nor Ali showed any reaction.

'The knife,' Holmes repeated. 'This man was knocked unconscious, dragged here, dramatically arranged in the doorway by two men wearing boots and robes rather than

39

trousers, and stabbed with that knife. His position shouts out "murder most foul". Of Jew by Arab. The shocking effect was deliberate.'

Ali turned to leave, but Mahmoud stopped him with a gesture, and went back over to examine the body more carefully. The three men studied the scuffed boots, the head wound, the pitiful skullcap, the marks on the floor, and above all the ornate dagger that had slowly taken the farmer's life. After a couple of minutes, Mahmoud rose. 'We cannot bury him,' he repeated.

'I agree,' said Holmes. 'It would raise an even worse uproar than this would. But given an hour or two, we could transform murder into an unfortunate accident. And if the two hired men might simply disappear for a while . . . ?'

Mahmoud reached up to rub at his beard, and his fingertips travelled briefly down the scar. He nodded thoughtfully. '"Allah is the best of tricksters." Yes. Better for all. But quickly.'

'It might also be best to remove your possessions from the vicinity. It is one thing for unburdened men to slip into the groves, were a stranger to come upon the farm; quite another to make an escape encumbered with mules and household goods.'

I could see where this was going, but truth to tell, I had no wish to assist in the doctoring of the site. I did not even want to think about what they would have to do to disarm the effects of this death. Oh, I protested, of course, but in the end I gave in gracefully to the combined demands of the three men that I take the laden mules and get them out of the area. I do not think I fooled Holmes, but I protested.

We loaded the animals, tied them so I could control all three with one lead, and Ali gave me instructions that a child could have followed, on how to reach a hidden place where I might wait until they joined me. He repeated the directions three times, until I turned on my heel and walked away with all the Hazr worldly possessions trailing behind.

After my proud little gesture, I was greatly relieved when I succeeded in finding the place without mishap. I had envisioned dawn breaking with me still stumbling about the countryside, trying to explain myself in yet more stumbling Arabic, but I found it, the ruins of a burnt-out and long-abandoned caravanserai – roofless, overgrown, and no doubt infested with snakes, scorpions, and other happy creatures. I hobbled the mules, found a smooth boulder to perch on, drew my feet up under the hem of my skirts, and gave my soul over to patience.

And to thought. The shakiness that had overtaken me on seeing the dead man was beginning to fade, but I still felt queasy, and my mind skittered nervously away from speculations concerning what my companions were doing. I firmly directed my thoughts to the question of what threat might be felt both by a family of Jewish immigrants and by a pair of wandering Arabs, and meditated upon the possible relationship between two Palestinian Arabs and a family of Jewish settlers. What was I not seeing here?

And what, indeed, was I doing here?

It was not a long wait, as waits for Holmes tended to go, but it seemed considerably more than two hours before one of the drowsing mules twitched up its ears and a low whistle came out of the night. This was followed by the sound of three men moving quickly; in less time than it takes to describe, we had become four men (to all appearances) and three pack mules, still travelling quickly.

There are no true mountains in Palestine, not by European standards and certainly not within a day's walk of Jaffa, but I could have sworn that our two guides had imported some for the occasion. We scrambled up and down precipitous if unseen hillsides, obliging me to cling to the pack ropes and let my sure-footed animal lead me in the darkness, abandoning all pretence of my being in charge of it. At some hour well before dawn, we quit the hills and took to a dusty road for a few miles. Finally we stopped. Ali pressed cold food into our hands, we swallowed mouthfuls of musty water directly from a skin, and then we curled up on the hard ground and lay motionless as stones until the sun was well up in the sky.

I woke to the sound of argument, unmistakable if unintelligible. I started to sit up, and sank back immediately, wondering if I had been beaten while I slept. Not a part of me did not hurt. I then remembered Yitzak, and blood, and I redoubled my efforts to become upright.

The name Jaffa – or Yafo – seemed to be central to the argument. Working from that clue, I decided that our two guides were proposing to double back and see what they could find out about Yitzak's 'man with the *mullah*'. Holmes, naturally enough, was objecting to this plan; if I knew him, he would propose instead that he himself return to Jaffa and investigate while Ali and Mahmoud cooled their heels here. Seeing Ali's expression flare into outrage, I judged that the proposal had just been made, and that perhaps it was a good time for me to step in.

'Holmes,' I called. 'Do I understand it aright, that they wish to go into Jaffa and ask questions but that you object?'

'But of course,' he began. 'How can I know—'

'Holmes,' I said, addressing my mentor, my senior partner in crime, a man nearly old enough to be my grandfather, a person revered by half the world. 'Holmes, don't be difficult. They're right, and you're wasting time. I didn't argue last night when I was sent away with the rest of the household goods, because it was the sensible thing to do. Now the sensible thing would be to let them get on with it. Painful as it is to admit, I can't be left alone here during the day – my Arabic wouldn't stand up to a visitor. Yours would.'

I allowed nothing in my attitude to suggest another reason that he stay where he was instead of haring off for a strenuous day in Jaffa; if he was not going to mention his half-healed back, I was certainly not about to bring it up. He glared suspiciously at me, and Ali looked flabbergasted at my effrontery, but Mahmoud glanced sideways at me with something verging on respect, looked up into the air, and recited in English, 'Would they attribute to Allah females who adorn themselves with trinkets and have no power of disputation?' He then arose, taking the argument as settled. Ali followed his example with alacrity lest Holmes change my mind, but before they went, Mahmoud went to one of the packs and dug out a grimy block of notepaper, the stub of a pencil, a wooden ruler, and a tidy skein of string with knots tied all through it. He handed the collection to me, and pointed with his chin to a spot down the dusty road.

'The tall rock with the vine?' he said in Arabic, and waited until I nodded. 'One hundred metres, with that as the centre. We need a map.'

'Why?'

It seemed a reasonable enough question on my part, but his answer was not helpful.

'"A subdivision of geometry is surveying,"' he pronounced.

'And . . . ?'

'"One who knows geometry acquires wisdom,"' he elucidated, then turned on his heel and walked away, with Ali close behind him. I looked at Holmes, let the crude survey instruments fall to the ground, and went back to my pile of packs to sleep.

However, further sleep was not meant to be, thwarted by (in order of appearance) an old man in a cart, a young boy with a cow, an even younger boy with six goats, three cheerful and extraordinarily filthy charcoal burners gathering fuel, the old man in the cart returning, and a chicken. All including the chicken had to pause and investigate our curious encampment, making conversation with Holmes and eyeing his apparently dumb but not unentertaining companion.

In the end, I threw off my cloak and my attempt at sleep, to storm over to the vine-covered rock and begin my assigned survey. I knew it was a completely pointless bit of make-work, given us by Mahmoud just to see if we would do it, but by God, do it I would, and in a manner so meticulous as to be sarcastic. Taunting, even. So I sweated beneath the sun with that length of tangled string, barking my shins on rocks and disturbing whole communities of scorpions and dung beetles, mapping out a precisely calculated square whose sides ran compass straight, placing in it every bush, boulder, and patch of sand. I measured, Holmes (when we were alone) noted down the measurements, and then I took a seat in the shade of a scruffy tree and rendered up drawings that would have made an engineer proud. Four drawings, in fact: the map; a topographical diagram; an elevation from the lowest point; and finally as precisely shaded and nuanced an artist's rendering as I could master.

Holmes chose a remarkably similar means of dealing with the frustration, impatience, and resentment of having been relegated to the side-lines, only instead of string and inert paper, he worked with words and fools. He sat on his heels, rolling and smoking one cigarette after another, while our visitors (except for the chicken) climbed out of carts or divested themselves of burdens and settled in for a long talk. Holmes nodded and grunted and wagged his head or chuckled dutifully as the conversation demanded, and the only time he even came close to leaving his scrupulously assumed position on the side-lines was when he asked the old man (on the cart's return journey) if things were peaceful in Jaffa. I pricked up my ears, but it was obvious the man knew nothing about Jaffa and was interested only in equine hoof problems – his donkey's and our mules'.

By dusk, Holmes and I were ready respectively to strangle a visitor and shred a notebook. He stood up abruptly, and with uncharacteristic rudeness all but lifted the garrulous old man back onto his cart, waved an irritable arm at the stray chicken to dislodge it from its roost on the heap of our possessions, threw some wood on the fire, and slumped down beside it. I tossed my ridiculously precise drawings onto the ground, took out my pocket-sized Koran, and went to sit beside him. I was physically tired and mentally frazzled, but I positively welcomed submitting to the lessons that followed.

Holmes had learnt Arabic nearly thirty years earlier during a sojourn to Mecca, and I had begun intensive lessons upon leaving London ten days before. I did not know if I would be able to absorb enough of the language in the time at my disposal to be of use, but I was determined to try, and Holmes, as always, was a demanding teacher. Our every spare moment of the past days had been given over to the lessons, in language, manners, and deportment. I knew to use only my right hand for eating, I had the most useful verb forms and the most basic vocabulary under control, and I was learning to adopt the small, tight hand motions and the head and body movements of the native Arab speaker.

I had also received a quick tutorial concerning the society into which we were moving, Arab (both *hadari,* 'settled', and *bedawi,* 'nomadic'), Jew (some of whom had ancestors here in the days of Temple sacrifice), and myriad splintered varieties of Christian. Until the war, with the Turk on all their backs, these disparate groups had existed as more or less amicable neighbours; but since the Turkish surrender, the cap was off, the long-building pressure threatening to erupt – complicated further by British attempts at even-handedness, the rise of Arab nationalism, and the growing number of brash Jewish immigrants, both Zionist and refugee.

The British government looked to have its hands full with this tiny country in the next few years.

None of which explained why Ali and Mahmoud had been so fearful of detection on the night we arrived. I looked up from the small leather book I had been puzzling at.

'Holmes?'

'Yes, Russell.'

'You referred to Ali and Mahmoud's "little games". Was that whole demonstration of caution a facade?'

'Not all, no. Certainly if we'd been caught by a patrol at that hour of the night we'd have had a most unpleasant time of it. I do think, however, that the good brothers were attempting to illustrate how very awkward our presence here will be. A fact of which any sensible person would be aware.'

'You don't think they wanted us here? Then why did Mycroft—'

'I don't think they wanted *us* here, no. Two young soldiers trained in desert warfare they might have tolerated, although even that I doubt.'

Lovely, I thought morosely. I was on the verge of my twentieth year, I had worked with Holmes for four of those, and I had just in the last few weeks succeeded in convincing him of my competence and my right to be treated as a responsible adult. Now I would have to start all over again with these two proud and no doubt misogynist males. I did not look forward to the task.

'Do you think they're trying to get rid of us?'

He did not answer directly but with another lesson in cultural identity. 'In the desert, Russell, your brother's abilities are all that stand between you and a burial in the sand. It is why the Bedouin's sense of loyalty is so absolute: He must have complete faith in the man who watches his back. These two don't yet know us.'

It seemed to me that Holmes was demonstrating a good deal more forbearance towards these Arabs than he would have had they been, say, from Scotland Yard. I said as much, and he only smiled.

'Patience is a virtue much valued in the Arab world, my dear Russell.'

'Patience, loyalty, and eating with the right hand,' I said crossly. His smile only deepened.

'Wait, Russell, and watch. But for now, how much of the foregoing can you put into Arabic?'

The fire burned low and my brain cells began quivering with fatigue, and at long last our two companions emerged from the night. Ali immediately seized a pan, stirred up the fire, and set about making a meal. Mahmoud stood looking down at the flames, his fingers travelling through his beard and over his scar. Not a word had been spoken. I stretched, and went over to fetch the drawings I had left lying on the ground. I dusted them off and handed them to Mahmoud, and because I was watching for it, I saw the brief twitch of astonishment as he looked through the pages, and something else as well – a dim gleam of chagrin? or amusement? – but he had himself well in control before he looked up, and merely gave me a brief nod of acceptance. He put them away – with care – in an inner pocket of his robe, and bent to warm his hands over the fire. When he spoke, it was in Arabic, the trickier parts of which Holmes translated for me, murmuring in my ear.

'The *mullah* who spoke in Jaffa is a wandering preacher, well known as a speaker of sedition and unrest.'

'Against—?' asked Holmes.

'The Jews. The British. The foreigner in general.'

'Against the Turk as well?'

Mahmoud grimaced. 'The Turk has held this land for four hundred years. The fez is no longer considered a foreign garment.'

'Where is this *mullah* now?'

'He has a villa near Gaza.'

I narrowed my eyes at his tone of voice. 'You sound as if you disapprove.'

Mahmoud drew a breath and blew it out through his nose thoughtfully. 'There is a saying: "A full heart or a full purse." A *mullah* is a man of God. Men of God seldom gather wealth to themselves. A man with a villa on the top of a hill is not a poor man.'

Holmes, being a man who assumed the worst about anyone, a man who would not have shown surprise had the Pope been accused of forgery, grew impatient with this discussion of ethics and morals. 'What of the men who were with the *mullah* in Jaffa?' he demanded.

'Ah,' said Mahmoud, brightening a little. 'That is interesting.' It was so interesting that he had to drop to the ground and make himself comfortable, taking out his embroidered leather tobacco pouch. 'The *mullah* travels with two servants, a secretary and a bodyguard.'

'It was not they who committed the murders,' Holmes said flatly.

'You think not?'

'Your friend Yitzak said "not his" before he died. They were either the servants of some other man or not servants at all.'

Mahmoud did not argue with Holmes; neither did he agree; he just continued to assemble his cigarette with close deliberation, and went on. 'There was another man, a tall, clean-shaven man in European clothing, not a uniform, who stood back and listened, watching the other listeners. Afterwards he was seen speaking with the *mullah*. The two did not appear to be strangers.'

'Ah! That is our man.'

'You think so?'

'Don't you?'

Mahmoud reached for the long-handled fire tongs and did not answer, not directly. 'In any case, he is gone, and no-one knows who he was.'

'Didn't you—' Holmes stopped. Mahmoud paused with the coal halfway to his cigarette and eyed Holmes. Ali bristled. I held my breath; but in the end Holmes did not voice his criticism, merely waved it away. 'It can't be helped. But you know where that *mullah*'s villa is?'

'And that he is away from home until next week,' Mahmoud replied.

'Good,' said Holmes. 'Then to Gaza it is.'

CHAPTER THREE

ت

Common folk have no great need for the services of religious officials.
– THE *Muqaddimah* OF IBN KHALDÛN

THREE NIGHTS LATER, THE REFRAIN that had run so steadily through my mind at the beginning was back again: What on earth did I imagine that I was doing here? I ought to be home, in bed this night, in England. I ought to be in Oxford, worried about nothing more uncomfortable than the next day's tutorial. Instead we had tumbled into this foreign land under the authority of two Arabs who told us the least they could about our goal and our setting. After delivering his report on Jaffa, Mahmoud had drawn back into his taciturn mode and Ali seemed positively to enjoy our discomfiture. It was, all in all, not an easy partnership, and if something was not done to change matters, the relationship between the four of us looked to descend from its current state of mistrust into open animosity. I had thought, for a brief moment earlier that evening, that the restraints were about to drop, but Holmes had inexplicably refrained from reacting at Mahmoud's terse orders, and the shaky truce stood.

The Arab's orders had been obeyed, and here we lay, draped on our bellies atop the precarious and crumbling remains of a stone wall, keeping very still despite the discomfort because our slightest movement sent small stones tumbling down the sheer rock face at my right hand onto the roof far below. It was five days after our arrival in the country, closer to dawn now than midnight, and we were supposedly burglarising the *mullah*'s villa. I say 'supposedly' because in fact Ali and Mahmoud were inside while Holmes and I were given the task of keeping an undetected watch lest we be discovered – although again, why we were next to each other, abandoning the majority of the house's perimeter to the unguarded night, had not been explained. We had been there some ninety minutes, although it seemed like nine hundred. The rock beneath me had drilled itself into my softer organs and permanently rearranged the bones of my rib cage and pelvis, while the cold had penetrated even the heavy sheepskin coat I wore. I turned my head where it lay on my forearms and murmured to my companion, whom I could touch if I wished, but could scarcely see now that the day-old moon had gone down.

'Holmes, will you tell me please what we are meant to be doing here?'

It was the first time I had voiced the question aloud. After all, I was the one to blame for our presence here, and if it had not exactly turned out the way I had imagined, this ungentle sojourn among the sites and sights of the Holy Land, I was not about to give Ali and Mahmoud the satisfaction of seeing us turn back.

Not that I hadn't been tempted to walk away from them, beginning with the first day on the road. We covered barely twelve miles that day, although most of it was spent far from actual roads, picking our way around cactuses and over endless stones, and I was dropping with exhaustion when we halted in the late afternoon among some pomegranate trees near a dirty, nearly deserted pile of slumping mud huts that Ali called Yebna. He came over to where I had collapsed against a boulder and all but kicked me in the ribs to get me up and helping to make camp. My fingers fumbled with the well ropes and the water-skin seemed to weigh more than I did, but I did as I was told, ate without tasting the mess of brown pottage that was dinner, and slept like a dead thing for ten hours.

I woke early the next morning, the first day of 1919, when the faint light of dawn was giving substance to the canvas over my head. The air was cold but I heard the pleasing crackle of burning tinder from the direction of the fire pit in the black tent. Holmes was gone from his side of our tent, his bed-roll in a heap against the far wall, and I thought it was the sound of him going out the flaps that had awakened me.

Oddly enough, Holmes and I had embarked on a similar quest the previous summer, taking to the roads of rural Wales in the guise of a pair of gipsies, father and daughter, to rescue a kidnapped child. Of course, that was August in Wales, and therefore wet and relatively warm, and in a green countryside populated with settled folk. Plus that, the goal of our time there had been clear from the beginning – nothing at all like this, come to think of it, although the sense of the companionship was much the same.

My gentle musing from the warm cocoon of my bed-roll was rudely broken by Ali's harsh voice commanding me to rise, punctuated by a boot against the side of the tent that nearly collapsed it on top of me. Stifling a groan, I unwrapped myself and started the day.

Only late in the afternoon and far to the south did it dawn on me what Yebna had been: I had slept the night, all unknowing, in Javneh, the birthplace of rabbinical Judaism. The Mishnah, that remarkable, convoluted, cumbersome, and life-affirming document that laid the foundation of modern Judaism, was begun in Javneh, at the rabbinical academy that had come into being following the destruction of Jerusalem in the year 70. I had been walking among the very tombs, in the self-same dust where Rabbi Johanan ben Zakkai had taught, where Gamaliel and Akiva and—

Mahmoud refused to turn back. Ali just laughed at me. Holmes shrugged and said, '*Maalesh.*' I mourned, and fumed.

South we had continued, moving towards Gaza but keeping away from the relatively fertile and more populous coastal plain. We entered the fringes of desert, the hardscrabble lands where rains brought short-lived carpets of wildflowers for a few days and bald drought the other eleven months, where the nomadic peoples coaxed tiny patches of wheat and barley to grow in odd corners, yielding a few handfuls of grain in a good year, and the slightly more settled peoples gathered around wells and deep, age-old cisterns, using buckets and primitive well mechanisms to water their melons and their olive trees. This was the desert of Palestine: not the brutal deep desert of sand dunes and camels but a thorny, rocky, dry, inhospitable place where one could carve a living if one was stubborn and smart and did not expect too much. A hard land and a hard people, with occasional flashes of great beauty and tenderness. My respect for them grew along with the blisters on my feet.

The following night we stopped short of Gaza, in a flat place within sight of a well but outside a small village. The two tents went up, the traditional black Bedouin tent shared by Ali and Mahmoud in front of our smaller canvas structure, and before the first flames of Ali's cook fire had subsided into coal, two men appeared before it, carrying letters for Mahmoud to read.

One of them had an answer he needed written, and for the first time I saw Mahmoud's brass inkwell, stuffed with cotton wool to keep spillage at a minimum, and watched him act as scribe to the man in the dust-coloured clothing. Ali went off and returned with a large and muscular haunch of goat, and after we had eaten, six men from the village showed up to drink coffee and say the evening prayers and then have the contents of a two-week-old newspaper read to them. A long discussion followed, for the most part incomprehensible to the odd, bespectacled, beardless youth in the background, who was nine parts asleep in the warm smoky fug that gathered within the low walls of woven goat's hair, lulled by the gurgle of the *narghiles,* or water pipes, and the easy rhythm of the speech of a race of story-tellers. Strange as it seemed, with the blood of an orange grower named Yitzak barely dry on Mahmoud's hem and without the faintest idea of our goal, I began to relax, safe in a desert place three thousand miles from the seemingly all-knowing foe who had dogged our footsteps in England. This was a simple place, as simple as heat and cold, pain and relief, life and death. At the moment, I was alive and comfortable, and the world was a good place to be.

The interval when Mahmoud might have prepared more coffee came and passed, and eventually the *narghile*s ceased their burbling and the men took their leave, their loud voices fading slowly into the night. I followed them out of the tent, and stood, staring at the bright sliver of moon in the black sky, surrounded and celebrated by a million sharp stars and the splash of the Milky Way. I was bewitched by the magnificence, enthralled by the utterly alien sky, and would have stood there frozen (and freezing) had Ali not grasped me unexpectedly by the arm and whispered harshly, 'Get your coat and come. Silently.'

I got my coat and I came, and I followed Holmes and the two others through the dark night until we came to this villa, and the wall, and finally to my petulant question to Holmes.

'Holmes, will you tell me please what we are doing here?'

His dry voice came back in a breath, inaudible two paces off. 'We are waiting to be relieved of duty.'

I lay for a few more minutes, watching the outline of the dark villa and its uninhabited grounds, and spoke again.

'What were they talking about, all the men tonight around the fire?'

'The usual topics of farmers. The lack of rain. The price of wheat. A *ghazi* – raid – one group of Bedouin carried off against another, that meant trampling two fields and killing a milch cow. And of course the manifold wickednesses of the government. Mahmoud,' he added, 'seemed most interested in the last, although equally careful that the others would not see his interest in politics.'

'I see,' I said, not altogether certain that I did. 'Is he after evidence about the murder of Yitzak and his two hired men, or something more general?'

'Both, I should say.'

I was rather relieved to hear him say that; for the past two days neither Arab had given the faintest indication that they were anything but itinerant scribes. I was even beginning to think that the two of them were no longer actively involved in Mycroft's affairs, and that we had been parked with them by mistake. 'Then why do I get the feeling that they're giving us meaningless tasks like mapping that site just to see what we're going to do?'

'Probably because that is precisely what they are doing,' he replied, sounding sardonic. 'It is becoming very tedious.'

'Mmm.'

Silence again, but for the inevitable night noises of a Palestinian village. Jackals cried in the distance, a donkey brayed below us, and the cockerel that had been crowing with monotonous regularity paused for twice its normal thirty seconds, then resumed. Someone in the house at the foot of the cliff treated us to another round of his tubercular cough, then quieted. My legs were now numb except for the sharp hot points of blisters on the soles of my feet and between the first two toes where the rough strap of the sandals had rubbed the skin raw. It was becoming difficult to breathe, I noticed. It was also extremely cold.

I thought about the two Arabs in the house and about the odd current of humour that had permeated Holmes' reply to my query – and, now that I stopped to think of it, one I had thought I detected at times over the past days as well. It was not like Holmes merely to follow directions patiently, especially when they were unreasonable directions such as guarding the villa from a single place in the rear. The country and the way of life were foreign to me, but not completely so to Holmes; the distractions that kept me from looking too closely at just what it was Ali and Mahmoud were doing with us would not apply to him. It was as if two people were blindfolded and led around in circles, one of them a stranger who did not know what was happening, the other a person who knew exactly where he was and yet allowed himself to be led about as well, thinking it a great joke. I could not understand it, and I was too cold and uncomfortable to try.

'You're certain you'd recognise Ali's jackal noise?' I asked after a while.

'He has not made the signal,' Holmes said firmly. 'They are still in the house.'

'Raiding the pantry and having a kip in the soft beds, I don't doubt.'

'Don't be peevish, Russell.'

I fell silent. Another twenty minutes passed. In the two hours we had lain there, nothing had changed except that the rooster in the village had been joined by another perhaps a mile off. At two hours and a quarter Holmes breathed again in my ear.

'Something is moving near the house.'

Before I could react I felt, more than saw, a dark shape moving across the ground towards us.

'*Ya walud,*' came the now-familiar voice, pitched low.

'Here, Ali,' said Holmes.

The man had the eyes of a cat, and picked his way by starlight over the uneven ground to where we lay.

'There is a problem with the safe. Mahmoud cannot persuade it to yield, and the dog and the guard will awaken soon.'

'Does he wish me to try?'

'You said you knew modern safes.' It is difficult to express nuances of doubt and disapproval in a whisper, but Ali managed.

'I will come,' said Holmes, and rolled cautiously off the wall, sending a minor shower of stones off the cliff and rousing the dog of the house below, but not, fortunately, the human inhabitants. Holmes made to follow Ali into the blackness, then paused. 'By the way, Russell, I meant to wish you many happy returns. Although I suppose by now I am a day late.' He vanished before I could respond, but in truth I had quite forgot that it was my nineteenth birthday. For which I had received a sunburnt nose, a matching set of blisters, a bone-deep bruise on my right heel, a stomach clenched tight with hunger, and whatever bruises my current wall-top position might leave me with. All in all, one of the more interesting collections of birthday presents I had ever received.

Much cheered, I resigned myself for another lengthy wait.

To my surprise, less than half an hour later there was another motion of a shadow approaching, and Ali reappeared, much agitated.

'The safe is open, but that foolish man insists on looking at everything it contains. You must tell him to close it so we can leave. There is no more chloroform.' I followed Holmes' example and allowed myself to roll off the wall, only to be knocked breathless by a large stone in the belly. Gasping as silently as I could, I got to my feet and staggered after Ali and into the house.

From the outside it had seemed a large building, and moving through the dark rooms – over smooth marble floors and thick carpets, through air scented with cooking spices and sandalwood – confirmed my impression that this was indeed one holy man who did not embrace poverty.

We turned into a corridor towards a dimly lit rectangle and entered the room, Ali closing the door silently behind us. I looked at the two unshaven men in dirty headgear and robes, bent over the papers, then at the man in garish dress beside me, and could only hope that the guard Ali had chloroformed did not wake, because if he had a whit of sense he would shoot before asking any questions.

Holmes sat on a low stool in front of the wall safe, rapidly but methodically sorting through the stack of papers on his knees. As we came in I saw him pause over a letter, open it, glance at it, and slip it with its envelope into the front of his robe. Mahmoud was looking more animated than I had ever seen him, standing over Holmes and clasping his hands together as if to keep from wringing them, or applying them to Holmes' throat. Ali held out one hand to me, gesturing with the other to the two men.

'Tell him,' he insisted. 'Tell him we must go.'

I studied Holmes for a minute, and thought I recognised the disapproving set to his features. I turned to Ali. 'What is he looking for?'

'We only wish to retrieve one letter. We have found it. We must be gone.'

'Is it possible that this *mullah* could be a blackmailer?' I asked. Ali's eyes slid to one side and Mahmoud growled something about the man in truth not being a *mullah,* both of which I read as affirmatives. 'Holmes doesn't much care for blackmailers,' I commented, but added to the man himself, 'It will be getting light out in another half hour.'

The only sign Holmes gave that he had heard me was a slight increase in the speed of his examination. There was no budging him, until twelve long minutes later he had reached the end of the stack, having removed several more papers, and stood to put the remainder back into the safe. In a flurry of activity Ali and Mahmoud returned the furniture to its place, closed and reset the safe, straightened the lithograph of Jerusalem that covered it, and hurried us out the door.

The sky was beginning to lighten. Mahmoud locked the villa's door and we slipped among the shadowy shapes of fragrant trees towards the front wall (this one high, well maintained, and topped by broken glass) that protected the grounds from the road. Again Mahmoud took out his picklocks and applied them to the gate, unlocking it and relocking it after us. A groggy bark came from the back of the house, but we were away, down the hill, across two switchbacks in the road and the terraces of olive trees they wove through. We retrieved the possessions that we had left there, harmless bundles of provisions and armloads of firewood bound with twine, and finally rejoined the road some distance from the house. When dawn came we were just another quartet of stolid Arab peasants about our business. Half an hour later a lorry of British soldiers passed us without slowing, its dust cloud applying another layer of grime to our clothes and skin.

When we neared our campsite we could see two figures, squatting like gargoyles just outside the front edge of the black goat's-hair tent belonging to Mahmoud and Ali. One was a young man, swathed in many layers of dust-coloured fabric; as we approached he stood up to thrust his wide, callused feet into a pair of once-black shoes that lacked laces and were far too big for him, but were the necessary recognition of an Occasion. The woman at his side remained hunched on the ground, a small heap of faded black with the married woman's red strip of embroidery travelling up the front of her dress. Her head and upper body were wrapped in the loose shawl called a *burkah,* which she had raised across her face immediately she saw us coming, to supplement the red-and-blue veil decorated with gold coins that she already wore. I wondered, not for the first time, why the women in this country did not suffocate come the heat of summer. Her coal-black eyes, the only part of her visible other than an inch of indigo-tattooed forehead and the work-rough fingers of her right hand, were trained on the ground, although when she thought no one was looking, she shot hungry, curious glances at us.

The man greeted Mahmoud as a long-lost brother, hanging on to his hand and talking effusively. We had been through this before, however, and I had read the sign of the borrowed shoes correctly, for rather than removing his guest to the more leisurely depths of the rug-strewn tent, Mahmoud merely dropped to his heels on the ground outside, away from the camel-dung fire that Ali was beginning to rekindle. This was business, then, not friendship.

The rest of us continued as before, ignored completely by the two engaged in their transaction and ignoring the quick glances of the woman (whom of course the man had not bothered to introduce, and who therefore did not quite exist). I took great care not to stare at her, despite my natural curiosity, since I was, after all, to all appearances a male. I had to be content with the occasional furtive glance as I dropped my bundle of twigs and sticks next to the fire and waited for Ali to empty the last of the water from the skin so I could take it half a mile to the well and fill it. Twice my looks caught hers, and on the second occasion she came as close to blushing as a dark-skinned woman can. It was a peculiar feeling, to be thought flirting with a woman, but I decided that if the poor thing took some scrap of pleasure in the idea that a travelling stranger, one who not only had exotic light eyes but flaunted a pair of mysterious and undoubtedly expensive spectacles over them as well, found her a source of secret desire, it could only do her good.

I slung the flaccid water-skin over my shoulder and walked off. It was the third time I had made this particular trip, and the track grew no less rocky, nor did the filled goatskin get any lighter. Similarly, the two camels belonging to the group camped nearer the well were just as surly as they had been before, although the dog did not follow me as far as usual, and the camp children seemed to have accepted the fact that I would not respond to their chatter, merely running out and watching me from under their child-sized *kuffiyahs*. When the woman before me at the well had filled her Standard Oil tin with water, balancing it easily on her head before swaying off without deigning to glance at this apparent male condemned to perform a woman's tasks, I found that not only did the track grow no shorter, but the blisters which this and previous well ropes had raised on my palms were as painful as ever. I filled the skin, arranged on my back the obscene, gurgling object (which, even after days of seeing it hanging near the cook fire, still looked to me like an animal putrefied to the point of bursting), and plodded back to the encampment, past the sounds of the invisible women grinding the day's flour and the visible men in the shade of their tents, talking and smoking and watching me pass.

When I returned, Ali had made tea and was busy whittling – a donkey, it was, small but lively. Holmes was not to be seen, and Mahmoud had his writing table set up and was busy composing a document of some sort for his client, who was still talking, telling Mahmoud something about his brother and a camel, although his speech was far too rapid for me to follow. Twice the young man consulted the woman, who was either a sister or his wife, waiting impatiently for her to answer in her low, intelligent-sounding voice, before resuming his monologue. Mahmoud wrote placidly, the dip of his pen into the brass inkwell a constant rhythm broken only when he paused to trim the quill with his penknife, until finally the page was filled with a beautiful, clean, precise calligraphic script. He signed it with a flourish, the man put his mark on it, and Ali was called over to sign for good measure. Mahmoud sprinkled the document with sand to dry the ink, tapped it clean, folded it in on itself, sealed it with wax, and wrote an address on the front. The man accepted it with effusive thanks and a payment of small coins, and then he and our resident scribe each smoked a black cigarette and drank a glass of water to bring out the full flavour of the powerful tobacco. Eventually Mahmoud's clients departed, the man still talking, to the woman now, who as she stood up was revealed to be greatly pregnant. She shot me a glance both shy and ardent before following at his heels.

Immediately they had disappeared down the track, Ali jabbed his vicious blade back into its scabbard (causing me to wonder fleetingly if Arabs ever disembowelled themselves when putting their knives away in a hurry) and then whipped out the flats of bread that he had cooked the previous evening, and we moved into the tent to break our fast around the fire. I was already very tired of this diet of damp unleavened bread, burnt in spots, which even when hot had no more taste than blotting paper. That morning, however, I was ravenous, and would have eaten the stuff gladly plain, but as recognition of the successful night's work Ali uncorked a jug of honey and placed it on the carpet between us. He then gave us each a handful of dates and another of almonds, and poured out four tin mugs of the sour goat's milk called *laban* that he had bought the day before from our neighbours. Holmes and Mahmoud, I noticed, had their food placed directly before them, whereas my portions were deposited very nearly at arm's reach. Ali did not like eating with a woman, and although he submitted to the necessity, he did all he could to demonstrate his dislike. Even Mahmoud put my coffee down on the carpet in front of me, instead of allowing me to take it directly from his fingers as he did with any male. I sighed to myself and stretched forward to retrieve my breakfast, and sat back on my heels to enjoy it.

When we had feasted, Mahmoud reached for the coffee-making accoutrements. Wordlessly, the rest of us settled back into our carpets, Ali with his carving and Holmes taking out pipe and tobacco from the breast of his robe, tucking the ends of his *kuffiyah* up into the thick black loops of the *agahl* that held it on his head, and proceeding to fill the pipe and light it with a coal lifted from the fire with the tongs. He had, over the last days, taken to smoking the black leaf of the natives, but this morning's pipe gave off the familiar smell of his usual blend, a small quantity of which he had brought with him off the ship. The homely smell was a jolt in this foreign and uncomfortable setting, and for the first time I was washed by a wave of homesickness.

He waited until Mahmoud had the coffee beans in the long-handled pan and the luscious burnt-toast smell was beginning to mingle with the pipe smoke before he put the tongs down next to the fire and reached again into his robe. He drew out the letters that he had taken from the villa's safe. There were five in all, four of which he tossed onto the carpet at Mahmoud's feet. The fifth he held out to me. Mahmoud's face went stony and Ali sat upright abruptly, his great knife held out dangerously in his right hand, the carving forgotten in his left.

'That is not for you,' he objected angrily.

'You two may be accustomed to acting blindly under orders,' said Holmes, concentrating on his pipe, 'but neither Russell nor I have accepted any such commissions. Speaking for myself, I do not care to put my hand into any crevice I have not examined first. The other papers,' he told me, 'are the usual – two incautious love letters from a lady in Cairo, a landowner in Nablus referring to the purchase of illegally seized land, and a police report about – well, never mind that one. And there is this.'

I satisfied myself that Ali was not about to use the knife on us, then took the sheet of paper out of its envelope and unfolded it. Seeing that it was in German, and there was a great deal of it, I lowered my backside to the ground to stretch my legs and give my thigh muscles a rest – and immediately had all three men hissing at me.

'Oh, for heaven's sake,' I objected. 'I can only sit for so many hours with my knees in my armpits. My muscles cramp.'

'It's your feet,' explained Holmes. 'It is extremely bad manners to point the soles of your feet at someone. Almost as bad as eating with your left hand.'

'Sorry,' I muttered, and folded my painful extremities beneath me.

With the coffee halfway to roasted, Mahmoud could not very well put it back into the pouch, but it was with ill grace that he continued the ritual. I had finished the letter and was rereading it when the tiny porcelain cup was brusquely set down in front of me. I sipped it absently.

'Interesting,' I said. Holmes did not answer. I looked at him and found that he was sitting with one knee drawn up and the other leg tucked under his robe. He was studying his cup with exaggerated concentration, one eyebrow slightly raised.

I had known Holmes for nearly four of my nineteen years, during which time he, along with his housekeeper, Mrs Hudson, and his old companion-at-arms and biographer, Dr Watson, had become my only family. I had studied with him, spent thousands of hours in his often abrasive but never dull company, and worked with him on several cases, including the intense and dangerous kidnapping the previous summer; by now I knew him better than I knew myself, and read instantly what his posture was telling me.

'Hum,' I grunted, a considering sound, and read slowly through the German document a third time with his unverbalised but clearly expressed scepticism in mind. After consideration I began to see what he objected to. 'You may be right,' I admitted, and only after I said the words did I notice the consternation on the two swarthy faces across from us. With the sweet flavour of revenge on my tongue I nodded my head deliberately, then folded the letter back into its envelope and returned it to Holmes.

'I should say the flourishes on the final *e*'s and the angle of the dots clinch it,' I said nonchalantly, and held out my cup to Mahmoud. 'Is there more coffee?'

That gentleman gave me a long, expressionless look before reaching for the brass coffee beaker, but Ali could not control himself.

'Is this a secret language?' he burst out. 'The hand signs are invisible.'

'Merely the communication of true minds,' said Holmes. Turning his gaze on Mahmoud, he continued, 'What Miss Russell has noticed is that one of the letters we so laboriously stole from the *mullah*'s safe is a fake.'

'A fake!' exclaimed Ali dramatically without looking at Mahmoud. 'What do you—'

'Planted by you.' Ali made a strangling noise. 'Written by you.' Ali began to protest in an increasingly theatrical manner, but Mahmoud began a very small and quiet smile deep in his eyes, and eventually Ali sputtered to a halt. Holmes' voice went hard. 'The night we landed, you had your fun, trailing us about and pushing us into heaps of rotting fish and mounds of refuse. I protested at the time, yet since we left the town you have continued to lead us a song and dance through the Judean hills. I have said nothing, and if you do not think Russell has been remarkably patient, you do not know her. I understand that you found it necessary to test our mettle; in your position, I might have done the same. However, this has gone quite far enough.' He waggled the letter, then leant forward and dropped it onto the embers. That neither of our companions rushed to snatch it to safety was all the confirmation needed. Mahmoud's forged letter from a purported German spy in Tiberius smoked for a moment on the coals, puffed into flame, and curled blackly. Holmes looked up from the fire. 'Five days of keeping us in the dark is about three days more than I should have thought necessary, particularly considering the way it began. Make your decision: Trust us, or let us go our way.'

It was Mahmoud, still giving his impression of an amused stone, who broke the gaze, flicking a glance at me before he bent forward to dash the dregs from his coffee onto the letter's crisp, trembling curl of ash, and continued the motion into standing upright. He handed his cup to Ali.

'We will go to Joshua now,' he said, and turned towards the depths of the tent.

'Ah,' said Holmes with a nod of satisfaction. 'Joshua.'

Mahmoud paused with his hand on the tent's central post. 'You know Joshua?'

'I know of him.'

Mahmoud studied Holmes for a moment, and then went on into the tent.

'Who is Joshua?' I asked. Holmes looked at Ali with an eyebrow raised, inviting an explanation, but the man merely dusted his robes free of wood shavings and moved off to begin breaking camp. 'Holmes?' I persisted.

'You know your Bible, Russell. Surely you don't need me to explain his *nom de guerre.*'

'Joshua is a code name? For one of the military officers?'

'This Joshua prefers to remain in a more, shall we say, unrecognised position than at the head of his troops.'

I thought about it, then suggested, 'The Book of Joshua; "He sent out two men to spy out the land"?'

'Precisely so,' Holmes agreed, and, knocking his pipe out on the stones of the cook fire, went to empty his possessions from our tent.

CHAPTER FOUR

ث

Weapons are unnecessary on the main routes . . . but advisable on the others, as fire-arms, conspicuously carried, add a great deal to the importance with which the 'Frank' is regarded by the natives.
– BAEDEKER'S *Palestine and Syria,* 1912 EDITION

'NOW' BEING A RELATIVE THING when burdened by tents, water-skins, cooking pots, and mules, we did not get away until the middle of the morning. I packed up our meagre possessions and helped fold away the bell tent Holmes and I had shared since leaving Jaffa.

Once on the road, we headed slightly north of due east, in the direction of Jerusalem, although Ali admitted that we were only going as far as Beersheva. We followed the pattern that had been established our first day on the road: Ali and Mahmoud went in front, holding to a steady pace and never looking back except for Ali to shout the occasional command over his shoulder, telling us not to lag or stumble or let the mules stray. The two men led by as little as ten paces or as much as half a mile, and spent the whole time talking – or rather, Ali talked, with voice and hands, while Mahmoud listened and occasionally made response. Then came Holmes and myself, either in silence with my nose in the Koran or with him drilling me on Arabic grammar and vocabulary or lecturing me on customs and history. Behind us trailed the three mules, clattering and banging with the pots draped about them, obediently treading on our heels and breathing down our necks until we entered a village, when we had to take up their ropes lest the dogs spook them, or if we heard the rare sound of an approaching motorcar in the distance, which usually turned out to be an ancient Ford Tin Lizzie.

I had come to realise that Ali and Mahmoud were well known in this land. Mahmoud, despite his rough appearance, was a respected scribe and public reader. I found that they moved up and down the countryside in a more or less regular cycle, stopping for an hour or a week to draw up letters to distant relatives, contracts between neighbours, and pleas to the government, and to read letters received, or old newspapers, or even stories. The florid Arabic pleas to the Turkish rulers might recently have given way to more concise English documents, and the payment he accepted was now in Egyptian piastres and even the occasional English coin, but little else had changed. As we went along I began to appreciate the freedom the two brothers had, for they were familiar figures, and therefore accepted, but it was also accepted that they were different: nomads without livestock; lacking womenfolk but apparently no threat to the wives and daughters they came near; possessing a valuable skill that yet set them apart and gave them a touch of mystery and power; from no particular place. So the oddities in accent and vocabulary among us – Holmes' proper *kuffiyah* and my own loosely wrapped turban, Ali's Egyptian boots of shiny red leather and his long, colourful jacket, our troop's use of mules in a country that classified people either by the plebeian donkey-and-goat or the aristocratic camel-and-horse of the true Bedouin, our blue Berber eyes with the brown of our two Bedu companions, and even my spectacles – were not so much forgiven as expected, as if we formed a distinct and idiosyncratic tribe of our own. Ali and Mahmoud had lived this life for at least ten years, an ideal arrangement for a neighbouring (now occupying) government needing to keep watch on the activities of the countryside.

I wondered if now, with the war at an end, the brothers' way of life was about to change. Would the government want spies in the land during a time of peace?

'Holmes, what do you make of them?' I nodded at the road ahead, where the two figures, in the Arab fashion that strikes the Western eye so strangely, were holding hands while Ali's free arm waved in the air, illustrating a point. In Arab countries men hold hands in public; a man and a woman emphatically do not.

'You find them intriguing?' he asked.

'I don't know what I find them. I don't know this country, there may be an entire populace like them, as far as I know.'

'No, I believe you could assume that Ali and Mahmoud are very nearly unique here. Even T.E. Lawrence and Gertrude Bell draw the line considerably closer to home than these two.'

It took a moment for his meaning to sink in, and when it did, I demanded, 'What do you mean? Are you suggesting they aren't Arabs?'

'Most assuredly not. Can't you hear the London in their diphthongs?'

'I assumed that Ali had been to an English-speaking school, his English is so good, but his accent is Arabic, not Cockney. And I don't think I've heard Mahmoud say more than two dozen words in English.'

'Not Cockney, more like Clapham, and the Arab accent is an accretion. You really must work on your accents, Russell.'

'What would two brothers from Clapham be doing here?' I demanded incredulously.

'Russell, Russell. They aren't brothers, surely you can see that? Aside from the complete lack of any physical resemblance, their accents and their acquired habits – table manners (if one can refer to such when there is no table), gestures, attitudes – are quite different. At the most they might be cousins, but personally I should not care to put money even on that.'

'Friends?' I asked suspiciously; this had to be one of his peculiar jests.

'Companions, who appreciate Arab dress and culture and enjoy the freedom of their gipsy life.'

'And do some work for the British government on the side.'

'For their king, yes. They are Mycroft's, after all.' Ah, yes, Mycroft, the older Holmes brother, everything the younger was not: corpulent, physically indolent, a life-long cog in the machinery of government. But like the Holmes whose apprentice I had become, Mycroft was brilliant, gifted with a far-sighted ability to discern patterns, and able to grasp instantly the central issue in a tangle. Too, Mycroft, like Sherlock, was unbendingly moral, a fortunate thing for the British people and for international politics, because Mycroft's power within the government was, as far as I could see, nearly limitless. Had he chosen to do so he could very probably have brought the government to its knees. Instead, he gently nudged, and watched, and murmured the occasional suggestion, then sat back to watch some more. If anyone was capable of shaping a pair of Englishmen into Bedouin spies, Mycroft was the man (although I was far from certain that Holmes had not been pulling my leg). I had assumed that whatever task Mycroft needed done here would be as subtle as he was; I had begun to believe that it was so subtle as to be non-existent. However, by the sounds of things, clarification would finally be given us in Beersheva, no doubt by the mysterious spymaster Joshua.

We stopped at one o'clock to water the mules and make tea, and when I had finished my tasks and came to sit by the small fire, I eased off the fiendish sandals and tucked my bleeding feet carefully under the hem of my dusty *abayya*. The sweet tea was supplemented by a handful of almonds and some rather nasty dried figs, and in less than half an hour Ali was putting things away. With a sigh I reached for the sandals, but was stayed by Holmes' hand on my arm.

'Wait,' he said. He scooped a handful of almond shells from the lap of his robe and brushed them onto the dying embers, then rose and walked swiftly over to where the mules stood. Pausing a moment to study Ali's complicated knotwork, he laid hands on the ropes and in a minute had one lumpy canvas bag both free and open. He dug inside, pulled out a familiar pair of boots that I had thought gone forever, closed the bag, and retied the ropes. When he came back to the fire he dropped the boots in front of me, then in one brisk motion he bent to catch up the flimsy sandals and tossed them on top of the burning almond shells.

The pair of stockings that I had stuffed inside the boots five days before were still damp with seawater and the shoe leather smelt musty, but I did not hesitate. I slid them on, did up the bootlaces, and returned the slim throwing knife that had been lodged awkwardly in my belt to its customary boot-top sheath. When I stood up in my old friends, neither Ali nor Mahmoud had said a thing, but my feet were shouting with relief, and I felt that I could walk to Damascus if necessary.

We travelled on through the desert place, seeing only the low black tents of other nomads like ourselves and a few hovels, until late in the afternoon we began to come upon debris from the battle of Beersheva fourteen months before: snarls of rusting barbed wire, the broken frame of a heavy gun, the bare and scattered skeleton of a horse, and strange tufts of rabbit wire reaching up to trip us – a mystery until Holmes explained that this was a means of laying a quick and temporary road for motorcars across stretches of soft sand. When the sun had completely left the sky, we stopped, ate a cold meal, and then pressed on in the almost complete darkness under a heavy layer of clouds.

In the daylight, thanks to my improved footgear, I had not found it difficult to keep up with our guides, but in the booby-trapped dark I fell behind again, and twice was trodden upon by the lead mule.

After about an hour of this the wind came up. An already cold night turned bitter, with the added pleasure of sand driven into our faces. I took off my spectacles, which were in danger of being sand-blasted into opacity if not actually blown off my nose, wrapped my *abayya* more firmly around my body, and followed the dim form ahead of me.

It then commenced to rain. Ali and Mahmoud appeared, waiting for us to catch them up so they could help control the mules. Soon the drops were pelting down; lightning and thunder moved in on us until the storm was directly over our heads as we pressed on, clinging to the halters of the skittish animals for fear our tents and pans would gallop off into the night. The track, never a road, turned slick, and then sticky, until even those of us who had four feet were having a hard time of it.

When the hail began I stopped dead. 'Damn it all!' I shouted at full voice, necessary against the rush of wind and the fast-increasing crescendo of pings of the hailstones on the big convex iron *saj*. 'Why is it so almighty important that we reach Beersheva *tonight?*'

Neither of our guides chose to explain. However, my protest seemed to trigger their own recognition of futility, because they did not insist on pressing on. We fumbled about in the maelstrom for a while until the wind seemed to lose a few degrees of strength and I realised we were against an outcrop of rock. There we hobbled the mules closely and removed their burdens. Ali retrieved the big tent, but rather than attempting to put it up in the gale and the rocky ground, we simply crawled under it and wrapped ourselves up in its folds, huddling together in a mound while the hail smacked at the goat's hair above our heads. It eventually died off into the silent whisper of snowfall; finally, towards morning, there was stillness and a deep, creeping chill.

I had drifted into something resembling sleep when the half-frozen tent shifted and crackled, and someone left our communal warmth – Ali, I decided, hearing his footsteps retreat. He returned a few minutes later, rustling strangely, and stopped near where we had tied the mules. After a couple of minutes he left the mules and came back towards where the three of us lay, and then stopped again. Up to now I had refrained from moving, theorising that if I continued to lie there numbly I might not awaken to the full force of the cold, but now I worked my hand up to where the rough tent lay across my face, and I pulled it away just in time to see Ali, crouched down on snow-covered ground and with his hands stretched well away from his body, strike at the flint he held. The spark set off a great *whump* of petrol-triggered flame: Instantly the wet bushes he had dragged up burst merrily alight, and we had a fire.

This morning, unusually enough, Mahmoud cooked. He began with a porridge of some odd grain, hot and sweet and laced with cinnamon, eaten with wooden spoons from the common pot. This was followed by the inevitable flat bread, except that for him the big curving *saj* behaved itself and produced a bread that was light and unburnt and cooked through, tasting deliciously of wheat and eaten by tearing it into pieces and dipping it into a tin of melted butter. Then Mahmoud sent Ali back to the mules – it was now light enough to see what he was doing – and he came back with a dented tin that lacked a label. Hacking it open, he handed it to Mahmoud, who upended it over a pan. To my astonishment, it landed with a spurt of fat sizzling, and the smell of bacon shot up into the frigid air.

Mahmoud cooked the bacon crisp, and then set the pan on the ground between us. He did not eat any himself, but took out his prayer beads and watched with his inscrutable look as the three of us polished off the meat and even ate a good part of the grease, dipping bread into it until we were near to bursting. Jewish (and I had thought Moslem) dietary laws prohibit the eating of pork, of course, and I normally avoid it, but that morning I swear it was a gift straight from the hand of God, and it saved my life. When we repacked the pots, the morning was just cold, not deadly, and my sheepskin coat, though damp, was nearly adequate.

It is a superstition among the Bedouin, Holmes had mentioned to me during one of his little lectures, not to begin a day's journey until the dew is off the ground, lest the spirits take the traveller. The custom reflects good common sense, as hair tents packed wet will not survive for long. That morning, however, had we waited for dry tents we should have still been sitting there at sunset, so we beat the snow and ice out of the black tent as best we could, redistributed the remaining load between two of the mules, and heaved the unwieldy thing onto the back of the third grumbling animal.

The desert sparkled in the fresh morning, washed clean

and without a cloud in the vast sky. Patches of snow lay on the highest hills, melting quickly when the sun hit them. Water pooled and ran down the wadi below us, and a bright haze of green lay over the rocky waste, with here or there a wildflower, to all appearances brought up miraculously overnight. The mules lipped up tender blades of young green grass as we went, their packs steaming gently as the sun gained warmth, and the world was a very contented place.

Except for our guides. Ali was silent as he walked, and Mahmoud seemed even more glum than usual.

When I asked Holmes if he had any idea why they might be downhearted, he shook his head, and I shrugged my shoulders.

Meantime, the Promised Land was unfolding in beauty around us, my stomach was full, and my feet did not hurt for the first morning in what seemed like many. It is an amazing thing, the difference to one's powers of concentration a pair of comfortable shoes can make. I seemed to be seeing my surroundings anew, including my companion.

'Your beard is coming along nicely, Holmes,' I commented after a while. 'Does it itch?'

'It begins to be tolerable. The first ten days are always the worst.'

'And are you wearing kohl around your eyes?' We had all taken extra care with our toilette that morning, both as a necessity, having spent the night in close proximity to a filthy, goaty, smoke-impregnated tent, and because we were going into a small city filled with curious eyes. Ali had curled his moustaches with care; Mahmoud had beaten the dust from his *abayya;* my boots were brushed off against a corner of the tent, and my hair was securely knotted into its shapeless turban.

'Every well-dressed Bedouin wears kohl.'

'It's quite dashing. Actually, you're beginning to look remarkably ferocious.'

'Thank you. Now repeat the conversation we have just had, in Arabic.'

We struggled through another lesson in my new tongue. I had now reached a state of fluency roughly equal to that of a brain-damaged three-year-old, and had yet to say a word in the language to anyone but my companions, but I had begun to catch whole phrases in conversations without having consciously to pick over the words looking for meaning, rather like Ali picking over the lentils for stones. In another week, perhaps, I might find myself actually thinking in scraps of the tongue. Until that time it would be exhausting work, this language with five different gutturals, six dentals, eight pronouns, and thirty-six means of forming the plural.

In halting Arabic I informed Holmes that the rocks were red and the small flower was white, that flies were a plague from Allah and that the mules stank. He in turn described the holy city of Mecca (forbidden to infidels such as he) and told me about the true Bedu, complete nomads who survived on camel's milk and goat's meat in the deep desert, who lived for horses and for raiding and who looked with scorn on any who tilled the earth. I took the thin opening and slipped with relief into English for a while.

'Your accent is Bedouin, is it not? It seems smoother than Ali's,' I noted.

'I learnt the language in Arabia proper, not among the fringe peoples. Mahmoud's accent is quite good.'

'But you still say they're English?' It would, I reflected, explain the bacon.

'Without a doubt. However, I should not mention it in their hearing, if I were you.'

Holmes dropped his voice at this last remark, since our two companions had halted to wait for us. When we were before them, Mahmoud spoke, to my surprise, and in English.

'Because the wadis are now full we must go into the city by the road. Amir must remain absolutely silent. He must not speak, no matter the provocation.'

'You are expecting provocation?' I asked. He ignored me.

'The one thing we must avoid is a full-body search of Amir. Even among the English, there would be consequences were a woman to be found dressed as a man. Remember: Silence.'

He was curiously impressive, was Mahmoud, not unlike Holmes in his intensity and his complete self-control. I followed behind, subdued and not terribly interested in Arabic lessons. After half an hour or so we dipped down into a small wadi, and there we paused while Ali took a wrapped parcel from inside his robe, added to it his pearl-handled revolver and another, smaller parcel from Mahmoud, pulled the rifle from deep in one of the packs, and held his hand out for the revolver Holmes carried. Last of all he unstrapped his gold wrist-watch (the hands of which had not moved in six days), and he wrapped it all in a sheet of oiled cloth from one of the saddle-bags and secreted the whole bundle in a niche, arranging some rocks in front to keep it in place and hidden, but making certain that we saw where he was putting the armoury. Natives such as ourselves were not encouraged to bear arms.

The area to the back of us was a network of wadis and hills, including the (now flowing) watercourse of the Wadi el Saba, up which the British Army had made its decisive push for Beersheva in October of 1917. To our right were the remnants of the Turkish trenches, dug into the flat plain and lined by barbed wire, lengths of which remained, rusted and lethal. We gave the defences wide berth, and soon came to the rutted track to the coast that passed for a road, built originally by the Turks, used now to link the Beersheva garrison with the coastal railway up out of Egypt at Rafa. A year earlier, when Beersheva and Gaza were the front-line cities of British occupation, the road would have been an ant's trail of military activity. Now the town was rapidly slumping back towards its usual somnolent state, and if the lorries still came and went all day and half the night, they did so with less urgency.

Unfortunately, this state of affairs meant that the soldiers stationed there, already disgruntled at having to wait for demobilisation as the weeks after Armistice crawled into months, felt both left out and itching for something to do, and at the check-point into Beersheva it quickly became apparent why Ali and Mahmoud were so apprehensive, and why they had rid themselves of their weapons.

Half a mile from the check-point, Ali guided the mules to the side of the road and inexplicably set about making tea. Lorries rumbled up and down, laden camels plodded softly along, and we sat a stone's throw from the road, sipping our tea. It was not a very leisurely tea break, however; both of our Arabs were wound tight, and sat on their heels smoking and drinking and never taking their eyes off the point where the road dwindled into the western horizon.

Without warning Mahmoud rose, tossed the contents of his just-filled glass of tea into the fire, and snatched mine from my lips to do the same. Ali, moving easily but wasting no time, gathered up all the equipment, shovelled it unceremoniously into a saddle-bag, and cinched it shut. Within minutes we were on the way east into the city, and because at Mahmoud's insistence I had removed my attention-getting spectacles, I had absolutely no idea what they had seen to spark such movement.

The bored soldiers at the check-point were pleased to see us, and obviously recognised our guides.

'Why, if it ain't our old pals Tweedledee and Tweedledum. And look, Davy, they got some friends today. Ain't that nice?'

'Even wogs have friends, Charlie.'

'Too true, Davy, especially when they're pretty as the skinny one.'

It was fortunate that the dye on my skin obscured any blood that rose on my cheeks, because their comments soon escalated, becoming remarkably graphic. Nonetheless, all four of us stood with our eyes on the ground until the two soldiers tired of talk, and one of them strolled over and slipped the point of his bayonet under the pack ropes. The mules skittered backwards to the full extent of their leads as our possessions rained down about their hoofs. In two minutes everything we owned was spread on the ground for the inspection of His Majesty's troops, who trod up and down and kicked the coffee-pots and tent pegs across the mud. They seemed most disappointed to find nothing more lethal than a paring knife, and I shuddered to think what would have happened to us had we retained our guns.

They were just tiring of this when I became aware of the approach of what Ali and Mahmoud had seen earlier: an entire caravan of Bedouin – men, women, and children, camels, dogs, horses, goats, and sheep. There was even a lone chicken, squawking in agitation from a rough cage tied atop one of the camels. The front of the caravan stopped dead at the check-point but the tail continued to move forward, spreading out until it blocked the roadway in both directions. Lorries ground to a halt, drivers leant out of their windows and shouted curses, and an armoured car, horn blaring, pushed its way through the crowd on the verge, trying to leave the town. The two British soldiers, forced to abandon us before they had finished their fun, contented themselves with loud remarks about the filthy thieving habits of the bloody wogs, then turned away.

Ali bent to retrieve a fragile porcelain cup. As the soldier named Davy walked up the line, before any of us could react, he slipped his rifle from his shoulder and casually swung it around to swat Ali a tremendous crack on the head with the gun's heavy butt. Ali collapsed amongst the kitchenware. I took one furious step forward, and felt Holmes' hand freeze like a vice on my upper arm.

Fortunately neither soldier had noticed our movements, and

they continued on their way to harass the camel caravan, but Mahmoud had seen my instinctive move and frowned at me thoughtfully for an instant before he bent to help Ali, who was already sitting up, holding his head and moaning loudly.

It seemed to take forever to bundle everything back onto the mules and slip away before the soldiers could return to us, but we made our escape into the streets of the town. Near the Turkish railway station we stopped to tuck a few loose bits back into the tenuous hold of Mahmoud's knots. The precarious load would not have lasted an hour on the road, but apparently we were not going far. Holmes and I helped Mahmoud by bodily lifting the bulge of one pack while he looped a few more lengths of rope about the whole thing, mule and all. When the knot was tied he paused to look over the mule's back at me.

'When the soldier hit Ali,' he said in a low voice and with perfect English diction, 'it looked as if you meant to attack the man.'

'Yes, I'm sorry. I didn't think.'

'But you would have gone to Ali's defence? Physically?'

'Under different circumstances, certainly.'

He did not seem angry at my disobedience, just puzzled. Finally he said, 'But women do not fight.'

'This one does,' I answered. He held my gaze, then looked sideways at Holmes.

'This one does,' my mentor confirmed.

'*Wallah!*' Mahmoud muttered with a shake of his head, recited something in Arabic, and went to help Ali to his feet. I looked at Holmes with a raised eyebrow.

'From the Koran, I believe,' he supplied. 'He used the same passage the other day; it seems to be weighing heavily on his mind, for some reason. Loosely translated his words meant, "Would Allah make a woman to be covered in ornaments and powerless in a fight?" A rhetorical question, of course.'

Of course.

CHAPTER FIVE

ج

And Joshua the son of Nun secretly sent two men out of Shittim as spies, saying, 'Go and look over the land.'
— JOSHUA 2:1

Beersheva, the place of oath, the settlement whence Abraham and Isaac set out on their ominous journey into the hill city of Jerusalem for the father's willing sacrifice of his beloved son. Before the guns of August had broken into their ages-old way of life in 1914, the residents were only slightly more numerous than in the days when Hagar and Ishmael had been turned out into the wilderness, and only marginally more technological. Now the town was an uncomfortable mixture of dust-coloured hovels older than the hills, a couple of modern buildings constructed by the Turks to demonstrate their determination to retain this border outpost, and a number of brisk, efficient structures the incoming army had thrown up to house its personnel.

Our destination was an ancient inn at the southern end of town, a single-storey mud-brick establishment of numerous rooms leaning shoulder-to-shoulder around a central courtyard. The instant we came onto the premises a shouted conversation began between Ali (increasing my respect for the hardness of his skull) and several men who appeared from nowhere to seize our mules and lead them off.

Halfway through the courtyard, an older man emerged from a doorway and swept up to Mahmoud, kissing him three times on his cheek to welcome him. He then took Ali's hand, clasping it briefly to his chest, and greeted Holmes and me with less familiarity but equal enthusiasm. We stood in a cluster for some minutes before he noticed that Ali was not his usual vigorous self, and on hearing of our mishap at the check-point, he threw up his hands in horror, bemoaning Ali's mistreatment at the hands of those sons of dogs soldiers (or such was Holmes' translation of the epithets) and examining the admittedly alarming knot concealed by Ali's *kuffiyah*. At Mahmoud's firm suggestion the landlord finally whisked his shaky guest off to a bed.

The shouting contest continued unabated even in Ali's absence, touching down occasionally on Mahmoud, who would grunt a monosyllabic answer that seemed to make no discernible impression on the questioner. They ignored Holmes and me completely, but led us all cheerfully towards the back corner of the inn. We were ushered in, the flimsy door was shut carefully behind us, and I soon was given the opportunity to add to my vocabulary the words for various vermin, as well as a few expressive adjectives.

The door flew open, crashing off its primitive hinges, and half a dozen lads staggered in carrying all our possessions aside from the livestock, which when deposited on the floor left us with only one room to move in, a room currently occupied by the snoring Ali. Mahmoud caught one of the boys by the shoulder, pointed to the tent sprawling massively sodden across the floor, and told him to take it up and spread it on the roof to dry. Out went the roomful of damp, smoky, goaty hair; the cheerful voices retreated, and were heard from the open window, until finally thumps and footsteps overhead told of the task being carried out.

Next through the doorway came a meal, a platter heaped with rice and hunks of tough mutton (a change from the tough goat's meat we had eaten most nights) and a stack of bread, with mugs of *laban* and bowls of dates and dried figs. The lads dribbled water over the fingertips of our right hands from a long-spouted pot, stood there talking over our heads for a while, and then went off, politely propping the door back in the doorway as they left. The three of us ate, making balls of meat and rice from the platter and tossing them back into our throats. I was gaining confidence at eating with my less dextrous right hand, but Mahmoud, long practised in the technique of eating without chewing, finished first. He wiped his greasy fingers on his robe, went to check on Ali, whose stentorian snoring never paused, and then came back.

'He sleeps,' he said unnecessarily. 'You remain here; I will return.' He wrestled himself out the door and left.

Holmes and I looked at each other, wrapped ourselves in our *abayya*s, and went to sleep on top of the baggage.

Ali woke us late in the afternoon, complaining mightily of a sore head and grousing at the cold food he had to eat. (I shuddered at the little footprints on the platter and averted my eyes.) Before long Mahmoud swept in.

'One hour,' he pronounced. Ali immediately stood up, deposited the platter and empty bowls outside the doorway, and he and Mahmoud began to turn out and reorganise our possessions. Two cups, a bowl, and the smallest brass coffee-pot, its handle snapped off under Charlie's boots, were set to one side, and everything else was bundled neatly into a surprisingly small pile.

When the tent was carried in a short time later, smelling of sunshine, it too was reduced to a snug roll in the corner.

Holmes and I sat on our heels out of the way and watched.

Our house restored to order, Mahmoud reached for his sheepskin coat. We made haste to do the same, and followed him out of the door.

The early evening air was sharp with the smoke of cook fires and the day's warmth was fast departing, as it always does in the desert. We walked in a leisurely fashion through the mud-brick town, past two wells busy with women and a mosque in a park, through a whirl of children playing what appeared to be an Arabic variation on cricket, ignored by soldiers and glanced at by the native residents. Finally we entered a large and very new-looking cemetery – a military cemetery, full of the dead from Britain and Australia and New Zealand, men who had died ensuring that this, the southernmost town of the ancient

Israelites, should be the first town prised from Turkish hands.

In the smoky gloom of dusk, we strolled to the end of the sad, neat little park, and then turned to retrace our steps. On our way into the cemetery we had avoided a canvas-sided army lorry that stood near the entrance – hardly surprising that Ali gave it a wide berth, as its driver was behind the wheel with a glowing cigarette. The only surprising thing was that we had not been intercepted and thrown out on our ears the instant we appeared, four untidy Arab natives daring to defile a British military cemetery. Indeed, as we approached the lorry a second time, coming closer to it in the near darkness, the driver's door opened. I braced myself for a quick fade into the twilight, but to my relief, instead of abuse, the head that came out merely said, 'You're alone,' and withdrew.

The motor spluttered and roared into life, the driver's door slammed shut, and we had barely time to tumble after Mahmoud up and into the back of the lorry before it was in gear and moving.

We stayed behind the canvas, though the back flap revealed the town fading behind us. The check-point on the Gaza road slowed us briefly, but the sentries did not bother to look in the back. Soon we were bouncing down the pitted road, clinging to the sides in an attempt to take the edge off the worst of the jolts. The night became colder and the road got no better, for what seemed a long time, after which we turned abruptly to the right, and the road grew worse.

Ten minutes of this, and the lorry dived into a pothole, gave an alarming crack from somewhere in front, and the engine died.

Convinced that we had broken some vital part of the machinery, I just sat. Ali and Mahmoud, however, struggled to their feet and dropped over the back. Holmes and I followed, straightening up slowly to allow our vertebrae to ease back into line.

'As the Irishman said when he was run out of town on a rail,' Holmes commented, *sotto voce,* '"Were it not for the honour, I'd rather have walked."'

'Are we there, then?' I asked.

'So it would seem.'

The headlamps of the lorry illuminated a heap of mud bricks topped with rusted sheets of corrugated iron that I should have taken for derelict but for the well-fitting door that opened on noiseless hinges at Ali's touch. The moment we stepped inside, the lorry lamps went out. Mahmoud shut the door behind us, I heard Ali in front of me move, and then another door opened, spilling light into the tight vestibule the four of us had crowded into.

The room beyond was a singular piece of architecture, long and low, with roughly plastered walls, a floor of packed earth, and lengths of unpeeled tree trunks holding up the iron roof. Squares of flattened petrol tins were nailed up in place of window shutters, the interior whitewash had long since flaked off the wall, and the entire structure appeared about to collapse into the earth, but looks were deceiving. The ramshackle building was warm compared with the out-of-doors, and not a chink of light had shown from the outside. The two long walls, twenty feet apart, ran parallel to each other for about fifty feet, at which point the left one halted and both walls turned ninety degrees to form an L. The building was heaped with stored goods – crates, bales, and canvas-wrapped shapes. There were no internal walls in sight.

However, my attention was not on the room but on the solitary figure it held, halfway down. He was a small, round man – round of body, round of head, his knuckles dimpled into the flesh of his hands – dressed in unadorned khaki and seated on a camp chair. He did not look up at our entrance, merely continuing his task, which appeared to be holding something on a stick a few inches above a paraffin stove. A plate with a few round objects sat on a tea-chest at his left knee, and another heaped high was at his right, but the incongruity of the sight kept me from acknowledging what he was doing until my nose brought me the smell, evocative of my Oxford lodging-house with its mugs of cocoa and of Mrs Hudson's kitchen in far-off Sussex: The man was toasting crumpets.

When he finished with the muffin on his toasting fork he removed it, laid down the fork, took up a knife and smeared the crisp round with butter from a tin, and then balanced it on top of the plate at his right. He pushed the plate a fraction of an inch towards Ali, who with Mahmoud had gone up to the man and dropped to his heels across the small stove from him. Ali took two muffins, passed one to Mahmoud, and as they began to eat, the man reached down for his fork and proceeded to spear it into another muffin.

Holmes and I made our way down the room to the scene of domesticity and source of meagre warmth, following a path through the stores and shrouded equipment. We ducked our heads around a hanging oil lamp, settled onto a rough bench, and waited.

When our host was satisfied with the current muffin, he buttered it, put it with his others, and then picked up the plate and handed it to Holmes.

'There's honey in here somewhere,' were his introductory words to us. 'I'll find it if you like. I haven't any jam, I'm afraid. I can't bear the stuff any longer, not since they started providing it in the trenches every night before a big push. I was only in France six months, but I can't even look at a bowl of jam now without smelling mud and urine and unburied bodies. If you will excuse the reference. Shall I go digging for the honey?'

We reassured him that buttered crumpets were sufficient, and set to demolishing our share of the crisp, buttery, delicious, and utterly English fare. Fortunately, the crumpets were solid enough evidence to restore a degree of reality to the setting.

The left-hand plate was soon empty, the right-hand one containing the toasted crumpets nearly so. The round man reached behind him for a kettle, set it over the flame, took a khaki handkerchief from his shirt pocket, dusted his hands, and folded it away.

'I must say,' he mused, sounding as if he were continuing a conversation, 'I was intrigued when I received word that you were coming here, Mr Holmes. Particularly when your brother suggested that we might put you to use. You and Miss Russell, of course,' he added, with a small bow in my direction. 'However, I will admit to a certain hesitation. After all, there is some difference between London and Palestine.'

'But I take it our two guides have set your mind at ease that we will not commit some glaring faux pas and do not actually require nursemaids to help us survive our time here,' Holmes said evenly, sounding more amused than perturbed.

'You have passed their little tests satisfactorily,' the man replied, his eyes crinkling in his round face. 'You did not drop from exhaustion or limp with sore feet, you did not lose your tempers or put your hands on a scorpion, you retained the appearance of who you are dressed to be, and you saw through the facade of the letter in the safe. And, Miss Russell, you make lovely maps. By the way, do call me Joshua. Everyone does.'

'"Sending spies into the land,"' I murmured in Hebrew, thinking how appropriate the word 'spy' was here, since in Hebrew its root meaning is one who wanders about on foot. I had the blisters to testify that this was what we had been doing ever since we arrived.

'Quite right,' he said in English, sounding pleased.

'And do your spies gather information, or spread rumours?' I asked him. 'Those of your biblical predecessor seemed to do something of both.'

'As with my predecessor, it is not always clear just what the purpose of my people might be. Perhaps, as you say, something of both, listening and speaking.' He showed us his yellow teeth in a smile.

'And now that we have proven ourselves minimally competent,' Holmes said, dragging the conversation back to the main matter, 'you have what my brother, Mycroft, might call a "task" for us.'

Joshua shook his head and looked mournfully across the steaming kettle at Mahmoud, then said something in Arabic. It sounded to me as if he were accusing Holmes of drinking uncooked coffee beans.

Holmes responded with a brief phrase of his own, which my ears translated as, 'When the dogs bark at night, it is [foolish?] to look to the sheep the next morning.'

I could not see what this had to do with coffee beans, but Joshua seemed to think it a worthy retort, because he nodded briefly. 'You may be right,' he said. 'However, I think in this case we may delay long enough for a cup of tea.'

He walked around to a heap of canvas and brought out a wicker basket, which proved to contain a formal tea service that had probably been designed as a picnic fitting for the boot of a Rolls-Royce. From it he unpacked five delicate flowered cups and their saucers, then a matching china teapot, milk jug, and sugar bowl, arranging them all to his satisfaction in our midst. Milk came from a small corked bottle sitting on the ground near his feet, and was poured into the jug. He performed the entire ritual: warm the pot, spoon the tea leaves, add the boiling water, wait the requisite three minutes, and then pour the tea through a silver strainer. When we each had a cup in our hand, Joshua sipped his twice and then rested his saucer on his knee.

'The problem is,' he said, again with the air of picking up a conversation that had been briefly interrupted, 'that if one is given only the mildest inkling of dogs at the sheepfold, it is difficult to justify turning out the entire house to stand defence. Particularly when the family has just spent the last few years eradicating the countryside of dogs, with all apparent success.'

Holmes raised a disapproving eyebrow and said sharply, 'Five days ago three men were killed in the outskirts of Jaffa. This is success?'

'An unfortunate incident, with potentially far-reaching

consequences, but an isolated occurrence. We have caught the men.' Ali grunted; Mahmoud put down his cup and took up his prayer beads, thumbing through them as Joshua continued. 'It seems to have been a revenge killing. Yitzak was responsible for the jailing of three young Moslem Arabs last year, for beating up a Jewish boy who had made eyes at their sister. One of the lads died in jail last month, of the influenza. The two men who have been arrested were the dead boy's uncles.'

'You would say then that it was a coincidence that Yitzak saw one of his attackers listening to a firebrand *mullah* the week before?'

'Not necessarily a coincidence. The *mullah*'s speech might easily have urged them to action. Tragic, and contributing to a state of mistrust, but nothing more, and certainly nothing to do with Yitzak's . . . association with us. We can only be grateful that his wife and children were not at home. I do not believe they would have been let alone.

'There is, however, another matter.' He gazed down at the dregs in his cup as if unwilling to raise his eyes to the men across the stove from him. Ali eyed him warily; Mahmoud's fingers slowed on the polished beads.

'Mikhail the Druse is dead,' Joshua said in a quiet voice, and then he did bring his eyes up, looking across at Mahmoud, whose face turned to stone. Ali's cup fell, shattering into a thousand pieces of porcelain against the hard earthen floor, and he whirled to his feet and strode rapidly away from the light into the dark leg of the L. 'He was shot,' Joshua continued implacably. 'There is no certainty, but it appears to have happened two or three days ago. There are jackals in the wadi.'

'Who?' Mahmoud's voice had gone hoarse.

Joshua shook his head. 'It could have been some woman's husband.'

'Mikhail loved women,' Mahmoud admitted slowly, his fingers wandering briefly to his scar. 'And he was often in difficulties over them. "The cupboard is not locked against a man with the key."' His heart was not in his aphorism, however, and it did not sound to me as if he believed much in a jealous husband.

'This was one of your men?' asked Holmes.

'Mikhail was mine, yes.'

'What was he working on?'

'I don't know,' Joshua admitted. Mahmoud stared at him, and I heard a brief stir from Ali in the dark reaches of the building. 'It's true. There were rumours, out in the desert, of problems. Nothing substantial. He went out to listen.'

'For the sounds of dogs amongst the sheep?' Holmes suggested. He even made it sound as if such pastoral imagery were his daily fare.

'There were no dogs. I'd have heard them, if there were.'

'Something more silent, then. Wolves.'

Joshua sighed deeply, his jovial face looking more troubled than I should have thought possible. He put his hand into his breast pocket, drew out a pouch, and began to roll a cigarette. Recognising the signs, I settled myself for a longish story.

'I do not know how much you two know about our war here, so forgive me if I travel familiar ground, but our situation is a delicate one. I spent the first months of the war on the Western Front,' he began. 'That war, as you undoubtedly are aware, consisted primarily of crouching in the mud a hundred yards from the enemy and occasionally, at immense cost of life, pushing his line back a few yards, or, conversely, of being pushed and losing a few yards of one's own. Here, it was rather different. Other than the catastrophe in the Dardanelles and the constant loss of life from submarines, we contented ourselves with sitting in Cairo, gathering titbits of information and protecting the Suez Canal.

'Until Allenby came.' Joshua's tone of voice when he said the name was not far from worship, although I thought this deceptively soft little man would not venerate another easily. 'Allenby was given command in June of 1917. Four months later – four months! – we found ourselves crossing the Sinai into Palestine. We took Beersheva and then Gaza, and by God, we were standing in the gates of Jerusalem by Christmas. Nine months later, a year to the day after he'd begun this impossible task, he gathered up his rag-tag army of camels and colonials and pushed, and before we knew it we were in Damascus.

'It was a brilliant campaign – elegant, meticulous, sly, and inexorable. The Battle of Megiddo was a mighty victory, a beautiful thing to behold. In two stages a mere twelvemonth apart, Allenby had the country, and four hundred years of Turkish rule were broken.

'And now he's stuck with it, and stuck with the job of keeping the country in one piece until they decide at the Paris talks how to cut it up. The French want it, the Arabs think it's theirs, the Jews believe they were promised it, the British hold it, and General Allenby spends all the hours God gives him driving from Dan to Beersheva, calming arguments among the factions.'

'While you hear the rumour of distant wolves,' Holmes prompted.

'Who the wolves are I do not know, but yes, I believe I hear them. And I am quite certain, when we come close enough to hear their voices, we will find they speak Turkish.' Joshua was talking to Mahmoud now, and Mahmoud was listening attentively. 'Not all of our enemy was taken, and by no means have all surrendered. Here as in Germany there are discontented young officers who blame their old regime for the losses during the war. They will be infuriated by the demands made by the Allies. The cost of their losing will be high indeed. A mistake, but what victor listens to counsel of generosity and reason when vengeance is at hand? We are looking here at the seeds of another war, with political ferment about to foam up around us and engulf us. Allenby believes we can salvage brotherhood; I will be satisfied if we can merely keep the upper hand. We will need it, soon enough.'

Holmes cut impatiently into this speech. 'What do you wish us to do about the situation?'

'Do? I don't want *you* to do anything.' The little round soldier was gone; in his place bristled a condescending and irritated military officer, putting a problematic subordinate in his place. 'If we were in London, Mr Holmes, I might permit you to act, might even permit you to lead. However, may I remind you that this is not your home ground? Ali and Mahmoud are my men. Valuable men. I have few enough of those at the best of times, but in the last three months, between demobilisation and accidents, I am down to about half strength.'

'What accidents?' Holmes demanded sharply.

'Accidents. My men are tired, and peace has made them careless.' Holmes met his eyes, refusing to be dismissed. 'One in a motorcar crash, the other went off a cliff.'

'And Yitzak with a knife, and Mikhail with a bullet. Do you normally lose a man on the average of one every three weeks?'

Joshua sat placidly, refusing to be drawn into an answer, but even I doubted that this was a standard rate of attrition. I also was beginning to think that Mycroft, whose job was accounting for odd fluctuations in the empire's resources, had not been unjustified in offering us this little problem.

One thing I did not understand was why this rotund English spymaster was insisting that the deaths of his men were more irritating than worrying. Perhaps the bureaucratic passion for keeping face extended here as well. His next words seemed to confirm this.

'None of this is your concern, Mr Holmes. You are here – at my sufferance, understand, not due to any authority you might imagine your brother holds – because I want my two men to have someone watching their backs. Let me be brutally frank, Mr Holmes: You and Miss Russell are expendable. I have used better men than you, and I have even used men equally renowned. Were you to vanish, there is nothing to point to me. You are to regard yourself as a back-up, Mr Holmes. You and Miss Russell have proven that you can pass for Bedu under a cursory glance, and Ali and Mahmoud by themselves are vulnerable. Four men – if you will permit me, Miss Russell? – are safer from casual attack than two. And the two of you might be of some use in running messages or holding a rifle. Frankly, despite your brother's influence, I should not send you if I had any others available. However, I haven't anyone else, so I will use you, and trust you far enough to assume that you won't get my men killed. More tea?' He held out the pot, as if his harsh insults had never been spoken. I retained my cup, but Holmes, looking more amused than angry, handed his over to be refilled.

'Tell me more about those insubstantial rumours,' Holmes suggested, as if he had heard nothing of what the man said. Joshua studied him, but was apparently satisfied, because after the tea had been poured and milked, he put away the pot and drew a map from another breast pocket. When the camp chair had been moved back he spread the map on the floor and sat on his heels like an Arab beside it, agile despite his bulk. Ali emerged from the shadows and stood behind us, looking on.

The map was of the southern half of the land, from Jaffa on the Mediterranean down to Akaba on the gulf and over nearly to the Egyptian border. Beersheva was roughly a third of the way down, surrounded by a great deal of emptiness. Joshua touched the map with the fingertips of his left hand, and then drew the side of the hand down the sheet towards himself as if brushing crumbs from its surface.

'The desert has been a place of retreat for the oppressed and a source of trouble for the authorities for thousands of years. Fanatics hid out here, establishing monasteries or raising armies; rebels retreated here to die the deaths of martyrs, or to regroup and gain strength. It seems a deadly place, empty and sterile, particularly in the summer, but the intensity of life here has spilled over onto human dreams and ideas.

'You ask what and where these rumours are, Mr Holmes. I wish it were so simple. What we hear are whispers and words. A man here' – he tapped the map near a city called Salt – 'tells a story around the fire one night, a tale of Arab conquest that ends with the unbelievers dead and the city of Jerusalem closed to all but the Moslem. A woman at a well here' – his finger rested on Ramleh – 'speaks of a man buying weapons. The wind has more substance, but it has voices as well, voices that Mahmoud and Ali are trained to hear. They will go about their business and listen; you will fetch water and do as they tell you.' The small uniformed figure paused to stare at Holmes again and, seeing no response, seemed satisfied that his point had been taken. He sat back and spoke to Mahmoud. 'The anti-Jew speeches are escalating.'

'The *imam* in Hebron?' Mahmoud asked.

'And others.' Joshua turned to explain. 'Until recently, Jew and Arab lived together in this country without severe problems. Not as family, necessarily, but neighbours. That is no longer the case, for many reasons. The Arab people fear what the Balfour and Sykes-Picot agreements might mean. They fear outsiders in general. They respect the British, and they revere General Allenby, but they need a focal point for their uncertainty, and the recent influx of Jews from Russia and Eastern Europe looks to be that. Unless something is done, the Jews will become the scapegoat. The *imams* and *mullahs* are encouraging it, those who are political.' The man ran a frustrated hand through his thin hair.

'The speeches are escalating, becoming more bloodthirsty every day. We've had several incidents of rock throwing, a Jewish shop burnt, wild rumours. The murders of Yitzak and his two men are the worst; had you not made it appear as if the poor man had fallen on his scythe and his two hired men fled with the petty cash from the kitchen, I have no doubt that we would have had a full-scale riot on our hands in Jaffa by midweek.

'General Allenby does his best, but he's only one man, and has only so much oil to pour on troubled waters. And there is so much misunderstanding – it's difficult to know where to begin. When the *fellah* hears from his betters that the real meaning of the Balfour agreement is that his ten dry acres are to be cut in half and shared with a Jewish family from Russia, he believes that is what the government means by providing a 'Jewish homeland.' He does not know of the Paris peace talks, does not trust distant politicians to protect him. All he knows is that the Turkish yoke was on his neck for four hundred years; now it is off, he will fight to keep it off.'

'Aurens used to say, "Semites have no half-tones in their register of vision,"' Mahmoud commented. The precision of the words sounded incongruous in his heavy accent.

'Colonel Lawrence being something of an expert himself in the matter of black-and-white truths,' Joshua noted drily.

'Still, it is true,' Mahmoud persisted. 'This is an emotional people, not an intellectual one.' Not entirely true, I thought, given the record of Arabic scholarship, but I was not about to quibble.

'Tell me this, Mahmoud,' said Joshua, addressing his teacup. 'Do you think this reaction could be a deliberate one, rather than strictly spontaneous?'

The simple question instantly galvanised the room: Holmes quivered to attention like a hunting dog on point, Ali straightened, and Mahmoud's eyes went dark. Holmes broke the silence.

'That is a most intriguing suggestion. May I ask what brought it to mind?'

'A certain degree of similarity in the . . . one couldn't call them "attacks", exactly, although some of them were. "Symptoms" is how I think of them. Arabic pamphlets that bear a strong resemblance to one another. Identical rumours springing up at two or more far-flung places before they are heard in the intervening countryside. Slanted translations of British policy statements that give signs of having been planted. An unexpected sophistication in the times and places where rocks are thrown and speeches made, and a marked tendency of the ringleaders to disappear without a trace.'

'The trembling of a web,' Holmes said to himself. There was a look of intense gratification on the few square inches of face visible between *kuffiyah* and beard.

'A web?'

Holmes waved the question away impatiently. 'Where is the centre of this activity?'

'This is a small country, Mr Holmes. If the roads were in good nick one could motor down the better part of it in a day, or ride it in a week. Most of the disruptions have been within the triangle formed by Jerusalem, Jaffa, and Haifa, but then most of the population is there as well. If there is a centre to the disturbances, I would guess it to be around Jerusalem, probably to the north of the city.'

Holmes controlled himself admirably, saying not a word against the idea of relying on a guess, which he regarded as a mental aberration, shockingly destructive to clean habits of thought. He merely mused as if to himself, 'If conspiracy there is, who are the conspirators?'

Joshua took it as a question, and settled back in his camp chair for another lecture. 'In Palestine, clearly there are three main parties: Christian, Jewish, and Moslem. I think for the time being we may leave aside the fringe minorities, the Druse, the Sufi Moslems, and so forth. And if we assume that the disturbances are aimed at increasing ferment and upsetting the status quo that the military government is struggling to maintain, then the Christians are unlikely to be the cause: Under British rule, they will be in the best position they have held since the Crusaders were evicted in 1291. Jews are more usually targets than instigators, although there have been several staged reprisals against Moslems, but it would be hasty to assume that this is a Moslem conspiracy. There are several factions among the Jews, particularly recent immigrants, who see the traditional complacency of the native Jewish population as the main obstacle to establishing a Jewish homeland here. Jews whose families have been here for generations tend to keep their heads down and pray; radical immigrants, the Zionists from Russia and Europe, can be firebrands, anxious to unite their people beneath a sense of adversity. It is worth noting that, Yitzak's farm aside, there have been no deaths or serious injuries in the post-war clashes.'

'Yet,' I muttered.

'This man Mikhail,' Holmes broke in. 'Where did he die?'

It was clear that Holmes had not heard a word of Joshua's peroration. The round spymaster scowled, and addressed himself to Mahmoud. 'Mikhail was found halfway down the Wadi Estemoa. Two boys chasing a goat spotted him. Sheer chance he was found at all.'

Holmes had bent to run his eyes across the map, and when he found the river-bed in question he pointed it out to me.

'You have no idea what he was doing there?' he asked Joshua.

'As I said, I assume he was listening.'

'Was he robbed?'

'There was nothing in his bag but the basics: flour and coffee – already ground – a bottle of water, his tobacco, that sort of thing. No money, and his gun was missing, but the two Bedouin boys took those. Had I forced them to hand their loot over,' he added in explanation, 'they would never report anything else they might find in the future, nor would their entire clan. Instead I gave the boys a small reward, and they admitted to taking the gun and the money, but swore they took nothing else. I believe them.'

'Was he from this area?'

'Mikhail? No. Despite his Christian name, he was a Druse, from the hills above Haifa. However, he knew the whole of Palestine intimately. He was a dragoman before the war, especially popular with the English and German tourists, I understand.' He caught himself. 'But Mahmoud knows this, and you do not need to. You're not investigating a murder, Mr Holmes. You are not investigating anything, in fact. You are here in a strictly subordinate role. Is that understood?'

'I hear you,' said Holmes ambiguously, although Joshua did not seem to take it that way. He relaxed, and when he spoke next it was with an air of admission.

'When I heard you were coming, I thought Whitehall had lost their minds. A man older than most of the commanders here, with no military background, and a girl, neither of whom knows the land or the language as well as they ought. Frankly, I refused. And was ordered to give you a fair trial, after which I might send you home if I wanted. When Mahmoud here approved, I thought he had been out in the sun too long. In my experience, Mahmoud does not approve of many. But he said you would do, and here you are. Good to have you with us, Mr Holmes, Miss Russell. I wish you luck.' He began to pack away the tea paraphernalia.

Holmes ignored the fact that we were being dismissed. 'I assume you have buried the body. What have you done with his possessions?'

'I have them.'

'I need to see them.'

'There is nothing of interest there.'

'Still.'

Joshua wavered on the edge of anger for a few moments; then, controlling himself, he shrugged.

'His pack is not here. I kept it at headquarters in Beersheva.'

'Shall I come there?'

'That would not be wise.' He sighed theatrically. 'If you insist on seeing it, I shall have it sent over. You won't remove anything?'

'Not without notifying you. We also need to know precisely where he was found.'

Again Joshua hesitated, but gave in more quickly this time. He squatted next to the map and showed Mahmoud the watercourse, asking him, 'Do you know the place where the wadi turns, and there are three large boulders in a heap with a small tamarisk on the hill above them?' Mahmoud thought for a moment, and nodded. 'Mikhail was found behind the westernmost boulder. His pack was about ten feet away.'

'He was killed by a revolver?' Holmes asked.

'If so, it was not his own. He carried a small gun; this one was larger, possibly even a rifle. The scavengers had been at him, though, so it was not possible to determine what damage the shot had done in the first place. The bullet was not in him.'

'I see. Well, let us have his possessions tonight, if you can. We shall let you know what we find.' Holmes rose and began to button his long sheepskin coat.

It was quite obvious that Joshua was not accustomed to being dismissed by his men, and he did not know whether to impose the might of military discipline on Holmes or to overlook his response. With a somewhat forced return of joviality he decided on the latter. Practically slapping our backs, he began to bundle us towards the door.

'You'll let me know if there is anything you need,' he said, meaning he was quite certain we would not ask.

'Actually,' I said. He stopped, looking at me quizzically. My three robed companions stopped as well. 'Another tent,' I suggested firmly.

'*Another* tent?' Joshua made it sound as if we had lost any number of them along our profligate way.

'Yes,' I said. 'Please.'

'No,' said Ali. 'It will look suspicious, three tents with so few people.'

'Either a third tent,' I said flatly, 'or Holmes moves in with you.' A woman's determination was not a thing with which any of these males (other than Holmes) had much experience. One by one their eyes dropped, and again Joshua shrugged.

'Very well. Another tent. It'll be a small one.'

'So much the better.'

CHAPTER SIX

ح

Desert dwellers do not possess luxuries. They use tents of hair, or houses of wood or clay, unfurnished. They have shade and shelter, nothing else. Their food is either raw or little prepared, save that it may have been touched by fire.

— THE *Muqaddimah* OF IBN KHALDÛN

THE ROAD BACK TO BEERSHEVA seemed even rougher than the outward journey, and was definitely colder. We were let out on the south end of town, below the ancient wells, and in five minutes we were at the inn. Although it was nearly midnight, Ali called out for coffee as we passed the kitchen. I went off to the latrines behind the inn, in no pleasant mood.

I had left the mud-brick building in the hills stewing to myself over Joshua's patronising words and attitude, and the long, jostling trip back had not dissipated any of my profound annoyance. I arrived back in the room on the heels of the coffee bearers, and waited impatiently while the thick brew was poured out. The instant the door was fixed into place, I gave vent to my irritation.

'"Some use in holding a rifle,"' I grumbled furiously. '"Running messages". Who does he think he is?'

Holmes did not answer, but Ali did. 'He is Joshua.'

'And I'm supposed to be impressed by the name? For God's sake, he's got a resource he won't even consider using.' I gestured to where Holmes sat on his heels, sipping from the delicate cup pinched between thumb and forefinger, his long mouth twitching in amusement. 'Holmes, speaking objectively, would you not agree that it is a foolish commander who neglects to make full use of the strengths of his men?'

He inclined his head to show agreement, but Ali gave out a guttural laugh.

'Strengths? What strengths are those? An old man and a girl.' He added an eloquent mock-spitting gesture of hand and lips, and that, on top of a solid week of disdain and the dismissive attitude of the spymaster, was simply too much. I leapt to my feet and stormed over to thrust my face into his.

'Hit me,' I ordered. Behind me, Holmes put down his cup with alacrity and moved out of the way.

'By Allah, it is a great tempta—' Ali began. So I slapped him. Hard. His face went purple and he surged up, reaching out to grab me by the shoulders, but before he had his balance I performed a manoeuvre that I knew would only work once on a man of his size and strength, when he was both unprepared and off balance. As he came at me, I seized the front of his robes and then hurled myself over backwards, kicking out hard to send him flying over my head and tumbling through the open doorway into the next room. Before he could find his breath or his feet, I was standing over him with one of my two throwing knives in my left hand. His eyes widened, his hand flew to his belt, and I half turned and threw the knife back into the main room, sinking it with satisfaction into the nose of a bearded face on a fly-specked 1913 calendar that decorated the back of the door. Then I turned my back on him and walked away, retrieving my knife and returning to my now-cool coffee.

Holmes dropped back into his place, working hard not to laugh aloud, and murmured, 'Do you feel better now, Russell?'

I did, of course, although I was also beginning to regret the insult I had dealt Ali even before he stumbled back into the room with his wicked knife in his hand and his jaws clenched in fury under his beard.

Mahmoud, though, was looking at me with more interest than he had yet shown.

'Can you do that with the knife every time?' he asked me, speaking in Arabic, but slowly.

'Every time.'

Of course, I then had to prove it by dispatching three large spiders, two pencil marks, and a flying apple core. Mahmoud seemed inordinately pleased at this unexpected talent of mine. Ali, predictably, sulked. After the halved apple core had fallen to the floor, he stirred.

'A clever circus trick,' he said dismissively. 'Have you ever used a knife? Drawn blood? Killed?'

Holmes cleared his throat. 'My dear man, she's lived in England all her life. Give her time.'

It was, I think, the first time Ali Hazr and I had been in

agreement, under the effect of Holmes' amusement. He was mocking us both, and had a knock at the door not interrupted, Mahmoud might well have been pulling the two of us from Holmes' throat.

The interruption proved to be a wary soldier holding two canvas-wrapped parcels and an envelope. The envelope he handed to Mahmoud, one parcel went to Ali, and the other he put into my arms before scurrying away from the fray. While Mahmoud settled down to extract note from envelope, I glanced at my bundle, and was pleased to find canvas: It was small, and it was worn, but it was a tent. I had shared close quarters with Holmes before, but not by choice.

The brief note eventually reached me. I took it and read, in handwriting so perfect I would instantly have mistrusted its author even if I had not met him:

I have just received word that your self-styled mullah *was shot dead in Nablus yesterday.*

'Ah,' I said to Holmes. 'One of those letters you removed from his safe came from a man in Nablus, did it not?'

'It is not uncommon for a blackmailer to push a victim too far,' he agreed distractedly. 'Mahmoud, when you first opened the *mullah*'s safe, did it look at all disturbed, as if you were not the only man to rifle his papers?'

Eventually, Mahmoud gave a shrug. 'It was untidy, but without knowing the man's habits . . .'

'One thinks of a blackmailer as being that alone, but in truth, if a petty criminal were to perform an illegal service for another, and if that other was in a more delicate or precarious position were the crime to be brought to light, well, it would make a solid basis for a steady income.'

'That is,' I clarified, 'a blackmailer may not also be a criminal-for-hire, but the criminal may easily turn his hand to blackmail.'

'A man may pretend to be a *mullah* in order to stir up dissent, but when his safe later reveals him to be a blackmailer, he reveals himself as a man of many parts,' Holmes elaborated.

'This is pure speculation,' Mahmoud objected disapprovingly, his English gone suddenly pure.

Holmes sighed. 'True. Let us see what Mikhail's bag has to tell us.'

We dropped to our heels to examine the possessions of Mikhail the Druse, primarily a bag of striped cloth containing the bare necessities for survival in the hills: flour, water, and dried lentils, tea and roasted coffee, part of a hard Bedouin cheese, a handful of dried figs, and half a dozen tiny muslin bags containing spices. He also had a flint and steel; a worn cooking pan and a small coffee-pot with pretty designs etched into it; tobacco in an embroidered pouch along with cigarette papers and a nearly empty box of vestas; a knife and sheath (which, judging from the bloodstains, had been removed from his person still sheathed); and a single .22-calibre bullet, overlooked no doubt by the boys who had found his body. The only two things that I thought marginally unusual possessions for a Bedouin were a small collapsible brass telescope and the stub of a pencil.

Holmes picked up the little muslin pouches one by one and

sniffed at them. One seemed to puzzle him, so he picked open the bag's draw-string to examine the contents. Poking his finger inside, he withdrew it, looked at what it held, and dabbed the fingertip against his tongue experimentally.

'Salt,' he concluded. 'Rather dirty salt. And mined, I should say, rather than taken from an evaporation pond.'

'The Dead Sea has both kinds,' commented Ali absently, turning the striped pack inside-out to finger the seams and examine the straps. 'If it is dirty, it is probably not government.' He threw the pack onto the floor. 'Joshua was right, there is nothing here.'

Holmes had picked up the pencil stub and was eyeing it; it was two and a half inches long and sharpened with a wide blade. 'No papers, diary, that sort of thing? Would your friend Joshua have mentioned if he had removed them?' he asked Mahmoud.

'Yes.'

'Mikhail was a friend of yours, I believe?'

'Mikhail was a friend.'

'What kind of man was he?'

'What does it matter? He is a dead man now.'

'A man is murdered because of what he is,' Holmes said, with what for him was remarkable patience. 'If you tell me what Mikhail was, we may more easily find how his death came to him. Unless you believe it was an accident.'

Mahmoud reached out for the box of matches, slid it open as if hoping for a clue, then closed it, turning it over and over in his fingers – which, I noticed, were longer and more sensitive than I had realised. 'Mikhail was a good man,' he said abruptly, eschewing maxims for the moment. 'He was an honest man, and he hated the Turks. They killed his entire family some years ago, destroyed his entire village. A massacre: his mother and father, two sisters, wife, and son died overnight. He had no great love for the British, but he trusted Joshua. Mikhail was very good at what he did. There was no accident.'

It was the longest speech I'd heard Mahmoud make, in any language, and it had been delivered in an English nearly devoid of accent. Holmes did not acknowledge the occasion, merely pulled shut the strings on top of the little bag of salt and tossed it back onto the small heap of possessions. He held out his hand for the striped bag, which Ali had begun to reload. Ali hesitated, then handed it over to him with a show of tried patience. Holmes upended it so that everything fell to the ground, turned it inside-out again, and set about examining it. In a moment his attention was caught by a small lump of something brown that had stuck itself to the seam. With a little 'Ha!' of triumph he took out his penknife and began to scrape at the lump, using tiny motions to get every bit of the substance. When it was free he held it up to his nose and sniffed at it deeply.

'Do you know what it is?' I asked him.

'I ought to,' he said, and held it out for me to smell.

'Honey!'

'Beeswax,' he corrected me. 'This is a short length of a candle that has been blown out, and left to go cold on a dusty piece of rock before someone scraped it off.'

'A bit of candle,' Ali said scornfully, and with heavy sarcasm added, 'Even heathens use candles at times.'

Without acknowledging Ali's remark, Holmes held the blob of wax on the end of his knife while he fished a bit of slick paper from inside his robe, and, taking great care to get all of it, scraped the wax onto the paper. He sniffed at it, wrapped it tightly, put the tiny packet inside his *abayya*, cleaned his knife blade on the knee of the garment, then said: 'We must go and examine the place where Mikhail died.'

'There is no point,' Ali protested. 'We know where and how he was killed.'

'We know no such thing,' said Holmes placidly. Still ignoring Ali's protests, he went to our pile of things, retrieved his wool rug, and proceeded to wrap himself in it. Sitting down on a portion of the rolled-up tent, he paused for a moment to fix Ali with a hard gaze. 'I do not work well in harness with others,' he said. 'If you wish to accompany me, I will permit it. However, I am not interested in your recommendations as to our course of action. Goodnight.' He pulled the rug over his head, curled up on the tent, and went to sleep.

As, eventually, did we all.

We woke at five o'clock to the banshee wail of the *muezzin* from the mosque. The hours between wakefulness and dawn were taken up with the final restoration of order to our possessions and with replenishing our supplies. After our breakfast (coffee, flat bread, and a mug of watery *laban*) Mahmoud rose, settled his knife in his belt, and looked at me. 'Come,' he ordered.

It was only the fourth time he had spoken directly to me, and I nearly tripped over myself scurrying to obey. He did not make me walk a full pace behind him, either, as if I were a slave or a woman; he merely kept his shoulder in front of mine.

There were few shops and not much in them, but he bought

a quantity of small, misshapen, grey-green coffee beans, some knobs of hard brown sugar and a pair of equally hard cheeses, one tin of condensed milk that had originally belonged to His Majesty's forces and was cause for intense bargaining, some millet, three kinds of pulse, two tins of tomatoes, a handful of aromatic mint leaves, a quantity of onions, half a dozen dry-looking pomegranates, two lemons, four small eggs (which were then wrapped in straw and placed in a string bag he had brought with him), four new tea glasses, two porcelain coffee cups and a bowl, a box of German matches and several packets of well-travelled Egyptian cigarettes, some dried fruits, a few small scoops of half a dozen spices, each wrapped into a tight square of paper with the end turned in, ten oranges, six carrots, and an antique cabbage. Mahmoud carried the eggs and the tea glasses; I was loaded with everything else.

From a side street came the sound of hammer on metal, and we were soon standing in a metalsmith's while Mahmoud searched the artisan's wares for a coffee-pot to replace the one broken beneath the British soldier's boot. The bargaining and tea drinking looked as if they would go on for some time, and since no-one was paying me the least attention I allowed my burdens to slip to the ground and moved off to look about.

My eye had been caught by a stack of bright colours through a doorway, which seemed to be a workshop adjunct to this one. The colours turned out to be, not rugs as I had thought, but a pile of embroidered robes. Some of them were the traditional garish red-and-orange on black fabric, but two were a striking, subtle blend of greens and green-blues on a natural, creamy cotton. The needlework was both strong and delicate, and had they not been so obviously women's garments, I should have been very tempted.

Mahmoud, however, had no such compunction. Before I heard him coming, the lovely thing was plucked from my hand. I turned, startled, to watch him walk back over to the smith and drop the dress in a heap onto the carpet beside the pot that was under negotiation. It seemed, I decided eventually, that the garment was to be a bonus to justify the ruinous price the artisan was demanding for his work. After another twenty minutes the bargain was completed, money changed hands, and Mahmoud picked up his eggs in one hand and the four glasses in the other. I shoved the new purchases into my parcels and staggered after him.

When we returned to the inn Ali was missing and Holmes was trying, with limited success, to oversee the packing of our possessions onto the mules. Mahmoud seemed undisturbed at the absence of his partner, and simply set to and directed the inn's servants in the packing and tying of loads. When we left town Ali had still not appeared. It was not until we were well clear of the check-point on the Hebron road north of town (manned by three taciturn but businesslike British strangers) that he materialised, sitting nonchalantly on a rock by the side of the road, in his hands a nubbin of wood and his great knife, at his feet the bulky parcel that we had buried in the wadi before approaching Beersheva.

Once the revolvers and rifle were distributed between their persons and the mules, we were away again, and I finally had the opportunity to ask Mahmoud to explain the transaction involving the dress.

'I wished to finish my business,' he told me. 'We would have been there all day.'

'You said something to him about a girlfriend?' He and the shopkeeper had laughed after Mahmoud's comment, one of those shared masculine laughs, the same in any language, that instantly raises a woman's hackles.

'I told him you wanted the *kaftan* for your girlfriend.'

'I see. Oh. Do you mean you bought it for me?'

'I paid three shillings for it. If you want it I will give it to you for four.'

'Truly? It's a beautiful thing, yes. I'd love to have it. Thank you.' He grunted and picked up his pace, but suspicion had begun to dawn, and I trotted to keep up with him. 'Mahmoud, did you buy the *kaftan* because you saw I wanted it?'

He glared over his shoulder at me as if I were mad. 'Of course not. I wanted to hurry the business. That is all.' He began to walk even more quickly, and I allowed him to pull away. I was very pleased to own the garment, but I wished I could understand quite how it had come about.

And I did not forgive him for that hackle-raising laugh.

CHAPTER SEVEN

خ

Victories often have hidden causes. Muhammad said, 'War is trickery.' A proverb says, 'A trick is worth more than a tribe.'
– THE *Muqaddimah* OF IBN KHALDÛN

NORTH OF BEERSHEVA LIES A strip of true agricultural land where the soil is more than a thin scum of dust on the surface of rock and there is water enough to encourage the crops. The small fields of green wheat and barley looked strange at first to eyes accustomed to the stony places, but when we entered a brief hollow where the green stretched out on either side and the trees along the edges of the track had miraculously escaped the Turkish axe, I was hit again by a flash of déjà vu, back to the previous summer as gipsies. Here we had mules clanking behind us instead of the creak and tinkle of a gaudy horse-drawn caravan, and the sky over our heads was brilliant and clear instead of grey, but the feel of being on the road incognito was very similar.

'This reminds me of Wales,' I said to Holmes.

'In Arabic!' he growled, in that language. This also was like our time in Wales, when I was required to maintain the disguise even when unobserved. Obediently, I reworded the sentence into something resembling Arabic.

Holmes corrected my vocabulary and pronunciation, and waited until I had repeated it, before he answered that yes, he remembered Wales, and then launched off on a completely unrelated tale of a Bedouin raid he had participated in while a guest of the Howeitat tribe, of which I understood every second word. My Arabic was improving, but it was a strain to have to think in a foreign tongue.

We lapsed into silence. A mile or so passed, the only sounds our laden mules, the occasional lorry, the tinkling of various goat bells, and from time to time the drift of conversation from the two men ahead of us. Ali seemed in high spirits; I wondered idly what he had come upon during his trip to retrieve the guns that cheered him so.

Mostly, however, my thoughts were on the previous night's curious encounter with the spymaster Joshua. His stubborn determination to present an unruffled, unworried facade in the face of what to me seemed some fairly serious problems had struck me as odd then, and seemed even more peculiar at a distance. And he certainly was no judge of men, if he thought Holmes would be deflected by pretty words and stern instructions. Indeed, had he wanted Holmes' interest to be piqued, he could not have chosen a better approach.

I stirred myself and trotted forward to join Holmes, who had drawn ahead of me while I was deep in thought.

'Tell me, Holmes,' I began, only to have him hiss at me in disapproval. I laboriously constructed a sentence in Arabic, which came out something like 'Consider Joshua want help you – your, or no?'

Holmes put the sentence right for me, waited until I repeated it with the correct inflection, and then said merely, 'I think you'd find that our friend Joshua is a very clever man indeed.'

Which was all well and good, but I personally would not trust the little man one inch further than was absolutely necessary.

By the time we made camp that night, having walked eighteen or twenty very uneven miles and heard nothing but Arabic since leaving Beersheva, I was exhausted. I did my chores and ate Ali's tasteless food mechanically, and sat slumped against a bundle in front of the fire in the black tent, dimly aware of Mahmoud pounding the coffee mortar and Holmes talking again, telling another story. Without making an effort of concentration, it was just a flow of Arabic, sweetly guttural noises that ebbed and flowed against my eardrums, until my attention was snagged by the sound of my own name. I bent my ears to his words and decided after a minute that he was telling Ali and Mahmoud the tale of our Welsh adventure; as I listened, an odd thing happened. Despite, or perhaps because of, my combined lack of sleep, physical tiredness, and psychic revulsion for the ubiquitous foreign language, I suddenly realised that I was able to understand virtually everything that was being said. It was as if some internal mechanism had clicked on and the strange and laborious patterns fell neatly into place, so that even individual words that I did not actually know were clear in their context. For half an hour I sat by the fire, drinking minute cups of thick, bitter coffee and listening to Holmes build an epic out of the case in Wales.

Holmes had always been a good speaker, but this performance was, I realised later, extraordinary, particularly coming from a man long critical of his biographer's habit of making romance out of what the detective viewed as an intellectual exercise. In the general run of things he scorned Watson's vivid adjectives, yet that night in front of the cook fire Holmes produced a narrative decorated with embroidery and detail that even Watson might have hesitated to include. It was an exciting story, and only when it had rung to a close did I become aware of the glances that our two companions had been throwing my way. When the air was still again but for the whisper of the fire and the distant bray of a *fellahin* donkey, Ali turned to me with a glare. *'Mouhal,'* he said: Impossible. *'El haq,'* I replied: The truth.

He continued in Arabic automatically. 'You climbed up a tree, entered the house of an enemy, and rescued this child of the American senator? Alone? A woman – a *girl?'*

'It is true,' I repeated, pushing away the irritation his naked doubt caused.

'I do not believe this story,' Ali declared fiercely. A female who could not only heave him across the room and throw a knife with potentially deadly accuracy but perform heroic rescues on top of it was obviously more than he could bear.

'You would accuse me of falsehood?' Holmes asked in a quiet voice.

Ali looked from one of us to the other, no doubt seeing hot anger on my face, cold threat on Holmes', and scorn in both. He even glanced at Mahmoud, but found no help in that blank visage.

'Exaggeration,' he said resentfully, in English.

'Very little,' said Holmes, accepting the word as if it had been an apology. He did not allow the subject to pass, however, but continued to study Ali as if the younger man were a schoolboy in danger of failing his course of study. This made Ali understandably uneasy. Holmes finally spoke, in a voice with cold steel in it.

'I can see we are going to have problems if you continue to think of Russell as a woman, and English. It could be highly dangerous. I recommend strongly that you stop, now. Think of Russell as Amir, a boy from out of the district who does not speak the local dialect very well. Refer to him using the masculine pronoun, picture him as a beardless youth, and you just might succeed in not giving us away.'

In the course of this speech Ali's expression had gone from a smirk to disbelief to fury. He rose, his fists clenched, Holmes' bland face infuriating him even further. He took a step forward. Mahmoud said his name, and he stopped, but turned to his partner and flung his hand out at Holmes in protest. Mahmoud spoke again, a phrase too terse for me to take its meaning, but it cut Ali off as with a blade. The angry man stared furiously at the calm seated one, then turned his back without a word and stormed into the night.

We all turned in shortly thereafter, but the night's silence was broken by the lengthy murmur of conversation, rising and falling, from the direction of the black tent. I could hear no words, but it sounded to me as if Mahmoud did most of the talking.

In the morning Ali seemed filled with brittle cheerfulness, Mahmoud was more taciturn than ever, and Holmes was distracted and anxious to be away. We broke camp while Mahmoud made tea, then stood and sipped the hot, sweet drink in the chill dawn before entering the wadi, the shadows still stretched long against the ground.

Here at the lower end of the watercourse the wadi bottom was damp with pools of clear water, but the going was firm, with only the occasional patch of mud. Holmes walked in front, ignoring the tracks in the sandy soil, tracks left by those retrieving Mikhail's dead body. His eyes were on the boulders above the wet line of the recent flood, and he stopped often to crane his neck at the top of the cliff above us.

The sun was overhead when we came around a bend to find Holmes standing on top of a group of three large boulders with a young tamarisk tree growing from the hill above them. We stopped. Ali gathered together a circle of stones and set about building a fire in the wadi bottom. Mahmoud retrieved his coffee kit. Soon the aroma of roasting beans filled the cold, damp canyon, but Holmes, oblivious, continued to quarter the hillside, stopping from time to time to finger a broken twig or bend close over a disturbed stone. Eventually I climbed up the rocks and joined him.

'There were at least two men,' he began without preamble as soon as my ears were within range. 'And it was not a revolver but a rifle, three bullets, from there.' He jabbed a finger briefly at the top of the opposite cliff before returning to his task of gently prising pieces of stone free from the crumbling face of the cliff with the knife from his belt. 'A first-rate marksman, too. He hit Mikhail's turban with his first shot, fifty feet above here, and wounded Mikhail with this, his second.' His long fingers came out from the crack in the rock at which they had been worrying, holding a misshapen wad of grey metal between them. He displayed it to me, slipped it into his robe, and scrambled down a few feet to trace a faint smear of red-brown on the face of the rock and a small spatter farther on. 'When the third one struck, he fell onto the boulder, as Joshua said.' On the boulder below, despite the intervening rain-storm, the stain was still clear.

We sat for several minutes, Holmes contemplating the sequence of events and I regretting the death of this man I had never met, until eventually the aroma of bread joined that of coffee, and we descended to take our midday meal.

When we had finished eating, the men lit their cigarettes and Holmes narrated the last scant minute of the life of Mikhail the Druse. 'He was coming down into the wadi. He must have known someone was after him, because he was moving quickly, at a greater speed than is wise on this terrain, which caused him to skid and slide. He may not have known that the man with the rifle was there on the other side until the first bullet went through his turban . . .' He paused to lay a tuft of white threads on a flat stone. 'He did wear the usual white Druse turban, I take it? I thought so. When the bullet went through it, he panicked, jumped and fell, caught himself on that rock with the black vein in it' – Ali and Mahmoud turned to look at the hillside – 'and the second shot hit him, a flesh wound that bled quickly. It was on the left arm; there's a partial handprint farther along. This was the second round.' He took the flattened bullet from his robe and put it beside the scrap of fabric. 'You can see the track of his flight down, even from here. Across the slide area, jumping to the boulder, he fell, rolled, and caught himself briefly on the dead tree, pulling it from the ground. He lost his bag then, turned to reach for it, and as soon as he stopped moving the third shot came, and he died. A short time later, the pursuer whom Mikhail was fleeing came down the same hill in Mikhail's tracks, at a considerably slower pace. He checked to see that the Druse was dead, then went through his possessions. I would suggest that he removed something that had been written with that recently sharpened pencil we found in the pack.'

'How can you know that?' shouted Ali. 'You were not there watching! Or were you?' he demanded, his eyes narrowing with sudden suspicion.

'Don't be a fool,' Holmes replied in an even voice. 'I read it on the stones. Ali, I know that Mikhail was your friend. I am sorry, but this is how he died, with thirty seconds of fear and a clean bullet.'

'And the knowledge of failure,' said Mahmoud bitterly.

'Perhaps we can change that failure.'

'But how do you know this thing?' Ali insisted. 'You found the bullet and the threads, but how do you know of the second man?'

'It could not have been the man with the rifle who went through the Druse's pack because the marksman was on the other side of the wadi, and by the time he reached this place the blood would have been dried. It was another man, already on this side, who reached Mikhail's body and stepped in a patch of wet blood. He tracked it over to where the bag had fallen, paused there, shifting his position three or four times, and then went down to the floor of the wadi, where marks of his passing have been erased by the rising water. He wore boots,' Holmes added. 'Stout ones. If you wish, I will show you the marks left by the bullets and Mikhail's passing.'

'That will not be necessary,' Mahmoud said. 'We have spent too much time here already. For all of us to examine the hillside risks attracting attention. Let us pack up and go.'

Ali was too troubled to argue. He merely rinsed out the coffee cups in one of the rain pools and stowed them away on one mule, tied the broad iron *saj* on another, and set off with Mahmoud up the wadi.

We followed them with the mules rattling along behind. After a while I asked Holmes, in cautious Arabic, if he knew where we were going.

'Mahmoud certainly knows,' he replied helpfully, and then ordered me to recount the history of my widespread family members. In Arabic, of course.

I stumbled over kinship terms and the stony ground for a long time as we continued our way up the wadi, rising always towards the tops of the cliffs. In the late afternoon the wadi's youthful beginnings, bereft now of easy sand, forced the four of us to scramble and crawl, tugging and pushing at the outraged mules, until finally we emerged onto a high plain, a vast and empty highland lit by the low sun of evening.

There was not a soul in sight.

To my astonishment, Ali's reaction to the emptiness was to tuck his skirts up a bit, settle his knife more firmly into his belt, and without a word of explanation set off towards the north in an easy jog-trot. He was soon out of sight. We followed at the speed of the walking mules, pausing to eat cold bread and let the mules rest when the last rays of the sun had completely disappeared, then resumed our march when the faint light from the new moon gave outline to the objects around us. As the moon drooped towards the horizon, bobbing lights appeared on a distant hill, and shortly after that Ali's shout came through the night along with at least half a dozen other voices.

The men greeted Mahmoud as a long-lost brother, kissing his hand and bestowing compliments with such exuberance that I wondered if perhaps, despite their appearance and manner of speech, they were Christians – or else Moslems who had overlooked their religion's injunction against alcohol. It appeared, however, that this group comprised a large percentage of the population of an isolated village, and visitors, particularly those not only known and useful but trustworthy as well, were cause enough for an intoxication of spirits.

Moreover, I thought that, unlike similar demonstrations of enthusiastic greeting we had seen in the previous days, this one was actually based on true friendship and long acquaintance. The vigorous middle-aged man walking at Ali's side met Mahmoud with a hard, back-slapping embrace and loud, easy laughter. What is more, Mahmoud responded, giving the man a grin of unfeigned pleasure and slapping his shoulders in return. The expression looked quite unnatural on his face, but it lasted while the other men crowded around and took his hands in greeting.

After we were introduced all around and the initial drawn-out welcome was giving way to a redistribution of burdens to the newcomers' backs, I witnessed an odd little episode. The headman, whose name had been given as Farash, held up the lantern he was carrying and peered at Mahmoud's face. He even reached out and touched the ugly scar with one finger.

'It is well?' he asked quietly.

'Praise be to God.'

'And now Ali.' Farash shook his head. 'You and your brother, you always come to us hurt.'

Mahmoud laughed – actually laughed. 'When Ali has a sore, he fears an amputation. His head is fine.' Then, so quietly that I could barely hear, he said to the man, 'Mikhail the Druse is dead.'

'Ah!' It was a sound of pain Farash made, and then he asked, 'Killed?'

'Shot.'

Farash shook his head again, mournfully this time. 'Another good man is lost,' he murmured. After a moment he stirred, and with a deliberate effort pulled himself back into good humour. 'But you and Ali are with us again, and we shall feast.'

The festive air of the villagers carried us across the uneven ground and through a couple of minor wadis until without warning we were parading into a tiny village, through a sparse collection of mud huts with lean-tos holding them upright, past a well and some bare trees and up to the grandest villa in town, a windowless box twelve feet square and so low that even Mahmoud, the shortest among the four of us, had to stoop. There were clear signs that chickens and at least one goat had recently vacated the premises, and the fleas were appalling, but the honour was great.

Every man in the village was soon in the hut with us, with the women crowded outside of the door. Cigarettes were taken and glasses of cool water given while coffee was made and distributed by the ancient village *mukhtar,* whose house this obviously was. After the coffee had been drunk, four men staggered in carrying a vast platter heaped high with rice that glistened with grease in the lamplight, topped with a mound of hastily cooked and venerable mutton. The combination of hasty cooking and the age of the animal did not make for an easy meal, at least for those of us who tried actually to chew the meat, but we filled our bellies on rice and bread and the less gristly bits, drank more coffee, and then sat listening to the fireside tales of wartime valour and pre-war derring-do until the wee hours, when the *mukhtar* abruptly stood up, shook our greasy hands with his, and departed, taking his village with him, all but a few shy and giggling children who lurked around our door until the morning.

The next day a bank holiday was declared, and all day long people from neighbouring tents and houses drifted in for the fun. Mahmoud was kept busy writing letters and contracts, Ali sat beneath a tree with needle and thread, repairing the mule packs and pads while talking easily to acquaintances, and Holmes squatted in the shade of our fine villa and absorbed the local colour and gossip. I, however, beat the dust and the wildlife from one of our rugs and took it out to a distant grove of bare fruit trees beside an irrigation ditch, trading fleas for flies and dozing to the rhythmic creaking of the mule that worked the *dulab*, drawing water from a deep well. I slept the sleep of the just and the profoundly weary, unconcerned about potential threats and undisturbed by the occasional passer-by checking on my well-being, until the noise of thundering hoofs made me bolt to my feet, certain that I was in the path of a cavalry charge or at the least a stampede. It was only a horse race, and it was won by a remarkably unfit-looking beast with a gloating, exuberant Ali on its back. Mahmoud, I gathered, won a great deal on his wager.

In the late afternoon the cook fires started. Following the afternoon prayers, I led the mules down to the nearest rain pool to scrub their dusty hides, accompanied by what seemed to me a number of children disproportionate to the population as a whole, who were soon wetter than the mules, if not as clean. The youngsters found me greatly amusing, a mute but comprehending boy who wore strange glass circles on his face and laughed at their antics, and I returned to the village in the midst of a noisy, wet entourage.

While I was restoring the animals to their hobbles, I heard someone call my name. To my surprise, when I looked around I saw Mahmoud, surrounded by a knot of men. He was tucking something that looked like money away into the breast of his robes with one hand, and gesturing to me with the other.

I brushed some of the mud off my garments, straightened my turban, and went to see what he wanted. To my even greater amazement, when I approached he flung his heavy arm around my shoulders and turned to his companions.

'Amir is a very clever boy with the knife,' he said, enunciating carefully enough for me to follow his words. 'I will wager his throwing arm against anyone.'

The juxtaposition of my grandiose name with my unprepossessing appearance had its usual effect, reducing the villagers to helpless laughter. Mahmoud grinned like a shark and kept his arm firmly across my shoulders while I stood and wondered what was going on in that devious mind of his, and what he had in store for me.

When the villagers realised that he was seriously proposing to bet on the knife skills of the youth with the ridiculous name, they made haste to accept before this madman had second thoughts. If he wished to give back all the money he had won from them during the day, who were they to object? A couple of the men scurried off to devise a suitable target, the remaining dozen began to sharpen their knives, and Mahmoud, giving my shoulders a final hard embrace, turned his head and whispered in my ear in clear English, 'Do not be too good at first, understand?'

I had a sudden coughing fit to conceal my astonishment, and turned away to watch the men bringing up a length of tree trunk and some stones to prop it upright. Mahmoud proposed to run a con game on these villagers, absorbing what remained of their hard-earned cash after Ali's unlikely victory at the horse race. Oh, I had done the same myself in English pubs armed with darts, but I had only done my opponents out of a few drinks, and they had always been people who could afford the small loss. This was something else, and I disliked the taste in my mouth.

I pulled myself up. Mahmoud knew what he was doing; these were his people, after all. *Maalesh,* I said myself – as no doubt the villagers would say before too long. I only wished I could feel so easy.

Under the tutelage of Holmes and a number of others, over the last four years I had accumulated a variety of odd abilities. I could pick a lock laboriously, drive a horse or a motorcar without coming to grief, dress up in a costume as a sort of amateur-dramatics-in-earnest, and fling a fully grown man (an unprepared and untrained man) to the ground. My only two real gifts, gifts I was born with, were an ear for languages and a hand for throwing. Be it a rock or a pointed object, my left hand had a skill for accuracy that I could in all honesty take no credit for, although I had on occasion found it tremendously useful. As I was about to again.

The men giggled at the sight of my thin and obviously inadequate little throwing knife, and they slapped their knees whenever my first throws went wide of the mark. Mahmoud began to look worried – well, not worried, but he took on a degree more stoniness and his right hand crept up once to rub at the scar – when three largish wagers were swiftly lost. The villagers were ecstatic. I tossed my knife in my hand and gave Mahmoud an even look, trying to get across a mental message.

Either he received it or he well knew how the game ought to be played. In either case he trusted me. He reached into his inner pocket and drew out a considerable stash of money, which he proceeded to count out, milking the drama. He laid it on the ground in front of his feet, and looked back at me.

We took those villagers for a lot of money that afternoon, with the rest of the village, men and women, looking on. I did try to lose a bit when the less prosperous men had their bets in, but it was not always possible. My losses ceased to concern Mahmoud when he saw what a good investment they were, both in the short-term cash returns when over-confidence blossomed and in the long-term benefit of goodwill. It is never a good idea to alienate your host by making him feel completely swindled.

But we did take the money of poor men. And I did not care at all for the way Mahmoud had manoeuvred me into taking it.

Eventually, enough cash had changed hands to lower the interest in the contest. My last challenger stood down, jovial to the end, if rueful. Mahmoud folded away a thick wad of filthy paper money, tucked two heavy handfuls of coin into the purse at his belt, and gave me a look under his eyebrows that was very nearly a complacent smile. As the crowd thinned, I looked over their heads and saw our companions, standing and watching with all the others. Ali gave me a sour look, Holmes an amused one. I squatted down to sharpen the tip of my blade on a stone, slipped it back into my boot, and joined them. Feeling, truth to tell, a bit cocky but more than a little ashamed.

A long Bedouin tent had made an appearance on the hillside behind the village, and the smell of coffee was heavy in the air. The children who had followed me when I washed our mules and had been kept at bay during the contest now swarmed back to claim me, but I gratefully escaped my enthusiastic admirers by insinuating myself far enough back in the tent to be among the adult coffee drinkers, perched between the *mukhtar*'s rather messy falcon and his equally ill-tempered saluki dog.

The evening followed the standard programme for a semi-formal soiree: coffee, food, coffee, sweetmeats, tobacco, coffee, and talk. An immense brass dish was carried in by six men, laden with four whole roasted sheep that had been stuffed with rice and golden fried pine nuts. Tonight the meat was delicious and actually tender. The rice was flavoured with a small, tangy red berry called *sumac* and the bitter, refreshing coffee that followed was fragrant with cardamom. *Narghiles* and regular pipes came out, the rhythmic drum of the coffee mortars fell silent for a while, the irritating 'music' of the one-stringed violin and the wailing song of its player ceased, and the stories began. To my surprise and pleasure, I found that I had no great trouble in following the thread of talk. Under the pressure of continuous use, my Arabic was improving faster than I had thought possible.

The *mukhtar* opened. He was a once-large man now reduced to bone, stringy muscles, and bright colours: blue robe, green turban (a claim to descent from the Prophet), and a beard reddened with henna (sign of a devout pilgrimage to Mecca somewhere in his past). His teeth were worn to a few brown stumps on his gums, but his eyes were clear, his hands steady on the *narghile* as he smoked and talked of his part in the recent war, shooting from the high ground at the retreating Turks.

Then his son – Farash, who had spoken so intimately to Mahmoud the night before and been told of the death of Mikhail the Druse – told a complicated story about some relative who had married a woman from another tribe and ignited a feud that had lasted for sixty-two years, although I may have misunderstood this. Holmes contributed a blood-curdling narrative concerning a Howeitat clan feud begun by a marriage ceremony that greatly amused the men, although I couldn't see quite why. Ali made a brief remark that seemed to link women and donkeys, but again, I did not understand the jest. He then told a lengthy and energetic tale about two men and five scorpions, and at some point it dawned on me that the two men he was talking about were none other than Davy and Charlie, the abusive British guards on the Beersheva road, and that the sly revenge Ali was describing explained his high spirits when he had rejoined us with the armaments on the road north of town. I laughed loudly with the others, earning myself an uncertain glance from the narrator.

Next came an ancient villager, speaking in a high and monotonous voice, who launched off on a story that wandered through people and places, touching down on the occasional battle, that nearly put me to sleep and made a number of the others restless. After half an hour or so the *mukhtar* reached decisively for his leather canister of coffee and the roasting pan, and the continuity of that story was soon broken by the serving of coffee.

When we had all drunk our compulsory three thimblefuls, Mahmoud handed over his tiny cup and began to speak.

Silence fell throughout the length of the tent as the children were hushed in the women's side, and all listened to the strong voice speaking of the outside world. Mahmoud was a good speaker with a compelling, even dramatic, manner, surprising for so normally reticent a person. The story he told the village concerned the final conquest of the Turkish Army three and a half months before.

The people obviously knew of the war's conclusion, but not in detail, and it was detail he gave them. His audience sighed at the first mention of the name of Allenby, the conquering hero whose very name transliterated into Arabic reads 'to the Prophet.' Mahmoud told of the fulfilling of prophecy, when the ancient tradition declaring that the Holy Land would be free of the infidel only when the waters of the Nile flowed into Jerusalem was realised, transformed from a declaration of hopelessness into actual truth when the British Army supplied water to the city, carried on the backs of a regiment of camels from its source in the Nile. He went on to tell of heroic fighting, of small groups holding off armies, of a single man who crept across a hill, invisible as a rock, to destroy the huge gun flinging shells across the miles at the distant British troops. Each of his episodes drew admiring remarks and much sucking in of breath from the audience, murmurs and exclamations of 'Wal' during the telling, and wagging of heads coupled with laughter at each conclusion.

The greatest applause came, however, with the story of Allenby's deception of the Turks and their German advisers. With his hands in the air Mahmoud sketched the land north of Jerusalem, his left hand describing the sea and Haifa while his right hand drew the Ghor, or Jordan Valley, that hot, miserable, malarial lowlands that separates Palestine from the vast deep desert to the east. Here Allenby had laid out his greatest trick:

He would convince the enemy that he was about to strike out on his right, directly across the Jordan, whereas in reality he planned to attack on his left, circling down on them from their western flank through the Valley of Jezreel, that is known as Megiddo, or Armageddon.

Mahmoud built his story with growing drama, beginning in Jerusalem, when the Fast Hotel near the Jaffa Gate was confiscated for army use and advisers in high-ranking uniforms openly filled the town, sure signs to the Turkish spies that Allied headquarters was moving to be near the river Jordan. He then described the stealthy moving in of troops on the left flank, always at night, only into tents that had already been in position for months. When he described the false messages given to spies, his audience began to nod in appreciation, guile being a truer sign of wit than mere cleverness was.

When he launched into a detailed description of the ostensible troop movements on the Jordan itself, however, the villagers began to grin in gap-toothed appreciation at a commander who would cause lorries to drag logs up and down, raising the dust of great activity, and who would direct whole regiments to march conspicuously into the eastern lines during the heat of the day, only to have them travel quietly west again under cover of darkness to their starting point. Out and back went the decoy soldiers, openly out to and secretly back from the Jordan Valley, a relatively few men giving the impression of a massive build-up of strength. Tent cities were planted and five pontoon bridges thrown across the Jordan while 'El Aurens' – Colonel T.E. Lawrence

– and his camel Bedu staged spectacular raids nearby.

But it was the fake horse lines that had Mahmoud's listeners rolling on the carpets with tears in their eyes: twenty thousand old blankets shipped up from Egypt and draped over shrubs, some of them propped up on wooden legs, from a dusty distance taking on the appearance of a massive accumulation of tethered cavalry horses.

The Turks fell for the entire ruse, supported by their German advisers, who believed the reports of their misled spies. The Turkish empire lined up the strength of its men and guns at the eastern borders of Palestine, ready to counter the attack out of Jerusalem; when Allenby threw his true forces instead onto their unprepared western flank, the Turks had not a chance. He swept them up, took ninety thousand prisoners, and broke the back of the Turkish Army in the most decisive victory of the entire world war, pushing the remnants in rapid and growing disorder all the way to Damascus and surrender.

Mahmoud's story was obviously the high point of the evening; anything else would be an anticlimax. With the typically abrupt leave-taking of the Arab, the party began to break up. Limp children were carried off to their beds, older boys clattered off into the four directions on scrofulous donkeys, and adults pressed the *mukhtar's* hand and that of Mahmoud before walking off into the night, reciting segments of Mahmoud's story to one another at the tops of their voices, laughing and calling and fading away.

Not everyone left. The close friends and family of the *mukhtar*, twenty-five or thirty men, stayed on, chatting and smoking a last pipe and conducting small business. I thought we were perhaps finished for the evening, and began to think with actual anticipation of my hard bed where at least I could stretch out my leg muscles without causing offence, when Holmes dropped a question into a brief silence.

'My brothers,' he asked, frowning in concentration as he rolled up a cigarette. 'Do you think the Turk is truly gone from the land?'

CHAPTER EIGHT

ﺩ

Writing is the shaping of letters to represent spoken words which,
in turn, represent what is in the soul.
— THE *Muqaddimah* OF IBN KHALDÛN

THE QUESTION RIPPLED THROUGH THE tent, silencing the men around the fire. I could hear the sounds of sleepy children on the other side of the cloth partition; someone shouted monotonously from the other end of the village. Holmes ran the tip of his tongue along the edge of the thin cigarette paper, sealed it, and reached for the tongs to take a coal from the fire. Men began to speak, in a frustrating jumble of voices.

Some, I thought, protested loyally that Allenby and Feisal had truly driven the Turk to his knees. Heads nodded, and hands reached for the reassurance of *narghile* and cigarette.

Some men, though, did not agree. The men of active fighting age, men whose faces were even more guarded than the average Bedouin's, quiet men with scars and limps, men who had done more than stand and shoot at a fleeing enemy, those men did not nod their heads and exclaim loudly at the cowardice of the Turk. They glanced at each other from under their eyelids and at Holmes, and they said nothing.

Holmes listened politely to the protestations of freedom, and allowed the subsequent conversation to drift away into a series of bloodthirsty reminiscences of wartime *ghazis*. I did not think, however, that he had missed the covert glances, and I was not surprised when, a few minutes later, he got to his feet and left the tent, nor that when he returned he settled down not into his former spot, but in the midst of three of the men who had been silent. One of those was Farash, the *mukhtar*'s son.

Reluctantly I had to agree that the questions he was about to put to the men were best done casually and quietly, so I stayed where I was in the third rank back from the fire. I looked to see what Mahmoud and Ali would do and saw that, despite the sour expression on Ali's face, they too planned to stay where they were and allow Holmes to continue his sub rosa interrogation. Mahmoud, moreover, tore his eyes from Holmes and turned to the *mukhtar*.

'Perhaps you have a thing you would like me to read?' he offered.

The eager look on the *mukhtar*'s old face, and on several others nearby, showed that they had been hoping for the offer. Three or four men scattered, to return with precious, tattered journals in hand. The *mukhtar* sent a rapid-fire set of instructions at the dividing wall. In an instant, a woman's hand appeared under the coarse striped fabric, holding out a worn copy of an English journal called *Boy's Own Paper* with a dramatic cover showing a troop of khaki-clad lancers riding furiously towards an unseen enemy. The dubious expression on the central horse was echoed by its rider, understandable in my opinion since the men were probably aiming their sharp sticks at an entrenched position of troops backed by machine guns, but logic has never been a major element of patriotism. At any rate, the magazine was obviously treasured by the *mukhtar,* who put it on top of the half dozen similar literary offerings made by the other men, laid on the carpet in front of the scribe and public reader.

Mahmoud took his time deciding which of the journals and books he would read from, although I knew the instant I saw a familiar cover emerge from a striped *abayya* which he would pick, and I was right. He passed over the *Boy's Own* and a *Saturday Evening Post,* hesitated over an Arabic translation of an American detecting person named Nick Carter, and finally reached out for the nine-year-old copy of *Strand* magazine. This he opened with care, checking that all the relevant pages were intact, before he settled back on his mound of bolsters and began to read, not so much translating as paraphrasing and considerably abridging it as he went. The story Mahmoud chose for the night's public reading was one that Dr Watson's literary agent, Arthur Conan Doyle, had called 'The Devil's Foot.' It featured a consulting detective by the name of Sherlock Holmes.

Mahmoud might have been reading a news article about the peace talks for all the mischief his face revealed, but I thought Ali would erupt with delight. Holmes, who had remained bent down to hear whatever was being said in the soft private conversation, jerked upright at the sound of his real name, badly startled. Mahmoud read on, stern of visage but with a faint breath of humour in the depths of his voice. Holmes pulled himself together, shot me a glance that dared me to laugh, and returned to his talk, safer from interruption now that the attention of the tent (both sides of it, I thought, hearing the heavy accumulation of breathing bodies pressing against the divider from the women's side) was on this rousing tale of greed and revenge and induced madness and terrible danger. Long before the end of it, Holmes was having difficulty in keeping his own group's attention, but eventually he sat back, obviously content with what he had learnt, and allowed them to participate in the climactic experiment Holmes had so rashly conducted on himself and Watson, the results of which were very nearly of a sort to which clean death might have been preferable.

Mahmoud very sensibly cut short the lengthy explanations of motive and method, simplifying both down to a few lines of dialogue and a dramatic conclusion.

It was a shining success. Much discussion followed, on how one might lay hands upon this magnificently lethal substance and the sorts of crime its use might best be suited to punish, and whether or not mere passion for a woman (and an unobtainable woman at that, for a Christian monogamist) was motive enough.

Eventually, when it became apparent that Mahmoud was not about to pick up Nick Carter's adventures or the story of the *Boy's Own* lancers, talk became sporadic and desultory: One man told his neighbours that his young grandson had been taken to hospital in Hebron and was not expected to survive the experience. Another man had a horse gone lame, and asked if anyone had some remedy for a cracked hoof that had yet to be tried on the creature. Ali made a casual enquiry about, I thought, banditry in the area, saying that he was concerned about travelling east of here with such a small group. The responses varied from an automatic and obviously ignorant reassurance to a disgusted agreement that no travel was safe in these troubled times. Then he mentioned the lone corpse found in the Wadi Estemoa, without identifying it by name.

A flurry of speculation sprang up like the last flames of a dying fire, and the presence of bandits in the hills to the south-east was debated. However, the hour was late and interest soon died down. Men began to wrap themselves in their *abayya*s and turn into cocoons on the floor of the tent. The four of us took our leave of our host and walked the short path to our flea-infested but honourable house.

Fortunately, this night we had outlasted the village children, and we could speak amongst ourselves in low voices without fear of being overheard. Somewhat to my surprise, Holmes did not hesitate to share what he had been told. I half expected him to pretend fatigue or at least surprise when the three of us rounded on him as soon as the door was shut, particularly following Mahmoud's stunt with the Conan Doyle story, but he did not. He would, of course, have told us what the men had said, even if grudgingly and with gaps, but I thought afterwards that the readiness of his response was by way of recognising the debt he owed Mahmoud for so willingly taking on the lesser role, distracting the others while Holmes questioned the men who might know something. He dropped to his heels, tucked back his *kuffiyah,* and started talking – in English, to my relief.

'The men I was with were all soldiers for the Turk during the first three years of the war. They deserted when the Arab independence movement began to make real headway.'

'Do not call it desertion,' Ali objected, also using English. 'They were slaves reaching for their freedom, not traitors.'

Holmes waved aside the niceties of definition. 'That is not important. What matters is that the three conscripts, even as long ago as 1917, were aware that within the Turkish Army, certain men were laying plans for what was to happen in this country if Turkey lost.'

'But in 1917, Turkey was winning,' protested Ali.

'So it appeared, but to a small group of officers, it was far from decided. One of these three was a member of a work party hiding supplies in a remote cave: food, clothing, weapons and ammunition, medical supplies, and detailed maps. Some of the maps, he remembers, were of El Quds. Jerusalem.'

'*Wallah,*' Ali breathed. Mahmoud smoothed his beard thoughtfully and dug his prayer beads from his robe.

'The supplies are no longer there – having been, shall we say, liberated by the men on their way home.'

'But if there was one cache . . .' Ali did not bother finishing the thought.

'Who were the officers?' I asked Holmes.

'These men knew the names, but said that, having had such a personal interest in the fates of their former superior officers, they made a point of hunting them out after the war. Of the half dozen they knew were in on it, all were either dead or in the custody of the British. Now all are dead.'

'Unfortunate,' commented Mahmoud laconically.

'Yes. They did say, however, that the six officers were not acting on their own, that orders came to them. And not from Damascus but from Jerusalem.'

We meditated on this for some time, and then Mahmoud asked, 'You have the names of the Turkish officers?'

'I do. Perhaps they will have left administrative tracks that could lead to their superior. Had the Germans actually been in charge of the army rather than merely advising, we could certainly depend on records having been kept. The Turks, however, were less concerned with order. I suppose Joshua is the one to follow that particular lead; can a message be got to him?'

'It can,' Mahmoud replied.

Ali shifted slightly, but before he could rise and signal that the day's events were ended, I stopped him with two questions aimed at Mahmoud.

'Are you suggesting,' I said carefully, because I wanted this quite clear, 'that what we are looking for is a group of Turkish officers who have escaped capture and gone underground? And that these officers are plotting to take the country back from the British?'

Mahmoud clearly disliked being put on the spot, but after a moment he answered. 'It is not so simple. It may be more a matter of encouraging the disorder and dissatisfaction that already exist here, hidden beneath the British rule of order. "A dust cloud hides all." Think of a man stirring up a cloud of dust so as to move around without being observed. When the dust settles, the man is where he wishes to be, with no-one the wiser.'

It was a picturesque image, if inaccurate (would not a stirred-up dust cloud attract suspicion?) and not terribly informative.

'His purpose being . . . ?' I prodded.

This time it was Holmes who responded. 'Joshua appears to believe that the unrest is intended to, shall we say, encourage the British government to withdraw at all haste from the expensive and unpleasant business of governing an intractable province. I think that with tonight's evidence, we may assume that the architect of the unrest further intends to be in a position to occupy the vacuum of power when the British depart. It is a plan both complex and simple, well suited to a patient man with a taste for manipulation.'

'You think there is such a man, then?'

'Or as Mahmoud suggests, a small coalition. As an hypothesis it wants testing, but yes, it is a strong possibility.'

'And he or they direct the *mullah* whose safe we robbed, and murder harmless farmers, and shoot men in wadis, and—'

'Russell, Russell. Joshua all but told us that the good Yitzak was not just a farmer. Am I right, Mahmoud?'

'A spy, yes, during the war.'

Great, I thought; yet another thing that had passed me by. 'Still,' I persisted, 'this is a fairly ruthless approach to politics. Why hasn't your man Joshua heard of him, or them, before this?'

Mahmoud answered me in Arabic. '"When the cat looks at

the feathers and says he knows nothing of the bird, does that mean the cat's belly is not full?"'

It took me a while to sort that one out, first the syntax, then the meaning. Eventually, though, I thought I had it. 'You're saying that Joshua does know that there is an actual plot to take over the country. That his vague maunderings about wolves in the sheepfold and his attempts to put Holmes off the scent were a ruse. My God, the man is more devious than Mycroft. So what we're searching for is a Turkish Machiavelli with the morals of a snake. Where do we look? Out here in the desert? In the Sinai? Jerusalem?'

Mahmoud answered with yet another aphorism, a long Arabic growl that translated something along the lines of, 'Jerusalem is a golden bowl full of scorpions.' Ali chuckled in appreciation, and without warning I was hit by a bolt of fury at Mahmoud and everything he represented. It was an accumulation of things, some of them to do with him – his flat assumption of command and his aloofness, the shadowy Joshua behind his shoulder and the patronising air with which he tended to answer my ignorance, his endless proverbs and convoluted epigrams and rawest of all the ease with which he had forced me to help him fleece the poorest of villagers. There were other vexations for which he could not be blamed, but in the blink of an eye, all the irritations that plagued me welded themselves together and pushed out a question I had not intended to ask.

'Tell me, Mahmoud, how did you come by that scar?'

The instant the words left my mouth I regretted them. Ali looked ready to succumb to an attack of apoplexy, and even

Holmes let out a small grunt of reaction at my thoughtlessness. I rubbed at my forehead in a gesture of tiredness and self-disgust.

'I am sorry, Mahmoud. It is none of my business, and even if—'

'I was captured,' he said flatly, his eyes glittering across the dim room at me. 'I was questioned. I was rescued. I was brought here.' He shifted to Arabic. 'Ali and Mikhail the Druse brought me to this village. The *mukhtar*'s family cared for me and hid me from the Turks. That was two years ago. Since that day they have been my mother and my father.'

I was struck dumb with remorse; I wished he had hit me instead of answering, or shot me dead. All I could think of was a gesture that left my English self far, far behind. I went onto my knees and put out my hand to touch his dusty boot. It was a strange thing to do, and where in my psyche it came from I do not know, but it was an eloquent plea for forgiveness in ways that words were not, and it reached him. After a moment I felt his hand on my shoulder, squeezing briefly.

'Don't worry, Mary,' he said, using English.

'I had no right—'

'Amir,' he interrupted, in Arabic now. 'Be at peace.' And strangely enough, I was.

CHAPTER NINE

ذ

The greatest number of marauders are found on the borders of the cultivated districts. The desert itself is safer.
– BAEDEKER'S *Palestine and Syria,* 1912 EDITION

IN THE MORNING WE MADE our farewells to the village and turned east. Before we left, I saw Ali take Farash aside, no doubt to press into the man's hand a piece of paper containing the names of six Turkish officers to be delivered to the spymaster Joshua. Heaven only knew where the answer would catch up with us. When the last of the children dropped, or was driven, from our tail, I turned to Holmes.

'Why do we go in this direction?' I demanded, in Arabic.

'You heard the talk last night, when Ali asked about the Wadi Estemoa. We are continuing to investigate the death of Mikhail the Druse.'

'I did catch the word *haramiyeh,* did I not? Bandits? To the south-east?'

'You heard correctly.'

'You think bandits murdered Mikhail?' I asked doubtfully. 'But he wasn't robbed.'

'They may or may not have been responsible, but if there are bandits, they will surely know who was moving through their territory at the time Mikhail was shot. Bandits are territorial creatures. They take careful note of who moves through their land.'

'They may know, but will they tell us?' I wondered.

He did not reply.

As soon as we were out of sight of the village we shifted direction, heading due south. That whole day we saw only innocent forms of life: women tending goats, a few clusters of black tents, once on the horizon a long caravan of camels wavering in the heat, going north towards Jerusalem. In the afternoon we dropped into a wadi to return to the lowlands, on the theory that robbers must eventually go where there are people to rob, and half an hour later a piece of rock in front of my feet popped into the air, followed in an instant by the crack of a rifle echoing hugely down the canyon walls.

The mules squealed in terror and sent me flying as they shot away down the wadi, and would have trampled the men in front of me had they not already leapt as one for the protection of boulders.

I followed their example with alacrity, and we all cowered in silence, except for Ali, who cursed the mules bitterly until Mahmoud shouted at him to shut his mouth. Another bullet pinged off a rock and another gunshot boomed through the wadi. A few minutes later a third one came, with no result other than to keep us pinned down.

I began to hear voices then, and thought at first that they came from above our heads, which would have meant real trouble, until I identified the lower tones as those of Mahmoud. I inched around to the back of my rock and could see the two Arabs arguing around the backs of their respective boulders. Actually, they did not seem to be arguing so much as Ali pleading for something and Mahmoud refusing to give permission. After six or eight minutes of this, punctuated by the odd bullet from above, Ali wore his partner down; Mahmoud, with the incongruous air of a parent giving in to a child's peremptory demands, flipped the back of his hand in the direction in which the mules had fled, then reached into his robe and pulled out his authoritative American pistol. He rose, pointed the long barrel in the general direction of our assailant, and commenced to fire.

Ali took off, racing down the rough wadi floor in the wake of our mules, his robes and *kuffiyah* whipping around him. However, the ploy was only marginally successful. After Mahmoud's fourth round, the man above must have risked a look and seen the fleeing Ali. Fortunately he was a terrible shot: None of his rounds came anywhere near the fleet-footed Arab.

After Ali had disappeared and the excitement died down, I wondered how long we had before the man above summoned reinforcements. One rifle we could hide from; two or three could prove uncomfortable. I could only hope Ali found the mules quickly and returned with our Lee Enfield, or else darkness fell, before the bandits regrouped.

'Holmes,' I whispered loudly.

'*Oui,*' came his reply. Yes, that would certainly confuse any listeners, to speak in French. I asked in that same language: 'I think I am in a better position to gain the top unseen. Shall I try?'

'*Non!*' That was Mahmoud's voice, not that of Holmes. '*Il ne peut pas le faire,*' he said. I wondered idly if his use of the masculine pronoun in referring to me was deliberate or due to an ignorance of French grammar.

'*Pourquoi pas?*' I asked. Why must I not go?

'*Ali va revenir.*' Ali will return.

'Holmes?' I asked for confirmation.

'*Oui,*' he said. '*Ça va.*'

Fine, I thought, and dug a little deeper into the lee of the boulder. We'll all just wait here for Ali to rescue us, or until we're picked off one by one.

We lay, cramped and still. Every so often the man above us would fire a couple of bullets into the wadi, and once he moved, forcing the three of us to scuttle around to the more protective sides of our rocks. However, he was such a bad marksman that we were in more danger from a ricochet than a direct shot. The day faded, my bladder filled, and then in a distinct anti-climax came a noise from above, followed by Ali's voice calling the all-clear.

We climbed stiffly up the steep wall and found Ali along with a man firmly bound by what seemed to be gardening twine. A rifle lay on the ground beside them, a piece of armament so antique it explained the man's wretched marksmanship. Ali was seated comfortably on the man's back, smoking a cigarette, and I looked in wonder at the surrounding landscape, which seemed to me utterly open, flat, and devoid of objects to hide behind. The same thought obviously occurred to Holmes.

'How did you manage to come up on him?' he asked Ali, who merely grinned at him.

'As invisible as a rock,' commented Mahmoud drily.

'That was Ali, who took out the gun over Jerusalem?' Holmes asked.

'That was Ali.' Mahmoud shook his head as if at the prank of a high-spirited son, then looked at his partner sternly to ask, 'The others?'

'A camp with three horses, two of them gone. This fool' – he paused to swat an all-too-conscious head with his open palm – 'thought he could act on his own.'

Mahmoud squatted down to peer into the bandit's face. 'When will they return?' he asked the man.

The man began to snarl threats and bluster, despite his position, until suddenly he screeched and began to buck his body up and down in an attempt to dislodge Ali from his back. Ali calmly took his cigarette from the man's backside and put it back between his lips. The air smelt of burning wool. The bandit groaned and began to curse, then went very still as the hot end of Ali's cigarette appeared three inches above his cheekbone.

'When will they return?' repeated Mahmoud, his voice even more gentle. The man stared through his one visible eye at the cigarette, and jerked violently when it dropped an inch closer to his face. Ali laughed; Mahmoud waited; Holmes looked on in stony silence; I tried not to look at all.

'When?' Mahmoud said for the third time. There was no answer. Showing no emotion, he took the cigarette from Ali's fingers, drew deeply on it, tapped off the ashes, and then whirled his bulky body around the man in a swift movement that trapped the bandit's head underneath one knee and against the other, grinding his left cheek into the ground. The cigarette end approached the man's eye, slowly, inexorably. I gulped and looked away.

The bandit began to scream, but in fear, not in pain, and there were words in his voice. His Arabic was too rapid for me to understand, but whatever he said seemed to satisfy Mahmoud because when I looked again the hand holding the cigarette was resting on the man's shoulder.

'Good,' he said in a soothing voice. 'I have one other question, then we will leave. Tell me about the men who killed a man in the Wadi Estemoa.'

'I did not kill him,' the bandit gabbled. 'I don't know anything about a killing in the Wadi Estemoa.'

'You did not kill him, no, but you do know who did. Tell me.' He lifted his hand, took another draw from the now-short cigarette, and touched it briefly to the man's ear. The man jerked as if he'd been shot. When the burning tip came back to hover above his face, he tried to focus on it with an eye as white rimmed and staring as that of a colicked horse. 'Who were they?' asked Mahmoud, his voice ever more soft and dangerous.

'Strangers. I have seen them!' the man shouted, almost sobbing as the burning tobacco came closer. 'Farther east, near the sea, I've seen them before. With the salt [something].' I missed the key word, but Mahmoud knew what the bandit was talking about, and so did Ali. Even Holmes nodded briefly.

'Those who work near Sedom, or San?'

'Mazra. On the [something].'

'Good. I thank you, my brother. And I hope very much that you have told me the truth because by the Prophet, if you have not, I shall come back and burn out both of your eyes.'

The man winced, but he held Mahmoud's gaze. Satisfied that he was hearing the truth, Mahmoud withdrew his hand. The man closed his eyes and shuddered in relief. Mahmoud patted his shoulder, and stepped away.

Ali got up from his seat on the man's back and squinted into the setting sun. 'I shall have to go find the mules that this son of a dog frightened,' he grumbled, and turned to kick the man's ribs in irritation. 'I will take his mare,' he decided. 'She looks fast.'

The figure at his feet squeaked at Ali's proposal but gave no other protest. Ali kicked him again for good measure and went over to where the horse was tied to a prickly bush. He undid the reins, threw himself onto the pad that passes for an Arab saddle, yanked the animal's head around, and kicked her into a gallop. Mahmoud went over to the saddle-bags that lay on the ground beside the bandit's rifle and went through them, removing various things and leaving the rest scattered on the ground. He then picked up the rifle, jerked his chin at us, and walked away.

When we had caught him up I protested. 'You can't leave him tied there. What if the jackals find him?'

'I left him his knife. He will be free before night falls, and his friends will find him by morning.'

'Holmes?'

'He won't die, although in England he would probably be hanged for his various crimes.'

'If you say so. What was that he said about the salt?' I asked Holmes.

'Salt?'

'The men who killed Mikhail were seen with the salt something-or-other, on the somewhere.'

'Ah. Salt smugglers, on El Lisan, the peninsula that comes out into the Dead Sea.'

'*Salt* smugglers?' I said in amazement.

'Anywhere a valuable commodity is controlled by the government, there will be individuals who circumvent regulations.'

I made a connexion in my mind. 'That's what Ali meant, that the dirty salt in Mikhail's bag was not government salt. Is there a link?'

'Between his having the salt and salt smugglers appearing later on in the case? Not necessarily. I should think smuggled salt is relatively common in this area. Mahmoud?'

'"He who feeds a lion is a fool,"' he said by way of confirmation. 'No-one buys government salt.'

We walked a couple more miles before I spoke again. We seemed to be making off rapidly in a new direction, and the desert is a big place. 'How is Ali going to find us?' I wondered aloud.

'Surely you can say that in Arabic,' chided Holmes, so I did.

'Ali will find us,' Mahmoud answered unhelpfully, and strode on.

And Ali did find us, trotting up in the dull moonlight on the horse with the three mules behind him. The large fire Mahmoud built may have helped, of course, but I was beginning to think there was some mind-reading going on here.

The rider dismounted, put the hobbles on the smug-looking mules, tucked the reins securely up behind the neck of the bandit's horse, and slapped her hard on the rump. She galloped off in the direction they had come from, her ears pricked.

'She will go to the wadi,' Ali said to me in explanation. 'I did not give her water, and she will smell it there. I would not want to be accused of stealing a horse.' He laughed merrily, pulled over the bowl of spiced lentils that Mahmoud had left near the fire, and ate with one hand while gesturing wildly with the other as he recounted the day's adventures.

This was not the same Ali as had sprinted away down the wadi that afternoon. Since we had left Beersheva – since Holmes had come down on his neck so critically, in fact – Ali had withdrawn into himself, had tended to avoid direct discourse and avoided looking at us, particularly at Holmes. Now, however, he was full of his previous good humour, and more. He seemed to have grown a couple of inches, and his beard seemed more sleek, as he joked and ate and explained (to all of us, not just to Mahmoud) how he had found the mules.

He almost crowed at his cleverness, restored to his sense of worth by having pitted himself against a superior force and decisively won the day, and it dawned on me that Mahmoud's air of indulging a child's entreaty, when we had first been pinned down in the wadi, was part and parcel of the affair. By pretending to deprecate Ali's dangerous, difficult, and life-saving act as a childish trick when we all knew the immense skill and nerve it had required, he was allowing Ali to flaunt his own feat as a game – neither man would have permitted himself the undignified braggadocio of mere pride.

I laughed aloud in pleasure at the analysis, and at the delicious complications to be found in human intercourse; Ali turned his head and laughed with me.

We did not bother with the tents that night, merely wrapping ourselves in *abayyas* and rugs for a few brief and very cold hours. The night was still inky overhead, spangled with the intricate spray of a million pure, bright stars, when Ali's tea-making sounds began.

Wrapped tightly inside my rug, I sat more or less upright and huddled near the small fire, my breath coming out in clouds before my face. When we started off I retained my rug, only returning it to the mule's pack when the sun had come up in our faces.

Over breakfast, which as usual was eaten in the late morning, I asked Holmes for the map I knew he had secreted somewhere in the folds of his robe. I ignored Ali's ostentatious display of checking the countryside for onlookers, as we had seen perhaps three human beings all morning (and those miles away) and I took the small folded paper Holmes handed me, spreading it out on my knees.

With some effort (the map was both small and highly

detailed) I traced our path out of Beersheva, through the Wadi Estemoa, up to a nameless square indicating the village, down into the other wadi where we had been set upon by a thief, and then straight east to where we now sat. I saw that in a short time we should come to Masada, or Sebbeh as the map had it, Herod's hilltop fortress that was the last stronghold of Jewish resistance to fall to the Romans in the year 74.

Masada was a natural hill fort on a cliff overlooking the Dead Sea. Directly opposite lay the wide peninsula called El Lisan – the Tongue – with the town of Mazra in its eastern crook and its northernmost tip given the unlikely name of Cape Costigan. The gap between our bank and the peninsula, however, was as I remembered: a bit far for mules to swim and, according to the depth lines sketched onto the water, too deep to wade.

'Will we go around the south to get to Mazra?' I asked.

'Too slow,' grunted Mahmoud.

'We swim, then?' I asked brightly, and added in English, 'What jolly fun.'

The facetious remark was too much for Mahmoud. 'That will not be necessary,' he growled repressively, and sent me to unhobble the mules.

It was a bare twenty map miles from the previous night's comfortless camp, but it was late afternoon when we reached the vicinity of Masada. The climb down the cliffs was too precarious to risk the legs of the mules in the dark. Ali again pulled his vanishing act, hurling himself down the precipitous path to the sea, leaving the tents and cook fire to us.

I briskly followed Ali's example. Before I could be handed a water-skin or a handful of tent pegs, I made my own escape, in the opposite direction.

I approached Masada from the high ground and made my way up the remains of the ramp that the Romans had used in their final assault on the fortress of rebels. Once inside the walls, I crossed the deserted plateau to stand with the last rays of the sun on my back, gazing down at the Roman camp and the sea behind it. Two years after Jerusalem fell, the inexorable might of Rome had thrown a circle around the hill and then, one basket of rubble at a time – carried by Jewish prisoners who, in painful irony, were safe from the arrows of their brothers overhead – built a ramp for their siege machines. The ramp was completed; the next morning the siege machines were brought up, the defences were breached, and the invaders stormed the walls to find: nothing. Nothing but death, an entire community – men, women, and children – that chose suicide over captivity. I wondered what thoughts went through Flavius Silva's mind as the Roman victor stepped onto the charnel-house of a mountain-top that morning. I wondered too what thoughts went through the mind of the man writing the account, a man who had actually commanded Jewish forces in that same revolt, who had been one of two survivors of another suicide pact that followed a defeat, who had turned his back on his people to wield a propagandistic pen for his new masters. Josephus the turncoat, I thought, was not a person to appreciate the grim irony of Masada.

The silence still lay here, a peculiar blend of triumph and devastation, the symbol of a stubborn people. The only sign of life below was the familiar dark shapes of a Bedouin encampment on the opposite shore. A hyrax came out and eyed me suspiciously; a vulture rode the air along the edge of the sea. The water was a dark bowl filled with the approaching night, but the air was warm and moist and slightly hazy. El Lisan lay before me; I wondered what arrangement Ali was making. With that thought I was called back to responsibility, and I took myself down from the brooding hill to hammer tent pegs.

CHAPTER TEN

The human body floats without exertion on the surface, and can be submerged only with difficulty; but swimming is unpleasant, as the feet have too great a tendency to rise to the surface.
— BAEDEKER'S *Palestine and Syria*, 1912 EDITION

FOR A SMUGGLER, I THOUGHT, the man seemed quite ordinary looking. I had met smugglers before, retired ones for the most part; on the coast of Sussex where I lived it was once a common enough profession. Salt smuggling, however, had struck me by its very prosaic nature as a vocation requiring a compensatorily flamboyant personality, but such was not the case here. He looked like a small shopkeeper, pleasant and settled and mildly hopeful that we might purchase something. Perhaps smuggling was an everyday occupation here, requiring not a modicum of derring-do. Ali and Mahmoud appeared immensely more criminal. Heavens, *I* looked more criminal than he did.

'We are interested in salt,' Ali had begun, some time ago, and Mr Bashir the smuggler took him at his word. He told us about salt. He told us about government salt and the taxes thereon, about the differences between the salt from the ponds obtained up near Jericho and those down farther in the Dead Sea and the hills near Sedom, about the misunderstanding that arose with the new officials and their English laws when the governments changed, strange foreign officials who were bafflingly immune, if not actually opposed, to *bakshish,* condemning that ages-old oil for all the machinery of the East as bribery, or begging. It was all so much easier under the Turks, he explained sadly. He talked about the subsequent difficulties faced by an honest tradesman such as himself, the uncertainty as to whether salt would even remain a government monopoly or be opened to free trade, which would certainly threaten his business, about the balance between purity and savour and price, the costs involved in mining it as opposed to the risks involved in illicit salt ponds. He talked with professional expertise about the Biblical story of Lot's wife, turned into a pillar of salt when she looked back on the destruction of her city, and ventured a humble opinion as to which of the pillars just south of here she might be. A wealth of information, our Mr Bashir.

Yes, he knew Mikhail the Druse. Not much of a customer in himself, but an amusing fellow, and as a reference there was none better. Very much to be trusted, was Mikhail. 'Which is why I am drinking your coffee now, gentlemen, truth be told. A friend of Mikhail's, you know?' Yes, he had heard the poor fellow was dead, truly a loss. How? Oh, news travels. And speaking of news, had Mahmoud heard of the affair of Sheikh

Abu-Tayyan's second son? No? Well, it appeared that he saw this woman one day, out walking to her well, and he decided that he had to have her. Unfortunately, she was already married. So, when he was down in Akaba one week—

The story, like most Arab camp-fire stories, went on forever and depended on an intimate knowledge of the people and customs and a peculiarly brutal sense of humour. Rather like the tales one overhears in a beery working-class pub, come to think of it, only more picturesque when told in the sober poetry of guttural Arabic beneath a black goat's-hair tent.

At any rate, this story, with the one Ali told afterwards (about a she-camel which was stolen and disguised, with another camel dyed to look like her, which second camel was then stolen back by the first camel's original owner – who, to crown the story, did not discover his mistake until the dye wore off), took the better part of an hour. Mahmoud then mentioned a mare Mikhail had owned, that possessed a strange ability to—

We were off again. Twenty minutes later that mare was put to rest, and a dainty feeler went out from Mahmoud. Did Mr Bashir perhaps know where Mikhail had gone this last week? Perhaps Mr Bashir had even seen Mikhail? Because there was a horse – not the mare with the strange trick, but another one – that Mahmoud was interested in, and Mikhail had been going to see the owner to make enquiries—

Mr Bashir was not fooled. Mr Bashir had been waiting ever since he had dropped from the saddle of his demure little mare onto the salty shore to hear what it was we truly wanted; furthermore, Mahmoud knew full well that the salt smuggler was not fooled, but it was all part of the way of doing business in the East, and neither of the adversaries was disappointed. Mahmoud nattered on about the miraculous if non-existent horse, and Mr Bashir smiled widely and drank coffee and laughed at the correct places and shook his head in amazement and distress, while my knees went numb and Ali picked a design with his vicious knife down the back of a thumb-sized wooden snake and Holmes watched it all under lowered eyelids, looking half-asleep.

After a long, long time, the normally taciturn Mahmoud paused to draw breath, and Holmes spoke up for the first time.

'There is another horse,' he said. Mr Bashir looked at him politely, and Mahmoud subsided. 'It is a family matter, you understand?' Mr Bashir began to look distinctly interested. 'There is a man, not from this area, but he comes to this place from time to time. There was a horse, a stallion, that once belonged to my father, and it was stolen, and the thief sold it to this man. This man then sold the horse himself, up into the north.' This put rather a different slant on the matter, I saw. Horse stealing was one thing, an honest sport, but theft for mere profit, without allowing the owner a chance to steal it back – this was not cricket. Mr Bashir might be a trader, but he knew honour. Holmes continued. 'Mikhail was the brother of a brother. I heard he knew this man, that he could find where the horse is now. If I found that place, my brothers and I could go there and bring back the horse of my father. You understand?'

Mr Bashir's eyes shone at the thought, both of the chance to earn a profit at little effort, and moreover at being given a role in the sort of story that might be told over fires from here to Aleppo. Holmes, holding the drama, reached into his robe and pulled out a small leather purse. He jiggled it on the palm of his hand a couple of times. It clinked heavily.

'I might be interested in buying salt, as well,' he said.

'I have much salt,' said Mr Bashir. 'I also may know the man you seek.' Holmes pulled open the top of the money purse and took out three silver coins. These he laid casually in a row on the carpet in front of him. He reached back into the purse, took out some more coins, and worked them back and forth between his long fingers while Mr Bashir continued to speak.

'I do not know where the stranger came from, but I agree, not from here. Damascus, or farther north, I do not know. He contacted me a month or more ago. He too was interested in salt. He did not mention horses,' he added, and his eyes crinkled at the subtlety of his joke.

Holmes took one of the coins he held and placed it on the middle coin in the row of three. This one was gold, and it would be difficult to say which gleamed the brighter, the coin or Mr Bashir's eyes. Holmes said casually, 'He was not interested in the salt from the ponds, I think.'

'No,' agreed the smuggler. He was enjoying this.

'He was interested in the other salt, that you take from the ground near Sedom.'

'Yes . . .'

'Or, shall I say, not the salt itself, but the means of extracting it.'

Mr Bashir did not even look at the pile of coins; this was a pleasure beyond business.

'That is true.' I glanced at my companions to see what they

were making of this, and saw a tiny smile cross Mahmoud's lips. Ali looked stunned.

'Are they perhaps items left over from the war? Perhaps having to do with the work El Aurens did on the Turkish railroads?' I knew instantly what he was working around: Colonel Lawrence was already a legend, famous for his guerrilla raids on the railways of the desert, laying explosives under the tracks and setting them off beneath a passing supply train to tip it neatly into the sand.

The smuggler slapped his thigh in delight. 'Do you wish some as well, my friend? I have a plentiful supply, and truth to tell the stuff is no good for mining salt. It is much too dangerous, can be heard halfway to Jaffa, and furthermore it blows the salt all over the countryside.'

'I do not wish any today, but perhaps in the future. Tell me, this *firengi*, this foreigner, has he already bought from you? Taken his purchases away with him?' Delicately Holmes placed another gold coin on top of the other, tapping it into alignment with his fingernail.

'I regret to say that he has. A week or more ago.'

'Which day might that have been?'

The smuggler hesitated, and Holmes' fingers hovered over the last coin.

'The night of the new moon.'

'Which way did he go when he left you?'

'In the direction of Hebron. He and two other men, with three horses and five donkeys.'

A third gold round joined the pile. 'How much did he buy from you?'

'He wanted everything I had, but I only sold him twenty-five.'

'Twenty-five? These are the one-pound sticks?' Holmes asked, sounding disappointed.

'These were bundles. Ten one-pound sticks bound together. And three detonators, of course.'

'Of course. Two hundred and fifty pounds of dynamite,' said Holmes in a light voice. 'With that, a man could surely remove a great deal of salt. I thank you, my friend. Would you please receive this, as a payment towards the salt I shall ask you to send me? There will be no hurry about it.'

Mr Bashir hesitated briefly, then took the coins and swiftly tucked them away. More coffee, a couple of rather subdued stories, and he stood up to leave. Ali rose to walk with the smuggler to his horse, but Holmes waved him back, and accompanied the portly little trader.

They stood talking for several minutes on the far side of the horse, then Mr Bashir mounted and rode away, but not before I saw Holmes press another golden coin into the man's hand. He came back to the fire smiling to himself.

'What did he not wish to tell us all?' I asked him.

'Ah,' said Holmes, dropping to the carpet and beginning to fill his pipe. 'It appears that while this stranger, this *firengi* from the north, was concluding his business with the good Mr Bashir, one of Mr Bashir's colleagues – I assume a son, as he was so embarrassed about the breach of hospitality – took the opportunity to glance through the man's bags, and happened to see, among other things, a revolver, a sniper's rifle with an enviable sight, and a monk's habit.'

He reached for a coal with the tongs, enjoying the effect of his dropped remark. Ali was much absorbed by the presence of a rifle, although frankly I had assumed the man would have had one. But a monk's habit?

'Was he certain? About the habit?' I asked.

'Mr Bashir's people are Christian Arabs. I am satisfied that his son knows what a monk looks like. Mahmoud,' Holmes said, interrupting Ali's muttered exclamations of revenge, 'where would you go, if you wished to find a monk in a habit?'

'There are many monks in the land. Many monasteries.'

'Not as many as there were in times past,' I commented.

'This may be true. Still, there are monasteries in the Sinai, St Catherine's being the most famous. There are the monasteries of St Gerasimo and St John and St George near Jericho, Mar Elyas and Mar Sabas and St Theodosius; Latrun, St Elijah, and in Jerusalem itself another St Elyas. Also St Mark's, the Monastery of the Cross, the Abyssinian monastery, the Armenian monastery, the—'

'Enough,' said Holmes. 'We are looking for a monastery within one or two days' journey from here on horse, in a lonely place, preferably in or west of the Ghor. A place a stranger could visit for a day or two without causing comment or disruption. A place . . .' He paused, tapping his pipe stem against his lower teeth and staring vacantly at the edge of the water a stone's throw away. 'A place with beehives.'

Ali looked at him dubiously, but Mahmoud simply recited, 'Mar Sabas, St George, St Gerasimo, St John, the Mount of Temptation, and Mar Elyas.'

Holmes took his map from his robe and spread it on the ground. 'Show me.'

Mar Sabas was to the north-west of us, in the hills between the Dead Sea and Jerusalem. The monastery of St Gerasimo was in the land between Jericho and the northern tip of the sea, with St John on the path worn by pilgrims between Jericho and the river Jordan to the east. St George was in a wadi to the west of Jericho, near the old road leading up to Jerusalem, the Mount of Temptation was to the north of Jericho, and Mar Elyas lay south of Jerusalem, off the Bethlehem road.

'There are of course many others, in the towns or else hermitages that do not permit visitors. These six meet your description. Although,' Mahmoud added with a faint air of apology, 'I will say I am not certain that the Mount of Temptation has bees, and none of them would be an easy matter to reach in a day.'

'These will do as a start.' Holmes folded up the map and returned it to his robe. 'We start for Mar Sabas tomorrow, then, and after that we shall see.'

'It is yet early,' suggested Ali. 'If we start now we will be at the monastery by nightfall tomorrow.'

'No,' said Holmes, settling back onto the warm, salt-rimed sand. 'We are comfortable here, and besides, Russell has yet to swim in the Dead Sea. One cannot come all this way and fail to float in the waters.' With all the appearance of a holiday maker he lay back on the beach, dug his shoulders back and forth in the sand to shape a hollow, and tipped his bearded features to the sun. Ali and Mahmoud looked at him sourly, obviously wondering what hidden purpose the man had in staying on here. Holmes opened one eye.

'Did you say something, Russell?'

'Oh, no. Not at all.'

'Good. You might go and fill the water-skin, then, if you have nothing better to do than sit and snort.' He dropped his head back onto the sand and closed his eyes.

I kept my face straight until my back was to them, then allowed myself to grin all the way to the spring. Holmes, ever the dramatist, would tell us all what he had in mind for the evening when he was good and ready.

Imagine my surprise, then, when darkness fell, the moon rose, and Holmes made no move to follow Mr Bashir or cross over to question the Bedouin encampment on the opposite bank. The haze that had lain over the sea all day dispersed with evening, and the reflection of the half-full moon was a bright, faintly quivering line stretched across the still sea, before Holmes stirred.

'So, Russell. Are you ready to bathe?'

I was completely nonplussed. 'You were serious?'

'I am always serious.'

Any number of answers to that rose to mind, but I kept them to myself. 'I have no bathing costume,' I objected, which I knew was ridiculous even as I said it.

'Russell, I shall stand guard and keep Ali and Mahmoud from ravishing your young body.'

The words hung in the air as heavy as the sarcasm in his voice, and made me uncomfortably aware of all the males in the world around me. I tried to stifle my discomfort by looking out at the sea, dark and flat. Portions of my skin had not felt the touch of water in days, and God alone knew how long it would be before I had the next opportunity. My scalp cried out to be free of its confining wrap. I stood up.

'May I have the soap, please?'

Holmes was as good as his word, turning his back while I scuttled through the pale moonlight between clothing and water. I scrubbed deliciously with soap and sand, rinsed everything and scrubbed again. The salt-heavy water stung ferociously at my myriad cuts and blisters, and I did not actually feel much cleaner, but when I judged the dirt gone and the dye threatened, I tossed the bar of hard soap up onto the dry sand and launched myself out into the sea.

Trying to rinse myself off by submerging had been a bit like pushing a cork into water, but floating was an extraordinary experience. The water was as warm and dense as a living thing against my naked flesh, and I found that if I remained perfectly still, my limbs stretched out limply and my hair in a great cloud along my arms and back, it was difficult to perceive where Mary Russell ended and the Salt Sea began. The air along my exposed front was slightly cool, but the sea's temperature was mine, and the heartbeats that thudded slowly through my veins became the pulse of the sea. The moon and stars gazed down as I floated on my back atop the buoyant salt fluid, and the loudest thing in the universe was my breathing, travelling in and out of my nostrils like a great wind.

It was hypnotic, and then it was unsettling, and finally I became aware of another entity in my universe, sitting on the shore two hundred yards away, smoking a pipe while he guarded against intruders. I sat up in the water.

'Holmes, I hardly think you need stand guard against the hyrax and foxes. Come in and have a swim.'

For a minute there was stillness where he sat, and then I perceived movement. In the dark and without my spectacles there was no danger of my witnessing anything untoward; nonetheless I turned and struck out into the sea.

We were both strong swimmers, accustomed to the cold waves of the English Channel, and we were nearly at the shore of the peninsula two miles away before we slowed, and stopped. Holmes had maintained a scrupulous distance, close enough for companionship but not in the least improper. I could see him as a ghostly shape, near enough for conversation.

Sitting upright was awkward, like a cork trying to float on end. Eventually I settled on stretching out in the water with my hands behind my head, which kept my ears above the water without having to work at it.

The slight disturbance of our own movements died away; the sea went absolutely still. There was no current here; this was where all the water of the Jordan Valley came to be turned to vapour; it flowed no farther. I was intensely aware of my own skin, vulnerable and safe in the thin moonlight, cradled in the warm, thick, sensuous water. I was even more conscious of Holmes, fifty feet away and in the same condition, and on the distant western shore Ali and Mahmoud, reclining by the faint glow that was the low-burning fire. And no doubt listening to our every splash and bit of conversation.

With Mahmoud in my mind's eye, and keeping my voice low lest it carry across the water, I spoke. 'Holmes?'

'Yes, Russell.'

'When Mahmoud says he was questioned by the Turks . . .' I stopped.

'Torture, yes,' Holmes confirmed.

'I thought so. It was stupid of me to ask. I should have . . .' Again the words drifted off.

'Guessed?' he asked sardonically.

'Known. I should have known. I did know – the scar had to have been linked in his mind with some mental trauma as well as the obvious physical one: His fingers worry it when he's under pressure.'

'I shouldn't worry, Russell. Mahmoud certainly doesn't seem to.'

'You think not?'

'If anything, I should say he feels mildly relieved, to have had it out in the open for once.' I had not thought of that.

The magic of the sea was somewhat deflated. After a while we swam back to the shore, took turns rinsing off the salt in the fresh-water spring, and resumed our dirty clothes for the walk up the beach to our encampment.

And thus to our beds, nestled in the soft sand and warm beneath the blanket of moist, salty, insect-free air that covers the Ghor.

Before I drifted off to sleep, I lay playing the entire evening over in my mind, and it came to me that it had been a gift, that night – a birthday present, as it were, given me by Holmes, slipped to me under the table without acknowledgement of either party.

A sly man, Holmes, but not without generosity.

CHAPTER ELEVEN

ز

*Mar Saba — Accommodation will be found by gentlemen
in the monastery itself; ladies must pass the night in a tower
outside the monastery walls. Visitors must knock loudly at the
small barred door for the purpose of presenting their letter of
introduction . . . The divans of the guest-chamber are generally
infested with fleas.*
– BAEDEKER'S *Palestine and Syria*, 1912 EDITION

WE CAME TO MAR SABAS on the afternoon of the second
day. The hard miles between our Dead Sea camp and our
first sight of that extraordinary monastery were a considerable
contrast to our dreamlike night on the beach. We picked our
way over mile after mile of loose, jagged rock, and although Ali
kept reassuring us that Mar Sabas was just ahead, I no longer
held much hope that I should see the place in this lifetime.
One of my boots was sprung, I had twisted my ankle taking an
incautious step, my tongue was swollen with thirst, my woollen
garments and the snug binding I wore around my chest chafed
and itched abominably, and the patches of raw skin, irritated

by the salt water, now stung fiercely when the sweat trickled into them. I had long since entered that timeless state of mere endurance, placing one foot in front of another until strength failed or I ran out of ground.

It was very nearly the latter. My mind had retreated from its body's discomfort and was miles away, reliving the strange sensations of that glorious night's swim, the unnaturally thick, slippery water followed by the tingling, all-over scrub in the clear spring, the half-moon that rode the black sky, the eerie colours the fire made burning the scavenged, mineral-laden drift-wood, like a hot rainbow in the circle of stones. I concentrated on the memories, my thoughts far, far away, until I did literally run out of ground. With no warning, my eyes fixed unseeing on the hazardous track, I walked smack into one of my companions, stumbled slightly to one side, and then Mahmoud's hand was gripping my shoulder, keeping me from stepping off into space. I looked down a sheer drop at a frothy blue ribbon six hundred feet below, and then raised my eyes.

'God Almighty,' I declared, not without reverence.

'It is a singular place,' said Holmes in agreement.

'It's . . . Yes.'

It looked like the home of a race of mud wasps infected with cubism. Directly across from us, the opposite wall of the wadi, which was light grey like all the Negev Desert and tinged with a seasonal whisper of green, rose up towards distant hilltops that were identical in colour and shape; to the horizons, all the world seemed made of grey, pitted rock. Then the eyes focussed on the facing rim, dropping down into the pits and shadows of erosion until they were caught by the sudden awareness that some of those pits were too square for natural artefacts, and that many of the shadows had remarkably sharp edges. Off to the right a worn path, little more than the track of a mountain goat, followed the striations of rock and led to an actual building, a small cluster of walls and roofs in a courtyard. Caves were fronted by low stone parapets, recesses were blocked off by high stone walls with doors let into them: Mud-wasp caves were rendered into human habitations.

Then to the left, the cubist tendencies of the wasps had gone mad, and a tumble of angular buildings, hard planes of stone and tile, spilled down into the wadi, beginning high above with a pair of square watch-towers planted firmly on the road that ran along the top of the western rim. Walls, windows, roofs, terraces, buttresses, and stairways, in varying states of repair, looked as out of place as an upended tub of monochromatic building blocks. The only reminders of organic shapes in the monastery's centre were two domes and a sprinkling of trees.

'Come,' Ali said. 'They will not admit us after sunset.'

We dropped down a faint pathway cut into the precipitous face of the wadi. A couple of hours later we had gained the bottom without serious mishap, hoisted our skirts to wade across a shallow place, and climbed up again to reach the gates of the monastery. The sun was low above the hills when Ali stepped forward to pound a demand on the small barred door. It took three tries, increasing in their authority, before the door edged open.

'Too late,' said the figure within.

'It was not sunset when first I knocked,' answered Ali.

'Come tomorrow.'

'Tomorrow we are gone.'

'So much the better.' The door closed, but on Ali's boot.

'We wish to worship,' he said, and then astonished me by adding, in passable Latin, 'Do not deny us the hospitality of thy gates, O holy one.'

'There is a party already in the guest rooms,' the truculent monk replied.

'We have tents, and do not wish to be greedy.'

'You must have a letter from Jerusalem. I cannot admit you without the permission of our monastery in the city,' the monk added with a note of triumph.

'I have a letter,' Ali answered. The monk sighed, and put his hand out of the door. Ali handed over a dirty and very worn piece of paper, but as it was not dated, and it was clearly signed, the gatekeeper had no choice but to admit that there was no dislodging Ali's foot. Besides which, the hinges might not have withstood a fourth assault. The door opened, brother porter handed the letter back to Ali, and stood back. We led the mules in, surrendered them to a servant, and followed the monk into the heart of the order.

The monk, once he had received our donation, led us on a desultory tour through the buildings, over the carefully tended terraces where they grew figs and olives, melons and vegetables. A great many birds made their homes here, and we noticed a hive of bees in a protected corner of one terrace garden. There was a domed chapel, ornate to the point of biliousness, which we were taken through and made to admire. We also saw a pile of skulls stacked behind iron grating to commemorate the disastrous Persian invasion of 614, the small patch of ground where more recent residents lay buried, and a cavern to the south of the monastery where St Sabas himself was reputed to have lived peaceably with a lion.

All the monks in that place, who numbered less than fifty, were thin and brown and leathery, and the entire time I was within the walls I remained acutely conscious that no other woman had entered these walls since the monastery had been founded in the sixth century. Unless, of course, she too had been in heavy disguise.

As the sun receded, the birds in the palms quieted; eventually, as the moon rose over the rim of the wadi, the water below could be heard, tumbling on its way to the Dead Sea. The monk left us, and then Ali and Mahmoud went away. It was utterly still, and cold, and the desolation of the rocks in the blue light of the moon was eerie. I suppressed a shiver.

'We could be a thousand miles from anywhere,' I said quietly.

'We are three hours from Jerusalem.'

The night seemed less cold; my spirits rose. 'Is that all? When will we go there?'

'Patience, Russell. We need data first.'

'But will we go there?'

'You yourself have told me that Jerusalem is regarded as the centre of the universe. I believe we will find that it lies at the centre of this mystery as well.'

'Did you find the thing you were looking for here?'

'It is not here. The candle in Mikhail's pack did not come from these bees.'

'How can you be certain?'

'The smell of the candles in the chapel here was entirely

different,' Holmes said, 'and the colour and texture were wrong.' I did not question his judgement; after all, beekeeping was the avocation to which he had devoted innumerable hours in the years since his premature retirement. I merely stood up and cast a last glance at the unearthly landscape of the wadi.

'Shall we go and see what Ali intends to inflict on us for supper?'

To my surprise we were once again installed in our tents outside the monastic walls. Ali produced a dish of some unidentifiable meat that tasted like chicken but had rather too many vertebrae, and as I perched gingerly on the inadequate carpets, picking meat from bones, I reflected on the incongruity of how difficult it was proving to keep kosher in the Holy Land.

The ground was very hard, and when Mahmoud began to make coffee I gave up trying to find a decent seat and perched on my heels. I removed my boots first, examined the sprung seam on the side of the one, and asked Ali if he had a needle and tough thread I could use to repair it.

'Why didn't we stay in the monastery tonight?' I grumbled. My threadbare stockings and the carpet beneath them were little protection against the stones, my twisted ankle hurt in the squatting position, and my backside hurt if I tried to sit. 'The ground inside the walls is considerably smoother,' I added, and then cursed under my breath as the blunt end of the needle buried itself in the thick of my thumb.

'Did you discover who are the occupants of the guest-chamber?' Holmes asked Mahmoud.

'There are no occupants of the guest-chamber,' Mahmoud replied. 'The servant who cares for guests is away, and the monk did not wish to be bothered with us.'

I removed my punctured thumb from my mouth. 'We could insist,' I suggested hopefully.

'The divans of the guest-chamber are generally infested with fleas,' remarked Mahmoud unexpectedly in English. For some reason this set Ali off on a gale of giggles. It sounded like a quotation, and was obviously a private joke.

'Have they had many guests?' Holmes asked.

'One week ago a party of four Englishmen, and a group just before Christmas. No-one at the time of the new moon.'

'I thought not. Very well, we shall go north tomorrow.'

The rocks remained every bit as uncomfortable as they had started out, to the extent that at two in the morning, flea-infested divans began to seem attractive. It was no hardship to rise early and return to the road.

We turned back towards the sea and north, and trudged for twenty dreary miles (how far I had come since the first sparkling day out of Jaffa, a bare two weeks before!) down out of the desert hills and into the Jordan Valley, where the river emptied into the Dead Sea. When it first appeared, I welcomed the green of palm and banana and sugarcane and the rustle of birds in the leaves, but with every step the air grew warmer, and so damp that it became a struggle to breathe. The mules plodded with their heads down, dripping sweat from their necks and flanks. Their humans did much the same.

The monastery of St Gerasimo was another disappointment,

as were the following day the various small monasteries around the site of John the Baptist's immersion in the Jordan. We pushed west through the thorns and the oppressive air towards Jericho, a squalid little settlement unworthy of its ancient and noble history. We were aiming our steps at the Greek monastery on the Mount of Temptation to the north of town, after which we would turn our faces towards the monastery in Wadi Qelt and then to those along the Jerusalem road, but no sooner had we shaken the town's mongrel dogs from our heels than we stumbled upon an archaeological dig inhabited by an elderly English woman with a passion for the subject as a whole, a positive lust for potsherds in particular, and a furious store of energy at her command. In our enervated state she had no trouble in seizing us and dragging us off to her home, where she questioned us and lectured us and put us up for the night, returning us to our path the following morning clean and fed if delayed and rather dazed by the assault.

From her peculiar encampment we travelled north towards the Mount of Temptation (it being a steep climb to the top, I planned on volunteering to stay behind and guard the mules). Before we reached it, though, about a mile outside of town where the track passed through a small plantation of young banana trees watered by the ages-old Jericho springs, a car stood waiting.

It was a heavy car, an open Rolls-Royce of the sort used only by the highest-ranking army staff officers, its chassis virtually indestructible over the roughest of roads. The driver sat on the running board, smoking a cigarette and watching us come along the dusty track. As we approached he straightened, flicked the end of his cigarette across the road, and nodded in a familiar way to Mahmoud.

'I've arranged for you to leave your mules and kit with the family in the next farmhouse,' he said politely in an English straight out of Edinburgh. 'General Allenby would like a word.'

CHAPTER TWELVE

س

Both the sword and the pen are necessary tools for a ruler;
however, at the start of a dynasty, the need for the sword is greater.
— THE *Muqaddimah* OF IBN KHALDÛN

IT WAS STRANGE BEYOND MEASURE, compelling and exotic, to sit motionless while the land flew past at a speed faster than legs could move one. Trees were no sooner sighted than they were gone, and I felt as though I was looking at the open-mouthed children on the roadside with an identical amazed expression on my own face.

We were in Haifa in no time at all, it seemed: one hundred miles, and it was still not too late for tea. We were driven up to a grand house (the palace of a pasha, I discovered later) that had a number of incongruous army lorries and armoured vehicles scattered about what had once been formal gardens. The driver deposited us at a portico, where a lieutenant wearing thick spectacles and a uniform that had never seen battle conditions took possession of our ragged persons with such an air of infinite politeness that one would have assumed that he ushered in similar guests every afternoon – as indeed he may have done.

The lieutenant clicked down the polished corridor, turned a corner, stopped before a door, opened it without knocking, said, 'The Hazr brothers are here, sir,' stood back to let us file in, and closed the door behind us. I was dimly aware of the sound of his heels clicking away, but mostly my attention was taken by the man in the room.

The room held two men, but I do not imagine that the world has produced many individuals who would be noticed in the presence of the man whose office this was.

He was big, although not extraordinarily so. His size was more an extension of his personality: taut with power until his uniform seemed at risk of bursting. He had eyes that probed and analysed and summed up the strengths, weaknesses, and potential uses of their target in seconds, a beak of a nose, a thinning tonsure of hair, and his bullet head was tipped slightly to one side as if listening for hidden currents. Behind his back, men called him 'the Bull'. This was the man of whose exploits Mahmoud had spoken in the village, the man who, in the space of sixteen months, had assembled his inherited hotchpotch of an army and moved it out of its static place in Suez in order to present the despairing British people with Jerusalem for one Christmas and the remainder of the Turkish empire for the next, the man who at that moment was the sole authority of all the occupied territory from Constantinople to the Suez Canal: the

Commander in Chief, General Edmund Allenby. He seemed to take up a great deal of space in the room.

We had paused just inside the door while Allenby swept us with those search-light eyes of his. After a long five seconds he let us loose and turned to the man seated across the desk from him, and told him, 'I shall give him a decision tomorrow, when I've reviewed his report. Now, time for tea. Ah,' he said, as the door behind us opened with a clairvoyant promptness. 'Good. Over by the fire, if you would, Arthurs. It's as cold as England here.' He emerged from his desk, holding a hand out to Mahmoud. 'It's good to see you again, Mr Hazr. I trust you are well again? Those knife wounds can be a nasty business. Mr Ali Hazr, a good day to you as well. And you two,' he addressed himself to us, taking our hands in his powerful grip – but not, I noticed, using our names until Arthurs had laid out the tea things and shut the door behind him. The big man then turned to his aide, one of those phlegmatic, sleek-haired, blue-blooded types the diplomatic corps treasures, and an unexpected sparkle bloomed in his eye. 'Plumbury,' he said, 'I'd like you to meet . . . Mr Sherlock Holmes.' As he spoke the words he peered closely at the aide's face, and was rewarded by a blink, apparently of astonishment. Allenby grinned as if he'd scored a point, and then the mischief was clearly in his face as he brought me forward to be introduced. 'And his associate, Miss Mary Russell.'

Plumbury's reaction was a clear victory for the Bull: not only did the startled man blink a second time at the unwashed Arab youth standing in front of him, he went so far as to raise a pale eyebrow. The general let loose a bark of laughter.

I decided to play along with the general's game. 'How d'you do?' I said politely in my best Oxford accent, and held out an equally languid if rather unsanitary hand.

'Er, yes, quite. That is, how d'you do?' Plumbury managed.

'You stand up to the costume very well, Miss Russell,' Allenby remarked.

'Thank you, General.'

'Colonel Lawrence used to dress up as a woman sometimes to get inside the Turkish lines, but then draping a man head to toe with an Arab woman's fittings is hardly a disguise – a person could conceal an orang-outang or a dancing bear under what those ladies wear. Yours is a different thing entirely. And you, Mr Holmes, look very much at home in your costume. I swear you look younger than you did, what was it? Nine years ago? Ten, that's right, just before my Lake Victoria trip. How is your brother?'

'He kept good health when last I saw him.'

'Good, good. Sit down.' After the briefest of hesitations, which I realised afterwards was probably the contemplation, and rejection, of having me, the only lady present, pour, Allenby picked up the teapot. 'I trust Earl Grey is all right. That's what they sent in the last shipment. And if you want milk, all we have is tinned, I'm afraid; I've never much cared for the flavour of goat's milk in my tea.'

The domestic scene was completed by a large plate of small, crustless sandwiches – anchovy paste on brown bread and hot-house cucumbers on white – and a silver tray of tiny iced cakes. We sipped from delicate cups, balanced plates on our knees, and patted our lips with dainty embroidered serviettes, and the only one of us who looked as if he belonged there was Plumbury.

Our polite social conversation consisted of reminders of the outside world. I was distressed to hear of the death of President Roosevelt, who had been a sort of distant cousin of my American father's family. Ali and Mahmoud were gratified at the news that the holdout garrison in Medina had at long last mutinied against their fanatic commander, surrendering to the Emir Abdullah. Then with the second cup of tea, business began.

'I was in Beersheva two days ago,' said Allenby abruptly. 'Tell me what you've discovered since leaving Joshua.'

Ali set down his cup and began his report, in flawless English. I was interested to hear him analyse the last few days without interpreting what we had done. He almost made it sound as if we had been following a clear course of action, rather than desperately casting back and forth across the desert for a scent. Allenby seemed to understand, however: He sat back with his cup of tea to listen without comment until Ali had brought us into Jericho and up to our abduction from that town by the general's driver.

'Problems?' he then suggested. Mahmoud answered this query.

'Not specifically against the English, although in the south your soldiers are making Britain no friends.'

'They want to go home, I know, and I badly want to send them. They're sick at heart and far from home, particularly the Anzacs. You heard of the barracks mutiny back in Sussex? A "soldier's strike" they're calling it, if you can believe it. Bad show, that. What else?'

195

'You have spoken with Joshua,' Mahmoud replied. 'You know what I know, that trouble is coming; you know what Joshua thinks, that it is a planned trouble.'

'Do you agree with Joshua?' Allenby asked.

'Someone wants the country, yes.'

'Who?'

Mahmoud gave him that curious sideways movement of the head that is the Arabic equivalent of the French shrug, and did not answer.

'Who?' Allenby repeated, this time with the threat of command in his voice. Mahmoud's back went suddenly straight.

'My general, you know better than I who it could be. I am a creature of the ground, and know only what moves on my own patch of earth, while you see all the land from Dan to Beersheva, and on into the Sinai. I sincerely hope that you know more than I, or we are all lost.'

Allenby seemed to waver on the brink of letting loose with a display of his famous temper, and I felt us all shrink within ourselves; then he relented. He even laughed. 'Very well, Mr Hazr, from the point of view of a lowly ground dweller, who do you see coordinating these incidents?'

'A Turk,' Mahmoud answered promptly. 'It stinks of Turkish methods.'

Plumbury's sleek head nodded in agreement.

'Hoping to take back the country while our attention is elsewhere?' Allenby said, though it was not a question. 'That would be the easiest time, when it was not expected.'

'And when the soldiers are weary of fighting and the English people sick unto death of war. This country is in a state of confusion, the ideal setting for a tyrant to take hold. Or a fanatic.'

'It would be nearly impossible to convince the British people to support a new war way out here, that is certain,' Allenby agreed. 'Even Whitehall would be loath to make the move up from a military occupation to all-out war. Still, no matter who started it, or why, the situation is beginning to gain its own momentum, and our task is to nip it in the bud, to kill it now, in a tight operation, not in six months. Or in six years on another battlefield.' He sat forward, and my awareness of his size, which had lessened somewhat under the influence of porcelain cups and crustless sandwiches, flooded back. 'This land has been fought over for thousands of years. A sea of blood has already gone into this soil. I do not intend,' he said forcefully, 'to supervise another bloodletting. I believe we have the opportunity to create a new thing in Israel: a land where neighbours are brothers, not enemies. I believe that if Weizmann and Feisal can agree, that if we can make a fair beginning, Christian, Jew, and Arab can live together. What we must have, however, is that fair beginning, and someone, some group, looks to be attempting to kill it in the early stages.' A look of vague embarrassment flickered across his face and he subsided into his chair. He continued gruffly, 'I can't be everywhere, putting out fires. If some man is setting them, I need help to catch him. I don't know that you, Mr Holmes, Miss Russell, can do much; I realise you're here for a brief time. But you two,' he continued, turning his hard gaze first on Mahmoud, then on Ali, 'are supposed to be good at finding things out. Joshua tells me you are his best. Prove it.

'In one month, on either the ninth or the sixteenth of

February, I intend to act as host to a meeting of representatives of the major faiths in Jerusalem. We will visit the Western Wall, the Temple Mount, and the Church of the Holy Sepulchre, and then we will break bread together at Government House. I wish to have this problem cleared up by then. Do you understand me?' There was a gleam of threat in the general's voice, and suddenly the tales I had heard, of grown men fainting or vomiting after a hard interview with the Bull, did not seem so fantastical after all. Ali turned three shades lighter, and the rock-like Mahmoud seemed to quiver slightly, as if the earth had shifted beneath his feet.

Allenby saw both reactions, and seemed satisfied. He nodded and stood up, saying, 'You will want to look over the reports.' We obediently put down our cups and got to our feet. 'Any questions? Fine. Goodbye, Miss Russell, Mr Holmes. I shall be leaving early for Tiberias, so I won't see you again, and I'm afraid I have to send Plumbury down to Jerusalem, so you can't even have his brain to pick. Still, let Arthurs know if you need anything during your stay.'

It was my first inkling that we were stopping the night in Haifa, but when I saw the accommodation, I did not question the decision: There was a bath. The room had high ceilings and once-proud imitation French plaster cornices and a gorgeous, deep feather bed with a canopy draped with mosquito netting, but most of all it had a bath, and the spigot ran hot when I turned it on. I had thought the dye on my skin was becoming darker as it aged, but it was only grime. The hard soap in the salt-rich sea had not actually cleansed.

We took our dinner in an upstairs drawing room, in what,

according to Ali, had been the *harim* or women's quarters when the pasha had built it. Over the soup I asked our two companions about an unlikely statement of Allenby's that had puzzled me slightly.

'When General Allenby said something about picking Lieutenant Plumbury's brain, was that a joke?'

Mahmoud gave a crooked smile, but Ali chuckled aloud. 'The lieutenant is a typical Allenby possession. He looks about nineteen, does he not? What they call "wet behind the ears" and about as effective as a string broom. In truth, he has double firsts from Cambridge in history and philosophy, he lived here for three years before the war, and he knows nearly as much as the general does about the country.'

The languid youth was another Allenby illusion, a sleight of hand equal to the fake horse lines on the banks of the Jordan. I nodded in appreciation, and wished I might have seen more of the great man before we left his country.

We took our coffee (English coffee, a pale and watery imitation of the stuff Mahmoud made) in an adjoining room, its table piled high with files and boxes. We read through reports of recent incidents, speeches and pamphlets and outbreaks of violence, until my head began to swim, although I could glean no pattern, or even a sense of a pattern, from them. At midnight I gave up and took myself to my feather bed. Which incidentally, after nearly a month of sleeping either on a ship's bunk or on the ground, proved more luxury than I could bear: I ended the night comfortably on the floor, wrapped in the bedclothes.

* * *

Of the next day I remember little, and those memories left me are both sketchy and disconnected. I recollect emerging from my heap of bedclothes on the carpet and indulging in a luxurious second hot bath. I can recall breakfast vividly: devilled kidneys and kedgeree, boiled eggs, toast, and kippers, taken from hot plates on the sideboard and eaten at a long, gleaming mahogany table with a smattering of men, uniformed and not, all of whom were preoccupied and none of whom appeared to think that we were in the least out of the ordinary breakfast companions. There were newspapers, even, from Cairo, Paris, and London – some of them less than a week old.

I definitely remember getting into the motorcar that was to return us to Jericho. It was a Vauxhall this time, that looked the veteran of many a battle with the hard roads. Mahmoud sat in front; I was behind the driver on the right-hand side; Holmes on my left in the middle; Ali next to him on the outside.

After that I have only three brief recollections of the day. The first is telling Holmes about something I had dreamt the night before, children playing on a beach with buckets and spades, and a donkey ride in the background. Next comes the clear image of a bridge over a stream, and a child with three black goats that had immensely long ears, all of them looking up at us. Finally I retain the impression of the motorcar gearing down to climb a hill, and rocky cliffs, and a few sparse trees.

After that, darkness.

CHAPTER THIRTEEN

شٍ

*The feeling of blood ties is natural among men, with rare
exceptions. It causes affection for one's blood relations, that no
harm should befall them. One feels shame when one's relatives are
mistreated or attacked.*
– THE *Muqaddimah* OF IBN KHALDÛN

I WOKE RELUCTANTLY, LYING ON my back with my left cheek
pressed into a soft pillow that smelt of sunlight. A foot from
my eyes was a rough wall, warmly illuminated by the steady
yellow light of a candle, or a lamp. I did an inventory of my
body, decided that my head ached abominably, my stomach
felt equally wretched, and the rest of me seemed to have been
run through a clothes wringer. Gingerly, slowly, I eased my
throbbing head over to face the room.

I was in an attic of some sort, judging from the low and
sloping ceiling. An oil lamp made out of clay burnt on a
tea-chest beside my bed, its small flame rising from the wick

as perfect and without motion as a Vermeer painting. I was not alone: A child sat on the floor on the other side of the lamp, propped into the angle formed by the opposite wall and the stack of wooden chests that had been pushed up against it. Her head was resting back against the wall. She was asleep.

I lay for a long, peaceful time, contemplating the pure, small flame and the pale throat of the sleeping child. She was wearing a light-coloured dress, blue, I thought. It had an embroidered yoke. Her arms were folded across her chest, elbows on her drawn-up knees, hands resting on their opposing shoulders. The sleeves of the dress had fallen back to reveal half a dozen glass bangles on each thin wrist. Her left earlobe gave off a gleam which, I decided after some thought, indicated a small gold earring looped through it. Nearer by, my spectacles lay folded on the tea-chest; I could see twin reflections of the lamp flame in the two lenses, and a long, tall reflection up the side of a glass of water.

It was very pleasant, lying there, and absolutely still, so silent I could clearly hear the light rattle of breath down the young throat. I did not know how I came to be here, but I did know that I wanted neither to move nor to remember, because both would cause pain. Although I was dimly aware that at a distance there was sound, a vague impression of voices and movement, in this room it was so quiet I fancied I could hear the tiny hiss of the oil burning off the wick. I was quite disappointed when the child snorted and woke, blinked once, and then looked straight at me. The bangles on her arms jingled musically as she rubbed her eyes.

'Hello,' she said, only it was not 'Hello' and it was not 'Salaam'. She had said 'Shalom.'

'*Shalom*,' I answered her, and asked in my childhood Hebrew, 'Where am I?'

'You were hurt,' she said, and then in Arabic continued, 'Mahmoud brought you here.' Switching back to Hebrew, she asked, 'Do you speak Ivrit, then?'

'Not well.'

'It sounds all right. I just asked because Mama said I should speak Arabic if you woke up.' And in Arabic she continued, 'Are you feeling better now?' Her speech sounded odd, and it took me a minute to realise what was wrong: She was using the feminine form, not the masculine to which I was accustomed.

'Where am I?' I asked, sticking to Hebrew.

'You are in a storage room in the top of our house. My name is Sarah.'

'And where is this house, Sarah?' I asked patiently. The child was even younger than I had thought.

'In Ram Allah,' she replied, which meant nothing to me at the moment.

'Where are my friends?' Much as I wanted the continued bliss of ignorance, memory was pushing against my mind with increasing urgency.

'Uncle Mahmoud went away after he brought you here, but he said he would be back. Ali went with him.'

And then it was all there, the car, the crash, and blood. My mouth, already dry and foul tasting, turned slowly to shoe leather and the cold began to trickle down my spine. 'What about the other men?' I demanded in English, and when the child looked at me nervously, I put the sentence together in Hebrew.

'There were no other men,' she said, puzzled.

'A car?'

'It was wrecked. That's how you got hurt, Uncle Mahmoud said, but we weren't to let anyone find you, so that's why we put you up here. It isn't very nice,' she confided, wrinkling her nose and glancing at the cobwebs.

None of her speech registered, only the fact that Holmes was not here. And hadn't there been a driver? I couldn't seem to remember what we had been doing and where, but I knew Holmes had been with me, and now he was not.

I could not lie here, not knowing; I had to know, and the first step was to move. Pain came with motion, but no agony, nothing broken or dislocated, as I shifted over onto my right side and began to slide my feet over the side of the low bed. I set my left hand against the coarse sheet in front of my chest, glanced down at it, and froze: It was caked with some dry and flaking red-brown substance. I lay back and brought my hands up before my eyes in the feeble light, and saw on both hands the same cracked brown stain smeared across skin, palm, fingernails.

There was blood on my hands.

'We were going to wash you but Uncle Mahmoud said it was better to let you sleep. It isn't your blood,' the child said, trying to comfort me. I closed my eyes and, putting my hands beneath me again, slowly levered myself up until I was sitting. My head gave a violent throb, my stomach heaved, but my feet were on the floorboards and I did not actually pass out, just sat with my head collapsed forward onto my knees, waiting for the worst to fade.

There was an exclamation from the doorway, and the child Sarah scrambled to her feet and flew across the room. I could not summon the reserves to raise my head, so my first sight of Rahel was her bare feet.

'My daughter, I thought I told you to come and fetch me when our guest awoke.' Her Hebrew was sweet on my ears; for a brief moment she sounded like my mother.

'Sorry, Mama. I was just going to come.' The woman had a lovely voice, and her hand on the side of my neck was cool. She did not seem to be feeling for a pulse or estimating fever, but rather was conveying sympathy and comfort, and I could have slumped on that pallet with her hand on my neck and her words in my ears for the rest of my life. Instead I asked her a question.

'There was another man in the car. Two other men. What . . . happened to them?'

'One is dead and one missing.'

'Which?' I had to force the question out, past my closed throat and the pounding in my head.

'The driver was killed. That is his blood you have on your—' She made a startled noise and caught my shoulders, said something rapid and urgent to the child, and held me firmly as her daughter scurried out of the room and came back a minute later carrying a bottle and a glass.

The brandy steadied my head and brought my stomach back to earth, and after a while, moving with great caution, I sat straight up. The oil lamp on the tea-chest stopped whirling. My head continued to throb, but I thought perhaps it would not actually come off my shoulders.

'Where have Mahmoud and Ali gone?'

'They went to look for your friend. He was taken away by the men who attacked your car.'

'When?'

'You were set upon at about noon. It is now ten o'clock at night. They left you here perhaps seven hours ago. How are you feeling?'

'I will live.'

'Nausea? Dizziness?' she asked in English.

'Not too bad.' It seemed more natural to remain in Hebrew – the switching back and forth made me feel dizzy.

She reached behind her and took up the lamp. 'Look at me,' she ordered, and held the flame up between us, moving it slowly back and forth while she stared into my eyes. She was not satisfied with whatever she saw there, or didn't see, and paused with the lamp in her hand.

'You look bad,' she said frankly.

I couldn't assemble enough coherent thoughts to come up with a lie, so I simply gave her the truth. 'I am beset by memory. I was in a motorcar accident some years ago, and this one has brought back . . . unpleasant things. It's not a concussion,' I added, using the English noun. 'I've had one before, and this is not as bad.' My hand went up to explore the outside of my skull.

'Good.' She put the lamp back on the tea-chest. 'Could you eat?'

'I don't know. Tea would be a blessing.'

'I will send Sarah up with some, and bring your supper in a short time. My name is Rahel. I ought to warn you, do not make any noise if you can avoid it. Mahmoud thought you were best hidden away.'

My two hostesses left me. Further explorations revealed one large and tender lump behind my right ear, an abraded shoulder, a scraped elbow, and many amorphous aches. Whatever had hit us, I seemed to have been fortunate. Even my spectacles, which I picked up from the table, were relatively undamaged, aside from two parallel scratches on the side of the right lens and a certain wobbly feeling as I put them on.

I was considering the risks of being on my feet when Sarah came back and saved me from immediate action. The tea she poured with great concentration from the brass beaker was mint, and sweet, and although it was not what I had in mind, it continued the work the brandy had begun. By the time Rahel returned with a tray, I was positively ravenous.

A light soup, a piece of bread, a small glass of harsh red wine, and I felt considerably more real. The next goal was to be upright, and with Rahel's assistance I achieved that, keeping a wary eye on the low rafters.

'Where am I?' I asked her as I hobbled up and down experimentally, her hand on my elbow.

'Ram Allah. About ten miles from Jerusalem, just off the Nablus road. You are in the attic of the inn. I am the innkeeper.'

'It is very generous of you to take me in,' I ventured. It was difficult to know precisely what arrangement Mahmoud had with this woman, and surely not wise to make assumptions.

'Mahmoud has helped me; I help him. He saved my life and the life of my daughter in the war. You have heard of the Nili?'

The name popped an immediate reaction into the front

of my mind, loosed from some dim corner. '*Netzach Israel lo Ishakar,*' I said promptly. '"God will not forsake Israel." The spy operation run by . . . the Aaronsons?'

'Yes. My husband and I had an inn in Nazareth until the spring of last year. Men talk in inns, and we sent a great deal of information to your government, until we were betrayed to the Turks. I was a dear friend of Aaronson's sister, who . . . died after being tortured by the Turks. A week later, they killed my husband. Mahmoud rescued Sarah and me, and brought us here. He can ask a great deal more from me than hiding a friend in the attic.'

I moved free from her support and walked slowly down the length of the room. 'I cannot stay here.'

'Where would you go?'

That was indeed a poser. Still, I could not simply sit. With every degree of returning energy came two notches of anxiety for Holmes. Who had taken him, and why? I found I was standing in front of Rahel.

'Did they tell you nothing?'

She put out her hand and took my shoulder. 'Those two have more soldiers in the field than the British Army. They will find your friend, and they will come back for you.'

She was right, of course. It would be senseless, and no help to Holmes or myself, to go out into the night, in an unknown city, and lose myself as well. But it was very hard.

And I had no wish to stay in the confines of the attic. 'Do you have guests in the inn?'

'The last customers are just leaving.'

'Servants you don't trust? Any reason to think there is someone out there looking specifically for me?'

'No,' she admitted.

She helped me dress and secure my turban over the lump on my skull. Leaning heavily on her arm, I lurched my decrepit way down two flights of narrow stairs, used the privy, and was given soap, water, and a stiff brush to scrub my hands. Sarah was sent to bed, I was settled on a bench in front of the fire with a rug wrapped around me, and Rahel, after throwing wood onto the coals, went off somewhere. I decided that she was hoping if she left me alone, warm and quiet, I might go back to sleep.

I did not wish to sleep; I was, in fact, leery of sleeping. My bruised brain could not yet piece together what had happened on the drive down from Haifa, but there was a car, and an accident, and a death, and every time I closed my eyes the images that seared across them were those of the automobile accident that had taken my family four years before: vivid, terrifying memories, of my brother's face and my mother's scream and nothing at all of my beloved father who was driving, over a cliff and gone in flames, the guilt-saturated stuff of the nightmares that haunted me still. I had never spoken of the accident to Holmes, had told no-one of the death of my family aside from one long-ago psychotherapist. I could not think why I had allowed it to slip out in front of Rahel, but no, I did not wish to risk sleep.

So I sat propped against the rough plaster wall, watching the flames die down in the hearth and alternating between drowsy half-sleep and abrupt, heart-pounding terror when it was all I could do to keep from tearing open the outer door and shrieking the name of my lost companion and mentor into the night.

This cycle went on for a couple of tiresome hours, and I had just twitched my way back down into a state of torpor when a stealthy movement somewhere in the building brought all my nerves jangling to life.

Gritting my teeth, I lifted my head to look into the room.

Mahmoud stood there; behind him Rahel, with a rifle in her arms and looking very comfortable with it there. The intensity of the joy I felt at seeing him, this phlegmatic, uncommunicative, and utterly trustworthy Arab, took me by surprise. I gulped back the tears of weakness, and murmured, '*Salaam aleikum,* Mahmoud.'

'*Aleikum es-salaam,* Amir,' he replied. 'Your injuries were not serious, I am pleased to see.'

'Have you found Holmes?'

'We know where he is.'

'Thank God,' I said explosively in English. I let the rug drop from my shoulders and tried to stand up. Mahmoud instead pulled a stool over in front of me and sat down on it. His dark eyes probed my face.

'You are in pain,' he noted.

'It will get slightly worse, then better,' I said. Little point in denying its existence, not with those eyes on me. He thought for a minute, then seemed to make up his mind.

'You are *Inglezi, firengi,*' he said: English, a foreigner. 'But you are also not *firengi.* If you were only *firengi,* if you were nothing but an Englishwoman, I would not have returned here tonight, because the *Inglezi* have no—they have a different sense of what is honourable. What was done today is a blood insult, you understand? You and your Holmes have eaten our salt, shared our bread. Blood ties exist, you understand?' He was speaking English, but a much simpler English than I had heard him use before. It occurred to me that he was thinking in Arabic and translating as he went. I assured him that I understood what he was talking about, and that I agreed. He continued. 'If those ties did not exist, the exercise of retrieving him would be only a task, a service to the English government. Ali and I would do that as we have done other jobs. But this is a matter of honour, and I believe you have the right to be there with us, if you choose.'

Were I in his shoes, I reflected, I should be asking how badly I in my feeble state might handicap them, but he asked no such question. I met his eyes evenly.

'I will come, if you will have me.'

He nodded, and stood up. 'There are arrangements to be made; I will return for you,' he told me. After a brief consultation with Rahel he went out. She followed, to return in a couple of minutes with another glass, this one containing two inches of a clear, brownish liquid.

'This will help you to ignore the pain. It will not remove the pain, but neither will it cloud your mind or slow you down.'

I drank it, and sat until Mahmoud came and led me away.

CHAPTER FOURTEEN

ص

Since desert life is clearly the source of bravery, the more savage the group, the more brave, and the more able to defeat other peoples and take from them their possessions.
— THE *Muqaddimah* OF IBN KHALDÛN

I FELT REMARKABLY WELL PHYSICALLY, for a person who had been bashed about in a motorcar accident. The bruises were going to be spectacular and my head throbbed mightily, but I was all right, as long as I did not move suddenly or think about the crash. Thinking about it brought on a rush of cold sweat accompanied by dizziness and a roiling stomach: hard, cold panic.

So I did not think about it, just pushed it implacably away from me, with such success that I never did remember the details. Instead, I gave all my attention to what Mahmoud was doing, and concentrated my entire being on the thought of Holmes and getting him back.

We slipped out of the back entrance to Rahel's inn into the stillness of a Palestinian town at midnight. A third figure fell into place behind us as we passed the back of a shop – not Ali. I thought he carried a long rifle in his arms.

The town did not take long to leave behind. Mahmoud marched ahead, his swirling robes casting wild shadows in the bright light of the full moon. The road stretched palely on ahead; the lights of Ram Allah dropped behind us, and Mahmoud slowed his pace. When I was beside him he began to speak – in English again, that there might be no misunderstanding.

'There were three men in the ambush. The car slowed to climb the hill, and the minor land-slide they had engineered across the road ensured that we should slow even more. They shot the driver from the hill behind us and over our right shoulder, and we went straight into a shallow ravine. Very neatly done.

'The driver was killed. You hit your head on the side of the car when we went off the road. Ali pulled you out. I followed him into the rocks. We waited for Holmes to come, but he did not, and when I went back for him, two men had him in another motorcar that had been hidden around a bend in the road. The third man was still above us with his rifle. An extremely good shot, he was. Had we not left our equipment in Jericho, if I had my rifle, I should have gone after him, but I did not.' He shrugged, as close to an apology as he could come, and I gave him the Arabic hand gesture that said *maalesh*.

'You know where these men went?' I asked.

'Now I do. We have people in that area.'

'Was he hurt? Holmes?'

'There was no blood on the road,' he said, a clear equivocation.

'Was he on his feet?' I insisted.

'He walked to their car under his own power. They held a gun to his head.'

'How did they do it? How did they know we would be there?'

Mahmoud sighed deeply, a sound, I thought, of shame, but did not answer me directly. 'I ought never to have submitted to a driver. A car is big and noisy and suited for conquerors in times of peace, not for scribes. I am a man who goes about on foot, and leaving that path was a foolhardy act.'

'Do you know why?' Why the ambush, why Holmes, why—

'Not yet,' he interrupted grimly, and then, shifting to Arabic, said, 'That is enough of the foreign tongue. We will go quickly and in silence to the house where he is being kept. If we are seen, we may have to kill. It is to be hoped that the deaths will be few. I, myself, take no joy in death. I am not a believer in the blood feud. If it is done correctly, there will be no killing, but with so little time, it is difficult to lay careful plans, and things may go wrong. I hope, at this time of the night and so soon after he was taken, only a sleeping house will await us, and you will have no need to act. If the house awakes, we may need you. Do you understand?'

'I understand.'

'Can I depend on you?' he asked in English.

'To . . . ?'

'. . . Kill,' he finished the phrase. I felt his eyes on me, probing in the moonlight. I stopped, and then I looked at him. His eyes were dark holes surrounded by darkness.

'I don't know,' I said finally.

To my surprise he nodded, in agreement or satisfaction I could not tell, and began to walk again.

'You will tell me if you begin to feel ill,' he ordered.

'My head hurts,' I admitted. 'Of course.'

That seemed to be the extent of his concerns. We walked perhaps four miles altogether after leaving the town, with the rifle-bearing man trailing behind us, until Mahmoud touched my elbow and led me off the road into an almost imperceptible path through a thicket of some Palestinian cousin of the gorse, all spine and grab.

At the bottom of it was a tiny mud hut; in the hut we found Ali. He greeted my arrival with a sour look.

'You brought him, then,' he said to Mahmoud.

'She has earned the right,' Mahmoud replied evenly. His deliberate use of the feminine verb ending was reinforced by the optional pronoun, to force Ali into a recognition of my identity, and my presence. The disgusted look on Ali's face did not change, but he said no more, merely ladled us each a mug of soup from the pot. It was hot and tasted of meat and onions, and I was quite certain Ali had not cooked it.

'Thank you, Mahmoud,' I said. When my cup was empty, Ali filled it again with soup, laid a piece of flat bread on top, and carried it to the leather flap that served as a door. He knelt down to put it on the stones outside, and came back to the fire. A moment later we heard a faint scrape of shoe-leather on stone as the man out there picked it up and returned to his guard. Ali took out his knife and explored the point with his thumb.

'Ali,' Mahmoud chided. Ali flung his hands wide.

'Good,' he snarled. 'Beautiful.' He stood up, stabbed the knife back into his belt, and began to kick dust over the coals. 'I am infinitely happy. Let us go.' He snatched up a pack from the floor, grabbed a rifle from where it leant against the wall, and pushed past us out the door flap. Mahmoud picked up the second rifle and another pack and followed. I trailed in their wake, stumbling awkwardly down the rock-strewn hillside, trying to keep the bobbing *kuffiyah* ahead of me in sight.

I smelt the horses before I saw them. Five horses, all dark and each bearing only the padded cloth that Arabs often use as a saddle. Ali and Mahmoud were already mounted. Mahmoud threw me a set of reins, which I was relieved to find were attached to a proper bridle rather than the plain halter many Arabs used, and I struggled to mount the rangy horse (which laid his ears back and looked as if he would rather bite me than carry me) without benefit of pommel or block. The third man leapt without effort onto the back of one of the two remaining horses and kicked it to the head of the small column. My own mount determinedly followed his mates, with me in disarray on the saddle pad, struggling to get my heel across his back.

Once upright, my eyes were drawn to the riderless horse behind Ali, and I was struck by an illogical but powerful feeling of relief, as if the very presence of a spare horse warranted the eventual addition of its missing rider. My spirits rose a fraction.

We rode hard, at a pace across the uneven hillside that would have had me quaking in terror under normal circumstances, but now seemed merely part and parcel of the whole mad enterprise. An hour later the sky was lit with a faraway flash, and a rumble soon blended with the beat of our cantering hoofs. The storm stayed far to the north of us and added a nightmare quality to our journey, dazzle followed by blindness, but even at that distance, the thunder and the slight breeze served to conceal some of the noise we were making. A passage I had laboriously translated from the small Koran Mahmoud had given me ran through my mind: 'It is He who causes the lightning to flash around you, filling you with fear and hope as He gathers together the heavy clouds.'

Our guide, or guard, slowed us to a trot that jarred my aching skull even more horribly than the canter had done. I was riding blindly now, hoping the headstrong animal under me would not carry me off a cliff, and soon we slowed to a walk, and then stopped. I clung, panting, to the edge of the saddle pad, unaware of anything but the need not to fall off.

Mahmoud's voice came from a place near my knee. 'Take and drink.' I held out my hand, groped for his, came back with an unstoppered phial, and held it up to my lips. It was the same mixture, tasting of herbs and honey and drugs, that Rahel had given me back at the inn, and it worked as well as it had before. My head slowly cleared. I gradually became aware of the three men moving purposefully around the horses. Their dark robes rendered them nearly invisible in the last light of the fading moon, and I was startled when one of them – the stranger – appeared beside me and bent to pick up my horse's hoof. The abrupt change of the animal's stance would have had me off, had my fingers not already been entwined in the animal's mane. I clung on, my brain struggling to work out what they were doing, until it came to me: The horses' hoofs were to be muffled. We must be near our goal. Near Holmes.

The moon went in soon after that, and the breeze died away. We rode slowly down what seemed a remarkably flat and uneventful track for a mile or two, after which we dismounted and walked another mile. It was black as a cave, and utterly silent. Even the jackals were asleep.

My horse stopped before I did, and then I felt hands on the reins, pulling them from my grasp. I followed the sound of the animals moving off, and the rattle of a bush being dragged, and then Mahmoud was whispering in my ear.

'Can you see?'

'Very little,' I whispered back, slightly ashamed. My night vision has never been good.

'Nor I,' Mahmoud admitted, to my astonishment. 'Ali will lead.'

We followed the younger man up a hill, through an orchard, beneath a wall, and I realised that I could see the shape of the stones against the sky. Dawn was not far off. An owl swooped over; the night was so still, I could hear the bird's feathers parting the air.

'There is an inner room,' Ali breathed at us. 'It will be guarded. Does . . . she . . . understand?' His deliberate use of the correct pronoun echoed his earlier disdain and doubt. Mahmoud answered before I could.

'Amir understands that hesitation may mean disaster. He will do what needs to be done.'

I wished I shared his confidence. I began to sweat, despite the cold air, and my stomach turned to rock.

There was a locked gate; Ali opened it. Beyond it lay a garden, and a stout wooden door. Ali unlocked that. Inside, the building smelt of stone and woodworm and something as heavy as incense but not incense; I decided later it had to be hashish. The corridor was long and bare, and the whisper of our clothing was a harsh susurration against the hard rock walls. Ali's feet were bare and damp, and came up from the stones with minute sucking noises. Mahmoud's stomach growled once. The corridor seemed endless.

Once we heard voices, unintelligible echoes a long way off, fading as soon as they had begun. A minute later we passed a door from which came the sound of a man snoring. When we had eased past it, Ali picked up our pace, past doors, a window, three more corners, down a flight of stairs, and then he stopped.

'Stay here.' I heard his feet pad away damply down the stones. After a minute they came back. 'Clear,' he breathed. 'But we must bring the guard out.'

'Amir,' whispered Mahmoud, 'take off your turban. Quickly. Your hair – loose it. Put away your spectacles. And give me your *abayya*. Now, you must call the guard out.'

'Me? How on earth—'

'Hurry! We must have the door open. The guard will not open it for Ali or me, and if we try to force the lock he will raise an alarm. You must bring him out, Amir. Your Holmes is in there,' he added.

As he had known it must, that knowledge steadied me. I straightened my shoulders and arranged my thoughts, then paused with my knuckles above the wood.

'What would he call his superior? The leader?'

'Try "commandant,"' suggested Ali. I had hoped for more surety than that, but it would have to do. I started to bring my knuckles down on the door, paused again to unbutton a few of the fastenings on the neck of my shiftlike robe. I was very uncertain as to technique, to say nothing of ability to carry it off: One thing my training with Holmes had not included was the art of seduction.

I rapped softly on the door, pinched my cheeks hard to make me look flushed, and began to breathe rapidly – which was not too difficult, with my heart already racing wildly.

When the slot in the door slid open I was on the far side of the corridor, crouching against the wall with my robe over my booted feet and peering up with an expression of what I hoped simulated terror on my face. It opened with a sharp crack of iron on iron, and I did not have to feign a start. I blinked up at the pair of eyes that I could see fuzzily, framed by the small barred window.

'What?' a male voice demanded.

'That man,' I whispered fiercely in Arabic. 'The commandant. He hurt me. Please, oh, please help me,' I pleaded. 'I want to go back to my village.'

'Who are you?'

'I live in the village,' I improvised, my voice choked, and then to my distress I felt my eyes actually well up and a tear-drop break free to run down my face. 'He hurt me,' I said with a sob.

The man laughed harshly and slapped the view slot closed; my heart plummeted. However, then came the sound of a bolt sliding, and the knob began to turn. He pulled the heavy door open and stepped out, and he was just beginning to say something about making me feel better when Ali, pressed invisibly against the wall, took one step forward and brought his arm down. The dull thump told me that he had used the haft of his knife instead of the blade; it was quite effective.

Ali and I between us caught the guard before he hit the stones and bundled his limp and immensely awkward form back through the door. When Mahmoud had shut it behind us, we let our burden fall with a thud to the floor.

I took out my spectacles and put them back on, half aware of Ali taking a ball of twine from his pocket and kneeling beside the unconscious figure. Mahmoud ducked through the inner door and into the dimly lit room beyond; I followed on his heels, and saw Holmes.

It is extraordinary, the preposterous things that shoot through one's mind at moments like that. At the sight of him, my body reacted as if it had been stabbed, but my mind's first thought was how typical of Holmes it was to ensure that the dye on his skin extended beyond the normally visible portions: scalp to toe, where he was not the colour of blood and bruise, he was uniformly swarthy. My second thought was one, incredibly enough, of exasperation, that the month-old injuries to his back, the results of a bomb that had been one of the reasons for our flight from London to Palestine, had been healing so nicely, until—

I became aware of Mahmoud's fingers digging deeply into my arm.

'He lives,' Mahmoud said, looking intently into my face.

'Yes, go ahead,' I said nonsensically, but he seemed to understand, and moved forward, sliding his knife from its scabbard as he went.

A length of rope was tied around each of Holmes' wrists.

Both led to a single hook in the beam above him. His feet rested on the floor, but his arms, pulled tight against the sides of his head, were at an angle that would have been excruciating after five minutes, and breathing must have been hellish. By all appearance he had been there for a long time. The injuries to his back, the small round burns and the long weals of the whip, were not the products of a few minutes' work.

Mahmoud was now standing facing him, but I could not approach. I was afraid to look into the eyes of my friend, my teacher, my only family: I was terrified of what I might see there. Instead, I watched Mahmoud watching Holmes, and I knew when Holmes opened his eyes and looked back at the Arab, because the bearded face crinkled slightly around the scar. A smile.

'By the Prophet, Holmes. You look like hell,' Mahmoud said. Reaching into his robes, he pulled out a small silver box, snapped it open with his thumb, and scooped out a quantity of some black, paste-like substance on the tip of his little finger. He leant forward and put it into Holmes' mouth, put the box away and was wiping his finger on his robe when we heard the heavy outer door open in the room behind us.

Many things seemed to happen simultaneously: hurried footsteps and a large angry stranger with his mouth open standing in the inner doorway; my hand, of its own accord and with no pause for thought, going down to the top of my boot, plucking out the throwing knife that lived there, and sending it in one smooth movement through the air straight at the intruder's throat just as Ali's moving fist, wrapped around the butt of his own heavy knife, materialised behind the man's head; another dull thump and the man jerked to one side and collapsed to the floor at the same moment my knife clattered and sang down the stones of the opposite wall. Time shuddered and began to move in a linear fashion once more.

With a look of wonder Ali peered down at his right arm, separating the neatly slit sleeve with the fingers of his left hand and dabbing curiously at the blood welling up in the long, shallow incision that ran from his wrist to his elbow. For a terrible instant I had a vision of Ali on the floor with my knife protruding from his throat: had he been just inches over . . . He stared at me, and then back at his arm, and an expression of sheer joy came over him. I thought he would burst into laughter. My apologies died in my throat.

From behind me came a noise, a curious, high-pitched cough that contained both gasp and groan, cut off instantly. I whirled to see Mahmoud, his knife still in his hand, easing Holmes' arms out of the cut ropes. Holmes took one stiff step forward and collapsed, but Mahmoud, in a motion so smooth it looked rehearsed, shifted along with him, so that Holmes half fell across the Arab's shoulders with another grunt of pain. Mahmoud straightened, and then he was carrying Holmes, all the lanky length of the man with the bloody back draped across those broad shoulders.

Mahmoud put his head down, aimed at the door, and went through it fast, scuttling sideways like a crab to thread himself through. Ali stood up from tying the gag on the second man, snatched up a heavy robe from the first guard's chair, and threw it across Holmes' back as Mahmoud passed, then followed them out into the corridor. I paused inside the door to retrieve my knife and a heap of clothing that I thought looked like Holmes'; and again outside to catch up my own turban and *abayya* from the corner where Mahmoud had thrown them. Then I ran, pulling on clothes as I went. Ali locked the door behind us with the guard's ring of keys, which he slid noiselessly under the opposite door, and then we were all three running, as silently as we could, down the stone corridors, up the stairs, and out, out into the cool, crisp, wet-smelling air of dawn. I would not have hesitated to kill were we stopped, I knew that now. In fact, I could taste the desire for battle and murder and revenge between my teeth; but no-one raised an alarm, and we slipped out of there with the ease of mice leaving a pantry.

It was not until we reached the perimeter wall that trouble came, and when it did, it happened so quickly that again, it was over almost before it began, certainly before I could involve myself.

Ali pulled open the gate and stepped back for us to pass. Mahmoud, still carrying Holmes and showing no sign of flagging, went through first. I followed perhaps three paces behind him, and had just cleared the wall when to my instant and complete terror a loud voice spoke at my shoulder, demanding that we stop and identify ourselves.

Or rather, he began his demand. He never finished it. Our eruption through the gate on top of him had apparently startled him as much as he did us; he was fumbling with his rifle as he spoke, and made the fatal mistake of assuming Mahmoud and I were alone. I have never known a human being to move more swiftly than Ali. Before I had rounded on our attacker, Ali's vicious blade had done its work, and when Ali's hand came off the man's mouth, there was only surprise there, no pain or fear. Just surprise, and then nothing at all.

I had seen men die before, but only men in hospital beds, when death released them from the terrible suffering of gassed lungs or torn bodies. This was a very different matter, this transformation of bone and muscle into a limp, empty thing that landed on the ground with the meaty slap of a dropped water-skin. A noise welled in me, pressing hard against my closed lips, but whether it was a scream or gales of laughter I will never know, because Ali saw it coming and cuffed me so hard my teeth rattled.

'Do not be stupid,' he hissed at me. 'Run.'

I ran.

The sun was nearly on the horizon, the sky dangerously close to full light, and Mahmoud with his flopping burden was all too clear a quarter of a mile down the road. It was quite a ridiculous picture, I thought with that portion of my mind not taken up by the sensation of cross-hairs between my shoulder blades, rather like a long-legged man mounted on a small donkey, but it was also very impressive, the strength of the man sprinting down the road with thirteen-plus stone across his shoulders. He had, I thought inconsequentially, not even paused when the last guard had appeared, merely trusted Ali to take care of the problem.

The bizarre tangle of robes and limbs ahead of me stepped to the side of the road and vanished. I slowed when I reached the place, only to be passed by Ali, who crashed into the narrow path between the bushes without slowing and dived down the precipitous path that lay there, moving at a dead run. Still, I saw to my astonishment, barefoot: his red boots were in one hand, the dead guard's rifle in the other. I slid and scrambled down the hill in his wake, and though I pushed hard, when I reached the horses, the only one there was our nameless guide, mounted, holding the reins of my mount, and looking nervous. No sooner did the reins hit my palm than he drove his heels into his horse's ribs, and I had a battle to persuade my own mount to wait until I was on his back before he followed his fellows down the narrow, dusty, stone-strewn track.

CHAPTER FIFTEEN

*When ambitious men overcome a dynasty and seize power, they
inevitably adopt most of the ways of their predecessors.*
– THE *Muqaddimah* OF IBN KHALDÛN

IT WAS PERHAPS THREE MILES before I caught the others up,
despite my horse's turn for speed, and then only because they
had stopped. The spare horse was still riderless, but the mare
Mahmoud had ridden was standing with her head down and her
sides heaving, sweat dripping from her flanks, while Ali reached
up to help Mahmoud manoeuvre a completely limp Holmes
down from her back. I was off my horse and standing next to the
men without being aware of dismounting. Holmes looked every
bit as lifeless as the dead guard, but when I helped Ali catch him,
his eyes were open, the pupils tiny, and the cry that had burst
from me changed to one of relief: He was drugged, not dead.

They had clothed him in an unfamiliar pair of baggy trousers and Ali's sheepskin coat, and now laid him on the ground, arranging him on his side so as not to cause further damage to his back.

'How much opium did you give him, for God's sake?' I demanded.

'Enough to keep him quiet,' Mahmoud replied. His left arm, which had held the full weight of his passenger, must have been numb, for he was kneading it with his right hand and working his hand vigorously to restore circulation.

'Almost permanently, by the looks of it. He's completely unconscious.'

'He will recover,' he said, and added less belligerently, 'He is mostly bone, little flesh. Perhaps I ought to have lowered the dose.'

'How long before it wears off?'

'Hours. Five, eight.'

'He needs to be in a bed before that.'

'It has been arranged.'

'Where?'

'Two, three hours,' he said vaguely. He gave his left arm a final shake and, catching up the reins of the spare horse, vaulted onto its back. Ali bent to lift the dead weight that was Holmes, but I put a hand on his arm to stop him.

'Wait,' I said. 'I'm the lightest one, by a considerable amount, and my horse easily the largest.' And the most contrary, I did not add. Ali and I waited for Mahmoud's answer.

'How is your head?' he asked after a moment.

'It aches.' Actually, it throbbed horribly with every beat of my heart and I felt both queasy and shaky, but I did not feel there was any threat of passing out. Not without warning, at any rate. I held his gaze coolly. He gave one of his internal nods and slid back down to the ground, lifting his chin at my own horse as an order to mount it. I handed him the burden of Holmes' possessions and mounted the horse, shifting back to the edge of the pad to leave room for Holmes. He and Ali lifted Holmes bodily up, threading one leg up and over the horse's withers so Holmes' back was resting against my chest. I could barely see over his shoulders, but I worried that I was hurting his back, and said so.

'He won't feel it,' said Mahmoud.

Insh'allah, I thought.

It took fully three hours. At some point the guide left us, only to come pounding up behind again half an hour later with a parcel of Arab sandwiches, spiced meat and bits of raw onion wrapped in flat bread. We ate while riding, and afterwards I felt considerably less shaky and not in the least queasy. My head still ached, though.

After two hours of alternately picking our way over rocks and loping on the flat bits, Holmes began to come around. It was easier to hold him as he became less limp; on the other hand, the pain in his back was obviously getting through to him. We had to stop, and while Ali and Mahmoud between them held Holmes upright, I slipped off the horse and then climbed back on, awkwardly, in front of him. We rode the next few miles with him slumped forward against me, dreadfully uncomfortable for me but easier on him. However, when he began to jerk about behind me I was forced to relinquish the reins to Mahmoud and be led, riding half doubled-over and with both arms stretched behind me to keep Holmes from tumbling to the ground. At about this time our guide turned calmly into another road and, without acknowledgement from either side, rode away. A few minutes later Ali turned to check on us, then kicked his mare into a gallop and left us trotting along in a cloud of dust.

Twenty minutes later, I nearly tumbled to the ground myself when a voice spoke, strong in my ear.

'Russell?'

'Holmes! Thank God – are you all right? It won't be much longer.' I waited. 'Holmes?'

There was no answer. I tried to turn and look at him, but his head was limp against my neck; he had faded again. A few minutes later the same thing happened.

'Russell?'

'Yes, Holmes, we're all here. You're safe now.' I didn't think he heard me. And again a few minutes later:

'Russell?'

'Holmes.'

We repeated this lunatic non-conversation any number of times before we finally emerged from the hills and made for a collection of raw-looking buildings set among fields, a manned guard-tower rising over all. Ali stood in a doorway beside a tiny apple doll of a woman with a kerchief over her grey hair. Mahmoud rode up to the small house and dismounted, then turned to the woman and with his right hand gave a gesture ridiculously like that of a man tipping his hat, which of course is quite impossible with a *kuffiyah*. The tiny woman smiled with delight, came forward, and actually kissed Mahmoud on his hairy cheek.

Before I could speculate on the hidden depths to the man, he and Ali were on either side of me, holding Holmes so I could slip out from under him. They let him fall gently forward, then slide face-down off the tall horse, but when they tried to lift him, one of them must have seized some tender part of his anatomy, because he stiffened and drew a sharp breath. His eyes flew open, and he looked straight at me with that wide-eyed, apparently alert but slightly unfocussed gaze of a drunk, or someone wakened from a heavy sleep.

'Russell.'

'Yes, Holmes. It's all right.'

'Yes?'

'Yes.'

'Good,' he said easily, and then his eyes lost all focus and he slumped into the supporting arms.

His wounds took some time to clean and dress. I did not have to take a hand in that; I felt that I had placed quite enough dressings on that back in the last two months, and the tiny woman was more than competent. She had introduced herself in Hebrew as Channah Goldsmit and apologised that she was not actually a qualified doctor, but was as close as we would come for some miles. I did not dispute her claim on the patient.

I was brought a tall glass of cold, sour lemonade, and it went down my dry and dusty throat like a taste of paradise, a sensation utterly disconnected from all others as I stood in that small bare room watching Channah Goldsmit clean and salve and plaster the raw, beaten, and burnt skin of the half-conscious man who was the centre of my life. The needs of action had been met, leaving me lost, bereft even. I felt, frankly, young and helpless and in confusion, and I did not like it one bit.

Even before this latest episode, I had been aware that I did not really understand my feelings about Holmes. I was nineteen years old and for the last four years this unconscious figure on the bed had been the pillar of sanity and security in my daily life. However, he was also my teacher, he was more than twice my age, and furthermore he had never given me the least indication that his affection for me was anything other than that of a master for a particularly promising student. Five weeks earlier I had been a maturing apprentice who was moving away into another field, but the events of the last month, both at home and here in Palestine, had shaken that comfortable relationship to its core. I had been given little leisure time in which to contemplate the consequences of my change in status from apprentice to full partner, from pupil to . . . what?

Channah Goldsmit finished an eternity later, tidied up the snippets of gauze and such, and turned to me, to give instructions I suppose. I do not know just what she saw in my face, but it caused her to drop the basin of supplies and push me into the chair beside Holmes' bed. More gently, she removed the glass from my hands and herself from the room, but in a minute she was back, with a heavy woollen rug she tucked around my shoulders and a glass of the local brandy that she pushed into my hands.

I had not even realised that I was shivering.

I was aware of noise, she was speaking but I did not answer, and she went away. A short while later I was dimly aware that she had returned, standing in the doorway, with Mahmoud's head towering above hers, and again there was the sound of speech, but eventually they went away and left me alone with Holmes.

The sound of his breathing filled the room. I could tell when he drifted into an unconscious state, when his breathing slowed and deepened. For ten minutes or so all would be well, and then with a guttural sound in the back of his throat his breath would catch, as wakefulness and sensation approached. For a few minutes he would draw only short, shallow breaths, until with a sigh he was again teased away into the depths.

I could not stop shivering. The only warm part of me was my right hand, which covered Holmes' where it lay on the thin mattress. The left side of his face was against the mattress, and I watched his right nostril move, his right eye twitch from time to time, the right side of his mouth pull and relax beneath the beard and the bruises. I watched him as if willing the very life back into him.

The afternoon wore on and the evening sun slanted through the window before I heard his breathing change again. He did not move, but he was awake, fully awake. I drew my hand away, and waited.

His eyes flared open. He blinked at the sight of my knees, looked sideways without moving his head, and saw my face. His eyes closed, and his throat worked two or three times.

'Russell.' His voice was hoarse and low.

'Holmes.'

'Haven't we done this once already?'

'What, me sitting in a chair while you lie in bed with bandages on your back? I'm afraid so.'

'It grows tedious.'

A bubble of joy began to expand in my chest, and I felt a stupid grin come onto my face. To hide it from him, I poured a glass of water and attempted to dribble some of it into his mouth, without much success. He closed his eyes for a few minutes, then asked, 'What damage is there?'

'Superficial injuries only. Nothing broken.' Including, thank God, his spirit, not if he could joke.

'Whose diagnosis?'

'We're in a *kivutz*. A communal village. They have a doctor. Actually, she's a midwife, but trained.'

'In all my years, I don't believe I have ever before required the services of a midwife, Russell.'

At that I did laugh, and at the noise Mahmoud put his head inside the door, then withdrew it.

'Mahmoud gave me something,' Holmes said suddenly.

'Opium paste.'

'Dangerous madman.'

'He apologises for the heavy dose. Still, it got you here.' There was no answer. I said quietly, 'Holmes?'

'The car crashed, did it not?'

'It did.'

'The driver?'

'Dead.'

'I thought so. You?'

'Minor bangs.'

'What?'

'I'll have a head-ache for a couple of days, that's all.'

'Fortunate.'

'We were both lucky.'

'Yes. He was going for pain, not damage.'

It took me a moment to realise who 'he' was. 'Your captor,' I said. 'What did he want?'

'Information. Joshua. Allenby.' His voice was slowing.

'Did you give it to him?'

He did not answer for so long, I thought him asleep. Then: 'I would have done,' he said heavily. 'The next session, or the following.'

'Who was he?'

'I wish to God I knew,' he said, and then he was asleep.

CHAPTER SIXTEEN

ط

True visions carry signs to indicate their truthfulness. The first
is that a person wakes quickly; were he to stay asleep, the vision
would weigh heavily upon him. Another sign is that the vision
stays, with all its details, impressed on the memory.
– THE *Muqaddimah* OF IBN KHALDÛN

WE STAYED AT THE *KIVUTZ* for three days. That first day, a
Saturday, Ali and Mahmoud took an early supper with
the Goldsmit family, borrowed fresh horses, and rode back to
the villa where Holmes had been held captive. They returned on
Sunday afternoon, and found the two of us sitting in the sun in
front of the small house, drowsing like a pair of pensioners on
the seashore at Brighton while the busy life of the *kivutz* went
on around us.

Ali snorted in disgust and led the horses away. Mahmoud
dropped to his heels in front of us, facing to the side. Both Arabs
looked grey with exhaustion, and I doubted they had slept last

night either. Mahmoud reached for his pouch of tobacco and began to roll a cigarette, his fingers slow and awkward. He lit it with a vesta, and I could not help an involuntary glance at Holmes.

His eyes seemed fixed on the burning end of the cigarette. With an obvious effort, he tore his gaze away and, with small, jerky movements of his strained arm muscles he eased his pipe out of his robe, filled it, and lit it. I took from a pocket the small pomegranate a child had handed me earlier in the day, and concentrated on the process of opening and eating it.

'Gone,' Mahmoud said succinctly.

'Who were they?'

'The villagers thought they were from Damascus, one man said no, Aleppo. Not Palestine, anyway, that was agreed. The owner of the villa is himself a Turk. He took to his heels in the September push, and it's been empty ever since. These men came three or four weeks ago. Around Christmas.'

'Any idea where they have gone?'

'Wherever it was they took everything with them. We went through the house with great care.' Mahmoud turned his head to look at Holmes, searching that bruised and inscrutable face for doubt or criticism, and finding none. 'In one fireplace many papers had been burnt, then pounded into ash. Thoroughly. The only things we found were recent copies of the *Jerusalem Post*. In one of them, from last Thursday, we found this.' He reached over and placed a small torn-out scrap of newsprint in Holmes' lap. It was not an article but an advertisement for a watchmaker in the new part of Jerusalem. Next to the box there was a small tick mark from a pen.

'You take this to mean they are going to Jerusalem,' Holmes stated.

'Do we have anything else?'

Holmes tried to shift into a more comfortable position, and winced. The scrap of newspaper drifted to the ground; Mahmoud picked it up and tucked it away in his robe.

'The monastery of St George,' Holmes said. 'Channah Goldsmit assures me there are no bees on the Mount of Temptation.'

I could not think for a moment what he was talking about; then it came to me that the two monasteries, to the north of Jericho and to the west, had been our next planned stops before General Allenby's car had appeared and taken us away from our search for monastic bees. Ages ago, though only four days on the calendar.

Mahmoud looked away again. 'Mikhail's wax candle,' he said flatly.

'Precisely.'

Mahmoud ground the end of the cigarette out on the earth and rose to his feet. 'Ali and I will waste no more time. We go to Jerusalem.'

'That is probably a good idea,' Holmes said. We both stared at him in astonishment. 'You go to Jerusalem. Russell and I will meet you there. Shall we say either Wednesday night at dusk or Thursday at noon, just inside the Jaffa Gate?' He blinked mildly in the bright sunlight at Mahmoud towering above him, though I could see in the sudden lines along his jaw that craning his neck was painful. Mahmoud shook his head and walked off. Holmes eased his chin down, and let out a breath.

'You're in no condition to clamber over rocks,' I said. 'And I saw enough of the landscape to know that's what will be involved.'

'I will be by Tuesday,' he said. For Holmes, that was a considerable concession to the body's weakness.

However, Ali and Mahmoud had no intention of staying at the *kivutz* with us, particularly not as that would also mean a further (and no doubt pointless) delay at the Wadi Qelt monastery. I caught them before they set off for Jericho, and took Mahmoud to one side.

'I wanted to say thank you,' I told him.

'One does not thank a brother,' he said in return, with a twinkle in the corner of his eye.

'Is that a saying?'

'It is the truth.'

'Well, brother or not, I thank you.'

He gave me a sideways shrug to wave it away, but I thought he was pleased nonetheless. Then he pursed his lips for a moment, looking off at the hills.

'Amir,' he said. 'Mary Russell. Do not try to protect your Holmes, these next days. It will not help him to heal. This I know.'

'Yes,' I said. 'I had already decided that. *Fi amaan illah*, Mahmoud.' Have a safe journey.

'*Insh'allah*,' he replied. If it be God's will.

* * *

Holmes spent the rest of that day and all of Monday sitting in the sun, eating, and sleeping. The nights, however, were another matter. Without either of us commenting on it, I left a small lamp burning all night. I had asked for a second bed to be brought in for me, as his arm muscles tended to go into spasms when he relaxed and I needed to be there to force them down and knead them into pliability. Again, neither of us commented on his inability to control his muscles; I just slept in the same room, listening to the sounds he made.

He did not sleep much, not at night. On Saturday night he had twitched and spasmed until in desperation I insisted on another, milder, draught of opiate. Sunday night he sat and smoked and read a book borrowed from one of the *kivutz* members, and sipped brandy while I drifted in and out of sleep. On Monday night he read and smoked, and then very late I heard him take himself to bed, cursing under his breath all the while. I smiled, and slept, and in the still hours of the night I shot upright, staring at my surroundings.

'Holmes?'

The thin howl, an eerie, unearthly noise like a soul in torment, cut off instantly.

'My God, Holmes, was that you?'

He cleared his throat. 'Was what me?' he asked, and I gave myself a hard mental kick. I of all people ought to know the shame of nightmares, and as I woke more fully, I was not even certain that I had actually heard it. I lay back down and pulled my bedclothes over my head.

'Jackals,' I muttered sleepily. 'Sorry to wake you.' Neither of us slept much more that night.

* * *

Channah had arranged for the *kivutz* lorry, a Ford Model T that had been converted to carry sheep and cows, to take us to Jericho. The following morning after I had helped with the morning chores, we climbed in beside the driver and bounced away. It was not a merry ride. Holmes had refused medication, I was tense with anticipation of another crash, and the driver, whose name was Aaron, was not one of the handful of *kivutz* residents privy to our secret. He was also on the Orthodox side and made no attempt to hide his resentment at being forced to chauffeur a pair of Mohammedans.

The drive went without incident, aside from one punctured tyre and a delay while a large flock of Bedouin fat-tailed sheep drifted from one side of the road to the other. Two hours after we left the *kivutz*, Aaron stopped on a deserted patch of road just north of Jericho and we let ourselves out. Looking straight ahead, he waited for us to fasten the rope that held the door shut, then drove off. The sound of the engine faded. A crow cleared its throat from a nearby tree, a goat's bell clattered in the distance, and it suddenly hit me how very alone we were. When I looked at my companion it grew even worse: He looked terribly ill, pale and sweating with dark smudges under his eyes, and he was slumped against a fence post, unable at the moment to stand upright. I began to feel frightened, and yearned for the abrasive presence of Ali and Mahmoud.

'For heaven's sake, Russell, stop looking like a lost schoolgirl. I'm not about to collapse at your feet.'

'Are you sure?'

'Of course. I've sustained worse injuries than this. I merely need to limber up. Just . . . lend me your shoulder for a bit.'

I supported his steps for a hundred yards or so, but the exercise did actually seem to do him some good. His back straightened, his limp lessened, and eventually he took his hand from my shoulder and continued, slowly but unaided.

We skirted Jericho to the west of the tell, although I was sorely tempted to call on the mad archaeologist for whatever help she could inflict upon us, or even for an infusion of energy. However, the thought of the subsequent enervation held me back, and we continued through the banana and orange groves to the farm where we had abandoned our mules and our possessions. Ali and Mahmoud had agreed to leave us one of the mules and basic provisions, carrying the rest to Jerusalem before us.

To take both our minds off our troubles, I fell back on a comfortable, long-established ritual: I asked Holmes about the case.

'Holmes, do you have any thoughts about the identity of the man in Western clothing seen speaking to the *mullah?*'

'Many thoughts, Russell, but no conclusions.'

'It could be anyone.'

'Hardly that,' he said drily.

'Perhaps not anyone. Just any male in the country taller than the average Arab – who comes up to my chin – and wears a hat instead of a headcloth.'

'Russell, Russell,' he chided. 'He must be either English or European, if he impressed Mahmoud's witness as not being in uniform. Too, it is unlikely that anyone who does not have an ear in the British camp would know enough about

Allenby's business to lay hands on the car transporting the Hazr brothers.'

I glanced over at him, then away. As I had hoped, the colour was back in his face as the working of his mind lessened the discomfort of his body. In addition to which, criticising me always cheered him up.

'How will we find him?' I asked.

'Wait for him to reveal some piece of knowledge unknown to others, perhaps. He will give himself away in the end.'

'The man who . . . questioned you. Could it be he?'

'That man was by no means British in his manner, although physical disguise is of course a possibility,' he answered, his voice even.

'But he did not know who you actually are?'

'He seemed to believe that he was dealing with a half-literate Arab, but I would not swear to it. I do know that he is a very clever man, when he chooses to exert himself.'

'If he thought you an Arab, that leaves out a number of possibilities as his informant.'

'Such as?'

'Joshua,' I offered hesitantly. Fortunately, he did not laugh at my suggestion. Emboldened, I also said, 'Half the men in Haifa.'

'And if for some reason the British traitor did not inform his master, or if the master was clever enough to conceal his knowledge from me, what then?'

'Then it could still be anyone in Haifa. One of the drivers, perhaps – the man who was killed, to cover up his treason? Or anyone privy to communication between

Joshua and Allenby, or between Joshua and Mycroft, or—'

'As I said, Russell: many thoughts, no conclusions. We haven't sufficient data.'

'What, then, do you recommend we do?'

'Keep well out of sight, keep our ears to the ground, and wait for the opportunity to trip him up.'

What we had been attempting to do all along, I reflected, with no great success.

We found the farm where we had left the mules; the place looked deserted. 'If they've made off with our things, I'm going to commit murder,' I said to Holmes, but when we came into the clearing amongst the tangle of brush and thorny trees, the noise of the dogs brought an old woman out to investigate. Her face was heavily veiled though her arms and legs were bare, and the skin on her arms gathered into a thousand sun-darkened wrinkles before it disappeared beneath several pounds of silver and gold bangles.

'Good day, O my mother,' I said to her. 'We have come for the mules and the . . . things,' I ended weakly. She nodded, but her eyes had the expectant look of someone who does not comprehend. Holmes intervened.

'My mother, a few days past we left our possessions here with your son.' She nodded. 'And two days ago some men came here and took two of the mules and most of the bags.' She nodded. 'Where is the remaining mule?'

She nodded.

Holmes and I set out to find our transportation, food, and bedding, followed by the amiable old woman and half a dozen equally amiable dogs. There were no outbuildings near the house, but a path led through the bush, and there were the prints of shod hoofs on it. At the end of the path we found one mule and two sacks filled with food, blankets, and water, precisely what Ali and Mahmoud had agreed to leave for us. We loaded up under the watchful eye of the woman and her dogs, and went back down the path and past the house to the road. We thanked the woman, and she nodded, then raised her hand with a mighty clatter and rattle of bangles to wave us goodbye. The dogs began to bark as soon as we crossed an invisible property line and became strangers once again.

'Why do I feel as if I'd just robbed a mental deficient?' I asked Holmes.

He nodded.

We stopped at the base of the wadi to share a cup of musty water and a handful of dates. I gazed sourly up the expanse of rough, uphill road that lay between us and the monastery, and drew a deep breath.

'Holmes,' I began. 'It is hot. The humidity is debilitating. We have a minimum of food, barely enough water, and there is a group of men somewhere out there who would happily kill us both. It is, in a word, no time for an argument.'

'What do you propose?'

'I will beg you, Holmes. I will go on my knees if you wish, but please, as a favour to me, would you be so good as to let the mule carry you up this hill?' I took care not to add aloud, So I won't have to when you collapse.

'Since you put it like that,' he said, and to my consternation he actually climbed on the mule's back behind the rest of the load. And I had thought he was getting better: such easy acquiescence was a worrying sign.

Once again we were travelling in the direction of Jerusalem, and once again we were to be turned aside from that goal – although this time, I hoped, it would be only a peaceful and temporary diversion. What could happen to us in a monastery? The road, however, was a place of vulnerability, particularly with its antecedents in mind. 'Holmes, do you know what road this is?'

'Russell, if you are about to tell me the story of Joseph and Mary with the pregnant Virgin perched on the donkey, I warn you, I shall not ride one step farther.'

'No, no, I was thinking of something much darker than that, although also from the Greek Testament. I believe this is the road where the traveller was set upon by thieves, and rescued by the Good Samaritan after his own people had passed him by.' I paused, and the balmy afternoon suddenly seemed to turn chill. 'Did you look to see that Mahmoud had left us one of the pistols?' I asked in a small voice.

'Oh, for pity's sake, Russell,' said Holmes, sounding reassuringly vigorous. 'This country is wreaking havoc on your already excessive imagination. Do try to control yourself. And yes,' he added, 'we are in possession of both pistol and bullets.'

We climbed up out of the river Jordan plain on the rough road that followed the southern side of the precipitous Wadi Qelt. The heavy, damp air made breathing difficult and a cooling breeze an impossibility, so we sweltered our way up the hill, all three of us ill-tempered and drenched with sweat.

A couple of boys on a scabrous and undernourished donkey passed us at a brisk trot, going uphill. They called out merry jokes until the next corner had swallowed them, and I decided to stop for a breather when we came to a cave-like overhang that might well have been the place where Obadiah hid a hundred prophets from Jezebel. I watered the mule and ourselves, and stood looking out over the Ghor Valley and the northern end of the Dead Sea, brooding and silent and lifeless.

'Herod chose to build his winter palace here,' I said to Holmes. 'He enjoyed the climate and the social life.' He did not answer. We went on.

The next party to overtake us was a group of English tourists, too high-spirited and well dressed to qualify as pilgrims despite the presence of Jordan River mud on their horses' hocks. Two women in silly hats and half a dozen young men in uniform trotted past us on their sleek mounts, paying us rather less attention than if we had been stray dogs on the road. We plodded on.

At long last, a track that was little more than a footpath branched off into the wadi to the right. It was very steep, in several places evolving into a stairway as it snaked down the sheer wall of the wadi, and in ten minutes we lost most of the altitude we had gained in the past two laborious hours. However, at the bottom of the wadi ran a deliciously cool, sweet stream, and we drank deeply and bathed our faces before starting up the path on the opposite side, towards the monastery that hung from a nearly perpendicular stone face.

If the Greek monastery we had visited at Mar Sabas was the product of mud wasps, I thought, the Russian St George's had been constructed by cliff swallows. It was a thing of arches and windows balanced on an outcrop of striated rock, and looked as if the slightest earth tremor would flip it whole into the valley below; nonetheless, it was a lovely setting, for there was water here, perennial water, and if the higher reaches of the wadi were the standard mixture of rock and scrub, down here there were trees – not a great number, true, but they were actual, recognisable trees.

The clean air smelt of wet stone and green things, of incense and quiet, of sanctity and – flowers.

'Bees,' said Holmes thoughtfully as we passed a smattering of small, yellow blooms beside the path where the insects were working.

'Beehives,' said Holmes reflectively two hours later as we stood in the gardens with our monastic guide, watching the dusk draw in.

'Candles,' said Holmes happily later that night, when we were led into a small chapel ablaze with the light from half a thousand thin, brown tapers that gave off the strongest honey scent of any beeswax I have ever known. He plucked an unlit candle from a basket, held it to his nose, drew in a deep, slow breath, and went out of the chapel door with it in his hand. Outside on the dimly lit terrace, watched by our guide (who was by now completely baffled) and by a large cat (who, judging by the state of his ears, had retired to the monastery following a full life), Holmes took a small object from his robe and unwrapped it: Mikhail's candle stub, which along with everything but his money and his knife had remained intact in his pockets. He worked the wax between his thumb and forefinger to warm it and increase the surface area, and then put it to his face. He smelt it deeply, then did the same to the candle he had just taken from the chapel, and again the stub. His bruised features relaxed into a look of satisfaction, and he turned to the uncomprehending and frankly apprehensive monk.

'I should like to see the abbot, please.'

CHAPTER SEVENTEEN

ظ

The bare necessities are basic; luxuries are secondary. Thus,
Bedouins are basic, prior to cities and sedentary people.
Bedouins are clearly nearer to goodness than are sedentary people.
— THE *Muqaddimah* OF IBN KHALDÛN

Abbot Mattias was a true creature of the desert, as hard, prickly, and unyielding as any bit of rock-rooted scrub we had avoided in the past weeks. Holmes took one look at him and abandoned all thought of pretence. The telling of our story, in which I played no individual role and which sounded more and more unlikely with each successive twist and turn, appeared to make absolutely no impression on the religious. He sat back in his heavy carved chair with his hands threaded together over the front of his habit, his eyes on Holmes, his only movement the occasional drowsy blink of his eyelids, like a lizard. The two candles on his table burnt down. Holmes talked. I sat. The abbot listened.

Holmes told him more or less everything, omitting only our true names and skirting around the details of what had happened to him at the villa north of Ram Allah. Eventually he had brought us from England up to the present, to our arrival at the monastery and the confirmation that Mikhail's candle stub had almost certainly originated here. He then stopped talking. The abbot blinked slowly, waited for a moment as if to be certain that his guest had finished, and then unthreaded his clasped fingers and wrapped his hands instead along the fronts of the arm rests. The seat was transformed into a place of judgement.

'May I see your back, please,' he said.

Whatever Holmes had expected, it was not this. His face grew dark. There was no reading the abbot, absolutely no way of telling if he sought confirmation of Holmes' story, wished to see if the injuries needed medical attention, or was simply curious. Perhaps he even thought to put Holmes to a test. If the last, he was remarkably perceptive: Holmes was not one to display willingly any signs of weakness or failure. I do not know what Abbot Mattias wanted, and I never asked Holmes how he perceived the request. I believe, however, that he saw it as a challenge, by a man in a superior position, and he responded the only way possible: He stood up and pulled his robe over his head.

I averted my eyes to study an age-dark painting of Virgin and Child, the maternal figure gazing out with the weight of the world's suffering on her accepting shoulders. After what seemed a very long time, the rustle of Holmes' clothing ceased and I heard the creak of leather that indicated Holmes' weight settling back onto his chair. When I looked back at the abbot I had the shock of finding his eyes on me. And very discerning eyes they were.

'What of your companion?' he asked Holmes.

'He—'

'I am a woman,' I said. I thought this came as no surprise to the good father, and indeed, for a brief instant I imagined a gleam in the back of his dark eyes. He leant forward over his knees for a moment, then pushed himself upright and moved across the room to an ancient, worm-eaten cabinet of time-blackened wood. The moment he moved I realised how much older he was than I had thought. Eighty? Ninety? His voice, speaking English with a light Russian accent, was that of a man half his age.

He opened the cabinet and took out a bottle that had no label and had, judging by the scratches and wear, been re-used any number of times. His gnarled hands eased up the cork and he poured the thick, black-red wine into three squat and equally abraded glasses. One he placed on the desk next to me, the second near Holmes. The third he carried back to his chair and cupped in his hands, looking into it as if consulting an oracle.

'That you were maltreated by a man who uses the methods of our late oppressors, I take as a sign in your favour,' he said without preliminary. 'That you were befriended by Dorothy Ruskin, the mad archaeologist of Jericho, I take as another indication of good-will. That you walk with the men known as Ali and Mahmoud Hazr confirms the impression. And last, that you act as champion for Mikhail the Druse, whose death has left this world a lesser place, leaves no question.' He looked up, and his face cracked into a thousand wrinkles that took me a moment to recognise as a wry smile. 'A monastery may not be of the world, but it most assuredly is in it. Particularly its abbot. What can I do for you?'

Holmes swallowed his wine, with more speed than manners, and began to speak; the abbot rose and went to his cabinet, bringing the wine back with him. He filled Holmes' empty glass, and sat down again with the bottle close at hand.

'Sometime between Christmas and the New Year you had a visitor here,' Holmes was saying. 'I do not know if he appeared as a brother from one of your other houses, or if he stole a habit from you, but I do know that when he left, he had a monk's habit in his bag. He also helped himself to the candles from your chapel. Do you know this man?'

'What makes you think such a thing happened, my son?'

'I have spent the last three weeks tracing his footsteps, ever since three men were killed near Jaffa: a farmer who helped the English during the war and his two field hands. The person who came here distanced himself from the murders, which he, shall I say, encouraged, if not arranged, but did not actually commit.

'On the night of the new moon this man was down at the Salt Sea buying a shipment of explosives from a salt smuggler. The smuggler's son happened to see a monk's robe in the man's packs. Sometime that evening the man stuck one of your chapel's candles on a stone, blew it out when it was down to the last inch, and left it.

'Mikhail the Druse found it. Mikhail was following this man, very probably saw his transaction with the smuggler, scraped off the candle when he came across it, and dropped it into his pack – not as evidence, I dare say, but for its intrinsic usefulness to a thrifty man like Mikhail, as a source of light or as a fire starter.

'Unfortunately for Mikhail, the man discovered him. He and his assistant turned and chased Mikhail into the Wadi Estemoa. There they murdered him, removing from his belongings a small notebook. They then left him for the jackals, and took themselves and their load of dynamite off into the countryside, or into Jerusalem, to hide it.

'I fear that Mikhail the Druse was not a man naturally gifted at espionage. I believe that when he recorded information in his notebook he either did not bother to encode it, or else used a code easily broken, because when the man we seek laid his hands on the notebook, he discovered that Mikhail's master was a man called Joshua, and that Mikhail had something to do with a pair of wandering scribes named Ali and Mahmoud.

'Between the night of the new moon, when Mikhail the Druse was murdered, and the night of the full moon, when the man arranged a motorcar accident, he sought out information from within the British camp, most likely using a source he had used before – a partner, even. This source revealed that the two scribes would be with General Allenby in Haifa on Wednesday, and were to return by motorcar to Jericho the following morning. He even knew the route to be taken.

'No doubt the central man would have preferred to seize one of the Hazr brothers, but as chance would have it, they were thrown free and I was thrown into the arms of the men laying the trap. *Maalesh*,' he commented with a crooked smile.

The abbot picked up the bottle and filled Holmes' glass again without speaking.

'This is what I know of him,' Holmes concluded. 'I ask you again: Do you know the man?'

'He is not a man.'

Holmes and I looked at each other, startled. 'Surely you can't mean—' Holmes began.

'He is a demon.'

'Ah.' Holmes subsided, and did not glance at me this time.

'But perhaps your vision of the world does not allow for the existence of evil creatures,' the abbot said.

'Well,' said Holmes slowly, 'yes. I should say that I have met evil, true evil. Not many times, but often enough to recognise it.'

'And you would agree that it is different from mere wickedness?' I thought perhaps the good abbot had a modicum of Jesuitical training somewhere in his past, or perhaps he came by it naturally.

'Oh, yes.'

'Then you agree that evil walks in human guise. I call that a demon. You call it what you may. And yes, he came here, three days after the Western celebration of Christmas.'

'How did you . . . know what he was? What did he do?'

'I did not know at first meeting him. A holy man might have done; ordinary human beings are not given such a degree of insight. I watched him.

'A . . . being such as he lives for the discomfort of others. He feeds off any degree of pain. He probably grew up pulling the wings off butterflies and graduated to hurting small animals.

Under a regime such as our past rulers oversaw, such a tendency would be a useful thing. It would have been fostered, put to work. Under the guise of promoting order, keeping disruption and revolt in its place, he was without a doubt one of those men allowed to feed his urges while serving his masters: politics and pleasure intertwined. I have seen other backs like yours, Mr Holmes. I have seen far worse. His sort is adept at inflicting torment; one might even call him a connoisseur of pain – both physical and, through the body, the spiritual agony of guilt and shame. Certainly he understands that injuries to the spirit tend to be longer lasting than those of the body.

'Now, after years of freedom to do as he wished under official sanction, he can no longer control his need for causing hurt as once he undoubtedly could. It is a compulsion. When he came here, he could not resist reaching for the hand of Brother Antoninus, twisted by arthritis, and squeezing it firmly. He had to seek out one of our younger brothers who is going through a period of doubt, and suggest further things for the young man to worry about. Similar events, little things, but, in a small community, potentially deadly. After the second day I had to let him know I was watching him. He left the next morning. I considered it fortunate that we only lost a few possessions, most of them easily replaced.'

'What did you lose, Abbot?'

'As you said, two habits, a dozen large candles and some small ones.'

'Two habits?'

'Two. Also one of our climbing ropes—'

'Climbing ropes?' I interrupted. It was only the second time

I had spoken, but the image of mountaineering monks was too incongruous for silence.

'We live on a cliff,' Abbot Mattias pointed out with a smile. 'There are times when we need to rescue the straying kid of a Bedouin flock or remove a boulder that threatens our heads or our roof tiles. Some of the younger brothers enjoy the task. I know I did when I was younger. Also a small amount of money,' he said, returning to Holmes' question. 'We never keep much. Our needs are met by our mother monastery in Jerusalem.'

'Does that house also dress in the same habits?'

'Of course.'

'Ah.'

'Yes. And one other thing. A small ikon. Not valuable monetarily outside the community, but of historical significance and of great value to us. A painting, six inches by eight, of the Holy Virgin Mother.'

'Have you reported any of this?'

The abbot just smiled sadly. This land had a long way to go before it could think of the police as either friendly or helpful.

'Father Abbot, may I suggest that your house in Jerusalem be warned to watch for any strangers who might be trying to pass themselves off as monks?'

'I shall write to them, yes. However, Jerusalem is filled with strangers in monastic dress, from all the corners of the earth.'

'One last thing.' My head came around involuntarily at the tightness in Holmes' voice. 'Can you give me a description of the man?'

The question surprised the abbot enough to cause his eyes to narrow. 'I understood that you had met him.'

'I . . . encountered him. I should know his voice if I heard it again, his smell, possibly his step, but I never laid eyes upon him.' Holmes' face was shut up, rock hard but for a tiny spasm of tension in his jaw. I looked back up at the Virgin, who seemed to tell me that she had seen it all before, but I did not find the thought comforting.

'I see,' said the abbot.

'I do know a great deal about him. I know that he was born in the vicinity of Istanbul approximately forty years ago. I know that he went to university in Germany and spent time in Buda-Pest. I know he is highly educated, thinks of himself as cultured, is near my own height, and right-handed. He is missing two or three teeth in the back of his mouth, and he prefers Western-style trousers and boots with soft heels. He bathes twice a day, uses a French hair pomade, and smokes expensive Turkish cigarettes. I know that he has read widely in European philosophy, that he speaks German, English, Turkish, and three dialects of Arabic fluently, and other tongues with a lesser degree of comfort. I know that he controls his subordinates with a combination of reward and fear, that they are terrified of his temper, which is cold and vicious rather than violent. I know that he enjoys causing pain in the innocent. I know he is a dangerous man. I do not, however, know what he looks like, because he never . . . approached me to my face.'

He was, I think, telling me what he had been through as much as he was answering the abbot, and my stomach turned at the picture. To be strung up with one's arms together so as to make turning the head impossible; to stare at a blank wall and have pain inflicted without even seeing it coming, by a person – no, the abbot was right, this was not a person – by a creature who was no more than an accented voice, an elusive drift of odours, a step of shoes, and a rustle of clothing.

The abbot blinked his lizard blink. 'Your ears and nose told you all this?'

'My mind told me this,' Holmes replied coldly.

'God has given you a great gift, my son.' It was Holmes' turn to blink. 'The man is, as you say, tall, perhaps an inch less tall than you, and heavier, but not fat. His hair is black and beginning to thin, his skin slightly swarthy, his eyes dark. His beard was full but neatly trimmed. Not a distinctive face, but his mouth betrays him. His lips are too heavy. His is a greedy mouth, never satisfied.'

'Would he appear European, if he had no beard?'

'No,' the abbot replied. 'Not the least bit.'

So, this was not the man who had spoken with the *mullah* in Jaffa.

'Any scars, marks, features that stand out?'

The abbot thought. 'A small scar, here.' He laid his finger at the outside edge of his left eye. 'And a mark, a mole, just past his beard here.' He raised his chin and tapped the right side of his throat. 'Also, I believe he was accustomed to wearing a ring on his right hand, although he did not have it on while he was here. There was a light patch on the finger,' he said.

'Abbot Mattias, you would have made a good detective,' said Holmes.

'And you, my son, in very different circumstances, might have made a good abbot.'

I had not thought to hear Holmes laugh for a long time. The sound cheered me a great deal.

The half-moon lit our way as we followed a sleepy brother up a path to a pair of cells – enlarged caves, in the hillside. The night was cold, but heavy wraps made it bearable, and I fell asleep quickly.

During the night a noise outside my monastic cell woke me: Holmes moving past, outlined against the moonlit sky. I slid from my pallet and went out onto the pathway, where I watched him make his way down from our quarters to the central portion of the monastery. He stopped outside the abbot's door, and must have tapped or called quietly, because after a minute the door opened and Holmes went inside. He was still there an hour later when I went back to sleep.

I did not awaken until the sun crept through the cave entrance. I knocked a scorpion out of my boots, fixed my turban firmly in place, and came out to find Holmes sitting on the ground in front of his cell, watching the small signs of life in the wadi before us. He looked rested: the bruises were fading, his eyes were clear again. I sat down ten feet away from him, and considered asking him about his midnight visit to the abbot. If it was about information, it clearly had no urgency about it, but there was also the distinct possibility that he had gone to the man for what could only be called pastoral care. In that case it would be best to pretend I had slept through his nocturnal excursion. We sat together in the morning sun and meditated on the life of the Wadi Qelt.

The sun heated the rocks around us, causing a smell of warm dust to rise up and mingle with the crisp odour of the wet stones of the stream below. Our clothing smelt, too, although I was becoming accustomed to that, and the air moving down the valley brought with it a hint of incense from the chapel, accompanied now and then by the rhythm of chanted prayer. Bells had sounded earlier, the dull clatter so different from the resonant English bells; now I heard a tiny scuffle coming from beneath a bare shrub, which proved to be a small brown bird scratching in the dry leaf fall for its breakfast. Other birds squabbled and gossiped in the fronds of a palm tree, an eagle rode the heating air high over our heads, a pair of lizards came out to bask on the rocks, and once I caught a glimpse of a turbanned head passing by on the track on the opposite rim of the wadi. I could begin to understand the appeal of a monk's cell in the desert. If only the vow did not include obedience . . .

Breakfast was bread and sour milk and dried apricots, and afterwards we went for a final interview with the abbot. He greeted us by holding out a letter.

'This is to my brethren in the monastery in Jerusalem. Would you please see that the abbot there receives it?'

'Certainly,' said Holmes, tucking it inside his robe.

'In it I mention the two of you. As you appear, shall I say, rather than as you are. It is possible you may need assistance in the city. That letter will ensure that you receive it.'

'Thank you, Abbot.'

'I wish you good hunting, my son. I shall pray for you.'

'Thank you.'

'And you, my silent daughter. Uncharacteristically silent, I suspect.' The gleam in the old man's eyes was unmistakable now; it was nearly a twinkle. 'I give you my blessing.'

I hated to disappoint him, but I had to tell him gently, 'I am not a Christian, Abbot Mattias.'

'God does not mind, my child. He was, after all, your God before He was ours.'

'In that case I accept your blessing, with thanks.'

'And now you have before you a long and dusty walk. I have arranged safe passage for you. Not, I fear, an armoured vehicle; you will have to walk. However, you need not worry about being seen by your enemy. Gasim!' he called.

The door behind him opened and a Bedouin came in, looking enough like Ali to be a younger brother. 'This is Gasim ibn Rahail,' the abbot told us in Arabic. 'His people are on their way up to Jerusalem. You will go with them. Gasim, these are my friends. Care for them as brothers.'

'Your word, Holy Father,' the young man said, and gave us a grin that made me wonder if he spoke in mockery. It was, however, merely affection untempered by awe, and it suited us very well. We took our leave of Abbot Mattias and his monastery, and turned our faces, at long last, to Jerusalem.

CHAPTER EIGHTEEN

ع

Jerusalem, the centre of three religions, is not at all a town for amusement.
– BAEDEKER'S *Palestine and Syria,* 1912 EDITION

WE CAME TO THE CITY in the afternoon, climbing up the dusty road from Jericho in the company of six tents of Bedouins, ten camels, and an uncountable number of goats and fat-tailed sheep. The Bedu chose to stop the night on an over-grazed flat to the east of the city near a well called the Apostle's Spring, the water of which was possessed of numerous small red wriggling creatures. After we had drunk a final cup of coffee with the sheikh (Gasim's father), been presented with all his camels, goats, and horses, given our own meagre possessions to him in return, then reciprocally given back each other's gifts with lengthy and painfully gracious protestations of unworthiness, we thanked him for his hospitality by declaring our worthless selves his slaves for eternity, and finally took our leave.

Walking towards the setting sun, we came to the Mount of Olives, a great sprawl of tombs and gravestones, and there at our feet lay Jerusalem.

She is a jewel, that city, small and brilliant and hard, and as dangerous as any valuable thing can be. Built in the Judean hill country at the meeting place of three valleys – the Kidron, the Hinnom, and the long-buried Tyropoeon – Jerusalem had moved uphill from the year-round spring that had made her existence possible. When I first laid eyes on her, some of her structures were already thousands of years old. It was 401 years since the Turks took the city, 820 years since the Crusaders under Godfrey of Bouillon had slaughtered every Moslem and Jew within the walls (and a good number of unrecognised native Christians as well), eighteen and a half centuries since the Romans had last razed her stones to the ground, and still she rose up within her snug, high walls, a nest of stone set to nurture the holy places of three faiths, a tight jumble of domes, minarets, and towers, dominated from this side by the flat expanse of the Temple Mount, the holy place called by Arabs Haram es-Sherif, the largest open space in the city, a garden of worship set with tombs and mosques and the enormous, glittering, mosaic and gilded glory of the Dome of the Rock.

Built towards the end of the seventh century, the Dome of the Rock cost its builders the equivalent of seven years' revenue from all of Egypt. It is constructed as an octagon of three concentric stages, at the heart of which lies the Rock, an uneven grey slab some forty-five feet by sixty. If Jerusalem is the *umbilicus mundi* – the umbilicus of the world – then the sacred Rock is the heart that drives the life-blood through the umbilical cord. The Talmud declares that the Rock is the earth's very centre. Here the priest Melchizedek offered sacrifice, here Abraham bound Isaac in preparation for offering his beloved son's throat to God, and from this place Mohammed entered heaven on the back of his mighty steed, el-Burak. The Ark of the Covenant rested on the Rock, and tradition maintains that it still lies buried beneath, hidden there by Jeremiah as the enemy entered the city gates. The Rock bears the imprints of the angel Gabriel's fingers and the Prophet Mohammed's foot, and ancient legend has the Rock hovering over the waters of the great Flood, or resting on a palm tree watered by the rivers of paradise, or guarding the gates of hell. In a small cave beneath the Rock, benches mark where David and Solomon, Abraham and Elijah all prayed; in the Time of Judgement, God's throne will be planted upon it. The Rock had been a sacred place to humankind back through the dim reaches of memory, and would continue to be so when the city before me had been buried yet again – either by the forces of destruction, or through being built up beyond recognition.

Beyond the Haram es-Sherif, the city itself clusters close, all whitewashed domes and pale golden stone. A soft breeze came up, and I watched as her colours deepened with the approach of night. When the sun lay behind her, despite the scurry of lorries and the dust and the smoke of the evening fires, she took my breath away, that city. There were tears in my eyes and a psalm on my lips, and for the first time I knew why Jews, as one, declare that we will meet 'next year in Jerusalem.'

The sun had gone and the lights were up before I recalled my companion, seated near me on the stone wall smoking his pipe.

'Holmes – I'm so sorry, you must be famished. It was just so beautiful.'

'Quite.'

'And the moon will be over it before long . . .' I said wistfully.

He stood up and smacked his pipe out against his boot. 'We don't have to be in the city until tomorrow,' he said impatiently. 'I shall find someone to sell us our supper. All my life I have wanted nothing better than to spend a night amongst the tombs on Olivet.' I ignored the sarcasm: It was a gracious gift, if churlishly given. I sat and waited for the moon to climb, peripherally aware of the night noises, pilgrims returning late from the Jordan, the occasional army lorry grumbling its way towards Bethlehem, the jackals and donkeys to which I was now so accustomed blending with the calls of the *muezzins* and the sound of church bells and the low, constant hum that emanated from the city of seventy thousand souls.

I ate and drank the food Holmes put in my hand, accepted the thick robe he wrapped around my shoulders, and watched, enchanted, as the city slept and changed shape beneath the waning moon, until in the morning the sun woke her and restored to her that bright, hard beauty. Holmes again pushed food into my hands, cadged a mug of coffee from somewhere and gave me some, and when the city across from us was veiled by the dust raised by lorries and donkeys and the sun on our shoulders held a promise of heat, we rose, and went up to Jerusalem.

The city had seen more activity and renovation in the last twelvemonth than she had the whole of the Turkish occupation. The roads into the city were crowded with lorries carrying boulders and timber and tiles, with donkeys carrying rocks, sacks, and provisions, and with thoroughly draped women carrying a little of everything. Upon reaching the valley bottom we inserted ourselves between a caravan from the east and an army lorry whose driver's accent declared him from the East End. At camel pace we circumnavigated the walls until we reached the Jaffa Gate, our lungs full of dust and our ears assaulted by shouts and curses, and I felt that had this not been Jerusalem, I might have turned on my heel and fled back out into the clean, simple, silent expanse of the desert.

We threaded our way among a fleet of horse-drawn carriages for hire and entered Jerusalem in the footsteps – literally, as he had chosen to mark his pilgrim's entrance on foot – of the conqueror Allenby. To our right rose the Citadel, somewhere to our left lay the Church of the Holy Sepulchre, before us sprawled the great labyrinth of the bazaar, and all around us swirled an informal market, a miscellany of goods and peoples. I saw none of these. I did not notice the picturesque Copts and the Armenians, did not register the toasted-sesame smell of the round bread loaves that passed beneath our noses on the panniers of a donkey, did not even hear the strange, flat clang of bells or the '*bakshish*' cries of the beggars or the polyglot of tongues. My whole being, my entire awareness, was taken up by a small, crudely lettered sign propped in the window of the Grand New Hotel: Baths.

I was suddenly aware that, aside from a cold hip-bath at

the *kivutz,* I had not properly bathed since leaving Allenby's headquarters in Haifa a week before: my turban had glued itself to my head and my tunic to my shoulders, my hands revealed black creases where the skin bent, my face was filthy with caked-on dust, and, not to put it gently, I stank. Even Holmes, who when in disguise had the knack of appearing far more unkempt than he actually was, who possessed a catlike ability to keep his person tidy under the most unlikely of circumstances (such as the time earlier in his career when he had arranged with a local lad to bring him fresh collars along with his foodstuffs while living in a stone hut on Dartmoor), even Holmes, as I say, was showing signs of wear, both visible and olfactory. The darkness on his face was not all dye and bruises.

'Baths, Holmes,' I breathed.

'I can hardly take you into a bath-house,' he said absently, scanning the area around us.

'Not a public bath-house, Holmes. A bath, in a hotel, with a door and a lock. Oh, Holmes,' I groaned.

'Patience, Russell. Ha! This will be our man.'

I tore my eyes from the beguiling sign and followed his gaze, to where a lad of perhaps ten or eleven years was hopping off a low wall. The child walked backwards a dozen or so steps in our direction, finishing up a spirited conversation with the handful of other urchins who remained perched on the wall, then turned his back on them, hopped over the single leg of one beggar and the leprous hand of another, scrambled beneath the belly of a camel and dodged both the rock thrown at him by the camel's owner and the front end of an army staff car to fetch up in front of us. He was as dirty and ill clothed as any

London street Arab, with a grin that could only have been born out of an intimate acquaintance with illegality. He looked like a pickpocket, would no doubt grow into a thief, and I knew instantly that he was a colleague of Ali and Mahmoud.

'You look for someone, I think?' he said in English, a cheerful conspirator.

Holmes' hand shot out, and seized the young imp by his collar, dragging him forward until their faces were mere inches apart. The boy's grin vanished and he started to struggle, but Holmes just held him and hissed in furious and colloquial Arabic, 'If you think I shall do any business with a donkey as stupid as you, child, you are too dumb-witted to live, and I ought to put you out of your misery. Get away from my sight.' He shook the boy, let go of him, and we watched him pick himself up from the dirty stones and flee. 'Come,' said Holmes. I followed him to a niche against the wall, and there we squatted, with the dust washing over us and our bellies empty, until eventually the chastened lad reappeared, carrying a basket of oranges. He sold a few to passers-by before he reached us.

'Oranges from Jaffa?' he offered, speaking Arabic this time. 'Juicy, sweet. Three for one piastre.'

'Six for one,' countered Holmes, looking bored.

'Four. Large ones.'

'Done.' The coin and the fruit changed hands; the boy faded away; we stayed seated and picked up our oranges. I rolled mine around in my hand, speculating on the chances that this particular fruit had been grown by the man I had seen bleed to death, and then I dug in my nails to peel away the rind. I grimaced at the black smears my fingers left on the damp skin, and separated the segments gingerly, trying to touch only the edges of the fruit's flesh with the very tips of my fingernails. When we had each eaten one fruit and wiped our hands on our robes, Holmes took the other two and stowed them in the mule's pack, then handed me the lead rope and set off in the direction in which the boy had gone. Down the narrow street, and there he was, leaning casually against the wall, the empty basket tucked under his arm and a half-eaten orange in his hand. Without looking up, he pushed away from the wall and wandered off.

He led us a short distance down the narrow, cobbled street, then turned left and left again, a circle that brought us back to a gateway we had already passed – reluctantly on the part of the mule, which had tugged at the lead rope, knowing his partners were within. We entered through a pair of high, stout wooden doors opening into a small cobbled yard with stables, a covered cistern, some bare vines growing up the stone walls, and several windows, all of them lacking paint and most of them standing open to the flies and the smells. Against the right-hand wall an ancient wooden stairway clung precariously, leading in two stages to a doorway twenty feet above the yard. On the very top step of the stairway sat Ali.

He watched us arrive, then dropped his attention back to the wooden figure he was working at with the long knife from his belt, the blade he used for slicing onions, carving figurines, and killing men. As the wicked steel blade caught the sun, it struck me that the reason he used one knife for such diverse and often unsuited tasks was so that his hand might know it as a natural extension of itself, carving donkeys and cleaning fingernails to make it the more accurate when the time came for violent applications. I swallowed hard and looked away.

There was no sign of Mahmoud. Our urchin guide ran up the stairs and perched next to Ali, who ignored him and went on shaving paper-thin curls of wood from the emerging figurine. I stood with the mule's rope in my hand, looking dull (with very little effort) while Holmes negotiated a pair of rooms. One room would have been more expected and therefore less conspicuous, but I had insisted, and he had agreed, that some risks were necessary. When I saw the rooms I was glad that at least I should not have to share the windowless cubicle and its narrow single mat on the floor: 'tiny' was an understatement, and if it was a step up from squalid, one would have to be remarkably generous to call it comfortable. Still, there seemed to be little insect life, be it crawling or hopping, and the dirt on the walls and floor seemed to be mere dust and debris, not actual filth.

There was a bath, of a sort, or rather two: a dank closet in one of the cellars where cold water sputtered from a dripping green pipe to form a primitive shower-bath, or a tin bath behind a flimsy partition on the open roof. I sighed, and walked down to the cellar.

Refreshed, if not precisely clean, I went back upstairs and found Holmes just coming down from the roof. He was whistling. He looked, and smelt, beautifully clean, and although he retained a moustache, his handsome salt-and-pepper beard had given way to startlingly smooth (if still dark) skin.

'You had a bath,' I said.

'A fine, hot bath,' he replied, radiating good cheer. I scowled at him.

'With one servant to pour hot water over my head, another to shave me, and a masseur who would make a fortune in the best Turkish bath in London.'

'May your eyebrows grow inward,' I growled in Arabic. 'May your hair itch and fall from your head. *Sabah el-kheir,* Mahmoud,' I added, greeting that gentleman as he appeared in the doorway across from mine. His room, I saw, was blessed with both window and the exterior door to which the stairway led, and a small but well-fed charcoal brazier glowed merrily from the middle of the floor.

'Allah yesabbihak bil-kheir,' he returned my good morning – using, of course, the masculine ending. I was quite used to it by now. In fact, if someone had addressed me using the feminine I might well have turned around to look for the woman standing behind me. 'Have you eaten?'

'We ate bread only, with the sunrise,' I told him.

'Let us eat,' Mahmoud said, and Ali, who was still sitting on the top step of the stairway, obligingly rose, leant over the side of the rickety topmost landing, and bellowed down at the courtyard that we wanted food, and coffee, with tea first, and did not wish to wait for it until the vultures were perched on our very windowsills. Abuse was traded, and soon Ali drew back into the room, nodded at Mahmoud, and they and I took seats on the mats and familiar bed-rolls that were piled up near the walls of the room. Holmes went over to the window and glanced out, first down at the courtyard and then up at the rooftop.

'Does anyone know we are here?' he asked.

Mahmoud answered. 'The boy and the innkeeper. Others know we are in the city, but not where.'

'Those two: Are they trustworthy?'

'Both, to the death.' He knew what Holmes was saying, and was telling him in return that however it came about that Holmes was captured, it would not happen a second time – not through Mahmoud at any rate.

Holmes nodded. 'Let the others remain ignorant.'

'Yes.'

Only then did Holmes take his seat on the impromptu bolsters with us.

'We expected you yesterday night,' Ali said. Coming from Mahmoud, the same words might have made a question, but in Ali's mouth they were an accusation. Holmes, however, did not respond to anything but the query.

'We chose to spend the night on Olivet.' Both men looked at us sharply. 'You slept among the tombs?' Ali asked.

'I slept. I do not think Russell did so.'

'You did not . . . object to the presence of the dead?'

'It was pleasant,' Holmes said. 'Quiet.'

Ali glanced at me, and then at Mahmoud, and resorted to pulling out his embroidered pouch and building a cigarette. I thought their fear of ghosts in a cemetery an amusing thing, considering everything else they readily put up with.

Mahmoud had his prayer beads out and was thumbing them methodically. 'What did you find?' he asked.

'It is to be soon. There is a false monk involved. And it will be a bomb,' Holmes replied, and reached for his pipe. Mahmoud appeared as untouched as ever by this terse summary. Ali waited, but when Holmes had his pipe going yet did not elaborate, he began to splutter rather as the downstairs shower-bath had done. It was left to me to give the details.

I was halfway through our conversation with the abbot when Mahmoud abruptly interrupted with a loud question about the price of a mare in Nablus. When I hesitated, Ali stepped in with a comment about her cracked hoof, and then I heard the footsteps on the stairs. In came fragrant rice and new bread, lamb cooked tender with onions, nuts, and some tangy green leaf, little bowls of chopped salads as garnish, with fresh tea to slake our thirst and a pot of coffee to follow. We fell silent while applying ourselves to the serious business at hand.

Afterwards, Mahmoud poured out the coffee and set a plate of sticky sweetmeats in the middle of the carpet.

He handed cups to Ali, then Holmes, and finally to me: This was the first time he had given a drink into my hand instead of laying it on the carpet in front of me. I met his eyes, nodded my acknowledgement, and sipped the tepid liquid with gratitude.

Ali sucked the honey from his fingers, then wiped them delicately on his robe. 'Why do you think all this adds up to a false monk with a bomb?' He did not bother to conceal the doubt in his voice.

'It is the only theory which fits all the facts,' Holmes answered.

'Which facts are those?' Mahmoud asked.

'You've seen them. The Jaffa murders, Mikhail's death and possibly that of the false *mullah,* Mikhail's missing notebook, the candle in his pack and the salt smuggler's odd customer, the attempt to torture information out of me, the widespread rumours that keep General Allenby busy, the strange visitor at Wadi Qelt, and the missing habits of the monks.'

'They are not necessarily related,' Mahmoud objected mildly. 'Strange things happen all the time here. You do not know the country, it all looks odd and probably sinister to you.'

'The country I know marginally; the criminal mind I know very well indeed.'

'Criminal mind,' Ali said with a snort.

'You do not believe that there is a threat,' Holmes said coldly.

'Threat? There is always a threat. This is a land of threats and blood feuds, your eye for mine, your brother to avenge my father.'

'And the ambush?'

'Oh, that was political, certainly. But Allah alone knows what the aim was.'

'And my . . . interrogation?'

'That was no interrogation,' Ali nearly shouted. 'There are those in this country who do that sort of thing for pleasure, don't you understand that, you stupid man?'

'Using insult instead of argument is the sign of a small mind,' Holmes said in a dangerously low voice.

'I apologise. But I do not see—'

'You do not, no. But you,' Holmes said, turning to Mahmoud, 'you, I think, have your doubts.'

'"Only God is sure,"' Mahmoud said after a minute. 'But you may be correct. There may indeed be some sort of bomb plot in the works. However, it is unlikely to be immediate; we have heard nothing at all while we have been in the city.'

'What about the watchmaker, the one whose advertisement was in the papers you found?' I asked him. The ornate golden watch on Ali's wrist was still not keeping time, but that did not mean they had not been to the watchmaker; as far as I could tell, he wore it solely as an ornament.

'He seems merely a businessman. We are having him followed.'

'General Allenby's visit to Jerusalem is in little more than two weeks,' Holmes said half to himself.

'It has been moved forward to this weekend,' answered Ali, reaching forward for the beaker of coffee to pour himself another cup.

'*What?* In three days?'

'That is correct. I believe he—'

'But why? Why has he changed his plans?'

'He does not inform us of his reasons; one has learnt merely to be grateful for any prior notice.'

'Are the rest of his intentions the same?' Holmes asked. 'Meeting with a few religious leaders, a tour of the Western Wall, the Temple Mount, and the Church of the Holy Sepulchre, and then a gathering at Government House?'

'I believe so, although I suppose he will also go to a church service in the morning, he usually does, and he will probably have less formal conversations with the governor, the mayor, the mufti, and any of a dozen others.' Ali blew across the top of his cup, although the coffee was now scarcely warm, and sipped deliberately. 'Also, the number of men invited to the tour of the city has grown. It now includes the Anglican bishop, the Orthodox patriarch, the Armenian patriarch, Governor Storrs—'

'A veritable gathering of the gods,' Holmes said weakly. 'The only figures missing will be Feisal and Lawrence.'

'It was suggested that the two fly in from the Paris talks for this occasion, although I do not think it will prove possible.'

Holmes had gone pale beneath his skin dye; Mahmoud's face was thoughtful, and his fingers slowed on the prayer beads; I felt distinctly queasy at the thought of the entire hierarchy of Palestine moving about the city with two hundred fifty pounds of high explosive unaccounted for. Ali stared at Holmes defiantly, refusing to acknowledge any cause for concern.

'You do not care for my theory,' said Holmes, 'because it is mine.'

'I do not care for it because it is wrong. You have constructed a plot against Allenby out of air. I need to see solid objects.'

'And if your brother Mahmoud had discovered this plot, would you believe him?'

Ali darkened in anger. 'You are not my brother, and you have no sense for this land and its ways. I have no reason to listen to you.'

Holmes fixed him with a look from those grey eyes that soon had the younger man shifting his eyes despite his anger. 'A dog on his dunghill, a cock on his fence, and a peacock on the hat of an unclean woman,' Holmes said quietly. Like most insults in Arabic it does not translate without its cultural context, but it acted on Ali like a slap across the face: he went rigid, and pale, then the blood rushed back and his right arm moved.

'*Akhuyi,*' Mahmoud murmured: My brother. Ali's hand froze on the hilt of his knife. Mahmoud spoke again, in the language I had heard them speak back in the mud hut in Jaffa; for thirty seconds he spoke, and at the end of it Ali, who had not taken his eyes from Holmes, seemed slightly to relax.

'My brother,' Holmes said, a deliberate echo of Mahmoud's Arabic word, 'Mycroft, would not be happy were I to allow General Allenby to be killed and another war to find its roots here. I would not wish to displease my brother.'

Ali sat for a long moment, and then, to my astonishment, his lips twitched. His gaze slid sideways to where Mahmoud sat, then back at Holmes, and then he removed his hand from his knife, reached out to clap Holmes on the shoulder, and began to laugh. He picked up his cup and drained it, the gap in his teeth leering out from his swarthy bearded face.

Never, never will I understand men.

CHAPTER NINETEEN

غ

Language is the expression by a speaker of his intentions. Its origin is in the desire to convey meaning, and it must become a habit on the portion of the body that produces it: that is, the tongue.
– THE *Muqaddimah* OF IBN KHALDÛN

'THREE DAYS UNTIL ALLENBY'S LITTLE party,' Holmes said thoughtfully. 'I require information. The *Palestine News* is out of date before it reaches the printer, and at that it seems to be primarily home news, recipes, and advertisements. Is there any way of obtaining fresher news, in detail?'

'There are dispatches, of course. What kind of news do you wish?'

'Everything. Anything. A stabbing, a burglary, Major Thing's dalliances and the Cairo shopping trip of Sheikh Hakim's second wife and the odd disappearance of Mrs Abdullah's son.'

Mahmoud gave that odd sideways shrug of the East, and

said, 'When there is a thing I wish to know, I attend a barber shop, and there is a professional beggar I know. And there is always the bazaar.'

'The bazaar,' said Holmes with a wry smile. 'Of course. I am getting old, and no doubt stupid as well. Still, I should like to see any of the official communications you might lay your hands on. Who is Joshua's man in the city?'

'A clerk by the name of Ellison, at Government House. He has a house, and a woman, in the Russian Colony. He tells me, by the way, that Joshua has traced all six Turkish officers whose names we gave him: five are dead, the sixth is in prison. There are, of course, any number of others still unaccounted for, but then that is only to be expected in the wake of a spectacular defeat.'

Holmes nodded absently at this news. 'You trust this clerk Ellison?'

'With my life, more than once.'

'There may be more at stake here than your life, before this ends. We may also need an expert in explosives, if we find something that wants disarming.'

'Ali and I can do that.'

Holmes eyed him, saw only quiet confidence, and nodded briefly. 'Now,' he said, 'I believe we have given you all that we know. I shall take up my place in the bazaar, imbibing many pints of coffee and smoking far too many cigarettes, while you two search out the precise details of Allenby's schedule and listen for words of strangers asking about those same details.'

'Do you know nothing solid about this Turkish opponent of ours that you have created in your mind?' Ali asked, careful this time not actually to sneer. 'You say he likes to hurt people, he has several men working for him, including an Englishman in the government, he stole a monk's robe and an ikon, and he has a motorcar and some horses. He could be anyone.'

'He thinks he is omnipotent. He is not, but he is clever and sly and completely cold-blooded when it comes to disposing of life. He knows the land intimately enough to be invisible and he has, as you say, resources, both men and equipment. He knows enough about explosives to work a bomb into his plan. All of which fits a hundred men between Cairo and Damascus,' Holmes agreed, before Ali could repeat his objection. 'I should tend to agree with Abbot Mattias' assessment of the man, that he has worked with the Turks, and that his area of expertise was probably interrogations.' Holmes added the last without expression.

I thought it might be helpful to add other, more concrete details. 'Holmes thought his accent was not that of a native of Palestine, although he speaks Arabic flawlessly, and he was educated in Turkey and Germany. According to the abbot, the man is perhaps forty, only slightly shorter than Holmes although heavier and with darker skin. He has black hair, dark eyes, a mole on his throat beneath his beard and a scar next to his—' I had reached up to lay a finger of my right hand next to my eye, a duplication of the gesture Abbot Mattias had used, when the words strangled in my throat.

'*Wallah!*' Ali exclaimed, jerking back from me as if he had been shot. His hand clapped onto his knife and his eyes flew around the room, from Mahmoud back and forth between the two doors, as if he expected the enemy to burst in then and there. Mahmoud, on the other hand, moved only his hand – his left hand, mirroring my own as he unconsciously reached up to finger the long scar that ran down the side of his face. He looked pale, his cheeks gone suddenly gaunt, and there was on his face an expression I had never imagined I might see there: I saw fear.

'You know him,' Holmes said, somewhat unnecessarily.

'That devil!' Ali cursed, and spat on the floor. 'He was reported to be dead. We thought he was dead. If I had known that *he* was in that house where we found you . . .'

'Who is he?'

'Karim Bey was the name he called himself.' Mahmoud's voice was without inflection. 'He was here in Jerusalem during the war. Most of the city had no idea what he was, just another Turkish officer. He was known to be friendly with children. When he was not helping with the orphanage, however, he was the special interrogator first for the Turkish police, and then during the war with the army. Bey was brought in when others failed. He did not often fail.'

'I see,' said Holmes. An uncomfortable silence fell for a moment. 'Was he then clean-shaven?'

'Clean, yes,' Ali answered, nearly spitting the words. 'His face, his nice clothes, his hands, always clean.'

'He has a beard now, and is certain to have disguised himself in other ways as well, particularly if, as you say, he spent some years here. He may wear spectacles, darken his skin, change his fez for a *kuffiyah,* that sort of thing. Chances are good he will be dressed as a monk at least some of the time. If he is as concerned with hygiene as you say, it would explain why he wished to have two habits.' Holmes started to rise, then paused to address Ali. 'Shall I take it that you are now convinced of the need for this operation of ours?'

'If the monk in Wadi Qelt saw a man who looked as he described, by God, yes. Most certainly, there is urgent need.'

Holmes nodded, and stood up. He ducked across the corridor to his room and came back in a moment pushing his tobacco and rough papers into a pocket and carrying his sheepskin coat, which he proceeded to put on.

'I expect I shall be back before dark,' he told me. 'If anything comes up, I shall try to send a message.'

'Wait and I'll get my coat,' I said, getting to my feet.

'You have some sleep,' he said firmly. 'If Mahmoud rounds up any newspapers or dispatches, go through them, see if anything catches your eye.'

'I don't need any sleep.'

'Bazaar talk is a job for one person' ('one *man*,' he said in Arabic) 'and I may need you tonight.' He left before I could formulate any lucid objections, a sure sign of my fatigue, so I went across to my own airless cubicle, jammed a wedge beneath the door, wrapped myself up on the mat, and so to sleep.

I awoke to the harsh, flat clang of bells. The crack of light around three sides of my door was dim, but natural, not from a lamp. I stretched, scratched myself thoroughly (the room had not been as free from insect life as I had optimistically thought), knotted my hair securely into my turban, and kicked away the wedge.

It was still daylight, but only just. There was no sign of Holmes, Ali, or Mahmoud, and no indication they had been back since I had gone to sleep. I felt sluggish my bladder was full, and my teeth were covered with fur. I took up my *abayya* and made my way downstairs, used the privy and ran some water from a spigot to wash out my mouth and splash my face, and began to feel human again. I have never been one for naps in the afternoon.

As I walked back into the courtyard, a voice hailed me from one of the open doors, asking if I would drink tea. I agreed, with pleasure, and I did so, squatting against the sun-warmed stones with the young boy who brought it. Daylight was little more than a deepening blue in the square of sky over our heads, but the tea was flavoured with mint, hot and sweet and revitalising. I blew and slurped at it with pleasure indeed, and ate a handful of the candied almonds he offered me as well. When we had each asked politely half a dozen times how the other's health was, and reassured each other that the tea was most agreeable, thanks be to God, I asked if he had seen my tall friend with the blue *kuffiyah*. The boy was heartbroken to admit that he had not seen the man since he had been seen walking through the gates into the street some time since, but he assured me that my friend would undoubtedly return soon, if it were God's will. As I suspected that even Allah had little influence over the actions of Sherlock Holmes, I thought I might go out and see for myself.

I thanked the boy for his hospitality and we wished each other peace and good fortune. As I went out the gate, adjusting my *abayya* across my shoulders, it occurred to me that I had just conducted my first true conversation with a native speaker.

Our inn was at the edges of the Christian Quarter, a place

well supplied with pilgrim hostels. I walked back towards the Jaffa Gate, and in the open place before the Citadel I turned past the Grand New Hotel and dived into the bazaar, picking my way cautiously down the slippery, uneven stones that were more stairway than street. On either side of me the sellers of carpets and clothing, mother-of-pearl knick-knacks, copper pots, and *narghiles* kept watch. When a European woman and her lieutenant escort approached, the raucous calls of *'Bakshish!'* and 'See my carpets, madam, finest quality!' and 'Olive-wood crosses from Bethlehem, *effendi!'* merged into a single sound which heralded their progress like the voices from a flock of crows. They passed by without noticing me, the woman looking harried and the officer furious, and for the first time I was truly grateful for my occasionally inconvenient disguise: No man there gave this dusty Arab youth a second glance, save to be sure I did not come within snatching distance of the wares.

With growing confidence I walked on, down the shop-lined alleyways, through the merchants of grain and seed and into an area where the streets were so narrow that the wooden lattice-work boxes over the upper windows nearly met in the middle. Then the vaulting began, and the open street became a stone tunnel. When a cart or a laden donkey came along (and once a mounted police constable) pedestrians had to squeeze to one side. I paused at a book-stall and made two small purchases, and wandered on until I came to a meat market. There I held my breath and scurried through the foetid air and the flies, slowing again when I came to tables heaped high with fruit. I bargained for a couple of withered apples at one stall, a clot of dates and a handful of sweet almonds at another, and nibbled at them as I passed through a baffling variety of hats, caps, turbans, and scarfs, long black robes and dust-coloured khaki, a Scotsman in a kilt and a Moroccan in his embroidered robes, a Hasid dressed in his best silk caftan and a wild-eyed ascetic wearing almost nothing at all. I listened to the rhythm of Arabic (understanding a great deal of it) punctuated by the cries of children and a waft of Latin that smelt of incense and the occasional murmur of Hebrew, breathed the scents of freshly watered dust and old sweat and young bodies, of gunpowder and petrol, turmeric and saffron and garlic, incense and wine and coffee, and everywhere the smell of rock, ancient stones and newly crushed gravel and recently hewn building blocks.

At the far end of the *souk* I perched on a high doorstep and ate the second apple while watching the residents of Jerusalem go about their business. Half a dozen urchins screamed up and down the steps after a fraying golf-ball; two oblivious grandfathers in gleaming white robes sat in an inner courtyard, playing chess and rubbing their long beards in thought; a trio of adolescent girls with demurely hidden faces huddled together and giggled madly when a pair of handsome young boys went past them. A police constable strolled by me, followed by a small group of fashionably dressed tourists searching for the place (forty feet above what would at the time have been street level) where Jesus stumbled and put out his hand.

A few minutes such as this could almost make a person forget the lives that had been lost on these stones, the Nazarene Jesus two millennia before, the British Tommy bare months ago. It was a precarious peace that a handful of us were fighting to maintain, a foothold of good-will and security that future generations might use to rise above the bloody past. If we failed, if Karim Bey had his way, the fragile structure of government would collapse, anarchy would reign, and tyrants would again walk these stones. Hell lurked just outside the city gates.

I finished my apple, watching the tourists go by. They would lose their purses to a nice peaceful pickpocket if they weren't more careful, I thought, and tossed the core of my apple into the gutter to follow them. Night was closing in fast, and the original purpose of finding Holmes had long faded from view – after an hour in the *souk* I had to admit that I had little hope of stumbling across him. I turned back towards the Christian Quarter, and there I took a wrong turning.

It is difficult to become seriously lost in a walled city that covers less than a square mile, and I had memorised the names of the principal streets that cut through the maze; however, with most of the streets lacking either signs or street-lamps and darkness settling over the already dim lanes, I mistook the Akabet et-Tekkiyeh for the parallel Tarik es-Serdi, and found myself in an alleyway of locked shops and few people. Wondering if it ended in a cul-de-sac, I put my head around the side of the one lighted shop I came across, and said to the man, 'Good evening, my uncle. I beg of you, does this street lead to the Jaffa Gate?'

For a moment I thought the man knew me, such was the look of delight that dawned on his rotund features, but when I looked more closely at the face under the incongruous bowler hat, I realised that he was merely filled with the bonhomie of drink. He started around the high piles of his goods (hats and shawls) with both hands out to greet me and protestations of undying servitude on his tongue. I backed away but could not avoid him entirely without being undeservedly rude, so I allowed him to grasp my hands and rant on while I smiled and nodded and tried to keep my distance. This went on for some time, and I began to feel more than a little ridiculous. Finally, I decided I had expressed enough politeness, so I brought my hands together, raised them in a tight circle to break his hold, and then took a step back – directly into two more sets of hands with two more friendly mouths breathing alcohol at me.

God, I berated myself as I tried to pluck six hands from their grasp on my person, leave it to me to find the only drunks in the Moslem Quarter. They were not intoxicated enough to be clumsy, only free from restraint, and they had me well and truly cornered – in a friendly manner, I admit. An entirely too friendly manner.

All good things must end, however, and reason was obviously no weapon against these three: flight would have to do. Bending over sharply, I scooted backwards under the arms of two of the men – and my concealing turban was plucked neatly from my head.

The three men blinked like owls at the mussed blonde waist-length plaits that were revealed in the lamplight. One of them hooted in amazement, and they came for me again. I moved back away from their reach, my head feeling peculiarly light in the cold night air, but I did not relish having to walk across half the city and into the inn without my turban. I backed, and backed some more, watching for a means of distracting them or a wide enough place to enable me to dash past them, snatch the length of cloth from the ground, and run.

As I danced backwards out of the grasp of those hands, my foot trod on some bit of slippery rubbish and flew out from under me. I hit the paving stones and rolled, coming up filthy and bruised and finally angry. The merchants did not appear to be armed, and I was just beginning to contemplate the pleasure I should have in trouncing the three sots when I heard a voice.

Those ringing tones would have been instantly recognisable no matter the circumstances or the language: Arabic or Rumanian or the King's own English, an alley in Jerusalem or a tunnel beneath London, cursing or wheedling, there it was, sardonic, superior, infuriating, and at that moment immensely welcome.

'Is it allowed for others to join in this game?' it said.

The merchants stopped their laughing advance and began to crane their necks to find the voice. I straightened. 'Holmes, thank—' I caught myself and blurted out in no doubt ungrammatical Arabic, 'I need your help.'

'Yes?' he drawled. 'You seem to be doing well enough.'

I had him now: in a dark niche above a stone arch that kept two walls from collapsing into each other. The distraction his words had worked was all I needed: I jabbed a knee into one man's groin, brought an elbow up smartly into the second man's nose, and put a shoulder in passing into the third man's belly, catching up the rag of my turban and scrambling upwards over wares and awnings to gain the heights. Holmes hauled me the last couple of feet, and before the merchants had caught their breath to raise an alarm we were off across the rooftops and away.

We paused atop a piece of twelfth-century stonework while I restored the covering to my hair. 'I won't even ask how you found me, Holmes,' I said. 'But you might at least have lent a hand.'

'What, and rob you of the satisfaction of dealing with three large men single-handedly?'

He was right. I was aware of an intense feeling of pleasure at what I had done, on my own. This was the first time I had actually used the skills I possessed of physical defence, and 'satisfaction' was indeed the word. Of course, all three had been drunk, fat, and clumsy. 'Not so large,' I demurred, and then in the faint light from a nearby window I noticed the stain on my elbow. 'And if you'd interrupted a little more effectively I wouldn't have that man's blood all over my sleeve. I'll never get it out.'

'I believe if you examine it you will find it's nothing so fresh as that,' he said mildly, and with that I stood up and saw the filth that was smeared the length of my robe.

'Oh, God, Holmes, it reeks! What is that?'

'Best not to ask. Come.'

'I hope we're going back to the inn.' The other robe I possessed had seemed too dirty to bear, but now called to me as a paragon of cleanliness. I was not surprised, however, when he did not even answer, only swung his legs over the wall and dropped softly into the roof garden below.

Muttering Arabic curses under my breath and searching for an unsoiled patch of my *abayya* on which I might scrub my palms, I followed.

We rejoined street level in the Jewish Quarter and picked our way through the alleyways until we came to an open place. Several men, Polish Jews by the sound of their accents, were walking purposefully off to our left, and I glanced towards their goal, an opening between two squalid blocks of houses. It wasn't until we had walked a bit farther and I saw the bulk of the Temple Mount rising before us that I knew where they were going. I stopped dead, and when I listened I could make out their voices, struggling to reach the heavens out of the alleyway and past the heads of the houses that had been built up against the holiest place in Judaism. My people were praying at their Wall.

'"We sit alone and weep,"' I recited, tomorrow's Shabbos prayer. '"Because of the palace which is deserted. Because of the Temple which is destroyed."'

'Russell.' Holmes spoke sharply in my ear. A pair of men walking by us, dark shapes in their black caftans and fur hats, stopped dead to stare at the phenomenon of an Arab boy reciting a Hebrew prayer. I politely wished them in Hebrew a good evening, and they looked at each other and scuttled off.

'That was not wise,' Holmes commented.

'"Let peace and joy return to Jerusalem,"' I told him a bit giddily. '"Let the branch put forth and blossom."'

'That is precisely what we are attempting to achieve,' Holmes said, and took my elbow to march me away from there.

'Where are we going, Holmes?'

'To see a Moslem woman whose baskets were returned to her, and then an Armenian priest with an interest in archaeology.'

Why was it, I wondered silently, that the only time Holmes gave me a ready answer to a simple question was when the response was cryptic to the point of being oracular?

'Will we have time to eat?' I asked hopefully.

'Probably not.'

Either cryptic or disheartening.

CHAPTER TWENTY

ف

*Muhammad said: 'Every infant is born in the natural state. It is
his parents who make him a Jew or a Christian or a heathen.'*
— THE *Muqaddimah* OF IBN KHALDÛN

OLMES' MYSTERIOUS MOSLEM WOMAN WITH the
reappearing baskets lived in the village of Silwan, or
Siloah, across the Kidron Valley from the Old City. We went
out through the Dung Gate near the southern end of the
Haram es-Sherif and walked along the outer wall of the city for
a space, then dropped down onto a rutted track leading across
the valley (which was usually dry, although at the moment it
had a trickle at the bottom) and up the other side. There we
found a village of tombs, taken over and added to by the living.
The inhabitants looked as rough as their setting, and I could
only hope that we appeared too poor to bother assaulting.

Holmes seemed to know more or less where we were going, and only at the far end of the village did he stop to ask a child for the house of 'the widow of Abdul the Ugly.'

The widow lived in one of the tombs, it seemed. A boy answered our salutation, a child of about ten who eyed us with all the suspicion we deserved, two strange men calling on a widowed woman after dark. However, either Holmes' gentle but firm manner, his reassurance that we were only wishing a few words and would happily remain outside for the exchange, or his mention of copper coins, softened the lad's manly role, and in a few moments the mother was there, swathed to her eyebrows and crouching nervously just inside the entrance to the erstwhile tomb while we remained outside to preserve the proprieties.

'Madam, we are interested in the tale of your baskets,' Holmes began. When the silence within was broken only by an exchange of harsh whispers between mother and son, he added, '*Sitt*, I assure you I am not a madman. I too have had a thing taken and replaced, and when I heard your tale in the *souk* today, my interest was great. I believe it is merely boys who have done this, but if a boy is creating mischief, it is best to know this early, while he is still young, do you not agree? These are hard times to raise boys in. The temptations are many, and they have no respect for their elders.'

How on earth Holmes, whose closest approximation to being a parent had been in hiring hungry street urchins to run his errands back in the Baker Street days, knew that this would lay down a firm common ground with an illiterate Arab woman, I do not know, but it did. She immediately launched into a mournful recitation of the difficulties in raising children today, using phrases I have heard in twentieth-century drawing rooms and read in the hieroglyphic epistles of ancient Egyptian parents. She had just used the phrase 'He's a good boy' for the fifth time when Holmes cut her off.

'*Sitt,* I wish to know also about your baskets. You lost them?'

'They were stolen,' she replied, her indignation fresh and showing no wear after what must, judging by the rolling of her son's eyes, have been much telling. 'Stolen from my wall, my front wall, over where the good gentleman is even now sitting.' A hand reached out from the *burkah* and pointed upwards. We looked up and saw a twisted nail driven between the stones of the wall above my head.

'Why did you leave them outside in the street?'

'They were very dirty, and I did not want them in the house. I like a clean house, *effendi,* though it is difficult, what with two children and being gone from the house all day.'

'What work do you do?'

'What I can find,' she said simply. 'I wash clothes for Miriam the *ghassaleh,* I pick rags, I break stone.'

'Were these baskets for your work with Miriam the laundress?'

'No! *Wallah!* These were dirty baskets, old and worn and without any beauty, sufficient only to carry rock and soil. I did not imagine anyone would steal such ugly things.'

'So you carried stones and soil in them?'

'The son of Daoud the stonemason was a friend of my husband. Old man Daoud gives me work when I wish it. It is hard work, and my hands and shoulders ache when I have done a day's work, but it pays well, and my children must eat.'

'But the baskets were returned. How long were they gone?'

'Oh, one month? Perhaps more.' She consulted with her son, but he was uncertain. 'One month or six weeks perhaps.'

'And they were just returned.'

'Thrown down against the door,' she agreed.

'In the same condition as when they were taken?'

'Oh, no,' she said scornfully. 'They were barely threads clinging to each other.'

'Did you throw them away, then, *sitt*?' Holmes' voice remained as casual as before, but I could hear the tension coiling tighter in his questions.

'I was going to, but I did need a new nest for the chicken. The two baskets together were hardly as good as one, but better than twigs alone.'

'*Sitt*, I would like to buy one of these baskets.'

There was a long silence, then a suspicious, 'Why?'

'To use it to accuse these prank-playing boys, if ever I find them,' he said promptly.

The next silence was shorter and punctuated by whispers.

'How much would you pay for the old basket beneath my chicken?'

'How much would a new basket cost you?' asked Holmes in return.

'One . . . two *metallik*,' she said after a brief hesitation.

'I will give you one *beshlik*,' he offered, twice her price (and, I suspected, the smallest coin in his pocket). 'For the lower of the two baskets under the chicken,' he added.

Our only answer was a movement inside, then a long

silence. We sat and waited, then she was in the doorway again with a frayed, warped circle of reeds in her hand. The chicken, it appeared, lived inside with the family. She held it out to Holmes, who put it on the ground between us. As a piece of domestic equipment it left much to be desired, and had not been completely protected from the hen's droppings by the remains of the upper basket, but in its youth it had been sturdy and closely worked, and I could see why she made use of its remnants instead of chucking it out for the neighbourhood goats to chew.

'You can see,' she told us apologetically, 'there was no sense in trying to repair it.'

'No. But now you can buy yourself a new one, *sitt.*' He reached for his leather purse and took out the *beshlik* coin. The boy frowned, and the mother hesitated, but for different reasons.

'It is too much,' she admitted. 'I can buy reeds to make three baskets for one *metallik,* and the basket was old to begin with.' The boy saw Holmes putting the coin back into his purse and began to berate his mother, but he fell silent when Holmes held out his fingers again to the woman. She looked at the silver *piastre* in her palm, and then at Holmes.

'For your honesty, *sitt,*' he told her. Looking at the son, he added pointedly, 'The rewards of honesty are many.'

With blessings and best wishes we withdrew, and with the basket under one arm Holmes set off down the hill, through the evening noises and cooking odours and the tinkling of many goat bells. On the other side of the wadi I asked him, carefully in Arabic, 'May we go around to the left?' We went around to the left, and came to a garden, and a stream, and at the head of the stream a rectangular pool surrounded by low buildings. The waters in the pool reflected a motionless half-moon, and looked much deeper than I thought they actually were. We leant over the railing, shoulder to shoulder.

'Did you have a look at Mahmoud's eminently trustworthy clerk today?' I asked him.

'Of course. Bertram Ellison is a good Kentish boy who took a second-class degree at the University of London and became a government clerk. He came out to Cairo ten years ago, then followed the government legal offices here last year. He lives more or less secretly with a Russian woman three years older than he, although he also has rooms in the Christian Quarter that he uses as his official address.'

'An ordinary, fussy little office clerk with a minor secret.'

'So it would appear.'

'Who happens also to work for Joshua, and through him for the master illusionist Allenby.'

I felt him smile, and he took out a rolled cigarette and put it to his lips.

'Why are we standing looking at a pond, Russell?'

'This is the Pool of Siloam,' I told him.

'I see it is a pool.'

'Where the man born blind was healed in John's Gospel?'

'This is of importance?' he asked, beginning to lose patience.

'It is of interest, because this water comes from the Spring of Gihon three hundred fifty yards away, by way of an underground tunnel cut through solid rock in the time of King Hezekiah, twenty-six centuries ago. The city walls were down here then, and this miracle of engineering guaranteed water inside the city walls even during a siege. Hezekiah's workmen cut from both ends – there was an inscription in the middle where they met. I remember reading that an American boy worked his way through the tunnel sometime in the 1880s and found the inscription. Inevitably, when word got around, thieves came down and hacked it right out of the wall. It's now in Istanbul, I think.'

'A most compelling tale.'

'Illuminating, one might say: There is good precedence for deception and the hiding of resources in this country.'

'The study of history is always a worthwhile endeavour,' he agreed piously.

'Not that it makes it any easier to pick a traitor out of a crowd, one "man in Western dress" from a thousand.'

'And treachery being what it is, it is always the person closest to one's heart who can wield a dagger with impunity.'

'I'd have said, however, that Mahmoud would be among the hardest to deceive, and he says he trusts this man Ellison.'

'True.' He drew a last lungful from his cigarette and before I could stop his hand, sent the burning end out into the pond where it hissed sharply and died.

'May we go now?' he asked.

I pushed myself away from the railing and took a last look at the pitch-black hole at the top end of the pool. 'It is said to be dangerous to go through the tunnel. The water in the Gihon tends to rise suddenly, and wash down the tunnel.'

'I regret that we lack the leisure to mount an expedition, Russell. Attractive as it may be to risk drowning several hundred feet underground.' This time he did not ask but set off up the steep road to the Dung Gate.

Once inside the city walls we turned left, through the jungle of cactuses and builders' rubbish and away from the Haram and the Western Wall, towards the city quarter traditionally claimed by the Armenian community, swollen now with refugees fleeing the Turkish massacres of four years earlier that had left more than a million dead. The lights here were sparse and the streets tortuous, but Holmes' sense of direction was as efficient as ever and in a few minutes we were, to put a cap on the evening's events, inside of a church.

It was a little jewel box of a church, strung with a thousand gleaming lamps on chains overhead and fragrant with the incense of ages. We were apparently between services, because there were only a handful of people in the building, all of whom turned to stare disapprovingly at our persons. One of them went through a door in the back, returning after a minute with a formidable priest, a bear of a man with black cassock, black beard, black eyes, and greying black hair, who bore down on us and herded us out onto the street again. To my surprise, however, he did not leave us there. Rather, he followed us out, then took Holmes' elbow and drew us around the corner of the church and through a small gate into a private garden, at which point he turned and threw his arms around Holmes, clapping my partner to his breast with an enthusiasm that must have been excruciating to Holmes' half-healed back. The priest's greeting on being introduced to me was less effusive, which was just as well, but then he and Holmes were obviously old acquaintants.

'My old friend,' he cried. 'I was so pleased to have your message. It has been half a lifetime! Come, we will drink tea. But first you may like to wash your hands.' He did not even look at my clothes when he said this, and perhaps I imagined the twitch of his nostrils.

'This is my companion and student, Amir. Amir, Father Demetrius. Amir is a clumsy lad; he fell down in the bazaar,' Holmes told the priest. His half-truth and the use of my false identity warned me that there were limits to their camaraderie.

I was grateful even for the icy water and rock-like bar of soap, but nothing was to be done about my garments, except hope that they were dry enough not to leave deposits on our host's furniture.

We drank tea in his tiny, crowded study, and ate Armenian pastries until I thought I should burst, while the two talked about men and events of the past. In the midst of all this catching up on old news it dawned on me that the reason Holmes could find his way around the city so readily was not that he had committed the map in his bosom instantly to memory, but because he had been here before. Somehow, it had never occurred to me.

'So,' said the priest finally with an air of slapping his knees, 'what brings you to my door again after all these years? Something to do with the object beneath your chair, perhaps?'

Holmes kicked at the frayed basket that he had dropped under his seat. 'This? No, this is another matter.'

'And if it were the same thing you would not tell me, I think.' I raised a mental eyebrow: This priest did indeed know Holmes. 'I thought it might be one of your little puzzles – a hat worn by a missing friend, perhaps? That is what brought you to me, oh those many years ago. But no. It is something else that interests my old friend.'

The basket did look rather like a straw hat, one that had been thoroughly run down by a lorry, and though the priest remained intrigued by the object beneath his guest's chair, he politely did not mention it again. Neither did Holmes. Instead he began what sounded like another round of catching up on local gossip, but I soon realised was not.

'What is happening in archaeology these days?' he asked. 'I know everything stopped during the war, but has it begun again?'

'Preliminary work only, my friend. Surveys and explorations. The Germans, of course, were doing so much a few years ago, and now?' Father Demetrius gave an expressive shrug and pursed his bearded lips. 'The English are in charge of it now, and they are not about to hurry.'

'Where in the Jerusalem area?'

The priest began to smile slowly. 'We are interested in the active sites, are we?'

'I have always been interested in archaeology, as you may remember.'

The priest's eyes flicked down to the thing under Holmes' chair, then away, and it occurred to me that no-one in Jerusalem, and certainly no-one who had gone anywhere near a building site or an archaeological dig, could mistake that basket for a hat.

'He wants to know where the digs are,' Father Demetrius told the ceiling. He stood up and went to the wall of books behind the desk, taking down a long tube from the top shelf. He slipped his big fingers into the tube and, striking it smartly at one end, pulled at the roll of maps that emerged from the other. Deftly, as if he'd done it a thousand times, he put his fingertips under the top sheet and, rolling the remainder briskly, allowed the outside map to unscroll onto the desk, then popped the remainder back halfway into the protective tube to keep the whole bundle from unrolling.

We were looking at a very large-scale map of the city and its surroundings. He had used a pen to keep it up to date as buildings came and went and streets were added outside the wall in the New City. It was a wealth of information. He set weights on the corners, and stood stroking his beard.

'Here,' he said, touching a spot on the map. 'Here. Here. Here. And for a short time last summer, here. Nothing much at this very moment, of course. It's too wet.'

Holmes studied the map, saying nothing but radiating displeasure. Eventually he asked, 'Nothing near the Haram?'

'The south wall, but again, not at the moment.'

'Then it must be a construction site.'

'Near the Haram?'

'Do you know of any?'

'Hundreds,' the priest replied with a laugh that rattled the cups. 'The British are rebuilding the city, don't you know? The bazaars are clean, there is a vast new supply of water, new roads in all directions, the police no longer seize men and beat them bloody in the Old Serai – not as often, at any rate. Cesspools are being cleaned that haven't been emptied since the days of Jesus Christ. General Allenby wields a mighty broom.'

'Is there a project in particular that involves taking away a considerable amount of rubble?'

'Ah.' The priest smiled as if he'd tricked Holmes into admitting something, which in a way he had. 'There are several. But perhaps you are thinking of the Souk el-Qattanin.' The Cotton Bazaar.

Holmes nodded as if he were not really satisfied, and then he turned the conversation and allowed it to meander through harmless matters. Much later, we took ourselves back to our inn through a city that was dark and lifeless and eerily silent. The inn was shut up and dark as well, and we had to hammer on the gates before a boy came to let us in. The door to the room Ali and Mahmoud shared was closed. To my relief, Holmes surrendered to the trend, and we went to our respective rooms and our hard beds.

CHAPTER TWENTY-ONE

ق

The income of the Bedu is not large, because they live where there is little need for hired work, and such is the basis of profit.
— THE *Muqaddimah* OF IBN KHALDÛN

THE MORNING BEGAN EARLY, WHEN a fist pounded on the door with a rhythm I knew well.

'Up, Russell! You have work.'

I tucked my hair into my turban and opened the door, to see a familiar sight: Holmes, not rising from his bed, but rather coming home after a long night. I wondered if he had slept at all. I yawned; he looked at me with that dreadfully cheerful, superior attitude of the earliest bird around.

'Are you going to give me breakfast while you tell me about it, Holmes?'

'No time for either.'

'Holmes!' I objected.

'Can you find your way to the Souk el-Qattanin?'

'The Cotton Bazaar? Er—'

'Straight down David Street past the jog where it becomes es-Silsileh, two hundred yards towards the Haram, then north on el-Wad, and the Souk el-Qattanin comes in on your right. Just follow the sound of looms.'

'Why?'

'Because the army and the Red Cross have begun to renovate the *souk* and restore it to its original purpose, thus creating jobs for—'

'No, Holmes: Why do I need to go into the *souk?*'

'The innkeeper has arranged work for you on the renovation project there.'

'Work? What kind of work? I don't know how to run a loom. And isn't today Friday? I thought everything stopped on Friday.'

'You won't be weaving. And it's mostly Christians today, of course. Ideal for your purposes; the other days it's mostly Arab women, and you wouldn't fit in.'

'But doing what?'

'Carrying rocks and dumping the baskets where you're told, I should think.'

'That's it? What, are we out of money? I think I'd rather beg. Surely you can make me up to look like a leper or a multiple amputee or something.'

'Don't be frivolous, Russell. You will watch. For anything unusual.'

'Everything's unusual, Holmes,' I pointed out.

He ignored my sarcasm. 'You'd better leave your spectacles here, too.'

'Then how am I to watch?'

'Listen. Perceive. For heaven's sake, Russell, use your brain. Now, you are already late. Take a cup of coffee down in the courtyard, and I'll see you in the afternoon.'

'What will you do?' I cried desperately.

He paused in the doorway to his cubicle, looking back at me sternly. 'I will sleep, of course, Russell. I am, you will be so good as to remember, an old man who is recovering from a serious injury. I must have my rest.'

His door closed softly in my face. I stood with the ancient wood in front of my nose for some time before I decided that I might as well follow his instructions and learn something as go back to bed and lie there scratching and wondering. Folding my spectacles into a pocket, I went down the shaky stairs and out into the bazaar.

The project in the Cotton Bazaar was, inevitably, under the auspices of the army. A bored sergeant leant against a wall, smoking an Egyptian cigarette and looking at the women and a few men who were clearing rubble from the derelict street.

The Cotton Bazaar was one of the covered markets, a filthy Mediaeval near-tunnel of crumbling stone and rotting timbers that had, understandably, been abandoned for some years. I could hear the rhythmic sound of a number of looms, coming from no place in particular but seeming a part of the air. In the section of the bazaar still awaiting renovation, two privates with spades formed one end of the line, a group of donkeys with panniers the other, and in between we, the workers, balanced the heavy baskets on our heads to transport the rubble across the uneven and narrow places where the donkeys would not go.

I had carefully constructed an explanation for my presence, as good a speech as I could manage considering that I had no idea why I was actually here, but I rapidly put together another explanation in broken Arab English for the sergeant. He was not interested. He just waved me to the waiting baskets without looking at me and spat onto the paving stones. I took a basket and joined the line of dispirited workers.

Two hours later I was very aware that my skull was not fully healed: It did not take kindly to the weight of a wide basket laden with damp soil and stones resting on it. My stomach cried out for food, even some of Ali's half-burnt, half-raw bread, and my hands, arms, shoulders, and back were on fire. I had done no serious physical labour since the previous summer's harvest: I was, after all, by profession a student.

Now, however, one of Oxford's finest was hauling rock with the illiterate workers of Jerusalem. How should I explain the state of my hands to my tutors, if ever I returned to those green and pleasant shores? Even the thing from which we had fled here as respite, some unknown, invisible, and apparently omnipotent foe in England after our blood, began to look attractive compared to this . . .

Later in the morning several of the workers broke off for a smoke and a gossip. Trying to look inconspicuous (that is, not as utterly exhausted as I felt), I collapsed slowly onto a heap of displaced paving stones and tried not to tremble. My companions, half a dozen women and three men, had accepted me as a decidedly stupid young man with speech problems, and talked over and through me. A man with an elaborate, gleaming copper contraption mounted on his back came down the street, selling glasses of tea. He passed slowly down the line of resting workers, taking each customer's coin and waiting while he or she drank before passing on to the next, when he refilled the glass and waited again. I bought two glasses, and was thinking about a third when an angel appeared.

My friend from the inn, the young cook's helper, came skipping down the slippery cobblestones, placed a hamper in my lap, and turned and trotted away. My life was saved.

I bolted half the food in the basket without tasting it, by which time my co-workers were heading back to their very different kinds of baskets. Reluctantly, I placed it to one side, but its rejuvenating effects were already taking hold. I smiled at the old woman in front of me. The dim *souk* seemed brighter. The language around me became comprehensible again.

It always astonishes me, what women will freely talk about, even in front of men. By the time we stopped for lunch, I knew more about some of these good ladies than I knew about my neighbours in the Oxford lodging-house where I lived, and I had thought that intimacy considerable. I learnt a number of new words that morning, although truth to tell I had to guess at some of the English equivalents. It became quickly apparent that neither the sergeant nor the two privates (who had been put to dig as a punishment) spoke a word of Arabic. They may have suspected the nature of the comments and raucous laughter, but could do nothing but practise being phlegmatic and British. I began to enjoy myself, and ventured the occasional brief remark which, as they were Christians, they were able to accept slightly more readily from me, a male, than had they been Moslems.

Halfway through the next work period, a statement was made which interested me greatly. We had finished clearing the first patch, and our sergeant had shifted us around the corner to a side alley, when one of the women, looking with interest at the heap of fresh mud there, said plainly, 'We moved this same soil yesterday,' to which another responded, 'And the day before.'

They both laughed, but I looked closely at this pile as it went into my basket and into the pannier. It did seem different from the heap we had finished with, wetter and somehow less organic, but only when I saw how the others deposited the soil on the donkeys did it occur to me just how it was different. They too were paying attention to the contents of their baskets, and instead of simply upending them into the panniers, they were taking the time to tilt and shake them attentively, watching the soil pour down. Even without my spectacles I could easily see the change in their attitudes; then, near the donkey, the woman ahead of me snatched something from her emptying load and hastily thrust it inside her robe. Something flat the size of a thumbnail; I thought it was a coin, and then I knew how this soil was different: It was old, and these canny diggers knew it.

I nearly missed the bit of treasure buried in my own load, would have missed it had my colleagues not decided I was little better than a half-wit. One woman, a thin, hard-faced little grandmother, paused after emptying her basket to watch me tip mine into the donkey's containers. Her hand moved, but mine was there before hers, and I had the object stashed away before she could even curse. Later I paused in a doorway to examine it more closely. Scraping the caked soil of the ages from it with a thumbnail, I found a tiny glass phial, no more than two inches tall. I felt eyes on me, slipped it away into my pocket handkerchief, and took up my basket again.

When we broke for lunch I rapidly shovelled the remainder of the picnic down my throat, then sat with the basket on my knees, dabbing up the crumbs with a damp finger while I racked my brain to think of a way to return the conversation to the subject of the woman's comment about the reappearing soil. Unfortunately, the women were at one end of the alley, while I was with the men twenty feet away at the other. The men's conversation was infinitely less interesting than the chatter I could hear coming from the other end, being all about injustices done and relatives wronged by the new government, until one old man began dramatically to recite a positive epic: One of his goats had gone missing the week before! The very next day, his neighbours threw a feast! Roast goat figured prominently on the menu! The old man's grandsons attempted a course of rough justice! The military police arrived! They put a halt to the fracas!

His long and emphatic recitation finally came to an end, and before any of the others could draw a breath I made a loud remark, putting my tongue in the front of my mouth to supply a ready mechanical explanation for any linguistic failures.

'My mother lost a chicken the other week, but whoever took it left a silver bangle in its place.' The smattering of tales sparked by this pale story were neither enthusiastic nor particularly apt, and when they started to drift off on another track I made another loud comment. 'We think it is an *afreet.*' As I had hoped, the entire alley fell silent at my reference to a troublesome imp.

'Why would an *afreet* leave a silver bangle?' the man next to me demanded.

'Why would an *afreet* take a chicken?' I retorted, my logic equal to his. '*Afreets* cause trouble. My mother's chicken gave us many eggs, but the silver bangle, when she tried to sell it, brought only problems, for a woman down the road said we had stolen it.'

This was much more satisfying. For ten minutes we swopped stories of false accusations and genuine theft, and then I gave a final nudge.

'Why do you think the piles of soil keep coming into the Souk el-Qattanin? The new piles with old coins?'

After a moment of silence a great babble of voices burst out, which only eventually was dominated by one man, who simply had a greater lung capacity than the others.

'—the coin to my brother and we cleaned it until it shone, and then we carried it to the cousin of my brother's wife, who has a shop on the Tarik Bab Sitti Maryam, near the place where Jesus stumbled, where many foreigners used to buy things before the war and are now beginning to return, and the cousin of my brother's wife sold that coin to a rich Amerikani just last week for two gold *lira,* although he only gave my brother and me twenty-five *mejidis.*'

The others politely waited until he had finished to contribute their '*Wal*' of appreciation and their own stories, which circled around the suggestion I had planted in their minds, that the rich soil was being placed there by some peculiarly subtle variety of demon. I listened with only half an ear, though, because my question had already been answered by the last speaker: Yes, there was a rich and therefore deep vein of soil being worked somewhere beneath my feet.

'My father,' the man was saying, 'blessed be his memory, found a purse of coins on the roadside, and when he was honest enough to report this, being a good Christian, the police beat him and threw him into the Old Serai for a week, saying that he had stolen some of the coins and wanted a reward for the ones he had left, although it was actually the police who stole them. Of course, they were Turks,' he added pensively.

'And my mother's father's second wife,' called one of the women . . .

The topic of archaeological discoveries was thrashed over until our sergeant reappeared and ordered us back to work, but I was well satisfied with the results of my own labours: Someone, at night, was depositing quantities of soil from deep underground onto the surface to be hauled away. Someone, perhaps, who had borrowed two baskets from the wall of a tomb/house in Silwan that he had happened to pass. Who before that had borrowed two habits, a rope, and a handful of candles, because he thought he might need them, and he was passing. Someone who—The consideration of the someone distracted my mind satisfactorily for quite some time. I queued up with the others to have my baskets filled, and followed them to dump the rubble, but was quite unaware of any of it until I felt a hand on my sleeve.

I looked down into the face of the young cook's helper from the inn, for whom I was beginning to feel a deep affection.

'You are required back at the inn,' the boy said.

'Who requires me?'

'Your friend.'

'I have a number of friends.'

'Your long friend in the blue *kuffiyah*,' he said, and then for some reason he covered his mouth with his hand and let out a giggle.

'I will come.' I laid down my basket and went down the narrow street on his heels, picking my way over the rough surface and avoiding the holes (one of the privates had graduated to a pickaxe). On the Street of the Cotton Merchants the sergeant stopped me. 'Oi, where do you think you're going?'

'*Effendi*, my presence is required elsewhere,' I said smoothly in English.

'You don't say.'

'I fear that I do say.'

'There's no pay for half days. All or nothing, that's His Majesty's way.' I doubted it very much, but was not inclined to argue over a pittance. I began to say something to that effect when my youthful companion nudged me to one side and began sweetly to cajole the dour sergeant. I left him to it, and threaded my way briskly through the bazaar towards the Jaffa Gate. I thought I heard the sergeant's voice raised in shouts, but then I turned a corner and left them behind.

Only as I was passing through the vegetable market on David Street, restoring my spectacles to my nose, did it occur to me that a British soldier might find it suspicious that a native worker would leave without the better part of a day's pay. I hesitated, and nearly turned back, but Holmes was waiting, and the cook's boy had seemed to me quite resourceful enough to get himself out of that sticky situation. I trotted on up the steps of David Street to the inn.

CHAPTER TWENTY-TWO

ك

With the decrease of civilisation, the land's riches fade. In countries where springs existed in the days of civilisation, when the countries fell into ruin, the water of the springs disappeared into the ground as if they had never existed.
— THE *Muqaddimah* OF IBN KHALDÛN

AN ARMY STAFF CAR SAT in the street outside the inn's gates. This sounds like a simple matter, but when the street in question is less than eight feet wide and the car more than five, it means that a laden donkey must be unloaded and all but the narrowest carts turned and taken another way. The driver, magnificently deaf to the shouts and curses of would-be passers-by and the pleas of beggars alike, held a cigarette in one hand and a yellow-back novel in the other. I sidled past and went through the heavy wooden gates into the inn's yard, wondering mildly whom an army officer might be visiting in this quarter.

I did not wonder for long. My soft boots made chuffing

sounds on the worn steps all the way to the top floor. I rapped on Holmes' door, stepped inside – and immediately bowed and scraped my panic-stricken way backwards into the hallway.

'*Effendi,* ten thousand apologies, I fear I have the wrong room, I did not intend—' I closed the door, stood and stared at it for a long, puzzled moment, before realising that even if the sergeant had his suspicions about a hastily departing labourer, he could not have arranged for this both immediate and high-ranking a response. Besides which – I reached again for the worn iron door handle and put my head back inside. 'Holmes?'

The sleek figure – shiny high boots, immaculate khaki uniform, polished belt, starched hat, perfect hair, trimmed moustache, and the swagger stick he had been slapping against his elegant leg – turned with a diabolical grin on his face.

'Good Lord, Holmes, what on earth are you doing in that get-up? You'll be arrested!' I had seen the man in any number of disguises, from paternal gipsy to ageing roué to buxom flower-seller, but none more outlandish, given his personality, than this one.

He just stood there and laughed at me. 'By God, Russell,' he finally choked out, 'it was worth the untold bother of this fancy dress uniform and ten thousand accursed salutes to see you cringe like that. I didn't know you were capable of it. You were slinking, Russell. Positively slinking.'

I didn't think it at all amusing, and told him so. 'You nearly gave me heart failure, Holmes. I thought you were here to arrest me for stealing antiquities. I ought to turn you in for impersonating an officer.'

He wiped his eyes and blew his nose, and began to divest himself of hat, stick, and military belt. 'I wear this uniform with the approval of the highest authorities – although it is a decidedly temporary commission,' he added. 'What antiquities have you stolen?'

I took out the tiny handkerchief-wrapped object, dropped into a squat on the floor, and opened the cloth parcel out on the floorboards. I picked up the little glass vase to examine it, rubbing the encrustations cautiously away, but the neck had a crack in it, and part of it came away in my fingers. A pity.

Still, it had spoken its message to me, even in pieces.

'This is a Roman phial, Holmes. Probably third or fourth century.'

'Yes?'

'So what was it doing among the rubbish being cleared from a Mediaeval bazaar?'

He sat down on his low pallet, a difficult manoeuvre while wearing rigid knee-high boots. 'You are the historian here, Russell. What would you suggest it was doing there?'

I set the two pieces on the scrap of dirty linen and made myself comfortable on the floor. 'This poor little thing was jerked forwards in time sixteen hundred years or so, and I should say it happened no earlier than the last couple of nights. Someone is clearing out an underground chamber.'

'Good. Oh, very good, Russell.'

I opened my mouth to begin the analysis of the someone's character that I had constructed while I was working, but before I could say anything he stood up and pulled on his hat and belt.

'I shall have a car call for you at seven o'clock. It is now' – he patted his various pockets until he found the one he wanted, dipped in with his fingers, and brought out a silver watch on a chain – 'three forty-five. That may even allow you time for a brief nap, although I suggest that you plan to devote considerable attention to the state of your fingernails.'

I held up my hands and looked at them. The nails were in a lamentable state, it was true, but if anything they added to the verisimilitude of my disguise.

'Why?'

'Because we are dining, of course,' he said in surprise, snapping his stick briskly under one arm. 'At the American Colony. Not formal dress, of course. After all, there has been a war on.'

'Oh, no, Holmes, you can't mean—'

He opened the door. 'I left a frock in your room. If there is any other thing I've forgotten, ask Suleiman the cook to arrange it. I shall see you at seven.'

I did seriously consider an outright refusal of his peremptory summons; I wanted nothing but to strip off my turban and collapse onto my gently rustling bed. However, curiosity got the better of me – that and the challenge, which had not been voiced but which I knew had been made.

My fingernails, however, defeated me. In the end, after a hasty consultation of my Arab-English dictionary, I went through the room shared by Ali, Mahmoud, and most of our baggage (the men were not there; the door was unlocked) and called down the outside stairs to Suleiman the cook that I needed a pair of women's gloves, quickly, and to send a boy out into the bazaar for them.

My hair, too, was in a sorry state, but I eventually combed it back into a sleek knot and examined myself critically in the mottled glass Holmes had brought to my cubicle along with frock, stockings, shoes, hairpins, earrings, and all the accoutrements of female preparation. He knew the routine, give him that: He'd even thought to include a small bottle of expensive scent, which I used rather more liberally than was my wont. Cold water does not actually cleanse.

Still, I thought I might pass, if I did not forget myself and drop to my haunches or let loose with a florid Arabic curse. The frock was of an outdated fashion, perhaps more appropriate here than in London, with a high neck, long sleeves, and low hem. It was a nicely made garment, in a dark maroon fabric with touches of white that clung and moved and distracted the eye from the tint of my skin, which no amount of rice powder would lighten.

I examined my reflection and had to wonder uneasily if Holmes had intended for me to look quite so . . . exotic. The young woman looking back at me seemed, shall I say, sensuous – loose, even, like some Eurasian temptress in a bad novel. On the whole, I thought perhaps the effect was accidental; had he been deliberately aiming at the effect, he would probably have included a bottle of hair-rinse to make my blonde hair colour seem artificial.

A selection of gloves arrived, and shortly thereafter Ali and Mahmoud came up the stairs. They stood in the doorway, frankly staring at me, but I absolutely refused to blush. Instead, I turned to them for their opinion.

'What do you think, the white gloves or the lacy ones?'

Ali just gawped. Mahmoud examined the two choices, and his lips twitched. I chose the long lacy ones, which, as they were more difficult to get on and off, might excusably be retained during dinner.

With no more self-consciousness than a pair of cats the two men watched me complete my toilette, tug the gloves into place, and check my hairpins. Finally Ali said, 'There is a motorcar in the road.'

'Why didn't you say so earlier?' I asked in irritation, catching up the evening cloak and pushing past them to reach the external stairway – it was dark now, and outside there would be less chance of observers to remark on the inn's bizarre guest. I was picking my cautious way down the stairs when I heard Mahmoud's voice from above me.

'Is your hair the colour that is called "strawberry blonde"?' he asked.

I stopped. 'I suppose so,' I answered. When no other enquiries followed, I shrugged my shoulders and continued down the stairs, but before I reached the cobbles, a strange noise filled the dirty little yard: a man's voice, a tenor, singing. It took a moment for the words to register, by which time a second voice, a baritone, had joined in. '"I danced with the girl with the strawberry curls,"' they sang, '"and the band played on . . ."' The old tune followed me out the gates, and as I was being handed into the car by the driver the words dissolved into laughter. I shook my head. It was like living with a pair of adolescent boys. And Holmes was at times no better.

We drove out through the gap in the city wall next to the Jaffa Gate, the hole cut in 1898 to enable the Kaiser to ride his white horse into the city. I had seen a photograph somewhere of the occasion, the German emperor dressed in white silk, preceded by brass bands and Arab horsemen, with his ladies following behind in the comfort of their touring car. Once inside, of course, there would have been no place for the motorcar or the bands to go – our inn was at the very farthest reaches of automotive traffic, short of a motorcycle, in this labyrinthine city. Symbolism, however, especially in Jerusalem, is all – which explained as well the contrasting entrance Allenby had chosen to make nineteen years later when he seized the city from the Kaiser's allies. The general walked up the hill in his dusty boots, surrounded by men in the same battle-worn khaki uniforms as himself, all pageantry aside as he addressed himself to the gathered representatives of the city before returning to the business of freeing the remainder of Palestine. Symbolism, indeed.

The American Colony, north of the Old City, was precisely what it sounded like: a family of Americans who had come over in the 1880s and stayed to do good work through increasingly evil times. Their main house, originally built by a Turkish pasha for his several wives, was a two-storey stone block surrounding a private courtyard garden, strongly Eastern in its character. The night was cold; nonetheless I surrendered my cloak and followed a young man, who despite his accent and skin tone seemed more family than servant, through rooms that combined the high, airy arches of the Orient with the heavy furniture and grass-plumes-in-brass-pots motif of Victorian decorating, into the courtyard that sparkled with hanging lamps and glowing braziers, made even more festive by the delicate play of a fountain. My hostess quite obviously had no idea who I was, but received me graciously and introduced me to all the men nearby. And most of the people in the garden were men, many of them officers with red tags marking them as being on the staff of General Allenby, with a very few wives and not one unattached woman other than the daughters of the house and myself. Holmes was nowhere to be seen. I wondered if he would appear at all, or if I was to be abandoned here to my own resources, having no idea whatsoever why I was here or what I was to do, and feeling fairly certain that my hosts were asking each other the same questions about this unescorted and slightly dubious young woman they had in their midst. I had to pull myself together and make a good show of it, but it was impossible not to feel uncomfortable. I cursed to myself, and resolved to give Holmes hell when he finally appeared to rescue me.

My sour reflections were broken into by a handsome young cavalry officer who came to stand in front of me and ask, 'May I refresh your glass, Miss Russell?'

'I beg your pardon?'

His confident moustache seemed to droop a bit at my response. 'Er, your glass? I wondered if you might not care for another drop. Perhaps, well, there are other things to drink. If you like, that is.'

I took a deep breath, exhaled, put my problems to one side, lowered my chin, and raised my eyes to his. 'I'd adore another refreshment,' I purred at him, and watched his pink face turn pinker and his moustache positively bristle with pleasure.

The glass he brought back might not have qualified as strong drink, precisely, but at least it was neither sweet nor fruity. I swallowed, and decided that if I had to play the role dictated by this dress and the extreme earrings Holmes had left for me, I was going to do it with all my heart. If Holmes wanted a nineteen-year-old not-quite-a-lady, that is exactly what he would get.

When Holmes finally arrived, ten minutes before the dinner bell, it would have been difficult to say which of us was the more taken aback at the other's companions: Holmes took in my collection of handsome and attentive young officers with a sharply raised eyebrow, and I finally felt myself blush under the glance of the man at his side. Neither of the new arrivals greeted me, which on Holmes' part I took to mean that I was not supposed to know him. His companion simply did not recognise me.

The two newcomers were taken the rounds by our pleased hostess, introduced by rank to those they did not know (of course, Holmes knew very few of them, and none knew him) until they made it to my circle of junior officers, who stood so rigidly to attention that they might have been made of stone. The general's permission to be at ease had little effect on their spines, or their tongues. The introductions finally came around to me.

'And this is Miss Mary Russell, General, a visitor here. Miss Russell, General Allenby.' On hearing my name the general's brows flew up; our handshake was delayed by a ferocious bout of coughing which necessitated the application of a large handkerchief to the lower half of his face. A glass of water was brought, the general's back was very tentatively patted, until eventually, eyes wet and dancing, he reached out and grasped my hand.

'Terribly sorry, Miss, er, Russell.' His face contorted as if he were stifling another spasm of coughing. 'Dust, you know. Awfully dusty country.' Allenby was having a difficult time controlling his mouth, so I thought it only kind to turn to Holmes and proffer my dainty, lace-wrapped hand.

'This is Lieutenant-Colonel William Gillette,' our hostess hastened to say. 'He is new here himself. Miss Mary Russell,' she said, sounding very uncertain of the meaning of all these odd undercurrents that were suddenly stirring the placid waters of her dinner party. Holmes bowed briefly over my hand.

'Delighted, I'm sure,' he murmured.

'Colonel.' I tipped my head a fraction.

'Pray don't let me interrupt your conversation,' he said drily.

'Oh, no, please join us.'

'Perhaps later. I am told you have an interest in archaeology.'

'I do,' I said obediently. 'An absolute passion for the subject.'

'Perhaps we may discuss it after dinner?'

'I shall look forward to the pleasure.'

'Thank you. Charming frock.' His eyes skimmed over me, perfectly in character. I felt the young men around me stir, though none of them could possibly object to the impertinence of a man wearing the uniform of a superior officer, and he knew it. I, however, was a girl buoyed by a roomful of admiring and admirable men, and I did not have to take it from him.

'What, this old thing?' I said with heavy emphasis, and quite deliberately ran my hand down my rib cage to my hip. 'It's scarcely decent.' His eyes went dark and he turned away abruptly. I tucked my hands through two nearby elbows and sparkled at my admirers. 'Shall we have another little drink before dinner, boys?'

There were signs of a hasty rearrangement of places at the dinner table, and I found myself thoroughly closed in by men older than my junior officers. I toyed with the idea of continuing my flirtation, but only for a minute; it would have been cruel to my hostess. So, I allowed the high neck of my dress to be demure rather than provocative, and subsided into polite conversation.

To my right was an elderly and slightly deaf legal gentleman who slurped his soup and seemed quite unaware of the conventions of dinner talk, because he never did turn from the colleague on his right to speak with me. This left the gentleman on my other side with a double burden. Fortunately, the man across the table from me noticed my predicament, and made an effort to include me in his talk with his neighbours.

I had noticed the man earlier in the courtyard. He seemed to be a member of the family, although of very different ethnic inheritance, being Levantine in appearance. He was in his middle fifties, I thought, slightly younger than Holmes, calm and even tempered, the sort of man who listens carefully and whose remarks are invariably intelligent, even wise. He and his companion, the legal secretary Norman Bentwich (whose Camel Corps had been responsible for bringing the Nile waters of prophecy to Jerusalem) were talking about the projected building of a grand hotel in the New City, and with Holmes' hint about archaeology in mind – his sole clue as to my direction of enquiry – I asked about the problems of disturbing archaeological sites in the preparation of building sites.

The man, understandably enough, seemed mildly taken aback at my question. 'You are interested in building, or in archaeology, Miss——?'

'Russell. Oh, archaeology, definitely. I think had I been a man I should have liked nothing better than to spend my life grubbing about underground, excavating the lives of our ancestors and discovering tombs and tunnels and things.'

I had hooked him with my first cast. He reached out to shift a candlestick to one side so as to see me more clearly. 'Not buried treasure, Miss Russell? That's a much more usual interest among amateur archaeologists. Some of whom, may I say, are women.'

'Oh, yes? How interesting. But I'm not particularly concerned with gold and such. I much prefer the objects of daily life, bead necklaces and pots and carved stone kitchen gods and such. I found a tiny Roman perfume phial in the soil the other day – broken, of course, but so much more real than the jewels of the aristocracy.'

Everyone in Jerusalem, it soon became apparent, is passionate about the artefacts of the past, and we quickly had an active little discussion group going over the soup and the fish. Our hostess glanced down at us, relieved if a bit puzzled. Holmes, seated to General Allenby's left, threw the occasional brooding look down to our end of the table. The subject flew south with a remark about the excavation of tombs in Egypt, but I ruthlessly dragged it home again.

'Tombs are so jolly, don't you think?' I asked brightly. 'I do so love dark and closed-in places. I should think there must be plenty of them hereabouts, come to think of it.'

'Well,' said the man to the left of the dark man, 'you've

certainly asked the right man about that. Jacob, tell her about your discovery of Hezekiah's Tunnel.'

I hadn't just caught a fish with my random cast; I'd struck gold. 'You're not *that* boy?'

'It was a very long time ago.'

'But you *were* that boy. You and your friend waded through the tunnel.'

'Swam through, more like. And I'm afraid Sampson was a broken reed – he became frightened of the darkness in the tunnel and ran back home. We were supposed to meet halfway, but he never appeared, and in the end I emerged down at the Pool of Siloam, completely terrifying the poor women doing their laundry there when I came out of the hole. They thought I was an *afreet;* I was fortunate to get away with a few bruises.'

'I was just saying to – a friend the other day how I should love to go through Hezekiah's Tunnel.'

'I wouldn't have thought it appealing to a young lady, Miss Russell. It's an extremely dirty and uncomfortable sort of adventure. Just the thing for a young boy.' The people near us who were listening chuckled, and I wondered briefly how he, and they, might react were I to describe how I had spent my day; however, I merely returned his smile. He added, 'I found out later it's actually a rather dangerous sort of stunt. The water at the Virgin's Pool has a nasty habit of rising without warning and filling the tunnel to the top.'

'Are there many such tunnels in Jerusalem?'

'Tunnels like that, no. Most of the tunnels in the Old City are either much newer subterranean aqueducts, or buried chambers.'

'Aqueducts.'

'Such as the one Herod built to bring water from the reservoir at Bethlehem. Now, that's quite an interesting engineering feat. Not as impressive as the Siloam tunnel, perhaps, but good solid work. Of course, most of it's redundant now, with the new British pipes. What a godsend that has been. Why, last summer—'

'Are they empty?' I interrupted.

'Sorry?'

'The old underground aqueducts. Are they still flowing, or empty?'

He sat back and pursed his lips. 'Do you know, I haven't the faintest idea. We all used to be so interested in that sort of thing, the whole town would come to see when something exciting was dug up, but somehow after the last few years, we just haven't got back to it yet. It's a bit like a hobby, you know, with the tourists looking on, but there just hasn't been the time or the energy. It was very bad here, you know, towards the end.'

'So I understand.'

'Of course, we didn't have bombs raining down on us as you had in London.' I had spent very little time in the city during the war, but I did not disabuse him of the picture.

'No, just monomaniacal pashas, uncontrollable troops, disease, drought, and starvation,' I said, stabbing a piece of succulent roast beef on my fork and conveying it to my mouth.

'Yes. Still, that's over, isn't it? The Brits are here, there's water and food. They've even taken over the care of the sick and wounded. Perhaps we can carve a few hours out of the week again for leisure.'

'Well, if you plan an underground outing in the near future, do keep me in mind.'

'I shall indeed. In fact, why not next week? We could organise a family picnic into Solomon's Quarries. Some of the younger children have never been in there. It might take a few days to clear the entrance of debris and check the roof for rocks that have worked their way loose, but it would be great fun. Do you know, I can't remember the last time we did anything just for the pleasure of it.' His sallow cheeks had taken on a degree of colour, and he looked younger than he had before.

'What are Solomon's Quarries?'

'An enormous cave directly beneath the city – its entrance is near the Damascus Gate. It was actually once a quarry, one can still see the chisel marks and a few half-separated blocks, but it's probably not, as tradition has it, the source of the Temple blocks. As I remember, the stone is too soft.'

It would have to be a very large cave indeed to stretch to the Cotton Bazaar, thus undermining half the city, but it was underground, and underground was where my interests lay.

'I should be very interested to see it. How far back does it reach?'

'I don't remember the exact measurement, offhand. Perhaps one hundred fifty, even two hundred yards.'

My interest increased. Five or six hundred feet was a goodly distance in the tiny city. 'How does one enter it?'

'There used to be an iron gate, just east of the Damascus Gate. In fact, our store here at the Colony used to sell tickets for a franc. Not since the war, though. Just let me ask – O'Brien! Say, have you noticed any tourists going into the Cotton Grotto lately? No? I didn't think so. We were just thinking of getting up a picnic down there. Miss Russell here—'

'What did you call it?' I interrupted urgently.

'Call what?' The intensity of my voice confused him. Several of our neighbours glanced over at me, but I paid them no mind.

'The cave. What did you just call it?'

'The grotto? Yes, that's the other name for it. Less grand than Solomon's Quarries, which is the name the tour books use. Locals go by the Arabic name. The Cotton Grotto.'

Chapter Twenty-Three

ل

The arts are well established in a city only after sedentary culture
has a long duration there.
— THE *Muqaddimah* OF IBN KHALDÛN

THE CONVERSATIONS AROUND OUR END of the table began
to founder around the bulk of my stunned silence, until
I pulled myself together, closed my jaw, and made some inane
comment such as, 'How very nice.' Voices started up again, but
I did not dare look down to the other end; I could feel Holmes'
eyes drilling into me, but there was nothing for it now. We had
to get through dinner first.

Fortunately, the pudding course was being set before us,
soon to be followed by cheese, and then we ladies would
excuse ourselves. Ought I to escape then? Or might there be
further information to be got across the dining table? No,

that would not be wise; I had not only monopolised a partner who was not my own but drawn attention to myself in the process. Best not pursue it now, I decided, and, gathering patience to me as firmly as I could, I turned to the small, nervous Belgian on my left. 'What brings you to Jerusalem, Monsieur Lamartine?'

My patience was chafing me badly by the time we left the gentlemen to their cigars. I followed my hostess with a degree of apprehension; I have never been good at women's conversation, for my mother died before I could learn the art of small talk with individuals who had no employment aside from needlework and children, and in addition I had not begun the evening with an image guaranteed to endear me to them. However, I need not have worried. In truth, I was impressed with these women, particularly the recently arrived Helen Bentwich, who had been active in the Land Army movement in Britain during the war. The war had changed us all, and although these ladies dutifully began with polite, shallow questions, we were very soon happily embroiled in three or four separate topics, the main two being Zionism's relationship to Arab nationalism and the means of preserving the historical purity of the Old City in the face of future growth. It was with some reluctance that we rejoined the men. Who, it appeared, had been talking about cricket.

'Had a good chat, then, did you?' asked one jolly colonel, rising. 'Settle the world's problems with babies and dress fashions?'

I spoke up over the rumble of masculine chuckles. 'Actually, we were discussing the Balfour agreement and the progress of the Paris peace talks. Any chance of another drop of coffee?'

I swayed over to the sideboard and took a cup of coffee from the hand of Lieutenant-Colonel William Gillette.

'Just black, thank you,' I told him, and when the voices had risen around us I murmured over the rim of my cup, 'I imagine Mr Gillette would be much amused, were he to find that the character he played on stage was in turn impersonating him.' The original William Gillette was an American actor who had cobbled together one of the first stage plays about Holmes, using bits of the Conan Doyle stories and adding a romantic interest. Holmes' opinion of the production was what one might expect.

'I thought it only fair. What did the gentleman across from you say?'

'He said many things.' I smiled across the room at my young cavalry officer, grown shy when seeing me standing with a lieutenant-colonel.

'Russell.'

'Don't "Russell" me. If I tell you now you'll flit out of here and I won't see you for two days. I did the work; I'm not going to allow you to have all the fun.' I took my cup down from my face and turned my smile at an approaching man. 'Governor Storrs, you must be quite pleased with the progress being made in the city – at least I hope you are. I was saying to Colonel Gillette here – do you know Lieutenant-Colonel William Gillette? Yes, he does look a bit like the actor, now that you mention it. What an amusing coincidence. I was saying to him not five minutes ago . . .'

Twenty minutes of politeness was all Holmes could abide.

I had counted on that, allowing myself to be drawn into a silly conversation about rescuing Arab girls from the gutter (Mrs Major's words, not mine) by teaching them needlework, because I knew that I would not be stuck there for the rest of the evening. The musical portion of the evening was about to begin. Brigadier-General Ronald Storrs, de facto governor of Palestine, had sat down to the piano to play 'Vittoria' from *La Tosca* when Holmes loomed up between Mrs Major and one of my young officers, baring his teeth at me in a tight grimace that passed for a smile.

'You said earlier you would appreciate a ride back to town. I'm going now.'

'Thank you, Colonel. That's very good of you.' I took my leave of my host and hostess, shook off two of my more persistent admirers, and was nearing the door when the archaeological Jacob came into the vestibule.

'Are you leaving so soon, Miss Russell? What about our excursion into Solomon's Quarries? How may I get in touch with you?'

'Er, I—'

'A message left at Government House always seems to reach one, have you not found, Miss Russell?' Holmes said smoothly.

'Yes. Yes, it seems to. I move about so much, you know. I may not even be in Jerusalem next week, but thanks awfully.' Before I could make an even greater fool of myself, Holmes dropped my cloak onto my shoulders and propelled me towards the door.

It was freezing in the car, and I wrapped my inadequate

garments about me and shivered. The temperature emanating from Holmes was even colder.

'I had not intended that you make quite such a spectacle of yourself, Russell,' he said in a low, brittle voice as soon as the driver had pulled out of the compound. 'This was a simple exercise in gathering information, not an eights-week ball.'

'That dress was your choice, Holmes, and in case you hadn't noticed, there are probably three other English women under the age of forty in the entire city, and those are safely affianced. How could I help being a spectacle? As it is, they will certainly remember me, but not because I asked a lot of questions about tunnels under the city. Which sort of impression should you have preferred I make?'

He did listen to my words, and the temperature in the car gradually rose a few degrees. 'Very well,' he said, 'I see your point. Next time, I shall choose the frock with greater care; I should hate to be responsible for your having to spend another evening parading yourself in front of young men in that manner. I admit I had failed to visualise quite what the frock would look like with you inside it.'

I looked at him sharply, but there was not enough light to see his expression. His voice had said that as a flat statement, with neither innuendo nor even humour. Had another man said those words, I might at least have considered the possibility that he had noticed what I looked like, that he had appreciated – I sat up briskly. Enough of that. Too much flirtation, in fact, for one night. It was a good thing I was not staying here long, definitely not as Miss Russell: being the object of adoring gazes of young men in uniform was clearly a heady thing. Time to crawl back into my robe, turban, and *abayya*.

I must have sighed or made some noise.

'Cinderella home from the ball, eh, Russell?' He was, however, smiling when he said it.

It was after eleven o'clock, and the inn was again shut tight. A yawning boy answered our summons, handed us a small lamp, and stumbled away. At my door I wished Holmes a good night, and he peered at me in the meagre light as if I were mad.

'We have work to do, Russell.'

'God, Holmes. You told me that same thing at some unearthly hour this morning, and I've been slogging hard ever since. My skull aches, my shoulders ache, my hands are raw; don't you ever sleep?'

'You're young, Russell,' he said brutally. 'You can sleep tomorrow.'

'Do you intend—? You do. We're going back out.'

'Just let me get out of this absurd outfit. I should do the same, if I were you.' He ducked into his room, and I closed my own door and wedged it shut while I was changing back into the Arab boy. I fixed my turban, took the wedge from the door, and took a quick step back as it flew open to admit the Bedouin Holmes. He shut it quietly and we squatted together on the floor with the oil lamp between us. Amazing, how comfortable that position had become.

'Tell me what your archaeological friend said,' he demanded.

'There are caves under the north end of the city, near the

Damascus Gate. They're called Solomon's Quarries by the guide-books, but their other name, the one they're known by to the locals, is the Cotton Grotto.'

His eyes glittered. 'Suggestive.'

'I thought it was. There's an iron gate that may be buried in rubble – he thought the cave hadn't been used since before the war. It's a big cave, extending about two hundred yards underneath the city.'

'That still leaves quite a way to go to the Cotton Bazaar. Four, five hundred yards I believe.'

'Funny, the coincidence in names, though,' I said provocatively. Holmes does not believe in coincidence. He did not respond, just sat. After a minute he pulled out his pipe, which always made the thinking process go more quickly.

'We need to see some maps,' he said. I waited. 'Father Demetrius is certain to have among his maps one that shows everything underground in the city.'

'Is it too late to go and knock him up?'

He scowled. 'Demetrius is a fine old man, but he had some questionable dealings with the Turks.'

'Oh, surely not.'

'The welfare of his people is the only thing that matters to him. Even his passion for old stones takes second place to the Armenian community. Twice for certain, possibly several times, he gave the Turks . . . someone they wanted, in exchange for which they freed Armenian prisoners. One can understand it, I suppose. After all, the Turks were aiming at genocide, and when a million of one's people are killed, it is apt to make one view outsiders with a different eye. What, after all, is an Englishman

337

or two compared to a trainload of your countrymen?'

'He's not to be trusted, then?' I asked bluntly.

'He's not to be tested. He might have the ear of the wrong man for our purposes, and we've shown ourselves quite enough in that quarter. There are,' he noted, 'a fair number of Armenians still rotting in prisons.'

'What about Government House? The army has undoubtedly done a survey of every inch of the city, above and below ground.'

He puffed furiously on his pipe. 'I am wary of Government House,' he said finally, sounding not happy.

'Ellison.'

'A good clerk is like a servant, invisible and all-seeing. Still, I find myself unconvinced about Ellison. For one thing, I cannot imagine why Haifa would have notified Jerusalem that they were reaching out for Ali and Mahmoud, allowing Ellison to overhear.'

'You think there is another informant, one in Haifa?' God, I thought; the holes in British security are like Swiss cheese. 'What about the driver, was he then killed to cut the tie, or because he had outlived his usefulness?'

'That is possible. Probable, even. However . . .'

'You do not wish to chance bringing Government House in, even if we could keep Ellison from knowing.'

'Not until we are more certain. Not for something as important as this.'

'So what comes next?' I asked, although I thought I knew.

He held his pipe away and examined the tobacco in the bowl. 'Did you notice the lock on the door of Father Demetrius' study?' he asked.

'It is a very old lock.'

His head came around and he shot me a grin. 'That's my Russell,' he said, as if everything had been decided. But then, it had.

We let ourselves out the small door set into the inn's heavy gates and turned down the black alleyway towards the Armenian Quarter.

'Just one thing,' Holmes breathed into my ear. 'It is assumed in the city that anyone walking through the dark streets without a lantern is no better than he should be, and wants arresting. We can't very well take a lantern, but if we are caught, you are to get away. Do you understand? They will be satisfied with one of us, and I'll come to no harm sleeping in a cell overnight, but I'll not see you in a man's prison, even for a few hours. Do what you have to do, but get free.'

I had to agree that the thought was not a happy one. 'All right.'

'I have your word?'

'I said so.'

'Good.' He slipped away down the alley and I followed, out to the open area in front of the Citadel, a maelstrom of activity during the day, now deserted but for rats and one scrawny cat. We skulked after the cat, around the sides of the echoing emptiness, over the entrance to the silent David Street bazaar, between the gates to the Anglican church compound and the steps of the Citadel (where the humble victor General Allenby had given his victory speech to the city), past the barracks, and into the Armenian Quarter. Twice we heard noises and plastered ourselves against the walls, but the only living things we saw had either wings or four feet. We came to the church, we went around it, and we eased our way through the gate and the garden to the door of Father Demetrius' study.

My shiny new picklocks, a Christmas present from Holmes, were in Mycroft's flat in London. Holmes' old ones did the job, and in minutes we were inside the room, which smelt comfortingly of books and faintly of coffee and incense.

Holmes stretched to remove the tube of maps from its high shelf, and carried it over to a wall of books, where he seemed to be perusing the titles. He moved, and after a while I heard a click, and a bank of shelves opened. We went through, he closed the door, and only then did he turn on his electrical torch.

We were in a tiny closet of a room perhaps eight feet by four, with a thin mattress on the floor and a couple of pots. The only air came from a ventilation grid the size of a hand. I tried not to feel claustrophobic.

Holmes had the maps out and was spreading them on the floor. I held the sides flat, and he paged through them until he came to what we sought, when he removed the others from the top of the stack and let them curl up tightly.

The city walls and a few landmarks were the only familiar shapes on this map. The Dome of the Rock, the Church of the Holy Sepulchre, and the Armenian monastery were there; the Tyropoeon Valley that had once bisected the city was sketched in with a pencil, a north-south dip that cut along the edge of the Temple Mount before the city literally grew up and filled it with the rubble and debris of its earlier incarnations.

And here, drawn in clear, sweeping lines, were the aqueducts.

The major one came from the south out of Bethlehem, taking a wide loop along the sides of the Hinnom Valley, around the Sultan's Pool to the south-west of the city walls, following the topographic lines back along the walls until finally, not far from the Dung Gate, its route crossed under the walls and into the city proper, following the curve of the Tyropoeon Valley until it reached the eastern half of David Street, one of the old boundaries of the changing city. There the line ducked due east, under the Bab es-Silsileh: under the Temple Mount. According to the map, before reaching the Dome of the Rock the aqueduct divided, one arm reaching down to fill the fountain known as the Cup, the other reaching up to trickle into the Birkat Yisrael, now a dry rubbish tip, once, perhaps, the miraculous Pool of Bethesda.

That upper arm excited my interest, for after the split at the gate to the Haram it turned due north, running between the Western Wall and the Dome of the Rock, less than fifty feet from where the Souk el-Qattanin became the Bab el-Qattanin, the Gate of the Cotton Merchants, which was the Haram entrance closest to the Dome itself.

Furthermore, there was another aqueduct, coming not from Bethlehem but from the Mamilla Pool to the west of the city. It ran under the Jaffa Gate, pausing to replenish the Patriarch's Pool near the Church of the Holy Sepulchre before continuing east in the vicinity of David Street towards the Haram. It too split, the northern half joining up with the upper arm of the Bethlehem aqueduct on its way to the Birkat Yisrael, the southern half crossing the Souk el-Qattanin and debouching into a bath just below the *souk*, the Hamman es-Shifa. This too was noted as a possible candidate for the Pool of Bethesda, in Father Demetrius' neat, tiny writing.

While I was gloating over all these riches, Holmes had whipped out his map of Palestine, which included a detailed street map of the city on the back, and was carefully duplicating the priest's marks, the lines for the aqueducts, the slope of the valleys, square cisterns and round fountains and shaded-in patches for built-over vaults. The Cotton Grotto, looking like a patch of spilt grey ink, reached down farther than I had imagined, half again the distance Jacob had suggested. It undermined the Moslem Quarter nearly halfway to the northernmost corner of the Haram, where lay Herod's fortress Antonia and the infamous Old Serai prison of the Turks, where the relatives of impoverished Arab diggers were beaten and Karim Bey had reigned supreme. The Old Serai, I saw from the notes Father Demetrius had made, was now being turned into a school.

I studied the jumble of signs and notations surrounding the Souk el-Qattanin, and tried to recall the details of past reading. Wilson's Arch was at the next Haram entrance down, but surely there was a shaft here somewhere? And wasn't there something odd about that bath? My knowledge of the city was quite good for the earlier periods, but anything more recent than the Crusades was a blank page.

'We need a Baedeker's guide, Holmes,' I whispered. He grunted, and continued with his copying.

It took an hour before, cramped and cold, we rose, rolled the maps, and prepared to leave the cubicle. Holmes switched off the torch, and we stood in the utter darkness for several minutes to let our eyes adjust before going back out into the study.

'How did you know this place was here?' I asked him while we waited.

'Demetrius showed me it. At the time it was a bit of a joke – he used to store good wine in here, the stuff that he did not wish to share with his parishioners. No doubt since then more valuable contraband has been hidden here. Ready?'

The hidden door clicked and we stepped back out into the room of books. Holmes walked through the blackness and I heard the roll of maps hit the shelf as I patted my way slowly towards the door. I reached it without mishap, but something seemed to have delayed Holmes, and I heard a faint, drawn-out rustling sound, as of fingertips running across an uneven surface.

'Close your eyes,' he ordered. I turned away, and my lids were briefly lit by a flash of light, instantly extinguished. When he joined me at the door, he found my arm and then I felt something being pressed into my hand: a little book, heavy for its size. I smiled, for I knew that on the red spine I should see the name Baedeker.

'Won't he miss it?'

'He has dozens. He hands them out to visitors, probably doesn't even know how many there are. Let us go.'

I thrust the guide-book inside my robe and we went out into the garden, ghostly in the light of the waning moon. I waited while Holmes locked the door, and we slipped out of the garden gate as silently as we had come. It was now about half past two, and my skin crawled with tiredness. I had forgotten to ask where we were going, but on the street he turned to the right, back in the direction of the inn, and I allowed myself a faint hope that the night might be over. I was not to know what Holmes had intended, however, because a few paces down the street a dark figure moved out from the edge of a building, and an instant later my ears registered a footfall behind us. I whirled, and saw another shape that nonetheless seemed familiar.

'You were surely not thinking of any interesting outings without us,' said Ali. The threat in his voice did nothing towards making me relax from the stance I had taken. Holmes, however, stood briskly upright and continued on his way, brushing past Ali, who stood belligerently in the centre of the alley. Mahmoud moved up from behind us.

'Of course not.' Holmes' voice trailed down the narrow way. We had no option but to follow him.

CHAPTER TWENTY-FOUR

ٱ

*Most Orientals regard the European traveller as a Croesus, and
sometimes a madman.
The traveller should be on his guard against the thievish
propensities of beggars.*
— BAEDEKER'S *Palestine and Syria,* 1912 EDITION

WE WERE LET IN BY the owner of the inn himself, and
went to Ali and Mahmoud's room, where we lit lamps,
drank the coffee the innkeeper brought up scarcely two minutes
after we had come in, and settled to business. Ali was simmering
with suspicion and aggression, Mahmoud was so stony I felt I
could strike a spark from him, and Holmes gave the impression
that he saw nothing out of the ordinary. In the face of all this
masculine antagonism, I sat back against the wall with my new
Baedeker's and opened it to the index.

Holmes tossed down three tiny cups of coffee in quick
succession, reached into his robe, and brought out pipe,

tobacco pouch, and map. He filled his pipe and put a match to it, allowing the other two to eye the worn, folded square, and when he had his pipe going and his audience seething, he thrust the stem between his teeth and leant forward to unfold the map onto the boards. When they had looked for a minute or two at his modifications to the printed sheet, he took the pipe stem from his teeth and tapped the paper with it.

'The good Father, all unknowing, has contributed to our knowledge of the city beneath our feet. Russell, would you be so good . . . ?'

I closed my little book and scooted forward, and explained the various lines, squiggles, and marks. Ali grew increasingly bewildered, Mahmoud increasingly interested. I then told them what I had learnt while working in the Souk el-Qattanin. I was amused at their expressions when I described my job. When I had finished, Ali protested.

'There are no roads beneath the city. This is not London.'

'Roads, no, but caves and tunnels, tombs and cisterns that may be connected up to form a virtual road.'

'These aqueducts,' Mahmoud spoke up. 'Are they not tunnels?'

'For a man the size of a cat, perhaps. But they can be enlarged, particularly in the sections north of the Dome where the pools they once filled are obsolete.'

'And this?' Ali asked, pointing to the grey ink stain.

'Solomon's Quarries. Also known as the Cotton Grotto.'

'They go nowhere,' said Ali dismissively.

'They go nearly a thousand feet under the city.'

'*Wa!* So far!'

'Have either of you been inside them?' asked Holmes.

Ali looked uncomfortable, but Mahmoud fingered his prayer beads thoughtfully. 'There were rumours,' he said, 'in the last days of the war, of a plan to destroy what your map calls the Antonia from underground. As I heard it, the British forbade the plot. They are sentimental about Jerusalem. However, I never paid the story much thought, since it was told me by Colonel Meinertzhagen. Do you know him? A complete madman, but a great warrior.'

'It is possible there has been a secret passage for millennia,' I said. 'It is said of King Zedekiah that he and all his soldiers fled by night "by the way of the gate between the two walls, by the king's garden." No-one knows just where they got out, although the king's garden was at the southern part of the city. And Josephus says something about one of the sons of John Hyrcanus being killed in an underground passageway near the Temple.'

Holmes tapped the pipe stem carefully against his teeth a few times, then reached into his robe for another piece of paper, laying it on top of the map. 'General Allenby's itinerary for the coming weekend,' he said. 'Meetings at Government House tomorrow; a ride into the desert in the afternoon, weather permitting; an intimate dinner with the troops followed by army amateur dramatics – the general is a brave man. But look at Sunday.'

We looked at Sunday, Holmes' scrawl of the information given him no doubt by the general himself on their way to the American Colony: breakfast with Governor Storrs; church services with the Anglicans; then at one o'clock in the afternoon, as a public appearance of good-will, the walk through the Haram es-Sherif with Governor Storrs and an impressive list of high-ranking officers and high-ranking officials among the Christian, Jewish, and Moslem communities. No rabbis, of course, not in the Moslem compound, but a handful of secular Jews had been included, and it was possible one or two rabbis would appear at tea in Government House afterwards. Two dozen names, virtually every shred of authority in Palestine, in one place, on Sunday afternoon, in the holiest site common to three religions.

The reminder was chilling: those people, in that place, with two hundred fifty pounds of explosive in the hands of a man like Karim Bey.

"'I will wipe Jerusalem as one wipes a dish,'" I murmured, "'wiping it and turning it upside down.'"

Mahmoud's lips moved soundlessly as his fingers continued to manipulate the beads, but Ali said forcefully, 'They must not go. Allenby must be made to cancel the meeting.'

'Karim Bey must be caught.' To my surprise it was Mahmoud who said it. 'Too, even if the men are not there, Bey will detonate the explosives regardless. The site is of greatest importance; taking the lives for him would be an extra.'

'I agree,' Holmes said.

'The Jews will be blamed,' I said slowly. 'If they lose no leaders, many will hold them responsible.' And another bloodbath would begin.

'No doubt Bey's intention,' said Holmes. His pipe had gone out; he struck another match and held it to the bowl, speaking around the stem. 'It is unlikely that Bey and his men are coming and going through the streets; at night, discovery is too dangerous, and during the day there are gossiping neighbours throughout the city. Either they come and go during daylight hours in a normally busy area or they come in a way that is unseen. In either case, we need to look at the cave.'

Ali's wince was minute, but perceptible, and unexpectedly endearing.

'Looking at it will not take all four of us,' Mahmoud said.

'I had the impression you did not wish to be left out of any little part of this investigation.' Holmes' face was smooth and without guile, although I knew he could not have missed Ali's apprehension at the thought of descending into the earth.

'We desire to be consulted. Ali and I will arrange the surveillance in the streets, while you and Amir go below. You do not intend to enter the grotto tonight, do you?'

'I should like to look at the entrance.'

I abandoned any hope of sleep that night.

Holmes and I had two scares crossing the bazaar in the small hours of Saturday morning. On the second we were forced to take to the roofs, but when we eventually reached the Damascus Gate, a pair of loud Yorkshiremen were standing guard. We retreated east to Herod's Gate and, finding that conveniently deserted, we slipped out of the city and worked our way back outside of the walls. However, uncovering the grotto proved hopeless at night with the moon into its final quarter and no chance to use lights: one tangle of brush growing over stone was much like another, and further complicated by an accumulation of rock fall and debris left during the years since the last tourist had entered Solomon's Quarries. We tried. For half an hour we beat the bushes (silently) for the iron-gated entrance to the grotto, but even Holmes had to admit defeat. Back at Herod's Gate we discovered that the two jovial Yorkshiremen had moved there. Breathing curses in various tongues we retreated to the Damascus Gate, found it unguarded, and entered the city – only to be spotted by a patrol and forced to take to the rooftops again. Trying hard to look on the positive side of this harassment, I decided it proved, at any rate, that anyone bent on criminous activity would have a difficult time moving men and equipment about the city at night.

It was five in the morning before we passed back through the gates of the inn, which was already beginning its day, the breakfast fires going strong. We were heavy of foot, our clothes and skin were torn from the bushes, and we both felt gaunt with hunger – Holmes looked positively grey in the light of the cook's paraffin lamp. We ate something hot, and fell into our beds just as the rest of the city was coming to life.

By light of day, on the other hand, the Damascus Gate proved quite a pleasant place. The afternoon sun sloped benevolently down on the graceful women with loads on their heads and illuminated the fiendish brambles that had done us such violence the night before. For the past two hours we had been sitting on our heels across from the city walls with a bag of pistachios on the ground between us, cracking nuts with our teeth and watching, with mingled amusement and apprehension, the activity in those bushes.

We had seen it immediately we came out of the gate: half a dozen Arabs swinging long knives, under the supervision of Jacob the archaeological adoptive son of the American Colony. He had since left, upon which the workmen promptly stopped work for a smoke. Eventually they had set again to hacking at the bushes, although with noticeably less energy than they had shown before.

Still, the top portion of the gate slowly appeared, and some of the men casually tossed their brush-knives away and took up spades. It was quite apparent that no-one had gone this way in some long time; however, we intended to, when darkness fell.

Jacob came back after a couple of hours, when the gate was almost clear. With his presence the rate of digging picked up again, and the iron door soon stood revealed. Jacob had a key, which he tried in the door. He tried it for so long that the Arabs' anticipation waned and they wandered away to smoke and gossip, keeping one eye on this man in European clothing bent over a keyhole, patiently twisting and wiggling. Every so often he would take up an oilcan and squeeze some oil into the keyhole, and wiggle it again, but finally, at about five in the afternoon, he gave up. Squeezing the oil liberally over hinges and hole, he gathered up his workmen and departed. As he walked his way along the busy road towards the American Colony, he passed three feet from where his dinner companions of the previous night sat, pistachio shells scattered around their feet, faces bent to the ground. Jacob paused; my heart stopped. A small coin landed in the lap of my robes; he passed on.

The mound of cut shrubbery Jacob's team had left made a good place for us to stash the caving equipment we had brought in our bags, just after dusk.

And the oil had worked a treat by the time Holmes got to work with the sturdiest of his picklocks, six hours later.

CHAPTER TWENTY-FIVE

ن

One quality of the human soul is the wish to know what is to
come, be it life or death, good or evil.
– THE *Muqaddimah* OF IBN KHALDÛN

THE UTTER ABSENCE OF LIGHT or sound pressed upon us
as if we had been immersed in a great black lake. I felt
the pressure of it on my eardrums, against my eyes, and it
was difficult to breathe. It smelt . . . dead. Cold and stale and
smelling of nothing more alive than raw stone. Not even bats
made their way in here. I nearly leapt out of my boots when
Holmes spoke.

'I don't hear a thing. I believe we may risk a light.'

My heart skittered about in my chest for a few beats, and
then it settled again. I cleared my throat and quoted in Arabic,
'"Take refuge in the cave, and Allah will have mercy on you and

bring about a kindly solution to your affairs.'" It was a poor attempt at whistling in the dark: The cavern swallowed the orotund phrases, giving them all the power and reverberation of a dried pea rattling about in a bottle. I continued more prosaically and in a smaller voice, 'I think going forward with no light would be the larger risk.'

The truth of this was demonstrated immediately he had the lamp going: The floor was pitted with holes, some of them both deep and abrupt. It was not a place to explore unprepared.

The cave we stood in was vast. Our lamps made small patches of light as we picked our way forward, only rarely reaching as far as the perimeter walls. Massive pillars had been left by the cautious stone-cutters millennia before, to support the immense weight of the cave roof and the city on top of that, although in one place the fallen litter was considerable, and the roof seemed to sag. Niches had been cut into the walls for the lamps of the quarrymen. The floor sloped continuously, in some places rapidly, towards what the brass compass I carried said was the southern end. We walked at a distance from one another, so as to examine the widest possible expanse of ground, but we reached the end having seen nothing other than stone and trickling water and a few Crusader crosses carved into the walls.

The cave ended in a chamber perhaps twenty feet square which demonstrated clearly the method used for extracting blocks of stone: chisel marks on the walls, several ledges left when the stone above had been cut away, one half-cut block, abandoned to eternity. One could not help speculating why it had been left. Interrupted by some invasion or other? Made unnecessary by peace? One stone more than was needed for the job at hand? Or was it just deemed unsuitable, the stone too soft and permeable, and the quarrymen gone elsewhere?

I sat on a stone ledge trying to distract my mind with these thoughts so as not to think about where I was, about the huge expanse of stone hanging over my head, yearning for the pull of gravity to re-unite it with its lower half, with me in the middle, about the continuous tremble of lorries and feet that contributed to the inevitable—

'Russell, I trust you are not about to succumb to an attack of the vapours.'

'Don't be ridiculous.' I stood and forced my eyes to focus. A thin layer of dust lay over everything (raised by falling stones, my brain whispered at me), including the shelf I had used as a seat. Holmes looked closely at the top of a free-standing block, poked once or twice at the surface, then turned to look at a hole in the wall behind him. I went over and examined the block. There was wax on it, the wax of numerous candles, but it was all covered with dust.

'Surely this isn't fresh?' I asked.

'From the guides, when they had tourist groups in here.' Holmes' voice echoed strangely, and when I turned I saw his head and shoulders emerging from the hole. 'Can you get in here, Russell?'

I eyed the black maw. 'Must I?'

'By no means, I shall be happy to try. Provided, that is, you agree not to make protestations of horror about the results on my back.'

'Never mind. I'll go.'

It was a tight and narrow hole, little more than a crack, too small to crawl through on hands and knees. Holmes boosted me up, and I pulled myself in, and I went less than four feet before scrambling out again to strip off the confining coat and *abayya,* leaving only the long, thin shirt and baggy trousers I wore underneath. The turban I left on, in the hope it might offer a degree of protection to my skull. I pulled myself in again, and wriggled, moved the torch a few inches, pushed with the toes of my boots, and wriggled some more. Occasionally the crack widened enough that I could nearly crawl; other times the walls closed in and I thought I should have to retreat. I inched forward perhaps as much as sixty feet, which seemed like miles, only to have my way blocked by a total collapse of the ceiling.

There was no way around it, or through, and I lay half on my side with the sweat in my eyes, and the fingers of panic that had been plucking at my mind suddenly grabbed, and squeezed me, squeezed me in the rock under the city where I lay, waiting for my light to go out, waiting to run out of air, waiting to be stuck, irrevocably.

In another half minute my rational mind would surely have given way to the panic and the horror that was pulling at me, urging me to fling myself against the confining walls and shriek, but Holmes must have heard the cessation of my scrabbling noises, because I heard his voice.

'Russell?' It bounced and echoed, but it was as revivifying as a hand from a lifeboat. I bent my neck and answered loudly in the direction of my feet.

'Yes?' My voice quavered a bit.

'Russell,' he said, slowing his voice so that the echoes did not obscure the words. 'It would be very inconvenient if I had to go and fetch someone to bring you out.'

My growing panic flipped instantly into fury. *Inconvenient, is it?* By God, I'll give him *inconvenient.*

I pushed my body backwards, drawing the torch with me, pushed again, drew the light, pushed and scooted the yards back to one of the wider places where, with a flexibility I had not known I could summon, I managed to do a kind of slow, sideways somersault, and made the remainder of the journey facing out.

At the end of the tunnel Holmes took the torch from my hand, put it on the ground, and hauled me bodily out and set me on my feet. I staggered a bit when he let go of me, but I was glad he had taken his hands from my shoulders, because I could feel myself – not trembling, but certainly vibrating. He thrust a water bottle into my hands, and I drank deeply.

'God,' I muttered under my breath. 'The one time I could actually do with strong drink. Oh, nothing. Holmes, that tunnel's a bust. It was certainly used at one time – there are chisel marks all along it – but the roof is down after about twenty yards, with no side openings.' I shivered, and when Holmes handed me my *abayya*, it occurred to me that I was damp with fast-cooling sweat. It was comforting to know that my reaction was at least in part physical.

Holmes took his lamp and went off into the main cave while I dressed, drank a bit more water, and chewed at some leathery dried fruit. All of which made me feel considerably more substantial.

'So,' I said when he returned. 'What next?'

'We have eleven hours.'

I looked at him bleakly. It seemed hopeless. We had agreed with Mahmoud that if he did not hear from us by twelve-thirty, Allenby's one o'clock meeting with the officials of army and town would be moved elsewhere and the Haram cleared. Lives would be saved, although the resultant turmoil from the destruction of the site alone was bound to be violent.

I stood up. 'Then we'd best be going.'

We left the small chamber, which seemed almost homely in comparison with the main cave. On the way out I saw on the wall, in addition to the crosses and some truly ancient Hebrew graffiti, the Square and Compass of the Freemasons. A busy little place, this, over the ages.

Holmes stood in the cave with his lamp held over his head, peering into the gloom. 'It would be difficult to discern the tracks of a rampaging elephant, in these circumstances,' he complained. 'Still, we can only try. You take that direction, Russell.'

We split up, and began to work our way in opposite directions around the outside walls of the cave, down the finger-shaped extensions and back into the palm of the central cave, down and around. There was less dust here, aside from places where the ceiling was beginning to disintegrate, but some of the pits were dangerous, portions of the floor slick with insalubrious seepage from above. I went carefully, watching for anything out of place, but there were no footprints, no signs of recent digging, no convenient mound of rubble with an arrow in it pointing to the Souk el-Qattanin.

I met up with Holmes before I reached the iron-gated

entrance, as my direction had possessed the greater number of fingers. He simply shook his head.

There was nothing for it but to quarter the expanse of the central cave, a process both painstaking and painful: two or three cautious steps forward, examining the ground, then shining our electric torches upwards and craning our necks at the nearly invisible dome of the roof, in hopes of seeing – what? A pair of waving legs protruding from a hole?

Two o'clock passed, two-thirty, and then, at nearly three in the morning, I heard my partner's unmistakable 'Ha!' of triumph. I took my eyes from the rock overhead and trotted across the uneven ground towards his lamp.

He was looking down at a patch of rock like any of the acre or two I had already scrutinised; it took me a moment to see what he had found. Then I dropped to my heels and held the torch directly over it.

'Soil!' I said in surprise. The clot was dry, and crumbled at my touch. Holmes bent down and brushed it into an evidence envelope, which I thought an incongruous thing for him to be carrying in this place, but I suppose habits die hard.

'From a boot-heel,' he said, and turned his attention and his torch on the ceiling. He began to pace up and down again, his light bouncing over the rough stone overhead, so I too returned to my own patch. Twenty minutes later I heard another 'Ha!'

He was studying the ground again, standing by the base of one of the supporting columns. Upon joining him, I could see no trace of soil there, but the dust and small stones that littered the whole floor had been scraped away to the underlying rock in two long patches slightly larger than a hand, approximately sixteen inches apart, and a broader patch between them, on the side away from the column. I shone my torch upwards.

A door, cunningly hidden, was nestled into a deep hollow next to the column. It was a small door and very old, its black wood set with numerous rusted iron studs. The marks on the ground were from a ladder that had been let down here.

However, there was no sign of soil on the stone floor.

'Access to a house in the Arab Quarter,' I said.

'I am relieved to see you did not leave your wits behind in that crack in the wall,' he replied drily. I followed him back to where he had found the lump of soil, and we began a minute examination of the rock on an imaginary line drawn between the door, the bit of soil, and the cave wall.

They had been careful. I found one more trace of earth ten feet away towards the wall; Holmes found two places where someone might or might not have swept something from the cave floor. It was now quarter to four. We stopped for a rest, and Holmes lit his pipe, staring fiercely at the bland expanse of rock.

'This caution is suggestive,' he said eventually. 'The man is little concerned with the intelligence of others, so he rarely bothers to cover his tracks in any but the most cursory of manners. In the past, he has not seriously believed that anyone would think to look for him, regarding himself as invisible to mere mortal eyes. Now, however, he has become careful. I wonder if he would demonstrate the same concern had he not had a prisoner taken from under his nose.'

'I was thinking about that yesterday, how Bey just takes whatever he comes across that might come in useful, regardless of the alarm it might raise. Although of course he's right, there is very little chance, given the chaotic state of the country at the moment, that the authorities would have noticed anything until it was too late. Assuming he's reasonably discreet and knows the dress and language well enough to fit in, who would have thought to look for a mastermind behind the disruptions? Allenby was only beginning to have his suspicions, and even Joshua, who I think is considerably more competent than he chose to appear, was only half-convinced.'

'He seems to vacillate between caution and carelessness, depending on which aspect of his unbalanced mind is in the ascendant mode. Now I think we have wasted enough of—'

'Holmes, no!' He froze in the action of preparing to knock his pipe out against a rock. 'Your pipe. Puff it again.'

Obediently he put the stem back between his lips and drew rapidly on it three or four times. The smoke moved.

In an instant he had knocked the half-burnt dottle out and taken a candle from our caving bag, lit it, and held it at arm's length. It flickered faintly, then burnt straight and unmoving. I took another candle from the bag, lit it from his, and we both moved over to the wall.

It was a slow business, holding the candle, waiting for the air from our movements to settle, and, when the flame stood straight upright, moving it again. Then, when Holmes and I were only a couple of feet apart, my flame dashed sideways and blew out. I nearly whooped for joy, until I saw where the air current was coming from: beneath a huge, half-cut block.

We lay on our bellies and shined our torches at the narrow

gap between the block and the floor. It appeared no more than a hand's-width high. There was no tunnel visible on the far side of the hole, only rock.

'It doesn't go anywhere, Holmes.'

'It must.'

'I know you wish it to, but—'

'Russell, use your eyes.'

I followed the beam of his light, and realised that of course there would not be cobwebs in a cave with no flies, that what I was seeing were threads and hairs.

And several clods of soil along the sides of the rock across from us.

'But there's solid rock! I can see it.'

'I do not care what your eyes tell you; I tell you they must have come this way.' He got to his knees and began to remove his *abayya*, but I stopped him.

'I'll go first. If I get stuck, you can pull me out by my feet. I'm not certain I could do the same for you.'

Again I stripped down to trousers and undershirt, and for the second time that night I inserted my body into the jaws of the earth, knowing in my bones that at any instant the earth would bite down.

Only it didn't. What was not visible from the cave was the curvature of the floor. When I pushed under the rock, I found myself going down into a recess, then up again, and when the slope returned to the height of the cavern floor, I had cleared the back side of the block. I moved the beam of my light across the surrounding walls, and found I was standing in a nice large, tidy tunnel, not quite tall enough for me to stand upright, but sufficiently tall and wide to walk in. I got down on my knees and put my face to the hole.

'There's a tunnel here, Holmes. Plenty of room, the floor drops away. Push the equipment through in front of you.'

I crawled in again, as far as my hips, and took the bag and lamps as he passed them through. I dressed again as Holmes slithered through gingerly and rose to admire the neatly carved rock.

'Very nice,' he said.

'A back door?' I mused. '"The king with his soldiers fled by night."'

'May we go? Or do you wish to take measurements for a research paper?'

'After you.'

The tunnel ran south for fifty yards, then gave a jog and turned slightly east. Holmes kept an eye on the compass and map, but it seemed we were making a more or less straight run for the Haram. Keeping in mind the sly entrance, we paused often to peer into uneven bits, particularly those near the floor. We found no alternatives, only the tunnel, five and a half feet high and something less than three across, gouged through living rock by men with chisels two thousand and more years ago.

Abruptly, the smooth track was broken. The tunnel stopped, turned due east, took six steps down, then turned south again. It would appear that there had been two teams of diggers here, as there were at Hezekiah's Tunnel in Siloam, teams who missed each other slightly and had to compensate with a ten-foot linking tunnel and half a dozen steps to join the two. The more eastern half continued north past the meeting place for a dozen or so feet, clearly the extent of one crew's work before the diggers realised they had overshot their mark. That truncated section of tunnel had been used to deposit a great heap of rock and slops of soil, some of it so recently added that the pile was still trickling water into the passage.

It did not look quite the same as the soil that had been added to the Souk el-Qattanin, but Holmes had no doubts. He held up a pinch of the stuff between his fingers and brought it up to his eyes. 'I believe a microscopic examination would show this to be identical to the traces in the basket of the widow of Abdul the Ugly,' he said, and wiped his fingers on his robes. I did not think it worth the effort to argue.

We continued along the featureless tunnel, going steadily downwards, and had travelled perhaps one hundred and fifty yards from the cave when something in the air changed. Holmes stopped, played his light ahead into the passage until it disappeared, then turned it off. The blackness once again closed around us.

'Hear anything?' he whispered after a while.

'No. But the air smells different.'

'Does it? You're right.'

Other than the occasional whiff of a leaking privy, the only smell the tunnel had contained thus far was from the heap of damp soil back at the join of the two tunnels. This smell was similar, sharp and slightly rotten; not offensive, just earthy, particularly after hours of nothing more organic than naked stone.

We went on with even greater caution than before. After a

time I decided that yes, I heard a sound, but it was not clear enough to determine what it was, beyond a faint flutter against the inner membranes of the ear.

Without warning, the tunnel came to an end, to all appearances debouching halfway up a stone wall. Peering over Holmes' shoulder, I glimpsed water below us, black water with no way of telling its depth. Into it water dripped steadily from several places, a continuous, musical echo that explained the unidentifiable sounds in the tunnel. There was also, somewhere, an opening to the sky above: I smelt bats.

Holmes drew back and handed me the torch; I shined it into the space ahead of us. To our left, massive stone arches held up a vaulted ceiling, with a similar flooded room beyond. Stones protruded from the wall around us at regular and rising spaces to form a stairway climbing over our heads. The wall to our right was featureless except for the very tops of three nearly submerged arches, much shorter than those on our left. I pulled my head in and whispered to Holmes.

'Up the stairs?'

'And to the surface, after all the effort they went to to remain hidden? Not likely. The stairs are for general access.'

'Why? What is this place?'

'A rain cistern.'

'It's huge. And ancient.' Herodian, even – but of course: this would be Herod's vast cistern, the rock from which went to rebuild the tower at the corner of the Temple Mount, forming the fortress called the Antonia (after Herod's friend Marc Antony). Somewhere down here, according to Josephus, in a dark underground passageway between the tower and the Temple, Antigonus, the brother of Aristobulus I, was assassinated. 'We must be at the foot of the Antonia,' I said, and reached for my compass. Holmes stopped me.

'It's approximately the right distance. Let us try those low arches.'

Before I could object he had hoisted his skirts and lowered himself into the dank water. It came barely to his knees. I handed him the bag, removed my boots, and followed him.

The rock underfoot was slick and dropped dangerously off to the left, but it was solid and fairly even. Holmes was leaning over to examine the first of the nearly submerged arches on our right, and as I waded towards him I was struck by how closely he resembled an old-fashioned housewife looking under the furniture for a mouse, her skirts hiked up and her head covered by a scarf. I began to giggle, and he turned and shushed me in irritation, which only made it worse. I snorted into the palm of my hand and dropped one of my boots into the water, and only with difficulty, blinking the tears from my eyes, followed Holmes through the middle arch and into the passage beyond. I pulled myself up onto the dry shelf, sat down, and took a deep, shaky breath. Prolonged stress can take the oddest outlets.

Chapter Twenty-Six

The youths sought refuge in the Cave, saying 'Allah will have mercy and bring us out of this ordeal.'
— THE QUR'AN, *xviii:io*

Sober now, I pulled on my boots and crawled down the narrow shaft after Holmes. From here on there was no neat passageway carved into the rock, no single track without choices. We were now in the position of creeping from one unpleasant hole to another; twice, we took wrong turnings that ended in a tomb or cistern leading nowhere. Fortunately, our predecessors had done a fair amount of clearing. Often we could choose the proper length of aqueduct or entrance to a collapsed street by the piles of rubble they had left at the entrance. They were not hiding their tracks. The farthest they had carried their clearings was from the tunnel entrance at the Antonia cistern to the abandoned scrap of tunnel at the meeting place of the two teams of diggers off the grotto, a distance of some one hundred feet, and that they had been forced to do lest someone notice the addition of several cubic yards of muck in the cistern. Now they just shovelled the rock and soil to one side or into the nearest hole.

We were going south-east, the compass assured us, parallel to the Haram, but the journey was far from the calm walk through rock tunnels with which we had begun: into a broken tomb and up some steps; a squeeze through a tumble of immense and terrifyingly precarious fallen stones; under a column (braced by some very inadequate-looking planks); a sheer drop into a nice dry Mediaeval tank and a scramble up the other side; into an ominously snug bit of aqueduct that I should never have entered had I not known it had been recently traversed by others; on our bellies across an utterly unexpected segment of Roman roadway, its stones scored to save horses from slipping; through an intact doorway and across half of a room with a mosaic pavement and scorched plaster walls that seemed to be someone's cellar; through a trickle of water that appeared oddly like a stream, which I judged to mark the long-submerged Tyropoeon Valley; down a shaft and through a bit of Solomonic masonry; picking our way along the ledge that ran around yet another cistern . . .

It was a nightmare journey. To save our torches we were using a lamp, and only one so as to conserve paraffin. The compass was useless, as we never progressed in the same direction for more than a few feet. We were wet to our thighs with slimy, musty-smelling water from a misjudged cistern, my head was throbbing, Holmes was moving in a stiff manner I knew all too well, there was a disagreeable number of complacent rats living down here, and at each step forward the chance that we would simply stumble into the arms of our enemies grew greater.

Worse, time was passing. The city above us was awake now; half an hour earlier we had been startled by the clop of shod hoofs ten feet over our heads as we went under a lop-sided archway that was holding up the paving stones. Once or twice we caught glimpses of daylight, and the silence of the depths was no longer absolute.

At eight-thirty I flung myself down on a flat stone. 'I must stop, Holmes. For ten minutes.' I had not slept for more than a dozen hours in the four days since we had left the Wadi Qelt, and I did not sleep then, but neither was I entirely conscious. Holmes lowered himself slowly onto the floor of whatever this wardrobe-sized space was and leant back gingerly against plaster that had been flaking since the Crusaders captured the city. I closed my eyes and we listened to the vibrations of feet and iron cart wheels.

After five minutes Holmes took out his pipe. I nearly roused myself to object, then decided, The hell with it. The scent of tobacco was a common enough thing, and could enter the nether reaches from any place.

After too few more minutes I heard the familiar sound of the revolver being inspected and given a cursory wipe, then the rustle of the bag. I sighed, and sat up to receive a swallow of the water and a handful of nuts.

'We're going to be down here forever, Holmes,' I said drearily. I had intended it to be a dry jest, but it came out a flat

369

statement; at least there was no fear in it. I was too exhausted to worry about the roof caving in on me any more.

He spat a date pip into his hand. 'I have had failures before, but none quite so spectacular as the Rock of Abraham flying into the air.'

'You haven't had many failures.'

'Too many.'

'Such as?'

'This is a delightful conversational topic you've chosen, Russell. No, no; you wish to know my failures. Very well, let me think. I have had at least four men come to me for help, only to be murdered before I could do a thing for them. Granted, I later solved the murders, but that hardly mitigates the fact that from my clients' point of view, the cases were not precisely successful. Irene Adler beat me, although that was a silly enough case. And that one with the submarine boat plans, what did Watson call that tale of his? Scott something? Howard?'

'Bruce,' I said. 'Partington. And that wasn't a failure, you did retrieve the plans.'

'I might as well have burnt them, for all the good it did. Twenty-five years ago, that was, and how many submarine vehicles did Britain have in the water during the war? We left the depths of the sea to the U-boat.'

'You think Germany stole the plans later after all?'

'I believe those plans are sitting in the War Office somewhere with a thick layer of dust on them. Yes, I do recall that story now – it also began as an act of treason by a government clerk. Wasn't that the one into which Watson inserted some romantic claptrap about a rose?'

'I think that was in the story about the naval treaty,' I said.

'Was it? What does that matter? Why on earth are you talking about this nonsense?' He stood up and began to shovel things back into the bag.

'I didn't—'

'On your feet, Russell. Your present surroundings are bringing out an unpleasantly morbid streak in you.'

'My present—why? Where are we, aside from being buried alive?'

'You are in a tomb, Russell. I believe you've been stretched out on top of a sarcophagus.'

Our obstacle course continued, turning west, south, occasionally doubling back north, but maintaining a general direction along the Haram. I thought we must have come right through the city, but Holmes said no, we had not even reached David Street, some three hundred and fifty yards (on a direct line) from the Antonia cistern. We went on, and on.

Then in a dry, snug space created by the fall of some huge quarried stones we found a cache of tinned goods, some of them still in their shipping crates. They were thick with dust, those that hadn't been kicked to one side, though their labels were still bright.

'I thought so,' Holmes muttered. 'Bey must have caught himself some smugglers and learnt the route from them. Under interrogation in the Old Serai, no doubt, during the war. Food was scarce, and smugglers sprang up by the dozen – we may find who they were when we investigate the house with the cellar door above the Cotton Grotto. Bey tucked the route away in the back of his mind, waiting until he might need it. By the looks of it, he's not been down here more than half a dozen times.' He stopped, and held up a hand. 'Did you hear a voice?' he asked, then turned out the lamp.

I strained my ears, and was about to say that I hadn't, when it came again, a high-pitched and unintelligible cry that wafted, not from the street overhead but out of the hole ahead of us. It sounded like a child.

Silently, and using brief bursts from the torch, we gathered our things and began to sidle down the passage, in this case a narrow space between two walls, or rather, what had once been walls and were now foundations. The child sound came and went, and another sound as well: the trickle of moving water. It grew more distinct, and then Holmes stopped.

'We've run out of floor,' he breathed at me, and, curling his free hand around the torch to make a tight beam, he flicked it briefly at the ground and again at the space ahead of us, and then we stood in the dark and thought.

There was no space ahead. At our feet, or rather, about four feet below our feet, was a masonry channel with sluggish, unclean-looking water in it. The large, flat covering stone had fallen into the channel, and it was the faint riffling noise from the water as it dribbled over the stone that we had heard.

The voices were definitely travelling down this channel, and now that we were above it, they became clearer: still no words, not that I could make out, but they separated themselves into two, possibly three children, calling and shouting at each other. The normality of the sound was completely unexpected, and I racked my brain to think where . . .

'The bath!' I said aloud. Ignoring Holmes' shushing noises, I tried to pull the recollection of my feverish reading of the Baedeker's guide. I whispered, 'This must be the Hamman es-Shifa. It's a big pool of rainwater set deep in the ground just south of the Souk el-Qattanin. It has a channel leading out of the south-western end of it, three feet by five, something like that.'

'Do you wish to investigate, or shall I?'

'I'll go,' I said reluctantly.

'I must say I am coming to appreciate this system,' he remarked, the humour in his voice clear despite the low volume. 'Why did it never before occur to me to have a vigorous young assistant to do what the Americans call my "dirty work"?'

'I'm your partner, not your assistant,' I snapped. 'And you'll have to let me past.'

'There's a foothold on the other side; I'll perch there. Ready?'

'Just a moment.' It was not easy to choose between letting myself into the water with no clothes, thus reserving a source of relatively dry warmth for after my immersion, or with clothes on, so as to keep the filthy walls away from my skin. In the end I couldn't face complete nakedness, so I left my long, loose undershirt on, and dropped everything else into a heap. Holmes shot the light on and stepped forward onto the channel's opposite side wall; I eased myself down into the freezing water and went instantly numb.

'Do you need the torch?' he asked.

'Actually, there's a bit of light in one direction. I'll go that way first.' There was light, beyond a bend in the channel, and I made for it, trying hard to keep my face above the water even if it meant rubbing the back of my turban along the greasy stones overhead. I came to the bend, and I was so entranced by the slice of light that beamed at me from fifty feet away and the simple noises of the two children splashing and shouting that I nearly missed the concealed opening.

What caught my eye was a chip, the fresh gleam of broken stone amidst the black-green slime that covered every surface. I could not see into the hole, but I did not need to. I went back to retrieve Holmes.

Once safely inside the hidden entrance, we dried ourselves off as best we could, using the cloth bag we carried, though I abandoned my undershirt in the tunnel and wore just trousers and *abayya*.

We also abandoned some of our caution. Holmes lit the lamp and we went on, faster now. This was another patch of actual passageway, perhaps built as an alternative to the channel, but higher and therefore dry. It ran in the same direction, and then, where I estimated the bath would be, turned right, then left, then in a short time right again. The compass told me I was facing east: We were nearing the Dome of the Rock.

Holmes halted again. I craned to look over his shoulder, first at the floor, then at a piece of wood covering a hole in the roof over our heads. There was a great deal of soil on the floor ahead of it, beginning directly under the hole. Two marks on the ground, the twins to those we had found beneath the door in the grotto, marked where the feet of a ladder had stood. There was no sign of the ladder here either, but whatever they were clearing, it was here, into the Souk el-Qattanin directly above our heads, that they had rid themselves of the debris from this final portion of their path. The presence of the British weaving sheds in the *souk* must have proved an annoyance, forcing them to haul their equipment all that long way under the city from the Cotton Grotto, but once they were here, the soil from the tunnel ahead of us could be easily disposed of in the streets above, and the occasional solitary man could find entrance from the *souk*.

There was no time to search the overhead access. We were almost under the wall surrounding the Haram es-Sherif, and I was intensely aware of how close we were to the Rock that is the heart of the city, the stone that had felt the touch of the Ark of the Covenant, of Father Abraham and his bound son Isaac, of the Prophet Mohammed and his legendary horse. The Talmudic saying, the Rock covers the waters of the Flood, ran through my mind over and over again, along with the Moslem one that says the Rock is the gate to hell. If we did not uncover two hundred fifty pounds of explosive in the next ninety minutes, we might well find that both traditions were true.

There were fresh footprints in the spilt soil, fresher than the two sets of boots that trod each other, back and forth, into obscurity. In two places, water had oozed down the rocks and turned the soil into mud, and in each of those a pair of new boots had walked, once in each direction, less than twenty-four hours before. It had probably been in the still hours of the night, when a twelve-hour timing device could be set to go off at the moment Allenby and his companions would be in the Haram. While we had been searching for one end of the long and laborious path under the city, Bey or one of his men had come and gone through the Souk el-Qattanin at the tortuous path's short end.

Unfortunately, in neither patch did he step on top of the previous mark, so we could not be absolutely certain that he was not even now waiting at the far end of the tunnel. Holmes doused the lamp, handed it to me, and took up his torch again.

We came upon the source of the soil that had been deposited into the Souk el-Qattanin: A length of roof had given way. Large quantities of rock and soil had been cleared and a few perfunctory wooden supports added to hold up the ceiling.

It is almost exactly three hundred feet from the Bab el-Qattanin – the gate into the Haram from the Cotton Bazaar – to the Dome of the Rock, and we crept, as silent as shadows and with the bare minimum of light, expecting at any instant to be met by sudden violence.

A little less than halfway we came upon the upper arm of the Bethlehem aqueduct, what was left of it. It obviously no longer went anywhere, for the water had no hint of movement about it, and smelt stale beyond words. We went on, under the Haram es-Sherif now, beneath the platform on which the Dome is set, where Allenby was due to make a speech of brotherhood in less than two hours. Holmes shone the light into every cranny, even pushed at rocks that might possibly conceal the dynamite, thinking it possible that the site for the bomb was here, but there was nothing.

On into the dark we pressed, torn between urgency and caution, between the need for light and the danger of discovery, forty yards, twenty (Holmes had the pistol in one hand now, the torch in the other), and then with a shock like an internal explosion we were looking at the end of the tunnel, where the walls bulged out into a small circular room. There was nothing there.

Until we took two steps into the room, and saw the hole in the floor, and what it held.

An explosive reaction is a curious business. Set loose on an open hillside, a charge will billow out in roughly equal proportions on all sides, and quickly dissipate. Confined, for example inside a gun barrel, all its energy is forced to find release in a single direction, and is thereby vastly magnified.

This man knew his explosives. Karim Bey had burrowed laboriously down into the rock floor of the chamber to direct his charge. He had then piled heavy slabs of rock high around the edges of his hole, shaping them to focus the blast directly upwards. Without that preparation, the explosive force would have shaken the Dome, stripped it of its mosaic tiles, and perhaps even weakened it enough to bring it down. With it, Holmes' vision of the sacred Rock popping into the air like a champagne cork was all too vividly possible.

I lit the lamp and hung it from a nail that probably had been put in the wall for that purpose, and when I turned, Holmes was lying on the stones, his upper half suspended over the mechanism as his fingers traced diagrams over the tangle of wires below, trying to sort out what went where. I took the torch from him, directing it to where his fingers pointed. The clock hand that would trigger the thing was alarmingly close to its mark, and I tried to comfort my racing heart by telling myself that Bey would have used only a high-quality clock, one that would be quite accurate. In truth, though, it was just as comforting to know that a prayer here was said to be worth a thousand elsewhere.

After several thousand of my fervent prayers, Holmes sat up and took out his pipe. The burning lamp in the corner was bad enough, but his flaring match made my stomach turn to ice.

'Shall we go for Ali? Mahmoud said he could handle bombs.'

'No need, this is quite simple,' he said calmly. 'There do not seem to be any tricks. I don't imagine Bey thought we would ever get this close.' Holmes set his pipe between his teeth and pawed through the bag, coming up with a little cloth bundle of tools which he untied and let unroll on a flattish rock to one side of the hole. He selected a small pair of snips from one of the bundle's pockets. Holding these in his right hand, he set his pipe down, then stretched out on his stomach over the heap of stone, his head in the hole and his feet sticking into the tunnel. He flexed the snips a few times as if to warm up an instrument, and I shifted around to ensure that the light from the torch fell directly on his work. Extending both hands out over the bomb, he began delicately teasing at the wires with the fingers of his left hand. When the wire he sought was free, he adjusted his right hand on the snips and began to move them over to the mechanism, and with that came three sharp cracks directly over our heads.

I nearly dropped the torch; Holmes nearly closed the snips convulsively on the wrong wire: Either would have been equally catastrophic. I gave a startled curse and stared upward, Holmes shuddered once with the effort of not reacting, and nothing else happened.

Slowly he drew back his hands and dropped his face into the

crook of his left sleeve to rub the sweat out of his eyes.

'It's a guide in the small cave beneath the Rock,' he said in an uneven voice, and cleared his throat. 'They pound on the floor like that to demonstrate the hollow sound.'

'Bloody hell.' My own voice was none too steady. 'Are they going to do it again?'

'Not until the next tour.' He took a deep breath, wiped his eyes again, and extended himself once more over the two and a half hundredweight of dynamite. His hands went still for a moment as he focussed, then he picked up the wire and cut it. As simple as that.

I began to breathe again. Holmes snipped and folded wires back, carefully removed the two detonators that, under the impetus of the clock's alarm hand, would have set off the explosion, and carried them down the tunnel. He came back and lowered himself onto the floor, resting his head back against the wall.

'I'm getting too old for this,' he said after a while.

'When I take off this turban, my hair will be white,' I said in agreement.

'I've lost track of the time,' he said, a considerable admission.

I took out the old silver pocket-watch I always carried. 'It's twelve-fourteen.'

'Can we reach Mahmoud in sixteen minutes?'

'We can try.'

'That's the spirit,' he said, half mockingly.

While Holmes swept the tools into his bag, I retrieved the lamp and then, feeling a little self-conscious, held it up so as to illuminate all the corners of the small enclosure, just in case.

But there was no sign of the Ark of the Covenant, hidden deep below the sacred Rock, no indication in fact that anyone had ever been here other than Karim Bey or his accomplices. I followed my partner as fast as we could go down the slippery stones, across the moribund aqueduct and on down the tunnel to the hole in the roof that led into the Cotton Bazaar. The door set into the access hole was neither locked nor actually a door, merely a square of blackened wood, which Holmes lifted easily from below and inched gently across the floor of the house above us.

Holmes prepared to boost me up, then he paused and handed me the revolver. 'They may have left a guard in the house. Be as silent as you can.'

I tucked the gun into my belt, put my booted toe into his joined hands, and was heaved up and effortlessly through the hole. I rolled instantly to one side; there was no response from the room. Taking the faltering torch from the inner pocket of my *abayya*, I looked around the filth of centuries that occupied the cellar, and spotted a ladder. I lowered it for Holmes, and once he was inside we brought it back up and put the covering back into place.

The house appeared empty. We picked our way up the worn stone steps, thick with the dribblings of the soil from the tunnel, and up above ground for the first time that day, into blessed daylight – though not much of it, given the architecture.

The actual door of the house was boarded over, but the windows, directly under which lay the oft-replenished piles of rubble I and the others had worked to clear, were neither glazed nor shuttered. The *souk* was empty of diggers today, as the soldiers took up more urgent duties elsewhere.

'Two of us in our current condition would be remarkable in the streets,' commented Holmes. 'Do you wish to go for Mahmoud, or shall I?'

'I'll go.'

I delayed my departure for thirty seconds to beat some of the encrusted mud from my robe and turn my *abayya* right side to, while Holmes searched for a marginally cleaner fold of the turban to pull over the rest. I went through the window, nearly bringing the rotten frame down with me, and into the pile of earth. Trailing clods of soil, I trotted away, and at the appointed corner found both Ali and Mahmoud, looking very tense. I slowed to a stroll, and as I allowed them to goggle at my condition I felt a grin grow, out of control and cracking the dirt across my face.

'Amir!' exclaimed Ali. 'What in the name of—'

'Are you injured?' interrupted Mahmoud. 'Where is Holmes?'

'We are both fine,' I replied, and when I came up to them I added quietly in English, 'The bomb is defused. You may tell General Allenby he should proceed.'

'By Allah, you cut that close,' said Ali. 'Where will you be?'

'Down the Souk el-Qattanin,' I answered, and he turned and sprinted off into the bazaar.

CHAPTER TWENTY-SEVEN

و

*And they schemed, and Allah schemed, but Allah is the master
schemer.*
– THE QUR'AN, *iii: 54*

'THE QUESTION IS,' SAID HOLMES, 'knowing what we do of
Karim Bey, will he remain in the vicinity to witness his
handiwork, or will he be well clear of it? Russell?'

'Why does this feel like an examination question rather than
a call for an opinion?' I wondered aloud. 'Of course he's going
to be where he can see the results. He'll probably even have
arranged to have a good view.'

'Would you agree?' he asked our two companions.

'Oh, yes,' said Mahmoud.

'Certainly,' said Ali. 'Karim Bey would not miss a moment
of suffering.'

Holmes plucked out his map and folded it to the city portion. 'Allenby and the rest plan to come into the Haram by the Moor Gate. They will visit El Aqsa Mosque, come by the Cup, cross to the Golden Gate, go back up and into the Dome for a few minutes before standing together on these steps,' he tapped the map, 'for speeches and photographs. Yes?'

'These things are planned carefully,' Mahmoud noted. 'It is the only way to be certain not to offend anyone.'

'And Allenby being who he is, it will run to time.'

'Undoubtedly.'

'Do they still expect to be in the Dome at one-thirty-five?'

'Yes.'

'The bomb timer was set for one-forty. Bey will allow perhaps ten minutes before he is certain that something has gone awry. There are a limited number of buildings from which the western side of the Dome can be seen. Therefore we ought to be able to see him as well. If, that is, you can get us four pairs of field glasses, a quantity of dark cloth, a handful of push-pins or small nails, and permission to take over these two small buildings here.' He touched the map.

Mahmoud said, 'I will ask for permission. Ali will make the necessary purchases.'

Ali nodded and the two men stood up, but Holmes put out a hand.

'Oh, and Ali? While you're in the bazaar, some food, tobacco, and another torch. Ours is finished.' Ali scowled at this menial assignment, but he left, with Mahmoud close behind him, through the window into the *souk*.

* * *

A hasty search of what remained of the house turned up nothing more than half a dozen worn baskets caked with soil and the few remains of meals that had not been carried away by rats. The only source of interior water was a puddle in the cellar where the rain from the street had drained – dirty, but still cleaner than our faces and hands. We wet and rinsed our handkerchiefs and scrubbed at our skin, and when that was as clean as we could make it we beat and rubbed our clothing and re-tied our head coverings. When we were through we looked like the poorest of *fellahin,* but at least we would not frighten the children or, more important, get ourselves evicted from the Haram.

Ali returned, with hot food, a flask of tepid coffee, four army field glasses, and a fresh torch. Holmes smoked a pipe, Ali a cigarette. Holmes cleaned the revolver again. I felt like sleeping for a week. It was ten to one.

Then Mahmoud's head appeared in the rotting window and we were back into action.

'I shall be repaying favours for twenty years,' he told Holmes. 'I hope you know what you are doing.'

'Have you a better idea?' Holmes responded mildly. 'Given the time at our disposal?'

Mahmoud shrugged and went down the alley into the *souk.* Ali followed a minute later; two minutes after that, Holmes and I were strolling towards the Haram. Our orange seller was back, I saw, the urchin with his criminally charming smile set to watch the house.

There was a stir brewing in the Haram, with British soldiers, Moslem guards, and the interested populace preparing for the entrance of the great ones. One at a time we peeled off from the crowd and took up places in two of the small buildings that lay around the great Dome – small mosques, perhaps, or classrooms. The soldiers standing near the buildings' entrances became blind for a moment, and I reflected that Mahmoud must have appealed to whomever was responsible for managing events within the Haram; to pull off such a slick operation in a scant half hour meant going straight to the top.

Keeping well back from the arched windows, Holmes ripped lengths off the black silk Ali had thrown inside and began to tack them up over the windows. We soon had all the north and west openings covered; there were no high buildings to the south.

Then began our watch. I was aware of the movement of Allenby and his entourage of official persons, growing to the south, approaching, then going off behind us to inspect the bricked-up Golden Gate through which the Messiah is supposed to enter. All the time we searched for sign of Bey. Our conversation went something like this:

'The curtain on the third window to the left of the minaret?'

A lengthy silence.

'A woman.'

Another silence.

'I thought I saw—No. Sorry.'

Pause.

'A brown robe on the roof at nine o'clock.' (Twelve o'clock being due north.)

A long pause while Holmes found the figure in his glasses, then, 'Too short.'

Silence for six minutes, aside from voices in the Haram.

'Black beard and spectacles, top floor, ten-thirty.'

'Half the population has a black beard,' I grumbled, but sought out the window, saw the man, leaning against the frame of the window, watching the unusual bustle below. Then he was joined by a small child, and when I saw him take the child up in his arms and point in our direction, I immediately discounted him, although Holmes kept an eye on him for a while.

The trouble was, the sides of buildings facing this way were now in shadow, and the buildings themselves, all of them stone, had such thick walls that the openings were often a foot or more deep, even at the upper storeys. All Bey had to do was stand back, wear dark clothing, and keep still. We ought to be beating down doors, not standing behind curtains with field glasses, I thought. Too late now. My ears registered the approach of voices, one of them Allenby's, and I stole a glance at my pocket-watch: twenty-eight minutes past one. They were early.

The meeting seemed to be going well, judging by the hum of voices as they passed by our doors. The translators were being kept busy.

A twitch of movement from high up, in a slapdash shed on top of a roof, one of a hundred such in sight, this one about one hundred twenty yards away on top of a large building just south of the Haram's north-western corner.

'Holmes—'

'I see it.'

I fiddled with the sights, praying for greater clarity. There was someone there, but no face yet. If it was he, he must be feeling the tension, as the group filed into the Dome nearly five minutes early. A white smear appeared, for an instant, not enough to see, but seconds later I saw Mahmoud, his hand casually raised to scratch under his turban and incidentally cover his face, walking down towards the next set of stairs, and a moment later Ali, his face unconcealed, walked past our curtained windows.

'You saw?' he hissed, and without waiting for an answer continued briskly to the upper steps.

They waited for us at the Gate of the Custodian. I glanced at my pocket-watch before I followed them out of the Haram: thirty-six minutes past one. Allenby and the others were still inside the Dome.

Once clear of the open space, we trotted after Ali and Mahmoud, who seemed to know precisely where they were heading. They turned right into el-Wad Street, then into a typical Jerusalem maze of minute passageways and stone walls and unlikely bits of garden before fetching up in an alleyway that ran along the side of a massive building.

'The Old Serai,' Ali explained briefly. 'Bey has come home, but it is not his prison any more, and he will have to come and go secretly. That door is one way. At that end of the alley is another, unless he has wings. You two stay here, and stop him if he comes out.'

The two men were gone before Ali finished the sentence, and although Holmes palpably ached to go with them, he could see the sense of it. He subsided, and we settled down beneath a tree to watch.

One-forty-two. No explosion from the depths, and no fleeing monk, only a piebald dog skulking over the stones.

One-forty-seven. Ali's head appeared over the parapet far above us. Even at the distance, his fury and frustration was visible and Holmes, seeing it, leapt to his feet and smacked his hand against his forehead.

'Wings!' he shouted. 'Of course he has wings – the rope he stole from the monastery! How could I be so stupid?' He snatched the torch from his robes, turned, and fled down the alleyway, back to el-Wad and, running now, dodging merchants and tourists, pious Jews and donkey carts, with church bells clattering in the air and me on his heels he pounded into the Souk el-Qattanin and, brushing aside the breathless excitement of the young orange seller, heaved himself up into the house and launched himself down the slick steps into the cellar. Ignoring the ladder that stood there, he dropped through the hole into the tunnel and began to run again, the torch in one hand, the revolver in the other. I started out on his heels, but without a torch I stumbled and banged into the walls and dropped farther behind. The bobbing light came to a bend and went abruptly still as, with a shout, Holmes flung himself to the ground. The echoes of his voice rang through the stone passageway, and I came up noiselessly and pressed myself against the inner curve of the wall to peer down the tunnel. Holmes lay nearly at my feet, his torch and gun both pointing steadily ahead of him at the figure of the bearded man in the monastic habit, now straightening incredulously and blinking at the light.

'You've lost, Karim Bey,' said Holmes.

'Who are you?' the false monk demanded, his voice imperious and shrill with fury.

'Russell, do you have your gun on him?'

'I do,' I replied, although the most dangerous weapon I possessed was my throwing knife, and Bey was both too far away and on the wrong side. The man's head jerked at the sound of my voice, and his hand went slowly away from the front of his habit. I heard noises behind me, and ducked my head to see first Ali, then Mahmoud tumble into the tunnel and begin to run in our direction, only to slow when their torches picked me out, my hand raised in warning. The three of us moved around the corner to stand behind Holmes' prostrate form.

Bey held his lamp up higher, and narrowed his eyes at Ali and me, whom he had never seen before. He similarly dismissed Mahmoud and was returning to Holmes when with a jolt his gaze flew back to the older man at my shoulder. I watched his wide, cruel mouth relax from the surprise of recognition into a smile distressingly close to intimacy, even affection. I could feel both of the men beside me react to that smile; I thought Ali would shoot him then and there, but Mahmoud seized his partner's arm and the gun stayed down. The man in the habit, still smiling, allowed his attention to return to Holmes, who lay unmoving, his gun pointing unwaveringly at the man's chest. Bey squinted down against the light of the torches, and then his eyes went wide and he took a step back.

'You!'

'I,' replied Holmes.

Silence fell, silence aside from the strained breathing of several people, which ended when Karim Bey seemed to make up his mind about something and gave an almost imperceptible nod. We all braced ourselves and Ali's gun went up again, but the man moved only his eyes, first to look at Mahmoud, then

Ali and me, and finally at Holmes. He held his gaze there for a long moment, studying his escaped victim, then lifted his eyes to a point over all our heads, raised his right fist, and swung it in towards his chest. I thought for a startled instant that Bey was giving some archaic form of salute until Holmes shouted 'No!' and started to scramble to his feet, but he was too late. When Bey's fist made contact with the front of his robe there was a muffled thump – not a big noise, but Bey flew backwards as if he'd been kicked by a horse. His lamp crashed to the floor and burst into flames, sending a great billow of burning paraffin down the tunnel towards us, but even as we flung ourselves around the corner, we could see the man in the monk's robes, crumpled against the wall of the tunnel, thrown there by the force of the spare detonator he had carried in his breast.

CHAPTER TWENTY-EIGHT

ى

Scholars are, of all people, those least acquainted with the methods of politics.
— THE *Muqaddimah* OF IBN KHALDÛN

W E CLIMBED OUT OF THE depths like four wraiths leaving a tomb, every bit as dirty and nearly as lifeless. Once we had lifted ourselves up into the derelict house in the Souk el-Qattanin, we collapsed to the floor with our backs against the walls, staring unseeing at the hole at our feet. Ali cursed monotonously, in Arabic and at least two other languages, and for once I was in full agreement. It was a victory, but not a clean one, and far from complete. Holmes, I knew, might look as if he was about to fall asleep, but his brain would already be worrying away at the sizeable question of how, with Bey dead, we were going to lay hands on his informant, and weighing the possibilities of it being the Government House clerk Bertram Ellison.

I dropped my head into my hands and waited for the ringing in my ears to subside, the flash spot in my vision to fade; all I could see was Bey's curious gesture, over and over again, that quasi-military salute with which he had gone to his death. That we-who-are-about-to-die-salute-you sort of gesture.

And I could not reconcile the salute with the man's scorn for his victims, neither the intimacy with which he had run his eyes over Mahmoud's scar nor the surprise on his face when he recognised Holmes. And surely a slap would have been a more effective way to set off the detonator, not the smaller surface of the fist.

And—

I shook my head. This was sheer phantasy, akin to augury or the reading of a crystal ball. What difference did it make if he slapped or he pounded? How could I know if the gesture meant anything to him beyond proud defiance?

But he had looked *up*, beyond us all. And his back had straightened. And his elbow had been raised to bring the fist straight on. Drawing himself up to meet death? Or . . . or a last, half-humorous salute to an unseen captain?

God, I thought, I'm losing my mind. Mahmoud is going to look down his nose at me and Ali will laugh in harsh scorn, but I have to say this.

'Holmes?'

'Yes, Russell.'

'Are we certain that Bey was the leader here?'

Ali jeered and Mahmoud looked, and Holmes leant back and closed his eyes. I persisted.

'He recognised you just now, but he did not know who you really are. And he certainly did not know me for anything other than an Arab boy. He had no clue that he was facing Sherlock Holmes and Mary Russell.'

'Because his information was incomplete.' He sounded so tired.

'But why? Was it because his informant didn't know? Or could it have been because his commander didn't care to tell him?'

'Russell . . .'

'It doesn't fit, Holmes,' I continued desperately. 'Everything we know about Bey makes it unlikely that he would suddenly decide to become political. He was more than satisfied with his position in the Old Serai, torturing prisoners and . . . well.' I thought perhaps I ought to abandon that line of argument. 'He seems to be in two places at once, killing Mikhail one night and the *mullah* halfway across the country the next; he is both a planner and spontaneous, cautious and heedless. You said yourself that he seems to be of two minds. I merely suggest that he is that in fact.'

'What Amir says makes a good deal of sense,' said Mahmoud. I turned and stared at him in disbelief.

'So you suggest that instead of merely cleaning up the rest of the gang,' Holmes said, 'we should be looking out for the other head. Perhaps the – if I may use the word – mastermind.'

'It is a valid hypothesis, Holmes,' I said. To my relief, he smiled.

'Very well. In which case, I think we ought to move quickly. In my experience, master criminals, political or otherwise, tend not to wait about for one to catch them up.'

* * *

The one glaring unexplored strand in this tangle was the house in the Moslem Quarter that had been used by Bey and his men to bring in the larger pieces of equipment, the tools and explosives that they had not dared carry through the Souk el-Qattanin. That heavy, iron-studded door in the roof of the Cotton Grotto opened into a house, and the occupants of that house had to have some part in the plot.

Unfortunately, there was no way of matching our knowledge of the grotto with the map of the streets overhead, not with any precision. Holmes took out the thin, damp, much-abused map and spread it out delicately on the floor. With purpose, a degree of energy returned to our little band.

After some thought, we decided that the house must be on the south side of Haret es-Saadiyeh, possibly in the vicinity of a cul-de-sac alley that cut into the block of buildings. We could, of course, turn the entire search over to Allenby, leaving his soldiers and police to seal off the area and do a house-by-house search, but none of us seriously considered that option; in that we were agreed.

We did need an authority figure, however, to keep us from being arrested for loitering or house invasion by an over-zealous soldier. All three of us looked at Holmes.

'Do you still have that uniform, Holmes?' I asked.

He sighed. 'I regret to say I do.'

'Then you can be responsible for keeping the police off our backs.'

'While you . . . ?'

It was my turn to sigh. 'While I get into the grotto and knock on that door. Loudly.'

'Very, very loudly,' said Mahmoud. He and Ali (particularly Ali) looked pleased at this division of labour, and I reflected that I, too, would much prefer to be assigned the task of standing on a street corner or roof top, waiting to catch the fleeing rats that my subterranean pounding would, with any luck, dislodge.

'Why do men always get the fun jobs?' I complained, and took out my pocket-watch. 'What time should I begin?' I looked at the timepiece, then held it unbelieving up to my ear. It had not stopped; it was barely half-past two. Allenby would still be at the Haram, talking.

'Forty minutes if I run,' Holmes answered.

Even considering the diminutive nature of the Old City, I thought that forty minutes would have him shedding *kuffiyahs* and doing up uniform buttons as he trotted down the steps of the David Street bazaar.

'Shall we say fifty?'

'Forty-five, Russell.'

'Very well.' As we all stood to go, I added pointedly, 'I trust that one of you will let me know when I can stop pounding.'

'*Insh'allah,*' said Holmes demurely. If God wills it.

'Damnation,' I said aloud, startling two black-shrouded women balancing jugs on their heads. The gate to the grotto that Holmes and I had locked behind us now stood wide open, and I could see movement within the entrance. I touched the handle of the gun Holmes had given to me, and went forward.

It was not exactly relief I felt when I saw the archaeological Jacob occupying the cave mouth, but at least I would not have to shoot anyone to be allowed inside. Although I soon began to wonder if it would not have been simpler for all concerned if I had just drawn my weapon and ordered them out of my way. It might well have been kinder.

'Hello, Jacob,' I said, when I had reached the entrance. 'Terribly sorry, but I was never introduced to you properly, and I don't know your surname.'

That good gentleman just gaped at me, blinking furiously with the effort of reconciling an educated English voice with the visage before him, and wondering where on earth he had seen it before.

'Mary Russell,' I suggested. 'We met the other evening over the dinner table. Dressed rather differently.' I tugged off my turban to allow him the clue of my blonde hair, and he stepped back violently. I could only pray that he did not suffer from a heart condition, and I laughed as if it was all a great joke. 'I know, I know – it's going to take some explaining, but there is an explanation, I promise you. Only not just now. It's urgent that I go into the grotto and make some noise, to show some friends above the location of the access door. Do you know the door I mean? No? Then perhaps you'd like to see? And – might I borrow that ladder?'

The accent, the femininity, and the appeal to his curiosity disarmed him, to the extent that he trailed along after me, mouthing frail objections. He even offered to carry the stout cudgel I had brought along for the purpose of noisy pounding. His men, three highly entertained Christian Arabs, followed in a procession, carrying the ladder across the uneven floor of the grotto.

I looked at my pocket-watch, and up at the concealed door

with the ladder propped beside it, and wished, not for the first time, that I smoked. Cigarettes do give one something to do while one waits, instead of reviewing grammar or making conversation. I decided that Jacob deserved some slightly more detailed explanation of events, if for nothing else than to reward him for not flinging me to the police, so in the seven minutes left before I could begin my rat-flushing racket, I told him a much-abridged and quite misleading tale with the essential goal intact: to bash away at that door up there until someone came to stop me. I stretched out the embroidery until it was time to begin, so as to avoid his no doubt pressing questions, and then stood up, seized the cudgel, and rammed it up over my head into the sturdy wooden door.

The boom was satisfying; the spray of dust and flakes of rusted iron that settled over me less so. I coughed, sneezed furiously, and squeezed my eyelids together, continuing to hammer away blindly. It was a strain, and about one blow in three missed the wood and bashed into solid rock, sending a jolt along my spine that rattled my teeth. After about a minute of this lunacy I felt something patting my boot, and Jacob's voice raised above the echoing din. He was offering to take my place.

In the end we all took turns, perched on the creaking ladder, walloping away at the iron-hard door. Jacob the gentleman obviously thought me insane and was waiting for me to tire so he might lead me away and put a cool cloth on my fevered brow, but the three Arabs were having a fine time.

I was taking a turn on the ladder, and beginning to think Jacob might be right about my mental state, when between one blow and the next the door suddenly went hollow. I nearly dropped the cudgel onto the heads below, fumbling to exchange it for the gun in my belt. The door scraped open, my audience gasped, and I was looking over the sights of the revolver at: Ali. A grinning, blood-streaked Ali who had patently succeeded in conquering the house above.

'So, you wish to shoot me this time?' he asked politely, and I reflected that each time I nearly killed him, he became increasingly friendly towards me. His broad hand reached down. I let the battering ram fall onto an unoccupied patch of floor, stuck the revolver back into my belt, and reached up to take his hand and be hauled bodily through the hole. He kicked at the door, and I could only call a hasty 'Thank you!' through the gap before it was down and bolted again. I agreed: This was no place for introducing Irregulars.

Ali caught up his lamp from the floor and made for a stairway.

'How many did you get?' I asked him.

'Four,' he answered cheerfully. 'All alive, none talking yet. By God, that Holmes of yours is a good fighter.'

That Holmes of mine was nursing a set of swollen knuckles and a reddened eye, and looked immensely pleased with himself. He and Mahmoud were dragging the fourth trussed and gagged body back into the building, where they tossed him down with his companions, looking like so many rolled-up carpets. Holmes shut the door authoritatively on the curious crowd outside, and we stood looking at our haul.

Then, slowly and dramatically, Ali drew forth his wicked blade, and four sets of eyes went wide, four foreheads went instantly damp with sweat. No: five. I too had no desire for that blade to be applied to digging out secrets. I put out a hand to touch Ali's arm, studying the men at my feet. Four dark-skinned men in Arab dress, not the clothing of the poorest inhabitants, but none of them was wealthy. One was young, scarcely my age, and he looked near to passing out with terror. I squeezed Ali's rock-like forearm once again for good measure, and went over to kneel beside the young man.

'I will not hurt you,' I said to him. His eyes flickered to my face, then glued themselves back on Ali. I shifted, to remove Ali's knife from the prisoner's vision, and then leant forward to untie his gag. He watched me settle back on my heels, waiting warily for my trick.

'We must know where your leader has gone,' I told him. 'Not Karim Bey. Bey is dead.' All four went still against their bonds, and the young man's eyes rose to Ali's figure standing behind me. I did not disabuse them of their belief that Ali had killed Bey, merely said, 'We must have the other. These men will kill you in order to find him. Slowly, and with great pain. Tell me now where the other man is, and you will not be hurt.' I waited while the young man thought about it, then added, 'He is not one of you. He paid you for the use of this house and for your silence; you have no cause to give your lives for him. He would not give his for you.'

The prisoner's gaze wavered, and slid sideways to the oldest of the other prisoners, whose face resembled his. Father? Uncle? In either case the two were blood relations. I went over to the older prisoner and pulled away his gag, too.

'Please,' I said quietly. 'Don't let my friends hurt the boy. It is a bad way to die, and why: for a *firengi*? Let the *firengi* deal

399

with the *firengi*' I suggested, nodding my chin at Holmes in his foreign uniform and hoping fervently that the man we sought, Ellison or no, was indeed British.

It was impossible to tell what the man on the floor was thinking. He just lay there looking at me, his face completely closed. He might have been stone deaf for all the impression my words made. Ali shifted restlessly behind me, and I felt a rush of despair at my failure to prevent atrocity.

Then the man's face changed, faintly but surely. I put out my hand to signal Ali.

'He has a house over a shop in the Muristan,' the prisoner said. 'The olive-wood seller's with the lamp in front on the Street of the Christians. The entrance is through the shop. The back way is down from the roof into the New Bazaar, between the seller of brass pots and the leather worker from Kabul. He has two men with him. All have guns.'

Holmes had told me that Ellison kept a house outside the Old City as well, for his illicit woman friend. 'He will be in the Muristan, not at his house in the Russian Colony?'

'I do not know that place, only this.'

'What does he plan?'

The man shrugged against his bonds. 'To disappear. That is what he always does.'

'Not this time,' I declared, and rose to my feet. I looked around at Mahmoud. 'Was there anything else?'

He shook his head slightly, looking as amused as Holmes was. Ali slid his knife away, then went into the next room and returned with another knife in his hand, equally vicious, and walked purposefully towards the young boy. The man at my feet gasped as if I'd kicked him in the stomach, struggled once convulsively against his bonds, and moaned softly through clenched teeth. Ali bent down to yank the boy's gag back up, then straightened, held up the knife, and hurled it down with all the strength in his right arm. It stood quivering, two inches of its steel blade buried in the floorboards three feet away from the boy's tied hands. When I looked down, the older prisoner's eyes were shut in the extremity of relief.

It would take the boy a while, but he would free himself, and his family, before we returned. I stooped down to pull the older man's gag back across his mouth, to give us a chance to get free of the quarter before an alarm was raised, but before it was in place he spoke again. 'He carries a knife in his boot. Beware of it.' I slid my own blade out of my boot top. 'Like this one?'

'Ah. It is a custom, I see.'

'Not exactly,' I said. 'I thank you for the warning.' Ali locked the door and we left the men there.

The Muristan was an open area just south of the Church of the Holy Sepulchre that had been variously a hospice for pilgrims established by Charlemagne, a Crusader hospital, an endowment to the Mosque of Omar, and property of the Prussian crown. Now it was a part of the city that combined bazaar and offices, where church and commerce, Moslem and Christian, pilgrim and citizen rubbed shoulders and went about their business.

We nearly missed them. Had our prisoners hesitated two minutes longer, had we paused to let Holmes resume his robe and *kuffiyah*, the three men would have been gone.

It was twice blessed that Holmes had remained in uniform, because it was his presence that gave them away.

We came to the Muristan at a trot, half winded from the climb up David Street, slowing to a walk as we turned the corner into the Street of the Christians. The narrow way was crowded with Sunday pilgrims and shoppers, and the three men entering it from the side would have been invisible to us had one of them not looked warily around, spotted Holmes' military cap towering above the turbans and headcloths of the shorter populace, and turned to run. The abrupt movement caught our eye, and we were after them, pounding down the busy street, shouting since all pretence was gone. Passers-by stopped to watch, but made no attempt to interfere.

We caught them up in the courtyard in front of the Church of the Holy Sepulchre. One of them whirled around with a gun in his hand and pulled the trigger wildly. The bullet missed Holmes by inches, and then Ali and Mahmoud were on him. One of the remaining pair sprinted up the path to the right, with Holmes fast on his heels; the other dived through the mighty doors of the Church of the Holy Sepulchre – from which, thanks be to God, Allenby and his notables were long gone. By the time I was past the startled Moslem guards and inside the dim, echoing space, he had vanished into the recesses.

And the Church of the Holy Sepulchre is nothing but recesses, one chapel after another, galleries up the walls, every square inch of floor space in this holy of holies heavily used and bitterly contested (hence the Moslem guards, who can be depended upon to treat each division of Christianity with equal scorn). Candles and incense, sparkling gilt and dark shadows, prayers in all languages and people shifting about – it was a confusion of the senses.

I stood for an instant, searching desperately for the robe and *kuffiyah* I had followed in, but they were not in sight – and worse, the guards had decided I did not belong here and were coming out of their station to do something about it. I had no choice but to plunge towards the more populous left side, hoping both to lose them and to find my quarry.

I found instead his robe, kicked into the corner of a small unoccupied chapel off of the main rotunda. I muttered a phrase most unsuited to the setting, popped out of the chapel, and was spotted by an irate guard, but before I could turn and dive into the crowd, a familiar figure loomed up from the darkness behind him and seized his arm.

Ali – and by God he'd never been a more welcome sight. I stepped behind a pair of high-hatted priests and continued my search, but for what, or whom, I did not know. What had the man – *was* it Ellison? – been wearing under his shed robe? The second habit stolen from Wadi Qelt? The habit of a nun? A city suit? I continued slowly, searching every cranny and every face for anything at all that seemed not to fit.

I had cleared the rotunda and was coming out of its adjoining Greek church when Ali joined me.

'He dropped his robe,' I told him. 'How did you get rid of the guard?'

'I said you were my troublesome younger brother and I would give you a beating you would never forget. Did you see our man at all? Was it Ellison?'

'I don't know,' I said in frustration. 'I've never met Ellison.

All I saw was a glimpse of the man's hand – his skin is light. Do you know if there are any exits back here?'

Without pausing to answer he slipped away, leaving me to press ahead into a corridor that curved around the end of the Greek church-within-a-church. Tiny chapels heavy with incense and the smell of candles lay on my left, then a set of stairs going down, where I hesitated.

Did our quarry have a gun? Almost certainly. Would he use it? Probably not, if he could avoid it. A gunshot would bring half the Christians in Jerusalem down on his head, and a handful of Moslems as well. Ali would return at any moment; until then, I just had to make certain that the enemy did not find a back way out.

I started down the stairs, my heart in my throat; when running boots skidded along the floor behind me I nearly shrieked.

Ali spoke in my ear, so low I could barely hear him over the sound of my heart and the voices from the space below. 'He did not get out through the monastery.'

'Do these stairs go anywhere?' I asked.

'More chapels.'

'But no exit?'

'Not unless he removes a solid stone wall.'

'Then we—' I froze as his words hit me, and whirled to look at him in horror. 'Oh, my God, you don't think he has—I mean to say, this place is hideous, but . . . dynamite?'

'Holmes said two of the salt smuggler's detonators were in the bomb, and Bey used the third.'

It was thin reassurance, but then Ali shook his head decisively.

'Whoever this man is, he is far from stupid. He knows he would never escape a blast. I fear rather that he has circled ahead of us and will be out of the door. Leave me to check down here, and you go up and watch the entrance; the others will be here any moment, and we can then do this properly.' He laid his hand surreptitiously on the gun he wore under his *abayya* and I nodded and turned up the stairs. At the top I glanced to the right, and then whipped my head back left so fast my spectacles nearly flew off – but whatever I had glimpsed out of the corner of my eye was gone.

It had been something very like a sleek gleam of pale hair, ducking into yet another doorway.

A bare head was an unusual sight even in London; in this country, I did not think I had seen more than a handful of uncovered adult scalps the whole time I had been here. And most of those had been over breakfast in Allenby's headquarters in—

No! In Haifa, yes, but not over breakfast, not that sleek head. Over a more intimate meal, in Allenby's office. Over tea and crustless sandwiches. He was here, back in uniform, although he had been unable to conceal the bulky hat under his now-abandoned robes.

'Ali!' I called sharply. 'Ssst!'

I could not wait for him. That pale head was a scarce thirty feet from me, racing up a set of stairs that led God knew where. I heard movement from behind me as Ali hurriedly abandoned the depths, but I was already launched. Just before I hit the stairs, Mahmoud strode around the corner coming towards me, with Holmes' khaki hat going off in the other direction –

the sight of them approaching must have been what drove our quarry back. I threw my hand up to attract Mahmoud's eye, heard him shout to Holmes, and I raced up the stairs with them on my heels.

The ornate chapels at the top of the steps were perhaps fifteen feet above the floor level of the rest of the church, overlooking the entrance vestibule where the guards sat. I thought he intended to risk the drop and the guards for the entrance and the crowds of the bazaar just beyond, but when I burst in, I found him instead with a massive silver candlestick in one hand, a knife in the other, and a cluster of furiously protesting monks standing sensibly just beyond range of the blade. He raised the candlestick and drove it, not onto a tonsured skull, but through a screen, on the other side of which could be glimpsed a richly coloured little room. That he was not using a door could only mean one thing: The chapel on the other side of the screen had its entrance on the outside world. One more blow like that and he would be through it. I took my inadequate little knife from my boot and started hauling monks out of my way. The candlestick went up again, and I shouted his name.

'Plumbury!'

He did not stop, but it startled him enough to spoil his aim. The candlestick went up for the third and no doubt decisive blow, and I had to move or I would find myself staring again at his fast-retreating back with the blue sky above him. There were too many monks in the way to risk throwing the knife, or using the gun; instead, I dived forward, shoving my way between some very solid monastic bodies, and stabbed blindly downward into whatever portion of Plumbury's anatomy I could reach.

It was his foot, and the heavy leather of his military boot trapped my knife. I tugged once and let it go, but before I could pull away his own blade flicked down and sliced open the back of my wrist. The press of monks that had held me from him was still there, blocking my escape, and as I scrabbled and pulled desperately at their robes, I felt more than saw the knife draw up into the air and slash down again towards my unprotected back.

A single shot rang through the sanctified expanses of the Church of the Holy Sepulchre. Its echoes called and faded and died off into the shocked and unprecedented silence, and then the heavy candlestick clattered to the ground, followed by the knife, and finally Plumbury himself.

Had I not been so occupied with reassuring the monks that I was not bleeding to death, I would have embraced Mahmoud with all the passion in my young, rescued body, embarrassing us both forever.

EPILOGUE

*The significance of the children of Israel's sojourn in the desert
is that forty years brought about the disappearance of the first
generation and the growth of the next, that had not known
humiliation in Egypt.*
— THE *Muqaddimah* OF IBN KHALDÛN

THE SLICE ON MY WRIST was bloody but not serious, and as
he bound it for me, Ali seemed to find the wound cause
for pride, a mark of honour rather than the sign of clumsiness
and near disaster. It gave me no problems and eventually left
the thinnest curve of a scar, but to make Ali happy I displayed it
openly, with studied nonchalance. Mahmoud approved.

Late that evening, though, I did cover it when, in clean skin
and a dress borrowed from Helen Bentwich (which felt more
like a disguise than anything I had worn since leaving England),
I ran the gauntlet of beggars and stares to take my place before
the Western Wall, leaving the scrap of paper with my prayer on

it between the stones. War wounds, I thought, did not belong in that setting.

After I had paid my visit to the Wall, we left Jerusalem, to travel northwards towards Acre and the boat that would take Holmes and me out of this country, back to the equally troubling case that awaited us in England. I had seen very little of the Jerusalem known to pilgrims and tourists. I did not wade up Hezekiah's Tunnel nor venture into St Anne's magnificent simplicity, did not walk the perimeter walls or tour the Citadel or poke among the finds of the archaeologists. I did not even go to gaze upon the ethereal beauty of the Dome or upon the Rock itself that I had helped save – not that time, at any rate.

I left the city without seeing these things, because they would not have fitted. They belonged to a different pilgrimage, and would have constituted a different set of memories, and one set was as much as I could assimilate just then. I also felt no urgency to 'see' Jerusalem: I knew that there would be a 'next year in Jerusalem.'

Besides which, I could imagine nothing that would top my memory of that Sunday afternoon when we trailed back to the Jaffa Gate and piled into a horse carriage to save us the uphill walk to Government House. We arrived there at sunset, and the spurious uniform Holmes wore was the only thing that kept us from being arrested on sight. We all reeked of sweat and sewage, bat droppings and paraffin smoke and burnt flesh, and other than Holmes' khaki shell everything about us was battered, blood spattered, and filthy beyond belief. The appalled military guard took our weapons and escorted us, very nearly at gunpoint, through the layers of army officialdom until we were brought before Allenby himself, who sat among the empty teacups in front of a blazing fire in the elegant formal drawing room, surrounded by the notables who had accompanied him on the peaceful, and peace-building, afternoon at the Dome.

Nothing, no memory of tourist beauties or pilgrim satisfaction, no royal commendation or scrap of ribbon with a medal on it, could supersede the prize I hold to this day, the image I retain of the facial expressions of the bare-headed men in gold-braided uniforms and the head-covered men in gold-trimmed Arab robes, of Governor and Mrs Storrs, the Bentwiches, the Mufti and the Kadi, several members of the American Colony, the head of the Red Cross, two rabbis, Father Demetrius, and sundry other Important Persons (including, to my incredulity, the small, shy, awe-inspiring figure of T.E. Lawrence himself, flown in secretly overnight from the Paris talks for the meeting), when they saw General Edmund Allenby, majestically clothed in his most immaculate formal dress uniform, ribbons and medals in obedient line and every thinning hair in place, leap out of his chair to clap the shoulders and pump the hands of two frightful specimens of adult Bedouin Arabs (one in garish flowered *kuffiyah* and stained red boots, the other scarred and scowling, both men dirty and dangerous and probably not house-trained) and their accompanying army officer (himself no prize, being badly in need of a shave, a bath, some sticking-plaster, and a lorry-load of discipline) before he waved those three unsavoury individuals over to silk-covered chairs among the fastidious dignitaries. But that was not the end of the adventure, for then (and here the expressions of astonishment and dismay turned to sheer, slack-jawed disbelief) 'Bull' Allenby – last of the Paladins, conqueror of Jerusalem, hero of the Middle East, and Commander in Chief of all the Holy Land – turned to the fourth noisome intruder, grasped that young Bedouin lad's black, bloodied, and bandaged hand gently in his own, raised it to his lips, and kissed it.

A NOTE ABOUT CHAPTER HEADINGS

Baedeker's guide to *Palestine and Syria,* 1912 edition

The *Muqaddimah* (Preface and Book One) of the sweeping *History* written by the brilliant fourteenth-century Islamic scholar Ibn Khaldûn. These quotations have been reworded slightly for the sake of brevity by the present editor.

Helen Waddell, *The Desert Fathers*

The Holy Qur'an

ARABIC WORDS AND PHRASES

Abayya	a robe worn over a long skirt or loose trousers and shirt
Afreet	a demon or troublesome imp
Agahl	a heavy ropelike wrap that holds the *kuffiyah* on the head
aleikum es-salaam	a greeting (response to *salaam aleikum)*
bakshish	a payment, tip, bribe, or donation
burkah	a concealing woman's garment
effendi	an honorary address
fellah/fellahin	peasant, countryman
firengi	a foreigner, a 'Frank'
Ghor	the low-lying Jordan River valley
Imam	Muslim religious leader
insh'allah	a saying: if it is God's will
kuffiyah	a loose headcloth
laban	a drink of sour milk or diluted yogurt
maalesh	a saying: oh, well . . .

muezzin	the man who calls the faithful to prayer from a mosque
mukhtar	headman of a village
mullah	a Muslim religious leader
narghile	a water pipe
saj	curved sheet of steel used to cook flat bread over a fire
salaam aleikum	a greeting: peace be with you
souk or *suq*	bazaar
wadi	water-cut valley, often dry but for sudden floods
wallah!	an expression of surprise: by God!
ya walud	an expression of greeting or to call attention

ALSO BY LAURIE R. KING

In England's young silent-film industry, the megalomaniacal Randolph Fflytte is king. Nevertheless, Mary Russell is dispatched to investigate the criminal activities that surround Fflytte's popular movie studio. So Russell is travelling undercover to Portugal, along with the film crew that is gearing up to shoot a cinematic extravaganza, *Pirate King*. But as movie make-believe becomes true terror, Russell and Holmes themselves may experience a final fadeout.

><><

To uncover more great fiction
and to place an order visit our website at
www.allisonandbusby.com
or call us on
020 7580 1080